THE THUNDER
BENEATH US

THE THUNDER
BENEATH US

NICOLE BLADES

KENSINGTON PUBLISHING CORP.
www.kensingtonbooks.com

To the extent that the image or images on the cover of this book depict a person or persons, such person or persons are merely models, and are not intended to portray any character or characters featured in the book.

DAFINA BOOKS are published by

Kensington Publishing Corp.
119 West 40th Street
New York, NY 10018

All Kensington titles, imprints, and distributed lines are available at special quantity discounts for bulk purchases for sales promotion, premiums, fund-raising, and educational or institutional use.

Special book excerpts or customized printings can also be created to fit specific needs. For details, write or phone the office of the Kensington Sales Manager: Kensington Publishing Corp., 119 West 40th Street, New York, NY 10018. Attn. Sales Department. Phone: 1-800-221-2647.

Dafina and the Dafina logo Reg. U.S. Pat. & TM Off.

ISBN-13: 978-1-4967-0459-7
ISBN-10: 1-4967-0459-2
First Kensington Trade Paperback Printing: November 2016

eISBN-13: 978-1-4967-0460-3
eISBN-10: 1-4967-0460-6
First Kensington Electronic Edition: November 2016

10 9 8 7 6 5 4 3 2 1

Printed in the United States of America

To all of those big, creative minds shoved into small, tight boxes, but refusing to just rest there quietly, here's to chasing your dreams and betting on yourself.

PROLOGUE

Montreal
December, Ten Years Ago.

I'm still looking up at the constellation when I hear the thunder. Only it's not clapping through the blue night skies. It's under our feet.

Bryant goes in first. He was carrying the bag. Swallowed up almost silently, he's gone before the sounds can sync up with the pictures. It takes another set of seconds for me to recognize that the fingers pinching my body, attempting to pierce me, drag at me from the inside, aren't fingers at all. It's the cold in the water, the ice, and it's trying to steal my breath.

There's this hollow, haunting, barking sound just behind my left ear. It's Benjamin. Thick slush and jagged, cracked plates try to flood his gasping mouth, but he's still calling for me. The cruel stars conspire to shine their brightest now as I catch a full view of what is happening. I see Ben's face, his eyes. All the familiar of him is wiped clean away; only fear is left. I want to tell him to stop thrashing, stop panicking, to save his energy for crawling out of the hole, and that we'll be all right, but there's a rattling noise and it's building; I can't even hear my thoughts. It's the bones in my jaw; they're clanging together. It's happen-

ing to Benjamin too. Somehow he's pulled me close enough
that I can see his mouth—still above water—shaking. But I can
also see the terror streaked across his face.

I need to get out. We need to get out. Everything's heavy.
Everything's slow.

He's pulling me again with that one free arm, this time with
the secret strength he had tucked in his thick leather jacket.
That goddamn jacket. I didn't want to hear another word
about his prized jacket just a moment ago, before the world
cracked and we fell in. Now I'm hoping somehow it saves us.

"You need to get fly, Bestba," Benjamin said as we approached the lake. "Feel the butter *smoothism* of this jacket,
though. Now check your wooly-mammoth styles and tell me,
honestly, who's got dopeness on lock?"

I swatted his proud hand away from my face. "Jesus. The
worst thing they did was buy you that jacket."

"Seriously, is Mum punishing you for something?" Benjamin said. "Is that why she's forcing you to wear that shaggy
shit the whole winter?"

"How much more material do you have on my winter coat,
Ben? Four, five more jokes? Because the whole bit is well and
old now. Time for something new."

"Exactly. Time for something new—for real. Maybe a little
leather might help you out of this whole Wookiee situation
you're rocking. But, then again, Chewie could be a cute nickname for you this year. You could work with that." He tossed
his head back, forcing that choppy laugh into the cold air
above us.

"Shut up, fool."

We walked arm in arm anyway. Bryant took his usual position—the quiet apex of our sloppy triangle—and started lead-
ing us back to the house.

It really was a beautiful leather jacket. I wasn't going to tell Benjamin that, though. Benjamin had enough hype men in his day-to-day. He didn't need his sister gassing up his head too.

"I have a shortcut," Bryant yelled back.

"Is it a real one, as in cutting the time it takes us to get back to Aunt Esther's," Benjamin starts, and I finish—

"Right, or is it one of your shortcuts that really means a ridiculous, winding detour so you can check out some random nerd crap?"

"It's a star," Bryant said. He stopped walking and turned back to us. He put some bass in his voice. "It's stars. It's not random, and it's not nerd crap either. It's Orion, the Hunter. If we head through that area there, closer to the lake's edge, you'll see it. You won't believe how cool it is, but you'll see it."

"I knew you were up to some shit when you brought that bag with you," I said, rolling my eyes. "It was a fair, as in games and cotton candy and gold-coin winnings, not a science fair. Leave the lab coat at home."

Bryant's shoulders and voice dipped. "Whatever. I don't have a lab coat in here." He shook his head and kept walking.

"Fine, Bryant. We'll do this shortcut, Hunter-watching business," Benjamin yelled ahead to him. "But when—not if— when we get back mad late, you've got to man up and take the hit." Benjamin nudged my ribs. "No mouse in the house bullshit this time. They never suspect you anyway."

I nudged Benjamin back. "Yeah, but somehow it'll come back to be about me, my fault," I said, growling. "You know I'm the reason for all the bad things, like some permanent jinx. I'm the only girl in this entire family, but they act like I'm the absolute worst. I should be walking on silky leaves or carried on your backs. Where's the princess treatment? Do I need to add more pink in my life—is that where I went wrong?"

"Pink won't change the truth: You are the worst. Nothing to do with you being the only girl, either. Don't get the facts jumbled, chief." Benjamin let his laugh loose again, then cupped his mouth, hollering ahead. "Yo, Bryant, we're taking your share of sweetbread when we get there. And your ham too. You've been warned."

———◦•◦———

Benjamin's writhing has slowed to a few, weak flutters, but the weight of him, on my back, my arms, my shoulders—it's drawing me in. My brain shorts out and I'm acting on reflex, instincts. I've gone animal and I wiggle out of my swamped coat. I know my legs and arms are moving wildly, only because I can see them pushing the frozen chunks of water around. I feel nothing. I hear nothing. It's all clogged. When I find that solid piece, I dig in and claw at it. Dragging my entire body along the smooth ice, I hear screeching. The noise fills my head, and I realize it's coming from me. I'm howling, afraid to move, afraid not to. Something from low inside, from the pit of my stomach, forces me to roll halfway over, nearly to my back. Again, the sky's lights seem to jump in wattage and I see Benjamin's head gleaming, bobbing, bobbing, nodding and then under.

My eyes open again. I keep them like that longer this time, open, moving around, waiting for awareness to seep in through the corners. There are more lights, but they're not beaming from above the earth. Bright and harsh one moment, warm and flickering the next, these lights have smeared colors: red, blue, maybe soft white. Sounds stay muffled. A clear thought finally arrives: If I close my eyes, I might hear better, filter through the muddy mix of noises and notes, and figure out why and how and what. A new thought crashes in, sabotaging the first one: If I close my eyes, they won't open ever again. I can feel something in my chest; a tightening that works its way in a rough spiral down to my stomach and up along my throat at once. It's my voice, or something like it—I'm screaming.

Pain and panic and crushing fright press up against me, and I'm roaring now. I call out to Bryant, to Benjamin and I reach for my brothers. The muscles in my arms are activated—I think—but nothing's moving.

———»•«———

"You're okay. You're okay, honey. You're fine. I'm Sandra Bishop; this is Dr. Delaney. You're in the emergency room at Montreal General. Squeeze my hand if you understand."

I don't squeeze. I don't understand. Instead I reach out again, with more of me. It's not fine here. I need to get out. We need to get out.

CHAPTER 1

New York City
October, Ten Years Later.

Coochie. *Vajayjay.* Box. Beaver. Taco. Vadge. *Bajingo.* Lady Garden. Call it whatever you want; the goddamn thing just killed my career.

When I get to Trinity's desk, she's squeezed into a corner looking serious, uncomfortable, cagey. This doesn't help. She had a similar cramped-up pose the last time I was called in to meet with JK like this, all vague and abrupt. If I walk in there and see anyone from legal, I'm not going to bother taking a seat. I already figured out which books in my office I'll pack and which ones to leave on the shelf for my replacement.

I'm supposed to be lightning in a bottle. That's what *Chalk Board* magazine called me in that "Media's Top 25 Under 25" piece last week. Mind you, I'm twenty-seven, but I keep popping up on these industry lists anyway. Honestly, it's just code for *Yes, we let the right one in. Check off the diversity box.* I'm totally cute, though, so that helps. *Mediagenic.* That's another word they like pushing up next to my name. Morning-TV producers think I'm hilarious, even when I'm feeding them warmed-over quips I thought up in the shower. *You're great. You're so great.* I'm not. I'm not great. I'm the opposite. Heinous and horrible, a feral beast capable of atrocious things like that night. Like that night with Benjamin. He didn't deserve that, and had those merciless tables been turned, he would have never done that to me. Benjamin, he would have found a different way, because he was good. I'm not. But people are drawn to me, never wanting to let me go (more from *Chalk Board*). They don't know any better. None of them. Fools. They've bought into it, this story of me being golden, blessed, lucky. They haven't clued into what I figured out long ago: that luck is nothing more than a burden.

It's that ignorance, blissful and simple, that makes people want me around, want me close in their circle. All of this should ease the choppy pulse behind my eye right now, send my shoulders down. It doesn't. Because I know I don't deserve good things. Getting fired from a fluffed-out women's magazine job: that sounds more up my alley.

I squeeze my hand into the shallow, front pocket of my jeans. They're extra tight, pencil-cut, and the stiff edge of the denim scratches my knuckles. I don't care about that; I need to feel the smoothness of my tokens.

For the last ten years, I've carried these two gold coins, clicking them together—sometimes loudly—like ruby slippers. They're not worth anything; cheap tokens from the winter fair. They were my brother's. You would think, after everything, I would remember which brother. But I don't. I just know that I need them. They're part of my story.

"You good, T?"

She shrugs, then nods and finally shakes her head.

Crap. I'm done. How am I going to look my dad in the face?

None of this is a surprise, though. As soon as I went from writing legitimate women's health stories to becoming the vagina reporter, that was the signpost and I ignored it—on purpose. Giddy at being special, held up to the light for my merit, not some unfair fluke, I pretended that I was worthy, that I deserved this goodness. And now look at me: mowed down by the vagina. At least I know how to get a bump-free bikini line. There's that. There's also:

28 Sex Moves to Wow Your Guy
9 Sexy Steps to Orgasm—Every Time
54 Sex Tips to Blow His Mind
101 BEST SEX TIPS EVER
32 Dirty-Girl Sex Tricks to Drive Him Crazy
The 7 Secrets to Bigger, Bolder Orgasms

All of this is intel that will help me after I get fired today. Clearly.

Fuck this. The vagina will not do me in. It can't. I need to play this thing arrogant, like there's no possible way I could have made another misstep in print.

I pull my posture up, drop the befuddlement, and add some certainty to my voice. "So, it's two o'clock," I say to Trinity. "Just go on in?"

She's moving her head in an almost circular nod. Trinity doesn't want to answer me and she definitely doesn't want to look at me. I try to read her jerky movements anyway. Trinity Windsong Cohen (yes, real) is the worst with secrets. All three of my promotions were spoiled by her; the good news blurted out while she was latched to my forearm, in a red-knuckled grip. I move closer to her, lean in, open my clenched torso for any impromptu choke holds and last-minute reveals, but I hear nothing, just the muffled swish of the year-round space heater at her feet.

"Um. Let me just check with James," she says, finally. Her words are run-together, her voice barely above a whisper.

The churn in my stomach returns, and I brace for what's coming. Maybe they'll skip the meeting; have Trinity walk me to the kitchen for cupcakes and put me down with one bullet to the back of the head, Mafioso-style. I really wasn't supposed to be here this long anyway.

Trinity slams the phone down and looks right at me. "They're ready for you."

"No cupcakes?" It falls out of my mouth before I have a chance to tuck the thing deep under my tongue.

Her face wrinkles.

"Sorry. I'm—I should go in."

JK meets me a few paces outside of her doorway, smiling, her eyes squinting. That's exactly what she did last time too. It's only been three months since I was here, walking toward JK's tight grin and stepping into a roomful of dead-eyed, dark suits. It was my first transgression, but nothing about it feels truly forgiven. I know they're all waiting for me to put my other pump square in the middle of the shit pile once more, and their collective doubt will be realized. No more waiting, suits, because here we go again—me being summoned to the office, again, for some mysterious reason. Again.

All right. So that this doesn't become Chekhov's gun, here are the three things you need to know about what we'll call The Mistake:

1. **Wrote a big cover story about a famous yoga instructor with A-list celeb clients, who occasionally taught classes for the Rest of Us out of her impossibly fabulous SoHo loft.**
2. **The impossibly fabulous SoHo loft, I found out, actually belonged to her married beau. The married beau is**

also the publisher of your favorite celebrity-gossip mag and blog.
3. **I slipped this slimy piece of info into the story. Cut to a threatened defamation suit, a horrifying deposition with legal, and a retraction and apology. The PR girls still spit when they hear my name.**

I want to pray or vomit. I can't figure out which will actually help. Instead, I clear my mind and step lively toward JK's giant snow-globe office (seriously, everything is dusted in white). She opens her arms, waving me in like a banking jetliner. As I clear the corner, I see that no one from legal is there. I let my deep breath out, slow and quiet. However, the stranger seated by the window—this gives me pause. Shit. Maybe they found out about the honor-killing story. I've been working on it in ultra-stealth mode for months. It's going to be my golden ticket, my way out of here. Of course, now it will be *literally* my way out of here. Not golden at all. More like gray, or whatever color goes with insubordination. I'm not technically supposed to be doing this story. But how did they find me out? These people here are barely journalists; there's not a newshound in the bunch. Unless the mailroom guys—*my guys*—fucked up, and this is what it looks like right before the bus rolls over you.

"Hey, superstar. Glad you could join us," Susie says, as if I had a choice. Her voice is a little shaky, odd. All curly, auburn hair and outsized Clark Kent glasses, Susie is always steady. This right now is the opposite of steady, the opposite of Susie. She's practically warbling. I plant my feet and slide into ready mode. I just decided, this minute, I'm choosing fight over flight. The only thing I don't like is that my back is to the door, not the wall.

I hear JK's voice coming up alongside me. "Yes, come on in, Best. Very excited to have you here."

Stranger Woman, her skin like tempered dark chocolate, barely moves. Only her eyes angle toward me. Already, she's not impressed. She remains seated, even though JK and Susie are standing.

"Make yourself at home," JK says. She gestures to the chair next to the woman. I want to say something strong, unfazed: *No, thanks, I'm good here.* But it's tense enough. I walk over to the white leather seat to the woman's right, leaving enough space between us for our mutual disapproval to rest. "Best Lightburn, meet Joan Marx," JK says. Her grin is a little too wide, eyes glassy, like she just took a toke.

Finally the woman moves. She stands up, her slim pigeon's body bends at the middle, a smooth, shallow bow toward me. Her hair is in micro-braids and her makeup is too much. She's dressed like the plainclothes detectives I see at the all-hours diner near my brownstone, but instead of a wrinkled silk tie to finish the look, she sports a large broach on her left lapel. It's silver and shiny with raised, colored jewels. The control panel, I presume.

I float my hand out to shake hers. The grip is fine, but her hands are clammy.

Strike one.

JK sidles up next to me and touches my arm, gives it a light squeeze—more a soft pulsing—call it whatever, it's her trademark nurture move, something she perfected in twenty-eight years of running magazines filled with disparate, desperate (and often disordered) personalities. It works; my heart rate is slowing. Her moves always work on me: the arm pulsing, the wink, the random clothing compliment in the hallway, and the masterful combo of all three. It makes Janice "James" Kessler seem approachable (but she's not) and makes you feel considered (but you're not).

Susie, still skittish, interrupts the tired magic trick and I get my arm back. "I'm actually a little nervous," she says. "Maybe we should start. Sooner we do, sooner I can get that martini." We all chuckle and mutter things, light, easy, like it's being recorded for background noise on a movie. Stranger Woman is back in her seat, waxen and stiff. Before anyone has a chance to wipe the tight, cheap smirks from our faces, Susie takes a dramatic breath. "Okay. So, here's the quick and dirty on our wonderful friend Joan here: She is the former deputy editor at *Sports World Magazine* and before that she was at *New York News.* And before that, she put in a tour of duty in local network news for a few years. And now here she is, ready to join our team, and we are absolutely thrilled to have her."

I nod in her general direction. JK catches me and her smile dims.

Susie moves through a series of quick, weird tics, the last of which is rubbing the top of her pen. It's annoying and awkward, like everything else about this meeting. If she removes her glasses next and buries them on top of her head, I might as well lean back, expose my neck, give them full access to my carotid artery. Maybe they'll let their New Black One do the honors and have the first cut, although I can't imagine JK being down with bloodstain patterns all over this whiteness. Master move, getting another black woman to do me, though. Who knew JK was so artful?

Another deep breath. "As you know, Best, I love this magazine. It's the child I never had." Susie pauses, looking down at her bouncing knee. "I'm immensely proud of it, and this experience—that's the best word for it, really—it's one for which I remain eternally grateful."

Wait. This is a resignation letter. She's leaving. Susie's leaving and Robot Joan is taking her place. I didn't realize it at first, but I'm shaking my head now as it clicks together. Talk about being clueless. Ten minutes ago, I was positive this meeting was going to be my last day at *James*. I was sure that The Mistake had somehow resurrected itself and was going to finally bite me in the ass. I had every detail planned too: whom I'd call first (Kendra, then my dad), where we'd go to drink right after (Seeks Same bar, the cornerest booth), and what my parting words would be to the entire edit floor of *James* magazine (something from either Jay Z or Biggie—this part was totally game time, but it involved the word *fuck*).

But this time, this whole thing, it isn't even about me. Actually, now I'm pissed. I almost shit my pants, and for what? An intro to Robot Joan? At this point, either tell me how this changes my world here or break out those martinis you mentioned. Make a move, because I'm on deadline. The vagina waits for no one.

"Oh, Susie," JK blurts out. "This is so bittersweet, I know." She turns her head toward me. JK looks legitimately sad. "As you may have already guessed, Susie is leaving us, leaving the company; back to the world of transformative long reads and spellbinding stories in hardcover. We'll be making the official announcement later, but we wanted to let some senior staff in on the news first. And I know you and Susie have such a wonderful relationship, Best, but I'm sure you'd agree that we're *all* going to miss her."

I should say something. That was my cue.

"Well, I am really surprised and also really excited for you, Suze." I turn my chair away from Robot Joan. Of course, it squeaks. "You've been my mama bird here for so long. JK's right: We're all going to really miss you, miss your spirit, miss your New York crazy anecdotes, and all that warm wisdom you share with us every day. And I'm going to miss our talks—I'll treasure them."

I hit all the right notes. Tears are pooling at the base of Susie's eyes. And JK's face is flushed. They exchange warm looks. The sincerity of it all curbs the weirdness that has been muscling through the room since I stepped in. I steal a glance at Joan. She's still in greetings-people-of-Earth mode.

Oh shit. She looked right at me. I must be smiling because she is trying to do the same now, but hers is crooked.

Clearly, this android is last year's model.

CHAPTER 2

Temptation is high tonight. I want to call Grant. All it would take is an easy tap on his little photo—the one I took of him sleeping in my bed—and it'd be ringing. He would answer too. But I can't call him. He needs the space. And honestly, I want to talk about me, not him or the progress of his mental state. I want to tell him about Susie's good-bye party. It was maudlin and tacky, but he always liked Susie Davis-Wright and especially my renditions of her wild *Did I ever tell you about the time* stories, complete with a spot-on impression of her delicate, lady-baby voice. He'd want to know that she escaped the nuthouse. Though I probably should stay away from talk of cuckoo's nests.

Mainly, I want to tell him about the Robot, with her tacky pinstripe man-suits she seems to fancy and those loose braids and nonexistent hairline. And I want to laugh at her, with him. I want him to help me plot out exactly how to destroy her, before she does me. I want us to come up with vile rumors—just egregious shit—to spread about her. Grant would be so game for all of it. His mastery of subversive passive-aggression and other dark arts have left me in awe of him countless times. But before we could even get to all the Robot fun, we'd have to trudge through the other woolly parts, the part about him getting better, about when he thinks he might come back to New York. We'd have to get through the *us* part, which would end up being a wrestling match, with Grant left bloodied and further bruised.

After the accident, I saw a family therapist here and there. Dr. Monfries was able to ferret through all my shit, through my anguish, and string together a theory. He said it was a pattern, my behavior—a glaring one. He even had some heavy, hyphenated word for it, though I never committed it to memory. Knowing what to call it didn't matter much then anyway. It wasn't quite manic, he said, and calling it a phase or acting out was dismissive. After the *tragic disconnect* (also Dr. M's words), I'd have these desperate moments—urges, really—where I wanted and needed to be physically close to someone, preferably a stranger and male—any category, color or creed. It wasn't always about sex. Sometimes it meant sitting close, like creepy-close to some man on the Metro or practically pressing myself up on him in an already-crammed elevator. The men never objected, but I knew how to pick them.

The sick and damaged part of this pattern came in when, on a dime, the thirst would vanish and all I wanted was to be left alone. That hardcore, *don't-touch-me-or-I'll-scream* level of left alone. I didn't even want to overhear someone else breathing near me. And these men, poor pawns, would be so confused, so frightened and unsure of what to do with me, this spiraling girl now pushing them away with all the force she could gather. And by *force*, I mean I've slapped many faces, punched chests, scratched and kicked and pummeled wild and blind, a dervish of heartbroken, angry energy.

This pattern started a few weeks after the funerals and ended rather abruptly when I decided to move to New York. Dr. Monfries said it had a lot to do with my making a decision for change. I didn't care why it ended. I was just relieved that it did.

———◦•◦———

None of it matters anyway. Grant probably had to turn over his cell phone weeks ago, and I'm damn sure not calling his uncle's landline. This week has already squeezed my brain enough. I'm no glutton.

I should just go to Flavio's showing. Fashion photographers are always a worthwhile distraction, and Kendra's been talking about Flav's big night for a solid month. Not going means having to endure her live-texting me the entire event—with her pretty pictures of all the pretty people. Flaking on this is not an option. If Kendra called the shots, I would be soaked in vodka or some other distilled beverage most nights. After everything with Grant, she made it her duty to keep me occupied and out of my low-lit living room. As she sees it, any evening I'm not stuck at the office working late (in super-stealth mode) on this honor killing, I need to be in some carved-out hole in the Meatpacking District with her, Flav and the fabulous bunch, a bar glass at my lips. But I don't need that level of distraction. It's wasted energy. I miss Grant—mostly in the middle of the night—but I'm not in danger of slipping under. I'll survive. That's what I do, apparently.

> eta woman?
> *Ken, don't freak. Still at office. Might not make it. Sorrrryyyy! :-(*
> wtf?? not freaking but still wtf. said youd come you know flav loves u&yr smart mouth. tell that robot who's boss and bounce. She don't own u.
> *All right, Tupac. I'll see what I can do. Sorry for real.*

> Save the sorrys &get yr fine azz over here. Many cute ones. Totally ungay.
>
> *Ok, ok. Be there soon.*

I've convinced myself that it's somehow easier to not give Kendra the full truth. Sometimes it's dumb stuff too, like telling her I'm still at the office instead of admitting that I just don't want to go. But it's the larger things, the lies of omission—those are the parts I feel shitty about. Kendra and I have been friends for five years, we speak or text at least fifteen times every day, but she doesn't know about my brothers, about the accident—she thinks I'm this only child with a classic, small-town escape story. Kendra's a born and bred New Yorker. When we first met at that coffee shop and she asked, "So what's your story?" I had already tucked away my other life, that fractured life with two brothers and one vile night, its bitter residue streaked over everything. I had assumed a new existence. The previous five years were not just a blur; they had completely vaporized. Instead, I served up the cliché: I was just a blank page in a simple notebook, looking to *make it in the Big Apple*. The full truth is, Kendra really doesn't know anything about me. She doesn't know this despicable brute walking around as her best friend. And in my mind, it's better that way.

> BREAKING! Lindee's coming! SHOCKING!! Shes in car service not too far fm yr office want her 2 scoop u?
>
> *That *is* shocking. Is she bringing rotten tomatoes?*
>
> LOL!! IKR??!! Text her to scoop u she wld do that for u &only u.
>
> *No. Walking to train now.*
>
> Soooo youre coming! Yasssss!!

Calm down. Still need to go home first. Calling Tyson to fix my face.
Glam down, bishh!! see u ltr!!!!

The evil twin is going? Now I actually do have to come up with a good enough lure to get Tyson over here. Jesus. It all really does spin into a web.

I met Grant through Tyson. He was doing the makeup on Grant's indie film. They got on well and Tyson said he knew we'd hit it off too. "I just like him for you, May," Tyson said. *Like him for you.* As if he were a pair of shoes or shade of lipstick that works on me. Tyson always introduces me to the "chill ones." Grant was definitely that.

When he swooped into Mo-Bay's, late and winded, it was clear. Everything that Tyson had raved about was true. Grant was cool. He was funny and smart and fine as hell. That face, flawless. Radiant and expressive, beautiful and refined. There was this old-school mystique and glamour about him; it drew you in, compelled you, made you deeply curious to know more, it made you want to talk to him—and only him—the whole night. Oh, and of course, he's Canadian—Vancouver—which is why Tyson said he'd bet his Beyoncé tickets that we'd click in the first place. And we did.

Tyson described him to me, down to the tiniest detail, weeks before our meet-cute at the restaurant.

"I'm going to say this, May,"—Tyson Turner likes to call his women friends May, or Sally May if they're over forty—*"and you need to hear me: Grant King's skin is organic maple butter for the gods."*

Tyson also likes to lead with the quality of a person's skin.

"Not a blemish, not a scratch. Then there's that body: lean and cut-up like the best steak. I'm talking Kobe beef, honey. And you didn't hear this from me, but homeboy is packing serious pipe

*too. That's what those lesser bitches in wardrobe keep telling
me, like I can do something about it."*

His body was pretty impressive; that's true. And I'm not
even into all that stuff. Make me laugh, don't have back hair,
smell freshly showered most days, and know the difference between *it's* and *its*—listen, you're halfway there with me, mister.
The fit body-muscle thing was never make-or-break in my books.
I've slept with the fatty, as well as the scrawny, the shorty, and
the black Hulk before. Interchangeable, all of them. The short
guy edges out by a nose, though, because he really puts his all
into it, and does the most with the least. But then sex was never
really high on my list of things. After a few close calls, my actual first time was in college, and it was gross. Not the bloody,
fumbling, dispiriting part. I'm talking solely about the guy
here—I'll call him Darren, because his name was Darren. Darren Andre Wilson. He was one of six guys in my Women in
Media class, and the only black one. Darren was earnest and he
took his time trying to get in my pants. He liked me; I knew
that for a fact, and it was the reason I enlisted him in Project
Virginity-free. I needed to get it over with, and he was cute and
kind and uncomplicated.

The actual moment I *became a woman* was decent enough.
Darren wasn't a jerk or incompetent. Where he really fucked
up, though, was the narrow shit stain that he left on my sheets.
I didn't see it until I was about to crawl back in the bed after
walking Darren partway down my dorm hallway. It must have
been three in the morning when—*whammo*—skid mark staring me in the face. I dashed those soft, unsuspecting yellow
gingham sheets in the garbage at the other end of the hall that
instant, and slept on two bunched-up duvets on the floor next
to my bed for the rest of the month. Couldn't shake the smear.
Darren dropped the class posthaste. Maybe it was the back-
to-back Ds he got on his term papers. Maybe it was the nick-

name that started trailing him: Shitty Sheets. (What? I told *one* person.)

With Grant, things got going early—as in, that first night after we stumbled out of Mo-Bay's. I didn't even have much to drink that night. Neither did he. We were talking and laughing about everything as we walked, aimless. How much we missed ketchup chips and Harvey's fries and Vachon pastries—Passion Flakie for me and for him, a tie between Jos Louis and Swiss Rolls. This wasn't an accurate tie, I insisted, since the latter in his snack-cake list was basically a smaller, rolled-up version of the former. He told me about his enduring goal to bring Major League baller Fergie Jenkins's autobiography to the big screen, and that when his wallet was jacked last year, he was in a near-dissociative state of panic wholly because his commemorative Fergie Jenkins stamp was in it. And I told him about my enduring crush on Michael J. Fox as well as my categorical reasons why Canada Post needs to hurry up and honor the man with a stamp too. Grant bet me that he could get a cab to stop for us extra-fast if he sidled up next to the dumpy blond woman standing on the corner nearby. He was right.

We slid into the car, across the warmed seats, sitting close enough that our heads gently knocked together a couple of times as we skimmed potholes. Then, while we were heading over the Brooklyn Bridge, it started. Hands and lips and gropes everywhere. By the time we got to my floor, we were *on the* floor, then the couch, on the counter, up against the fridge, bottom of the bed, in the shower. It was hot and sweaty and good. He stayed over. (Not my style.) I called in sick. (Also not my style.) We made breakfast together early that next morning and ate it sitting tucked beneath a pillow fort he made on the living-room floor. We lay there, tangled up like vines, and watched old game shows for hours. It felt good with Grant then. It felt normal. But it was never going to work. I'm not built for that.

When he called me the next week I was a little surprised. I was sure that he had only put my number in his phone because his Canadian insides would not allow him to treat me like some throwaway hookup. Appearances.

"Hey. It's Grant."

"Hey."

"I know. I didn't wait the customary—what?—ten days before calling, but I want to see you again. So, I'm calling today."

I smiled, but slid the phone speaker away from my mouth. He's an actor. They're trained to pick up on even the slightest nuance. "Yeah?"

"Yeah. Do you want to come hang out?"

"Maybe."

"Okay. We're doing this, we're playing that game?"

"Not a game. I don't know what you're going to propose; I'm maintaining a holding pattern. Can't fault a girl. You Hollywood types are freaky."

"Right. There's always the creep factor to consider. I get it. Me being a *Hollywood type* and everything, it's probably not going to help with what I'm about to propose. I mean, it's kind of far-out."

"Why, are you about to *propose* propose?"

"*Yo.* Not that far-out. But it does involve a hotel."

"A hotel."

"Yeah, I know. It's a long story and it's boring. Studio shit. Courtship for contract re-ups. My agent, Shawna, only told me about it two hours ago. Look, it's ridiculous and excessive and whatever the opposite of flattery is, but I'm doing it, apparently, to keep the waters calm."

"Wait, are they naming a penthouse suite after you or something?"

He laughed—a giggle, really, covered over in a breathy chuckle that slipped through his nose. It was cute, wiggling its way through the phone to the soft middle part of me just below my heart, and I knew I was about to say yes to whatever he was about to say next. I was in the net, trapped. That laugh of his— *infectious* doesn't quite describe it. The way it would start, in the base of his throat, tickling him as it rose up to his nose and then dancing on his lips. I liked when he would let it fly, loose and wild, his mouth open, actual *ha-ha's* tumbling out, his shoulders shaking and his head flopping off to the side. There was something so honest and joyful in it that left you surrendered, open, willing.

When I got to the hotel, Grant answered the door wearing the classic plush bathrobe along with a pair of thick, black-rimmed glasses.

"Are you seriously answering the hotel room door naked?" I said, stepping into the room despite my clear disapproval. "If there's a half-drunk bottle of Jack and some small coke mountain piled on a glass-top table in here . . . then congratulations on being a total cliché, sir."

Grant smiled, big and crooked. "You don't mince a word, do you?"

"Well, do you blame me? You invite me to your publicist-arranged, studio contract, carrot-on-a-stick thing and then answer the door nude."

"Bathrobe," he said and tightened the sash around his middle like a miffed housewife.

"Fine. Almost nude, in a bathrobe." I stepped in a little farther and scoped the grand suite. Whatever wasn't white was chrome, and the windows were as tall as the walls. It was the picture of luxury and excess, and it was inviting.

"I think once you slip this robe over yourself, you're going to want to be nude—sorry, *almost* nude too."

"Is that right? Just a complete panty-dropper, huh?"

"Feeling is believing, homie. I even took out my contacts— like my eyes wanted to be on that freedom flow too. Go in there," he said, making an easy motion with his head toward the wide bathroom. "There's another one—it's your size, smaller. I hung it on a hanger behind the door. Just slip it on, even over your clothes, and—you know what? No spoilers. You're your own woman. Go in there. Take responsibility for your life. I'm going to order up some French fries since that's kind of the only way you can really enjoy cocaine and Jack Daniel's. That's what I read in my *Hollywood Clichés Handbook*," he said, his face straight and staring right at me.

I shook my head and bit back my grin. "All right, then. Let me investigate this overpowering terry cloth."

"Actually, it's bamboo."

I narrowed my eyes at Grant and he broke. His giggle-chuckle pushed its way out and attached its cheerful self to my sleeve. And that was it: the marked moment when this man, with his singular laugh and movie-star chisel and helpless heart, descended into my brain, into my being, and started to build a home there.

———◆———

"Those fries, they almost taste like the ones from Harvey's," I said, pushing the tray toward the foot of the huge bed. "Actually, they kind of remind me of the fries at Mikes restaurant—did you guys have Mikes in Vancouver?"

Grant shook his head. It was so slight, it could have been a nod or shrug. He was lying back, propped by pillows, and his robe had opened all the way down to his belly button. I wanted to run my hand along the ridges of his cut-up abs. It looked smooth, taut. A flash of heat moved from my ears down to my ankles; it tickled. I smiled, but Grant didn't. His face was straight and serious, but not steely. He leaned toward me, resting his head on the edge of my pillow pile, and I met him there. The kiss started soft. Grant's warm hand was sliding up the inside of my robe, along my leg, stopping just below my waist and pressing his fingers into the flesh, clutching at my hip bone. His lips tasted exactly as I wanted them to and his breath was hot and a little sweet. I felt that kiss; felt him everywhere. I didn't want it to end.

He pulled away first. Asked if I was okay. "I don't want you to feel like I'm forcing you into this. I mean, I am a Hollywood weirdo—or was it freak?" He pulled back some more and winked. And I actually liked it. I liked his corny wink. I liked him.

"We should update your name from Hollywood Weirdo to Prom Night Tease. I think you just gave me blue balls."

He laughed his laugh. "No, no. Never that. I'm just trying to . . . I don't know"—he paused and repositioned himself, sliding deeper into his bed—"slow things down."

I shuffled over, away from him, and nestled into the bed as well. "Okay. So, no more kissing?"

"No, no. Most def kissing. Yeah, lots of that. Like, so much that. I just . . . I guess I just want to talk a little bit. Does that sound wack?"

"Not at all. I like talking. You probably figured that out."

"Yeah. I did. You do. I like it."

"What do you want to talk about?"

He rolled onto his back and stared up at the ceiling for a stretch. "This is going to sound . . ." He paused even longer.

Something bubbled up in my chest, a strange need to rescue him from the awkward moment brewing right there next to us. It was this weird pull toward him. I wanted him to feel safe and at ease; I almost reached out to grab his hand and clench it in mine. Instead, I just started talking.

"You would never know this unless I told you, but I went to an all-girls Catholic high school. I actually wanted to go. It was this ancient convent that was completely converted into a school. In my second-to-last year there, a new student came. She was a boarder from northern Quebec named Marie-Claude.

Poor Marie-Claude Bouchard, spinal bifida leaving her with full-length leg braces on both deformed limbs. She had to use the rickety elevator that was reserved for the staff and any disabled students, which was just her at the time. A handful of us were tasked with escorting Marie-Claude on the elevator to her dorm room, to the gym on the lower level, cafeteria, chapel, everywhere. There was a schedule and we would ride along with her, sometimes chatting about our classes and listening to the weird clanging sounds of the old counterweight system, hoping it would never fail us like it had Kira, the time she got trapped in that box for two hours with Marie-Claude. Kira had to change Marie-Claude's adult diaper. Scarred for life, Kira was."

Grant's face warmed up again, and I could almost see the weight of whatever was happening in his world lifting off his body. He was rapt and inching his way over to me on the bed as he listened to each word leaving my mouth.

"Anyway, Marie-Claude had this journal she took with her most everywhere. It had drawings, magazine pages, and cutouts, and there was a thin strip of paper on the front cover that said *For the Shitty Days*. Her best friend from home made it for her, she had told each of us at different times on our elevator rides. One morning, I found the journal left behind in the bathroom and I flipped through it. But then I decided to write in it. I scrawled a bunch of vile shit about her, like how she smelled like piss and sour milk. Just mean for no reason. I felt bad about it immediately after I did it, and when Marie-Claude's handler for the day found it and showed it to her—that was pretty awful. I never admitted that I did it. I actually told myself that it's just what teenagers do, that being horrible at being a person was necessary for us to figure how to be better. But deep down I think I knew that wasn't true. I think I knew that there was something else in me, something black and menacing, arching its way up to the surface." I took a breath, unsure that I wanted to continue. But the words, they were coming, and I knew there was no way I could stop them. "And this thing inside me, it stayed there, showing up later, unwanted but sticking around anyway, for the shitty days and beyond."

"Jesus, Best. You can't hang onto things you did as a kid. If we all did that, we'd suffocate. We'd stop functioning and choke on all of it. I wouldn't even be here if I stayed fixed on everything from my shitty childhood."

"What do you mean?"

"I mean I wouldn't be here; I'd be dust." Grant propped himself up on his elbows. "I was a really unhappy kid. Moody, sad, miserable most days. For a long time, I didn't think I would make it. I didn't think I could do life, you know? But my mom"—he shook his head—"she wasn't down with that. She saw a different version. Like, she could see the pages laid out before they were even written. She hooked me up with someone—a therapist—and things started to just look better."

"Sounds like she was an extraordinary woman, your mother."

Grant dropped flat to his back again. "That's what I was getting ready to say before . . . Tomorrow. It's my mom's birthday tomorrow. She's been gone twelve years and it still doesn't seem real. I know in my brain that it's true: she's gone, she's not in our house, she's not locked away in the garage in her studio, she's not on this earth anymore, but large parts of me just won't believe it. It's like I can't believe it. I can't accept it."

"Because it's unacceptable," I said, and pulled myself close to him.

He turned his body toward me, our eyes lining up exactly, and he wrapped his hand around my wrist. "You're right. That's what it is: It's unacceptable."

We stayed that way, as if looking into a mirror, quiet and fading, resting on each other's calm for what could have been an hour or three. And all I could think was the whole thing—

the kiss, the bathrobes, French fries and beer and pillows—I wanted it to last forever and let everything else blur away. But it could never be that, and I knew this. It could never be happy and consumed and dazzling. Those things aren't meant for me. And poor Grant will soon know this too. Like everyone else who's tried in earnest to pull me in, pull me closer, he'll figure out that I'm not worthy of any of it.

> **Ty—you in BK?**
> *depends*
> **Need your beauty services. Plus, I have Stoli.**
> *Say that 1st next time homegirl*
> **Bring cranberry juice too, pls!**
> *My bruno maglis don't mix with bodega*
> **Fashion fool! Just hurry up. Kendra's waiting on me.**

Time with Tyson, even when we're both sober, is always good. He makes me laugh until my face is sore, and somehow still pulls off minor miracles with my makeup looks. He's my best-kept beauty secret. We've had some of our grandest moments sitting on the floor of the cramped disaster zone known as my closet, digging through forgotten fabrics and somehow finding treasures. But we rarely talked about Grant back then. And Grant knew he was the third wheel when he tried to squeeze into our vodka-laced cackling closet sessions.

When things fell apart for Grant, we left that day, raced up to Connecticut to his uncle's. And when I got back home alone, Tyson didn't phone or text me back, he came right over—within the hour of my distress call. Tyson sat with me on the illegal roof deck. He cooked his grandmother's gumbo for me. He watched back-to-back-to-back *Golden Girls* episodes and played Stevie Wonder for me on his iPhone, splitting his earbuds and getting me to sing along with him out loud. And he never once uttered Grant's name. But we both felt something wedged between us on the living-room floor, like a ghost neither of us could see or even be sure really existed.

Temptation returns. I want to call Grant. This space everyone keeps saying he needs—that I need and we need—I want to fill it with pillows and build a King-style fort and crawl inside of it and eat dry cereal and kiss and read thick, slick magazines, and call in sick to everything.

CHAPTER 3

Before I can clear the elevator door, Trinity pounces. "Did you hear about Miyuki?"

I raise my brows, then my Starbucks cup to her eyeline. "She got promoted. Senior Ed."

"Miyuki *Butler*?" I bark before saying it again, quieter and checking over both my shoulders as we continue down the hall.

"I know; it's crazy," Trinity whispers. She grabs my free arm and stops me from walking. "I've been here longer than that girl and do way more work by lunch than she gets done all fucking day."

It's true. Trinity has put in serious work at Millhause-Steig. Four years under JK—that's a decade in editorial-assistant time—and before that, she was an intern in Nikolai Steig's office. Oz himself. Most kids quit that post and run screaming like freed demons after six weeks. My Titi, only daughter of hippies turned lawyers, held it down for eighteen long months.

The muffled knocks and thumps from random high heels streaming by us make Trinity look even more anxious. She keeps scanning the hallway, forcing her hot words through the side of a clenched jaw; lips folded extra-thin. I nudge her and we move into the meditation room. It's a dim, padded closet near the pantry primarily used for crying. But crying has never been my thing, and doing it at work just seems reckless, even hidden away in a closet. I use the room when I need to call home to Montreal. The thick silence and darkness of the stale room somehow make it easier for me to talk to my parents. I don't have to look at anything when I'm in there; my eyes won't wander to my bookshelf or to the old tea tin filled with my green pens or my absurd, expensive purse hanging on its very specific hook. And I don't hear anyone laughing just beyond the door. I can focus on my father's words, listen closer for what he means to say. There have been times—rare—that I even heard something like joy underneath his stories. I don't think I would have caught it if I weren't in this dull closet.

"Okay. Run the bullet on this." I close door behind us and set my cup on the grimy ledge. The tea is already cold and I already know from Trinity's damp forehead that I'm not going to be in the mood for sipping anything after she gives me the full story on Miyuki Butler.

"It was Joan's idea, from what I understand," Trinity says. I want to give her a tissue, my coat sleeve, scarf—anything to wipe that sweaty brow, but she's about to unleash her tucked-away Southie accent and go on a speed-taking blitz. Mattified skin won't change a thing here. "Total fucking bullshit. *Gawddam* fucking bullshit. Four ye-ahs, four fucking ye-ahs I'm doing this, shovelin' awl the shit, and this bitch comes awn boawd—"

"Wait. Hold up. Did JK just go along with this?"

"Yeah, kind of. She's been backseat on a lot lately." Trinity frowns at me. "You've seen her at the meetings. *What do you think, Joan? Let's check with Joan and circle back. I want to hear Joan's two cents on this.* At first I thought it was about making her feel welcomed and needed those first weeks, but now—Jesus Murphy, it's like Joan is full-awn runnin' this shit."

"Let's focus, T. Facts only. Do we know what sections of the book Miyuki Butler will be handling? Or will there be a duty split with any of the other editors, the effective ones, like maybe, Isabelle?"

"I'm not sure."

"Does Robot—uh, Joan's assistant—have any intel?"

"No. That idiot is still trying to figure out how voice mail works. She's always got a shit-ton of questions about everything every day, all day." Trinity has no tolerance for slowpokes. "Hey, are you going to be okay?" she says.

I can't fix my face. I know it's contorted. "This is just . . ."

"Bullshit, I know. *I know*. Anyway, I should get back. JK's husband is getting some award this week and she's speaking at NYU on the same day, so I'm basically on beta-blockers duty. She's probably pinging me now." Trinity cracks the door and slips her head out, looking left and right. "Clear," she says, glancing back at me. "Drinks later?"

"I think that's our only choice."

We part and I beeline it to my office, slide the frosted door shut. I'm among the lucky few to have an office. It's actually a cubicle boxed in by thin walls and frosted glass. Smoke and mirrors.

My cell phone practically jumps into my trembling palm, and I'm jabbing the keys like it's whack-a-mole.

"Go for Kendra," she says. Kendra never offers a simple hello.

"I want to stab her neck with a dull pencil."

"Hello? *Who is this*?"

"Kendra, I'm not in the mood."

"Robot again?"

"Yes. She's just making it all terrible. All of it."

"What'd she do this time?"

"Just woke up breathing."

"Best, I know it's not funny, but the intense hatred you feel for this woman? It's pretty fucking funny."

"She resents me. She resents what I'm about, what I represent: a young, black woman sitting at the table, being noticed, being heard. I'm a sharper, smarter, cooler her, and she resents me. I'm out here highlighting her inadequacies every day. Of course she resents me. Please. I'm sure that's been bumped up to *hate* at this point."

"But wasn't she in the newspaper game for years? And she's married to that old sports columnist—what's his name? Gordon Gartrell or whatever. That's got to buy her some cred, no?"

"It's Gordon Gregory, and no. It doesn't buy her shit. Her ideas are wack. Mine are perceptive. She's this stiff, boring, unoriginal, navy-blue suit, and I am color, wit, and charm. I know what this audience wants to read about, what they care about. No one has to explain what the Bulgarian love lock is to me."

"Wait, please tell me that you're making that part up. The Bulgarian love lock? Gross. Who had to explain *that* to her?"

"Exactly. She wanted to edit the reference out of my story. That and the other five hundred and ninety-seven words I wrote, basically. And she's always bottlenecking everything that I try to do. You know what, I'd bet a fucking Birkin that she's stealing my ideas and presenting them to JK as her own brilliance. Susie never did that bullshit."

"Why are you even writing about the Bulgarian love lock— so gross. That job of yours . . ."

"I know. I could do better."

"Come on, Best. It's vaginas and penises and *tittays* all day. What's better than that? Plus, you regularly get to sit and giggle on morning TV—in full hair and makeup, I should add— with that silver fox. That man is hot as hell. He's been on my could-get-it list since I was in middle school."

"I'm sure Robot Joan is going to put an end to that too."

"That would be a dummy move. You're beyond fabulous on

TV. People love waking up and seeing your gorgeous face talking about how to get off."

"It's not all sex stuff."

"Um, the Bulgarian love lo—"

"I'm just saying I also write about health and science and psychology."

"Best, you're the one always complaining about being the *vajeen* queen. I'm just saying that you're good at it. The *James* magazine people know that. Even this Robot Joan woman knows it, which is why you're a threat and she's trying to make you throw up the white flag."

"Maybe I need to break out of my lane, then. Do something big and important, outside of my *vajeen* purview."

"Start by never using the word *purview* again, please."

"You sound more like your sister day by day."

"Twin power, baby."

"Not a compliment."

As always, Kendra's laugh starts to chip away at my scowl. I feel my face sliding back to calm. She catches her breath, clears her throat. "Look, are you serious about quitting this time?"

"Quitting? I'm not quitting. I'm talking about showing off my wingspan."

"By dunking a basketball or something? *Wingspan?* Jesus, Best."

"Listen, you're riding my nerve right now, Kendra."

"What do you want—you're talking about purviews and wingspans. This is not Best Lightburn language."

"That's what I mean. I'm going show the Robot that there's more here than penises entering vaginas. Whatever. I'm going to pitch that honor-killing story."

"Good Christ. That story is awful. Like I said *last* month, just give up on that story already. Why get into all of that?"

"Because I've been working on this for almost four months,

Kendra. And I'm so close to getting through to her, getting an actual phoner with the surviving daughter. I know I can get this interview and the Robot—scheme all she wants—can't swipe this story from me and claim it as her own. This story is it for me. It's weighty and compelling and heartbreaking. It's meaningful. It's a meaningful story that I have to write. I need to write it."

"It's also an ad-killer. Do you think brands are going to be clamoring to buy space next to that gruesome story?"

"We've run other edgy stories before. Like the S-and-M guide or the new sex-positions illustrated guide. And then we did the anal-sex thing—"

"Right, *Butt Seriously*. Who can forget that one?"

"You know what I'm saying, Kendra. We've done other stories before that were pushed up against the line that you're not supposed to cross. The advertisers didn't recoil, clutching their pearls."

"That's sex. This is murder and religion—specifically Islam, which is not having a banner decade, my friend. It's grisly. How are ads for mascara and tampons or worse, the pill, going to hold up next to a story like that?"

"But I'm not talking about the grisly stuff, the killings. It's going to be about living, about moving from death to life, without shame or guilt." I spin around in my chair and notice a figure looming by the door. No idea how long they've been there, but they have good timing. "Kendra, I gotta bounce."

"Please think this through, Best. That honor-killing thing is not a good idea," she says in a rush. "Not even a little bit."

"Miss Singh, please, let's do this lecture later, okay?"

"Wait, one more thing—is writing fashion content for our site still *out of the question*? 'Cause we just launched a new Tumblr. You'd crush that shit. You know I'm always good to talk to people here, pull strings, twist arms, crack skulls."

"From vadge to fashion?"—I whisper—"Oh, that's exactly what I need to do to establish myself as a serious journalist. Let me just go. Shadow at the frosted pane."

"Meet us later? Me, Flavio, and some friends are hitting Pop Bar."

"Maybe. I'll see what time I get out. And this better not be some blind-date bullshit, Kendra. Grant's just down, not out."

"You sure about that? Did you see the latest post on *Tell Me More*? Grant King is getting the *Where's Waldo?* treatment. Not a good look for your man."

"Do I have to say it in Bengali next, Kendra? I have to go."

"Fine. Just don't threaten me with the Bulgarian Love—"

"So much. I hate you too much. Bye!"

I can already sense who's at the door: Robot's assistant. She smells like black licorice and oppression.

"It's okay to knock, Kristen." I slide the door open and try to keep my smile easy.

"I know, sorry. I saw that you were on the phone. I didn't want to disturb you."

"What's up?"

"Joan wants to see you."

"About what, did she say?"

"She did, and I wrote it down, actually on a sticky note that I was going to leave on your desk if you were out or on your door if you were on the phone or something, like just now, but I forgot it on my desk along with the FedEx stuff I have to drop off at the mailroom. I was thinking about heading back to get it, but then figured I should probably just wait and tell you instead of running the risk of you stepping away while I stepped away and then missing you altogether. Sorry."

I'm dizzy. "That's okay. Do you remember when she wants to meet?"

"Yes. Now."

"Next time, don't bury the lede."

"Sorry, there's just a lot of catch-up and the last girl didn't leave much of anything to help me transition."

"That's because there was no last girl. Susie didn't need an assistant." Reel it in, Lightburn. She's a direct line to this woman. "But clearly there needs to be one, right? So that's good."

"Right. Thanks. And sorry about the long story."

"No apology needed, Kristen." This faux-smiling thing physically hurts. "Thanks for letting me know." Oh, shit. She's lingering. "So . . . you should probably do that mailroom stuff now, right?"

"Yeah, crap. Yes, ohmigod. Sorry. Thanks."

⎯⎯⎯⎯◦✦◦⎯⎯⎯⎯

The massive yellow door is ajar. Susie's old office is totally transformed. What was cool and cozy (and kooky in some spots) is now cold and starchy. Gone are the soft mood lamps, the mustard paisley chair, the blue, button-tufted mini-sofa, and that ridiculous, empty wooden birdcage. Just vanished. Where Susie had a collection of wild photos that told their own stories, the Robot has just two pictures in thin, simple frames—facing her. The one I could glimpse is black-and-white, old, with a tall person leaned up against a bicycle. The other one is slightly larger, horizontal, and angled so that you can only make out the edge of a waterfall and some jagged, dark rocks. Everything else on her oversized glass-top desk is about work: folders, galleys, pens (mainly red ones) jammed into a steel cup.

On the ledge behind her stuffy wingback are the required smoke-up-your-ass plaques and awards—hers largely pertain to sports journalism and being a black woman—plus her farewell *Sports Illustrated* mock cover was hung most prominently.

Even in that photo, she's cheerless, holding some manila folders against her boring blazer. One of the coverlines on the faux
mag mentioned her "severe" Mets fandom. That was, like, strike
18. I mean, *baseball?* Jesus. When she shared this tidbit as one
of her *great loves* at that first edit meeting, it was like, my king-
dom for a cow patty to hurl at her chest. But I actually played
it shrewd and told her that I was a brokenhearted Expos gal,
"You know, back when they were from Montreal." Complete
fiction. Like my father, I never liked or respected the game. We
use to give Benjamin so much shit for watching baseball and
then—the *nerve*—asking to play it when he started high school.
He was good too, but then there wasn't a sport created that
Benjamin Lightburn couldn't master. Sometimes, when I first
moved here, I would turn on a late-night Yankees game on the
clock radio—AM—just to have in the background, white noise
to help me sleep. But I would end up dreaming about Benjamin, and I couldn't have that. Now when I can't sleep, I grab
a pill or drink NyQuil.

More than bonding over the silly sport, I told the Robot the
baseball lie so I could slip in the part about my being Canadian, a Montrealer, and rather unlike the usual black American
women she's encountered in the office over the years. Yeah, no
go. She has remained as uncharmed and impenetrable as when
we first met.

<hr />

I knock on the open door anyway. It's what I always see
Kristen do. The Robot's not alone. Miyuki, all horse teeth and
glitter eye makeup, is sitting to her right. Three other senior
editors—Ashley, Isabelle, and Maggie—are also there, with
their skinny legs crossed twice, trying to look effortless on the
edge of those hard chairs.

"Just finishing up, Best," Robot says.

The others are looking at me, head to toe. I need to concentrate. No fear, no flinch. "Sure thing. Do you want me to come back later?"

"No, just hang out there in the hall," Robot says. "We'll only be a minute or so more. Editor stuff. Don't want to bore you." All of her smiles look penciled in.

I can sense Miyuki gloating, feel her relishing every minute of this bullshit inner-circle moment, and I want to spit. "Of course. No problem. Just give me a shout when you're ready."

"Oh, actually, Best,"—the Robot says; she sounds almost pleasant—"could you close the door for us? Thanks."

My name is not Alfred Pennyworth. *Bitch, please.*

"Sure." I know my smile looks plastic, but I doubt the Robot can tell. I make sure to keep it spread evenly across my face while pulling the door toward me.

This is fine. Waiting in the wings gives me a chance to straighten up, breathe out the bitter and focus on the work, gather my words. I see Trinity zipping around in the background. We make brief eye contact, and she points her finger gun to her temples, pulls the thumb trigger. I send her a quick up-nod and start a light pacing near the Robot's door. As the minutes click by, agitation stirs. I can't hear anything coming from the inside. What are they, whispering?

Pacing is over. Now I'm staring at the door, plain and overt, hoping it magically tells me something. (The fact that all of the top editors have heavy, yellow doors—not frosted sliding ones—is probably some mind game. I'm sure there's a funded study that can back me up.)

Kristen's still not back at her desk. She truly is useless. Just as I take a step towards her little assistant area to see what I can spy, the Robot's door opens. Maggie's the first one out, as usual.

"Hey, girl-pie," Maggie says.

Yeah, I don't know what it means either. She says it every single time we cross paths. She's either oblivious to how grating it is or she already knows and couldn't care less. I vote it's the latter; Maggie takes assholery to new levels. She's a thoroughbred Upper West Side New Yorker. Old money, father's side. This magazine gig is about annoying her grandparents. She also uses her mother's maiden name, just to add more salt to things.

"Maggs, what's up?"

"Same old hustle, you know. On my grind. But it's all good." (Note well: Margaret Martin is a walking urban dictionary. She makes sure to use all of the words all of the time, pushed together like a run-on sentence. I can only nod when she gets going.)

Isabelle and Ashley float out next. Here comes a compliment from Ashley in 3, 2 . . .

"Such a cute belt, Best."

"Thanks, Ashley. I've had it forever."

"You always say that. Still cute, though."

Ashley and Maggie head off. Isabelle's close behind them, but stops and turns back to me. "After your meet, stop by my desk, okay?" she says. Isabelle is lukewarm and flat in her delivery most days, all about business. She's also German, so I just pin it all on that. "I'll have a big folder and tons of links for you on Heidi," Isabelle says.

"Wait, links on Heidi?"

"Oh, Joan and Miyuki will fill you in. Talk later." Isabelle starts down the hall before I have a chance to step over the turd she just dropped on the carpet between us.

This drive-by-shooting-style of assigning stories to me used to happen a lot when I first got here. Ashley told me it was because the Yellow Doors really liked my voice. "They say I write like a slightly more knowledgeable best friend, full of cool, but minimal condescension," she said. Plus, I write that shit quickly. Things I learned from my super-brief internship at *GQ* before *James* snatched me up one month in. The two most important rules of magazine writing: 1) Locking in on tone, and 2) meeting your deadlines. Oh, and one more: Knowing how to stifle an eye roll. But that's more a useful lesson for general life. That last one definitely comes in handy when working under a loveable narcissist like the one Janice Kessler.

Example: JK came in one morning wearing these shoe-boot sandals. And they were all of those things at once—a shoe, a boot, and a sandal. A reporter from the *New York Times* was shadowing her for part of the day, doing a story on our magazine's issues issue (domestic abuse). The reporter, a man, noticed her *shooboodals* (let it settle). He called them provocative, I think. After he left, JK turned to me and said: "I'm so glad he noticed my shoes. There are only six of these in the world. I had these shipped in from Saudi Arabia two weeks ago." Eye roll of life issued; totally undetected.

<hr>

"Best, come on in," Robot says. "Oh, you didn't bring a notebook?"

Fucking Kristen. "No, sorry. I didn't know what this was about and Kristen didn't—"

"Do you want to borrow a sheet from Miyuki?"

"I'm good. Thank you, though."

The way I held my tone just then, my relaxed jaw and softened brow—that's some award-winning poise, cultivated with care by Miriam Annette Cumberbatch Lightburn. My mother— the original version, not the hollowed-out one you'd meet today—was a master at that kind of thing. She never let on that underneath those sweet grins and gentle eyes, there was a dragon, breathing fire, judgment, disapproval, and bitter loathing. My father often joked about it, this illusion, and called my mother Teebee, short for *tamarind ball*. I didn't get it until we took our first family trip to Barbados. He made a big production out of buying us kids a bag of tamarind balls—brown and small and rolled in fine sugar—to try that first afternoon there, as we headed back from the beach.

"Chil'ren," he said, his Trinidadian lilt turned up on high, "I want all yuh to wait and bite the tam'rin at once, together. And I wan' take a pick-cha with yuh ma pose up behind all yuh as you do it." He was all teeth, standing there, backing the rocky road, gripping his clunky Canon and counting down from three.

It was so bitter, this dishonest treat. Our faces puckered as my father laughed and laughed. All into the evening, it would erupt from his belly and spill out over his face. Soon enough, it spread to us and we started laughing too—even my mother chuckled. I remember Benjamin elbowed me: "Do you think he's ever going to stop cracking up about this?" I told him, "Never. We're going to get sick of hearing it."

I wish I could remember what it sounded like, that laugh. I wouldn't get sick of it. Never.

The Robot looks over at Miyuki, like she's waiting for the *go* light to flick on. "James and I have been talking and we want to get the jump on the next big-issue theme," Robot says. "James and I really believe that we can use this issue—this whole book, really—to shed light on real and profound challenges that our girl is going through."

The Robot is talking to me, but constantly looking over at Miyuki . . . who is still fucking sitting in here, sparkling like a fake gem. And "our girl"? That's classic JK-speak. She always refers to the reader as "our girl." I'm nervous again. I don't know where this whole thing is going.

"The senior editors and I were brainstorming new themes to cover this year, and we've got a pretty great list going. Isabelle tells me that, in years past, you've been a key player in the big-issue issue, so we'll have you do the anchor in the feature well again. We really want to hit the ground running this time and go showcase here. I'm thinking we can throw some story ideas at the wall today, see what sticks. Then go off, sharpen our pencils and come back to it."

What in the entire fuck? How many cornball clichés can one android use in fifteen seconds? That was ridiculous and gratuitous. Yet there's Miyuki, grinning and nodding like she's in a minstrel show.

"Did you have anything to throw out now? I know you didn't bring your notes."

"Actually, I do have something, an idea that I've been cooking for a bit. We've covered diseases, disorders, and various abuses in issues past—domestic was a big one; we actually did it twice." I pop up two fingers and try not to cut my eyes at this basic bitch. "We've also focused on addiction. JK's charity, of course, played large there. But I wanted to look at the thing that too often connects most of these issues. The thing that allows so much of these disorders, these addictions, to fester and too often leaves the victims drying up in the corner in silence. It's shame. Guilt is in there too a little, I guess, but it's really about the shame of it. I say we do a no-shame issue, where we help the reader do away with the useless thing for good."

"Okay," Robot says. "But what would the feature be about?"

Keep eyes gazing just past Robot's shoulder, take a beat, and go. "Right. So there's this really horrible news story, a crime story, out of Scarborough, Ontario—which is basically Toronto. Canada." (This is the only moment I look over at Miyuki.) "This father, Bashir Imam, a Muslim, stands accused of killing his four daughters. He drug-poisoned them first, then drowned them in the vacationing neighbor's pool. And the son helped."

"Oh my God," Miyuki blurts out. "That's so awful. This happened?"

"Yes. Anyway, the newspapers called it an honor killing. He did it, they said, because the daughters brought shame on the family, picking up grubby Western habits, that kind of thing. One of them even had a Portuguese-Canadian boyfriend."

"Best, I don't think—"

"There's more. One of the sisters survived. She was pretty beat up, obviously, but she made it. She survived this horrific thing. This horrific thing brought about from shame. I think if we interviewed her, maybe an as-told-to or something, we could really dig into something meaty and meaningful and powerful."

"I don't—"

"She wouldn't talk about the crime of it. That trial is long over—it was practically a lock on guilty from day one. We'd talk to her about what's left behind after a crime like that."

Miyuki looks at the Robot and at me and over at her again.

"Look, Best, I don't think that this story works for our girl. It's not a good fit for *James*. At all."

"Yeah, I have to agree with Joan here," Miyuki rushes in. "I mean, even if there was some part of it that might work for *James*, why would she talk to us? Why would she talk to you? I mean, that totally sounds like the Canadian newspapers and media and stuff would've been all over it already. Especially an interview with the survivor." She looks at the Robot, who's of course giving deep nods. "But that poor girl, though. Oh my God, seriously, I can't even imagine. Is the mother not around? Or did he kill her too? Sick."

"No, he didn't kill the mother, Miyuki. She died some years back, before they moved to Scarborough."

"Awful. This story gets more awful by the minute," Miyuki says. She puts her hand to her chest and gasps. It's all over-done.

"In any event, this won't work, Best. I'm sorry." The Robot's top lip is crimped. I want to rip that glossy, gummy sneer clean off her—*Jesus, be a fence!* And that gaping asshole over there, I want nothing more than to sink my five-inch heel square in her face.

"But I think there's something there, Joan. Even if we don't get to the daughter for a face-to-face or even a phoner, a story on her—on what happened—could be really gripping." I'm trying the locked gate again. It's what my father would do. "We've covered heavy, heady stories before—the breast-cancer spread, for example. That was pretty unsettling. Those photos? We could do that again. We should do it; do serious, disturbing, pivotal stories. These readers are ripe for that shit." Miyuki shifts in her seat, shoots a look at the Robot, like this is church. "I'm sorry. I just think that this is the kind of story that we should be doing, and I feel very strongly about it."

"While I agree about us taking deeper dives on the serious topics, this one is not it," the Robot says. She glances down at her note cards, as if there's anything remotely original and honest on them. Did I mention that? She puts everything on large index cards. Blue ones, like she's a talk-show host. I can't decide what's more annoying: the pretense we're all adopting that whatever she has written on her crutch cards matters or having to stare at the sloppy parts at the top of her braids-head while she looks down to consult them.

"Let's keep going," Robot says. "Is there anything else?"

"Maybe we could do something about mental health, depression, and how the shame around it usually stops people from getting help," Miyuki says. "We can come at it from Best's other beat: relationships. Like how you can help your best friend or sister or girlfriend or something step out of the shame and get help. We could use Lana Scott as our angle."

I want to roll my eyes and maybe spit.

The Robot is clearly lost. She's frowning. "Lana . . . Scott?"

"Oh, she's that model-turned-writer. She's beautiful, just stunning. She's African-American too," Miyuki says, nodding at the Robot and me. "Back in January, she tried to take her own life. It was everywhere. So shocking and sad."

I knew Lana Scott, but just on the margins. The handful of times that our lives crossed and we spoke, I thought she was gorgeous, exceptionally so. Then everything that held up that beauty began to seep through her perfect nutmeg skin. By the third meet-up, Lana started to sound a little lost or lonely or a sad mix of the two, and we both knew she—not only an It girl, but a black It girl—wasn't really allowed to be any of those things.

"I see," Robot says. "But if we were to tackle depression, we'd have Ashley get one of her top-shelf health writers on it. Now that I say that, I'm thinking we should move the Heidi Morrison story over to health too." She turns to Miyuki. "Be sure to tell Isabelle of this change." The Robot returns her lukewarm interest to me. "For you, maybe something on sex— sex and shame. Do you have anything there?"

"Story ideas about sex and shame?" I bite the inside of my cheek. I taste the blood and bite again. It's strangely soothing, in that weird can't-stop-touching-a-hangnail way. "Just general shame around having sex?"

"Oh, totally. There's like so much seriously crazy stuff happening in the boudoir," Miyuki says, only her syllables are all fucked up and she rests hard on the "r"—*Boo-DWAR*—completely oblivious to how dumb she sounds. Miyuki also says *IN-surance*, in case you're keeping notes. Tiny ants spread across my skin, pinching as they race-crawl to their final destination: my last nerve.

"Really? Crazy stuff, you say." My brand of mockery is so nuanced; don't worry. It's way over the head of hill folk like Miyuki Butler.

"No, really. I was watching this thing,"—it's never *reading this thing* with her—"about sex addiction last week, and they were talking about how the American Psych Association wanted to add it to the DSM as a legitimate thing: hypersexual disorder."

"Actually, that proposal was rejected. *By* the APA. It's not considered an official psychiatric disorder at all, so . . ." *Get that shit out of here.*

"Right, but the whole show was about the shame around sex addiction. And honestly, having the APA totally deny you as legitimate probably adds to things, you know what I mean?"

"Good point, Miyuki. Why don't you go back to the boards, Best, and put together three to five story ideas around sex and shame. We can circle back end of week and call some shots from there. And on your way out"—dismissed without a second breath—"just set time with Kristen for Friday and we can hash it out."

"Should I check with Trinity for JK as well?" I'm nodding, but Robot's face is twisted.

"No," she says, still squinting. "Just you, me and Miyuki."

"Miyuki?" Now I've got sour-face.

"Yes, she's going to run point," Robot says.

I'm blinking, or at least I think I am. "Oh, when you said 'run point' I assumed that meant—wait, Isabelle always does first edits on my stuff and moves it to Susie . . . which is you, now."

"Miyuki's the new Isabelle for you, now." She gives me that curdled half-grin. It's clear that I've angered her. But fuck that. I'm angered. Miyuki Butler editing me? In what fucking Mars-as-the-sun universe does Miyuki Butler edit me? I take a breath and focus on Miyuki. I let my eyes blur and like that, she's nothing but shadows.

When I was a child, I had this keen ability to stare at someone for just a short time and they would start to fade away, as if a thick black curtain was drawn before them. I did it mostly at home, when one of my brothers was annoying me or my mother was going on about the indignities of her geriatric patients and I couldn't bear to hear another sound leaving her mouth. A few times I was able to pull this off at school, but I needed to be extremely agitated, and that wasn't easy to do back then. I was a pretty calm kid, especially for the baby of the family. Miss Carter, my grade-five teacher, called me phlegmatic. She wrote it in the parent-teacher notes section on my report card. I looked it up, of course, before handing the thing over to my folks. My dad told me it was a good thing for me to be, but as an adult.

"You're too young to be phlegmatic," he said. "Children need some emotion close up, right on the surface."

I nodded, but didn't really understand what he meant. About a month after that report card, I got into a fight at school. My first one. My only one. It was with Jean-Luc Caron. He called me a black shit. Actually, he called me an *ugly nigger black shit*. I punched him directly in his pointed nose, not because I was insulted. Clearly, that dumb Québécois kid just grabbed a bunch of words and hurled them in my direction. I punched him because it just seemed like the right thing to do right then in the frosty schoolyard. I also did it to show Miss Carter that she shouldn't be so goddamn presumptuous.

"Was there something more?" the Robot says. "You look confused."

It's a side effect of the blackout trick. I hadn't faded anyone in so long, I forgot about the stupefied look that takes over my face afterward.

"Oh, no. Not confused. Just thinking about ideas." I make that silly clucking sound with my tongue, the one that usually goes along with a wink or thumbs-up.

"Good." The Robot's eyes are bouncing between the door and me. Subtly is not easy for these droids.

"Right, so I'll check in with Kristen."

"Good."

"Open or closed—the door?" I know I'm pushing it, but it's fun. A little.

"Doesn't matter," she says. Her displeasure is palpable.

"Great. Thanks for the meeting, ladies." Before she has time to deliver another exasperated squint, I quickly spin on my high heels, to the point that I wobble a bit, but keep it moving. I just need to get back to my foggy little cube and start making some calls. Top of the list: my father. I know he still has his hands swishing around in the crime-reporter pools. Of course, this means going through my mother first. I'm going to need a day before I make this call. Maybe three.

<hr />

Both my desk phone and cell are ringing when I get back to my office. I answer the work one; mute my mobile—both calls are from the same person. "Kendra, why do you insist on doing the double call? It's so—"

"Best." She's using her flat and serious voice. "You need to see the breaking news on *Tell Me More.*"

I jiggle the mouse, wake my computer, but the quiet new-mail chime is clinking along on loop and I watch as my new e-mail counter cycles up in number. I glance down at my phone monitor. The voice-mail notification is lit up and keeps blinking: fourteen missed calls, all unknown numbers.

"Listen, it's not good," Kendra says. "Actually, it's a fucking mess. They know about Grant's whole *mental snap* situation . . . and they know about you too."

I heard her, but I didn't hear her. More than anything, what I heard was my heaving breathing through the phone—panting, really. My brain started to go down the line of possible permutations: They know about me and Grant? They know about me and Grant and Connecticut? Or, they know about *me*?

"You still there?" Kendra says.

It clicks right then. Kendra wouldn't be this chill and gathered if the *Tell Me More* story was about *me-me.* She'd have way more shit to say to me than *you still there?*

"Yeah . . . yeah, I'm still here. I don't know . . . I guess, I'm just kind of over the vulture-ing of Grant's story. When does it stop? Give the man a minute."

"I know," she says. "But they're going to keep digging—you know that, right?"

I shake my head. "I guess."

"That's why maybe it's better to live your life out in the open. Just keep it real. No surprises, no secrets."

My chest tightens a little, and the quiet building on the phone begins to feel heavy. "I should bounce. I'll see you there?"

"Hells-to-the! Sex-shop galas are always a good way to end the workday. Don't gotta ask me twice. Finishing up two things and I'm out of here. I'll cab it over. Catch you later, sk—"

I hang up before Kendra can get the full word out: skater. It always low-key bothers me when she calls me that. Of course, she wouldn't know why it stings me, and I want to keep it that way.

CHAPTER 4

Eye contact. Always maintain eye contact. If I had a dollar for every time my father told me that, I could buy a small studio overlooking the promenade. (It's Brooklyn Heights—do the math.) The eye-contact thing was important to him, to his job. But then, as a crime reporter, he was usually interviewing liars, people who knew something about what had occurred behind the yellow tape, but who were either too frightened or foolish to speak up about it. Eye contact is a reporter's way of letting the subject know that you're listening beyond the words, he would always say.

"It's also our most accurate lie detector," he said. "The truth lights up in the eye like a strobe."

I wonder what he'd say if he saw me now, struggling to do anything more than squint at Candace Collins, the owner of Sexistential, as she strokes the demo anal massager debuting at this elaborate press event tonight. *What color is her strobe light, Dad?*

But it's more than the massager or even Candace's inflated excitement about it that's rooted under my skin. It's that shitty *Tell Me More* post. Yes, it's ridiculous and out of line, mean and sloppy, gotcha-style gossip, but I can't shake it. I know those girls near the coat check were talking about me when I came in—all the sideways glances and high school whispering. It's only a matter of time before I walk out of a bathroom stall to a set of slightly shamed faces of some dummies talking about the post—about Grant, about me. I can't even begin to consider the idea of Grant having read it. He's already trying to process enough hard truths up there; he doesn't need this. And there's my own rock-hard truth: I should have broken up with him before all of this, back when it made sense for me to just do what I always do and push him far away with both hands.

I've tried to Sherlock this thing. There were only a handful of people—seven, max—who knew about Grant and me, and by extension, about his Connecticut "getaway." Each one of them—from Kendra to Tyson—is a total vault. On Grant's side, he's so used to people prying into his private life; he's fiercely quiet about it. He had to tell his agent that he needed time off, but didn't really get into any deep details about it. His best friends, the two of them, are galaxies away from the Hollywood bullshit: Luke's a physical therapist in Toronto and Big Kev's living large as an eighth-grade math teacher in Vancouver. They've been keeping Grant's secrets since elementary school. No leaks there.

Trying to think who would gain from pushing him—us—off a cliff like this, and I've got nothing. Unless . . . unless this is some long-game payback for The Mistake. I knew that all was not truly forgiven. Maybe *water under the bridge* really means *let's set the whole fucking bridge on fire, with Best standing on it.*

Candace pats my arm a few times and looks around the full room. "Where are those men when you need them? Anyway"— she returns to the gleaming toy that's shaped like a very poorly thought out—and possibly painful—spinning top—"you can meet the manufacturing team later. Back to the good stuff." She lolls out her tongue. It has the required piercing as well as an obscene, weird white coating. I go back to avoiding any significant eye contact with her.

I don't dislike Candace. She's on my short list of people I'm barely tolerating. She always smells like fruity lube, but she's one of the less creepy sex-shop owners I've met in the last two years of being on vadge detail. Although, there was that time she shared how much she enjoys penetrating her then new boyfriend Glen, with her big toe. "He gets a real *kick* out of it," she said, before breaking into her throaty cackle. I ended up transcribing that phone interview on my own. I couldn't bring myself to ask some clean, green summer intern to do it. Their eyes are already like saucers.

"It's compact, phthalate-free, has a dual motor," Candace shouts above the K-pop pounding our eardrums. "We called it"—she rolls her tongue out again and runs it along her top lip—"The Pepper Grinder. Isn't that fucking *fabulous*?"

"Dead fucking fabulous," Kendra shouts from behind my shoulder. She slides over to Candace and rests her hand at the top of her broad back. "Honey, do you mind if I steal this one?"—Kendra tilts her head my way—"She's a star, as you know, and in high demand. The people want their Best."

Candace smiles, nodding like a new puppy. "Of course, of course, sugar. Just don't keep her all to yourself, now. I want to introduce her to our manufacturing partners—all men, and they love themselves some hot chocolate." Candace winks. Her affected Southern-belle routine grates. "And don't you dare leave without getting a special gift bag. Oh, my word. You are gonna love all of it." She wiggles the top of her body and leans hard on Kendra, who plays right along, pouting and shimmying to the hammering beat. Candace loves Kendra. She's become my instant plus-one at any event Candace puts on.

"Oh, we don't want to miss out on that good-good," Kendra says. She is talking over the music without sounding like she's yelling. One more spot of shine to the golden, enviable life of Kendra Singh. Gorgeous and endlessly fabulous, the example of easy charm; it's almost preternatural. Almost, because it isn't truly singular: there are two of them, identical twins. But even Lindee—born first by a full two minutes—covets her sister's life. If I believed in things like luck, I would say that Lindee was robbed of all of it. She's almost blighted; the shadow twin. Example: Six years ago, the sisters were sharing a taxi. Kendra got out of the cab a block before it crashed into a double-parked FedEx truck. Lindee smashed face-first into the Plexiglas divider and shattered almost everything inside of that beautiful nutshell. It was a horror show, right there in Midtown. Lindee attempted to sue everyone in a ten-mile radius of the accident, extending her vendetta to include two of her facial-reconstruction doctors. (She felt they weren't up on the latest developments in plastics, and left her with a "forever-fucked-up" nose.) Much of Lindee's face is held together by bits of bones borrowed from her hip and lower leg. She still walks with a slight limp and can get a headache from chewing too much.

"Just holler if you got questions, sugar," Candace says. "Make me look good in front of the manufacturing guys."

"You got it, Candie," I say, before giving her shoulder a light squeeze and bumping hips with her. (Kendra's not the only one with charms.)

I lean into Kendra, who's still shaking to the beat. It moved from K-pop to Bollywood hip-hop fusion, and Kendra is nodding deep into the groove. "Any minute now, you're going to strip down to the sari you're wearing under that Zac Posen two-piece, right? Lotus hands and everything."

"That's why I dragged you away from old foot-fucker Candie," she says. "I want you to meet the DJ. She's my cousin. Well, our cousin"—Kendra gestures toward the glass booth. "Lindee just showed up."

"Wait. I thought Lindee hates sex and everything related to it."

"I know, but she's stressin' about work shit; some new director is chapping her ass. They'll probably end up getting married—watch. Then I saw on the e-mail invite thing that our cousin Tina's spinning, so I told Lindee. I hope it's okay that she tagged."

"Candace loves you. Whenever I show up at one of her things without you she looks legit heartbroken. It's fine. I'm just surprised that Lindee agreed to come to a sex shop."

"A sex shop called Sexistential, by the way."

"I can taste her bitter all the way from here. Such a broken bird, that one."

"Hey, hey. That's my twin." Kendra stops her dancing short. "I can say shit about her, not you—especially not you. You're an only child; you have no idea how this thing works." She starts moving her upper body again. "But maybe your parents will adopt a baby from Malawi like my mom's neighbors did. It's like the new thing for bored empty nesters. Even better, your parents can request a preteen or tween or whatever—skip the diapers, but you know, still stay busy. Then you can be the pissed-off big sister proper, talk all the shit you want about your annoying brat brother stealing all your thunder."

I'm saying the words in my head, but they're tumbling out of my mouth and there's no way to draw them back behind my tongue. "Is that supposed to be funny?" I'm right up in Kendra's face, my nose nearly scraping her cheek. "You don't know the first thing about my parents. Why would you even say some shit like that? Like you know anything about them, what they need."

"Whoa. Slow down. What just happened? I should be the crampy one here—but I'm not, because it's jokes and we're in a sex shop, celebrating an anal probe. So let's relax, okay?" Kendra tilts her head at me. "Wait, is this about that *Tell Me*

More post? Watch, soon some reality-show D-lister will show up at an event wearing a giant condom and nothing else. Everybody will be focused on her instead. People have ADD, Best. Their memories are Swiss cheese. And BFD, the hotty-McHotts King was knockin' boots with fierce bitch Best all this time and no one knew. In the grand scheme, who cares?" She takes a beat and looks at me. Her smile drops. "Or is this about Grant himself, you know, the mental-break part? It's got to suck for him to be outed like that. What's up with his costar—ferret face? How you gonna just shove your teammate onto the third rail like that? What a dick."

"No. No, it's not about that. It's not about Grant. Not everything is about Grant!" I can't even try to contain it now—the words, the fire; all of it is spilling out fast and fresh. I'm yelling and don't care who hears me. "He had a temporary mental-health episode, Kendra. That's it. He didn't go all the way under. He survived. And it has nothing to do with being lucky or chosen or whatever. He survived. Sometimes people just survive!" It's obviously too late to try saving myself here. The only option left is to storm off.

I can feel Kendra's eyes, wide and wild, burning holes into my back as I hustle off the floor hoping for an unlocked door in the back office. Trying to remember any of Dr. Monfries's go-to phrases, calming chants for moments exactly like this, is a losing game. I consider my sessions with Dr. Monfries largely a waste of time; too many questions (for me), too little answers (from him), but he did know his way around a calming mantra. Of course, I discovered this in retrospect and am drawing a complete and fateful blank right now, when I need to remember most. My mind is empty of anything useful or quiet. I reach for my coins in my skirt's pocket, but they're missing too. I forgot to transfer them over from my cardigan—which is hanging in my office. I feel the panic crawling up the back of my throat and hurry into a darkened aisle near the "classics" DVD section. My eyes are watery, but I can still see clear enough across the room to the DJ table. Kendra, Lindee, and DJ Tina are bundled like nesting dolls. Kendra is tossing her head back; her long hair rolls against her like a thick, black wave. Lindee is wearing her cousin's jumbo headphones and fiddling with something on the chrome table. The cousin points to something else and all three of them turn their attention above them. Watching them huddled together looking to the sky—their narrow, brown faces made golden by the soft lights above the DJ's table—I clutch my stomach, trying to grab hold of the loud, jerky gasp burning up through my chest. My right eyelid starts twitching and I think I'm going to vomit.

And just like that, the moment—the clear, haunting one I had chased away years ago—returned. I was sucked back into the hole beneath me, reaching for Benjamin, slowing into a cold and sick silence, unable to move or process that my brothers were dead and dying and that I was surely next. I hear those sounds; the realness of it tries to choke the trembling life out of me. I'm gasping and step back farther into the shadowy aisle, reaching my hand for something sturdy. I don't want to pass out here with only Linda Lovelace and the other dusty porn stars around to hear my fall. It's all spinning around me, strange and unsettled. I can barely keep my head up. I dig my hands into my left pocket once more, knowing that those coins aren't there, but at this point I'll take anything—even the idea of my golden safety tokens will do.

CHAPTER 5

"So did you have this grand-mal freak-out *before* or after you called me a broken bird?"

"Jesus. It's been over a week, Lindee. Is this why you invited me out—to rub that salt in good and proper? I've already apologized at least eighty different times. Can we all let it go now?"

I knew she was avoiding me, but this no-show completely seals it: Kendra's fully pissed. Lindee asked me to come with her to pick out a birthday day gift for their mother. It was such a twin thing that I was honestly surprised to see that Kendra wasn't joining us.

"Is that why Kendra didn't come with you?"

"We don't have to die together too, you know," Lindee says. She's such a sour bitch, and most days I love it. I stopped asking questions a long time ago when it comes to Lindee. She tells me all the time how obnoxious my "reporter mouth" can be. *Always asking, never telling*. She's right. My general curiosity—let's just call it *comprehensive*—makes me a good reporter, but also downright nosy. It's annoying, all the questions—I can see that. Kendra doesn't mind it as much, so I often get sidebar scoop on whatever's happening with Lindee from her.

Their mother's birthday is either on Christmas Day or Boxing Day, I can never remember. Kendra just sends her to a super-luxuriating spa in the city for a full day. She has her assistant make the call to the spa too. Actually, I think the assistant set up a standing annual appointment for the mother, auto-billed to Kendra, years ago. There's operating on minimal effort, and then there's Kendra, right below that. But Lindee likes to search out the perfect gift for the woman who she says "was my only real friend during the roughest phases of my life." More than her own identical twin, her mother is the one person who has Lindee's unwavering respect and love. It's sweet to see Lindee sweet.

Every gift suggestion I toss out is quickly deemed "not good enough." I get why she started looking a month early.

My mother never wanted gifts from us on her birthday. And getting her to accept anything store-bought on Christmas morning was its own struggle. She was of the *you children are gift enough* set. Crafty attempts, no matter how sloppy and hardened with globs of glue, were always welcomed with wide arms, though. When we got older, long past the scribbly Crayola days, she only asked that we each write her a letter for her birthday. She really did treasure us, all that we were.

"Are you coming over this Thursday or what? Thanksgiving dinner, remember?" Lindee says.

"Was that an invitation?"

She barely raises a brow. "You're doing that question-with-a-question bullshit again? Because I'm not into it. Kendra already invited you. So are you coming?"

"First I'm hearing of it."

"Jesus Christ on a bleeding cross. This is all Flavio's fault." Lindee chucks a leather bag she'd been inspecting into a neat, expensive pile and drags her feet to the next display. She's rough and loud and deliberate about all of it, and pays no attention to the sighing, gawking salesgirl with the thick coating of chalk-white foundation and her hair pulled high and tight into a blond bun. Lindee's quite used to people staring at her, trying to understand what's happening with her face: the beautiful features slightly lopsided and the odd sliding step to her gait. "Him and that pretentious show he's putting on in Italy—it's all he has her thinking about right now. Swear, if he wasn't so skilled with that thick dick, he would be such an ex. He knows it too."

"Good God, the number of times I've heard about this man's penis—"

"Almost as much as you've heard about his whole pussy-eating obsession, I'm sure," Lindee says, her face straight and stony.

"Gross. So, lunch is just not happening today, then?"

"Off topic, unimportant; that's all Flavio will ever be. Just come to the dinner. It's not like you have some other Thanksgiving gathering to avoid. When do you Cafuckians celebrate again, middle of July?"

"October, numbskull. And *Cafuckians*? Is nothing sacred to you?"

"Cows." She scrunches her face, looking down at a pair of flat, low-cut leather boots in disgust. "Most cows."

"This dinner, is it at your parents' house? Is it friends and family or mostly family and oddball me or—"

"It's dinner in Queens. Relax. Plus, it'll help smooth all the stuff between you and Kendra."

"The stuff between me and Kendra? I didn't know there was *stuff between me and Kendra*. What stuff?"

"Bitch, please. That doesn't work on me. Of course there is. You know that."

"All I did—"

"All you did was embarrass the shit out of her with your Hulk-out in the middle of the dance floor. Look, if it was me, whatever. You know I ran out of fucks to give back in the early 2000s. But my sister, that's a different deal. She's soft under it all, like Mother. Kendra has a high tolerance for a lot of bullshit. I mean, Exhibit A: fucking Flavio. But the one thing she's not going to do is be humiliated. Please. Kendra is not the one. Our stepdad Gary tried it when we were young, like no-tits-yet young. He was laughing at her for getting some shit wrong on our chemistry homework. Just steady mocking her for no real reason—boredom or whatever white-guy patriarchy bullshit he was trying to pull with his new Indian wife and her brown twin daughters. Whatever. Kendra set that fucker straight one night when Mother was out with her cousin—DJ Tina's mom. She unleashed a torrent of insults and swears calling his entire gene pool into question. Bumbling fool. It was excellent. I wanted to slow-clap that shit. He never bothered her or us again. Didn't matter how late we would sit at that creaky kitchen table doing homework, that guy didn't dare step into our radius. He would go sit in the back room and watch TV like some bad dog on punishment. Oh, Gary—no one misses you, asshole," Lindee says, then makes a quick sign of the cross along her chest and points her middle finger to the ceiling.

"You really are a broken, bitter bird." I put my hand on a powder-blue cashmere hoodie. Lindee scowls before I can pull the hanger off the rack all the way. "It's just, I don't always do well with families and aunts and cousins and all that."

"I bet you don't," Lindee says, adding a loud snort. "You don't even want to be around your own family. Kendra said you're always trying to dodge your parents. Going home for Christmas is like walking to the gallows for you."

I open my mouth. Only a long, low breath dribbles out. Lindee rolls her eyes.

"Please, Best. You've cut all ties to family and familiars. Basically, anyone who knew you before New York? Deleted. No trace. You don't even have that bullshit middle-school friend popping up on your Facebook talking about CrossFit or the *problem with the government these days*. For all we know, you could be a black Russian spy or a rampant sociopath. But *I'm* the broken bird. Or was it bitter bird?" she says.

All I can do is shake my head, and we continue walking the waxy, bright-white floor in silence. Lindee seems to prefer it this way. I can feel High Bun trailing me, watching each piece of overpriced crap on which I place my hand. Lindee may be accustomed to the stares and assumptions, but I'll never be, not all the way. I'm kind of hoping that High Bun will step up her game and say something blatantly shitty, like *Let me show you the sale rack*, just so Lindee can unleash the dragon and belch that fire the Singh girls were born with in their bellies. But another customer calls High Bun away.

I walk toward Lindee. She's holding a low-cut boot in one hand and thumbing something into her phone with the other. "Okay. I'll come," I tell her. "What should I bring?"

"Don't bring your cell phone, I can tell you that much."

"Wait, what?"

"My mother doesn't allow cell phones in the house," Lindee says, without looking up from her screen. "She's freaked about vibrations, so keep that shit tucked deep in your bag." Lindee lifts her head and stares right at me. "I'm serious. Once Flavio tried to sneak his phone into the house in the front pocket of his tight-ass skinny jeans—what a dummy. Mother complained about neck pain the whole evening. Fucking Flavio. And on top of that, he asked if it was okay to smoke—*inside the motherfucking house.*"

"Okay. No cell phones—because that's not weird at all. But I meant, what should I bring, like food-wise?"

"My mother makes turkey and dressing, but that's it on the traditional bullshit. Everything else is straight-up Indian food. Bring an empty belly and eat what's served. No imaginary food allergies or dumb-ass no-bread diets or whatever. You eat for real at this table. Mother would be insulted otherwise."

"And you're sure Kendra was planning to invite me?"

"I'm not up for this, okay? You're invited. Make a fucking decision. Bring someone, if that helps you stop being such a limp dick. Speaking of, Flav will be there, of course. He's still trying to get in the good books. Spoiler alert: Never going to happen, *fratello*. I'm going to bring this guy with me—maybe. He's still walking the wire."

"Which guy?"

"From work, sort of. His name is Mark—yes, another Mark. Kendra calls him New Mark, and it's kind of sticking. He's a director, slumming in TV commercials for a minute. He worked on this big campaign for us in Amsterdam. He used to live there a few years back—he basically lived everywhere, born in Malta. Doctor parents, disaster relief workers—it's a whole indie movie. Whatever. We got him dirt cheap, so someone's winning."

"Ooh. A noble artist with humanitarian roots. Cute?"

She gives me her dead-eyed look. "Bitch . . . please."

"Well, is it serious? It's been awhile for you, Kalindee."

"None of these things are ever serious."

"Right. I don't really have anyone to bring—serious or hookup-ery."

"Well, according to *Tell Me More*, it's probably safer that way—for the dudes."

"Are you serious? That's what you're quoting here?"

Lindee rolls her eyes and clenches her teeth. I can't tell if she's trying to stifle a smile or dealing with her usual jaw pain. "Oh, calm down. Is that what made you go off on my sister, the stalkerazzi?"

"Christ. I keep getting these calls at work from this one reporter. E-mails too. It's like he can't just let this go. I didn't *ditch Grant because he went nuts*. I mean, Jesus. On Twitter, my mentions are in shambles. Everyone thinks I'm the worst kind of bitch. They actually type that out: *Best Bitch*. That's what they're calling me, and you know that's only a short walk to *Black Bitch* . . . keep the alliteration thing going."

"Hmm. You know what? *Best Black Bitch* sounds dope as fuck, like some raw punk band. You should own that shit."

"Own it? They're saying that I caused Grant's mental break, that I'm *the reason*. I ruined their special King. Why the hell would I want to own that?" I shake my head hard, as if that will make these awful thoughts tumble out of my ears. "I can't own that. I'm not a monster!"

"Wait. Who's going to the monster level on this? Seriously, you're overreacting. It's a gossip rag. Complete piece-of-shit thing that people scroll through when they're waiting in line to order coffee—oh, wait. That's it," Lindee shouts through her twister mouth. "That's it: Bitch Black. Yes, yes, Bitch Black is fucking excellent. That could totally be the name of a nail polish or lip color or skinny cocktail. My agency would be all over that and making bank on it too."

She walks off nodding, moving on to go knock over another neat stack of folded-down T-shirts. But Lindee was gone long before she walked away. Probably stopped listening to me a while ago. I rub my hand along a neat stack of fluffy cardigans. It's a soft spread of color and oddly, it's making my thoughts linger on my mother. Moms are always cold, always chilly. No matter the season, you know? Even in the eye of summer, there was always a breeze for my mother. Ice in her veins, she said. She was joking. But it's not very funny, is it—ice in the veins?

Mum was funny in her way, I guess. Like with my name. My mother's the one who came up with this ridiculous thing. Best. Really, it's Bathsheba. My father, quiet soldier that he is, just went along with it. He got to name the sons Benjamin and Bryant, so it was her turn for the girl child. My mother decided to keep the "B" thing going, which was fine. Brenda. Briana. Bobbie, spelled all cool. Even Blaire. I would have been the one black girl you know named Blaire. No. My mother went all the way up to the boundary of common sense and trotted back home with Bathsheba. Making it that much more appalling is the fact that she didn't pull it from the Bible, like you'd assume. It's the name of the fishing village in Barbados where she grew up. Benjamin, first son, couldn't pronounce it—naturally, no one at school could, either—and he wound up saying *Best-ba*. We dropped the *ba* a few years too late for my taste, and I became Best. I maintain that Bathsheba was her own private joke, quiet payback for being the one child who almost truly killed her during delivery.

"What the fuck are you doing?" Lindee snaps.

I have one of the cardigans slung over my shoulder, its softness cradling the entire side of my face as I lean into it. Lindee is peering at me, as are High Bun and two other randoms who are shopping the racks nearby. I'm confused, embarrassed. My face warms to searing in an instant. "I—I'm—I, uh. I don't know what that was, sorry." I turn toward High Bun and rattle off a string of disconnected stories and words, apologize for me and for Lindee, but she looks completely horrified by each utterance. The whispers, off to my left, they're getting louder, longer, mixed with barely muffled chucking. This is my fault, though. I said too much at once. Talking just to move the stiff air between us all.

"What is happening with you?" Lindee says. Her voice hasn't softened and neither has her glare. She finally decides to stop barking at me from across the sales floor and comes closer, dragging that left leg as always, and stands near my shoulder. She lowers her voice to clenched-jaw whisper, but purely for effect. "Are you going to smash the display cases next? 'Cuz, let a bitch know beforehand."

I shake my head, but my heart is racing and I have no idea what will happen next. A wild rhythm is thumping in my ears, punching in my chest. Everything is blurred now. Sounds are muffled. I'm swooning and there's nothing I can think to do to stop it. "Don't lock your knees," I say to myself, an instant too late, as the rest of my body buckles.

Fainting was never my thing. Even at the funerals, they had two nurses at either side of me, and never once did I waver. "Don't lock your knees," the older one whispered to me as we all stood for the first hymn. "The blood will pool in your legs; make you pass out," she said. I wanted to share this intel with my father, urgently. He was sitting next to the nurse on my right, the one who smelled like fresh lilac, and it took him a long, agonizing time—maybe twenty seconds—before he could gather himself up enough to stand with us. I needed him to know this, so he could stay up, stay standing, despite his missing heart. They didn't bother coaching my mother on anything. She was sedated and told to remain seated through it all. But when we found our way graveside—the matching caskets resting on their perch—the nurses doubled-up, flanking her, holding her, helping her take the seven horrible steps to the edge of the deep holes. I heard it, when my mother asked to be left alone there. And after a tense half-minute, her pillars agreed to retreat. Like everyone else, I watched her, unsure if she would teeter or tumble or jump. My mother removed the black, curved brim hat that her church sister fitted on her (they pinned a classic pillbox on me) and she bowed her head. She stood there for—it felt like a year—not moving, probably barely breathing, until my father stepped forward and placed his gloved hand on the middle of her back. That's when the sickest sound rumbled from the basement beneath the basement of her ruined heart and poured out of her mouth. It was a sound, a wounded howl, I hope to never hear again. She dropped to the cold, damp ground, still clutching that hat. The oldest nurse got to her first, followed by the pallbearers, and they, with my father, gathered up all the pieces of her, escorting her back to the stretched black car. I remember staring at the hat, dragged along the dirty snow. The church sisters rushed to my sides, shoring me, gripping me, certain that I would fold next, but I didn't. I stayed up, my knees soft like my mind and my eyes as dry as chalk, and I listened to the pastor's words—words that I can still recite without thinking.

We have entrusted our brothers Benjamin Errol and
  Bryant Eric to God's mercy,
and we now commit their bodies to the ground:
earth to earth, ashes to ashes, dust to dust:
in sure and certain hope of the resurrection to eternal life
through our Lord Jesus Christ,
who will transform our frail bodies
that they may be conformed to His glorious body,
who died, was buried, and rose again for us.
To Him be glory for ever.

Then we all said it, together with precision and passion: *Amen.*

———————

I'm leaning on the door in the cab, trying to keep my breath even. Lindee said she didn't want to run the risk of my hurling all over her new boots. Kendra isn't looking at me. She keeps her head straight, eyes trained on the foggy Plexiglas divider. But Lindee, squeezed up in the middle seat, is practically burning a hole in my temple with that glare of hers. I can feel her breath on me too, but can't look at her. I try to stay focused on what's going on outside the taxicab's window: a muddle of trees and gravel and steel gliding by. But my mind keeps falling back to those many other times riding in cabs with Kendra. Better times, when all we did was look at each other, giddy and laughing, talking about everything at once. I already miss her and it's only been a week—exactly nine days since my stupid mini-meltdown. I want Kendra to look over at me, to start talking about the latest, ridiculous thing her dum-dum assistant Stacey said. I want her to assume, naturally, that she's coming over after all of this to slather homemade mud masks on our faces, eat room-temp pineapple salsa with fancy water crackers, drink cheap bodega beer, and search for "Where Are They Now?" updates on all of MTV's *Real World* casts, because it's what we do. Or what we did.

Lindee called her sister when I passed out. Kendra was still at the showroom three or four blocks away. I was sitting on slippery fold-up chair in the boutique's scruffy backroom when Kendra walked in behind Lindee. She gave me a bottle of water and weak smile before turning to Lindee and starting that wordless twin-talk thing they always do, comprised of rough shrugs, quick nods, sighs, and eye-rolls.

The cab ride has been silent, save the drone of the sports radio show playing louder in the front speakers than in the back. The driver's not even talking on his cell phone through an earpiece, a rarity that only serves to up the awkwardness in the stuffy car. I'm trying to think of what else I could say to Kendra beyond what I have already. "You didn't have to come."

"But I did," she said, and handed me the wet bottle of water.

I want to apologize, but also don't want to say another word. I can't be sure of what's going to rush out of my mouth in trying to explain the outburst, explain anything. There's so much she doesn't know about my life—the old one—and once that thread is pulled, the unraveling will be ugly.

I feel Lindee's hand slipping over mine. Of course it startled me—nothing to do with how cold her fingers are—but it jolts me back into the moment and I know what I have to do.

"Call in tomorrow. Stay home," Lindee says as I drag myself out of the cab, parked badly on the curb.

"Lindee's right," Kendra says, leaning over but barely turning my way.

"I have meetings, deadlines. I can't." My voice is scratchy

and everything else about me—hair, clothes, coat—is disheveled.

"Fuck them," Lindee says. She does an elaborate hand gesture, her elbow and fists flapping about. "They need you. Not the other way. Fuck. Them."

Kendra nods.

"Miss, you say two stops," the cabbie shouts back at us. "Can't stay here." He has a vague South Asian accent, but his irritation is unambiguous. "You say two stops. No waiting." He taps his meter. "Waiting, extra charge."

"Listen, Mr. *Goswami*, there's no waiting charge, okay? We're not idiots. It's seven-thirty; you're already getting the peak-hour weekday charge. It's right there"—Lindee juts her finger through the dingy plexi opening, toward his meter and face—"one dollar. And the second stop takes you back to Manhattan, all right, so calm down, please."

He mutters something. It's not English.

"Oh, don't start down that road," Lindee barks. "I know all those Hindi bad words, sir. Bengali too, so you'll need to try harder, my friend."

Kendra shakes her head and—at last—looks at me, exasperated, a grin curling up one side of her face.

"Lindee, you need some meditation," I whisper. I nod at Kendra, a thank-you floated out into our weird, wordless space.

"And you need to figure out what's going on," Lindee says, her flat delivery returned, as if the ugliness with the cabdriver never happened. She elbows Kendra. "Right? That was a panic attack back there. Or a mini-exorcism. I mean, what was all that *ashes to ashes Amen* shit you were mumbling before you fell out? Were you speaking tongues?" Lindee chuckles and nudges her sister harder. Kendra shakes her head. "You should have seen that shit, Ken. Total hysteria in the middle of the store. Everyone in that place freaked the fuck out when she dropped.

You know she can't go back to Delle Donne boutique. It's a wrap on that place for her."

"Lindee, enough," Kendra says, frowning at her sister. She looks sad, or maybe it's pity mixed with a little horror—I can't really tell. I know that I've seen that same look on other people's faces before, a lot, like when I finally went back to school three months after what happened happened. None of my friends talked to me. The teachers pretended I magically faded into the walls. And the nurse and counselor worked diligently, pulling whatever scheme—hall passes, work at home, tutors, "rest time" in the infirmary—to get that high school diploma in my hand and me out the door.

Lindee cuts the tense quiet with one of her snorts. "Face facts, Best. This shit is serious, whatever's happening with you." She moves her stiff neck, shifting exaggerated looks between Kendra and me. "Oh, okay. Ken won't say it, so I will. Get checked out. I'm not saying that crazy in contagious, but homeboy *did* just crack his marbles a few months back . . . at your place so, maybe burning some sage isn't the—"

"*Kalindee*," Kendra snarls.

"What? You're thinking it too. Grant goes nuts, now she's flipping out. It's not a little strange to you—"

Kendra shoots an eye-dagger right into her sister's face.

"Whatever. Like I told you, Best: that motherfucker was never intact to begin with. But I'll leave that alone. Don't want to upset you—again."

I'm still not prepared to talk about any of it, and spinning this long lie thicker—I can't pull that off, not tonight. But my brain is so pinched I can't come up with a proper diversion. It's dark, damp, and I just want to get inside. "Listen, you guys didn't have to ride all the way home with me—thanks."

"Are you going to be okay?" Kendra says. "Do you want me to come up?"

"No. No, I'm fine. Just tired and hungry and embarrassed. I'm fine. Thanks."

"Kendra, you should just go with her. Make sure."

"No, really. We did tell the guy two stops." I push for a smile. I'm sure I look pained. The cabbie shakes his head. He's listening in on our convo and I'm embarrassed all over again. I know I won't see him after this awkward moment, but mortification is never concerned about the details.

"Whatever with this guy," Lindee says, waving her hand at the back of his head. "He's a cabbie and he really doesn't know who he's dealing with back here." Lindee doesn't give him a second side look. "We can come up for a bit. Watch *Golden Girls* or *Friends* or some shit."

"Guys, no. Look. I'm good." I nod. "I'm good, really."

"All right, but if you change your mind, text Kendra. She can double back—maybe with some sticky green or Xanax or something."

I nod and keep doing it until my jaw feels tight. The cabdriver's impatience has spilled onto me. I need to get inside. "If I say *I'm good* for the twentieth time, maybe then you'll believe me? Really. I'm fine. We'll talk later, Kendra." She folds her lips together and half-nods—the best I can expect from her. "Sorry I messed up the birthday-gift thing, Lindee."

"Oh, whatever, bitch. You were no help to begin with." There's that smirk. "All right, get off the corner, ho. We better get this guy back to the *real* New York City before he throws sulfuric acid on us."

Lindee can't close the car door all the way before the cabdriver takes off. He truly doesn't know who (what) he has in back of that cab. Poor fool.

There's this spot on my rooftop where I like to be whenever I make calls home. When he asked, I told Grant it was about long-distance calls and janky cell-phone reception. I don't use my landline. It's white, corded, and has no displays or fanciness to it all—it's completely ornamental, and I'm quite serious when I say that I don't know the number to it. So the bad-reception story sold. But the real reason for my being in that specific spot on the roof has everything to do with the view. Unlike the crying closet at work, up here—especially on a crisp night, taking in all the bright pops of Brooklyn light—it's beautiful. I can see clean across the buildings, with their patchy peeling covers, over to this soft glow that I believe is JFK Airport. And, of course, there's the bank clock tower looking back at me. I'm not allowed to be on the roof, though. Technically, no one is. "It's illegal up here," the landlord said a few times on move-in day. "Big no-no on parties or grilling. It's not safe." But he didn't know what he was talking about. It's the safest place.

I dial the number and get into position—leaned up against a cracked asphalt shingle—and count the number of telephone rings. (Maybe it's asbestos, not asphalt, and that's what Mr. Bernhardt meant by "illegal" and "unsafe.") My parents, even before the accident, never answered the phone in any timely way. And their answering machine too: it goes on for like ten rings before anything clicks over. I can't imagine how many callers just hung up and never tried them again. I've been tempted.

"Hello," my mother says, her voice soft, sweet.

I don't bother with pleasantries anymore. I know how she's doing. "It's Bathsheba." I gaze over at the clock's red face, waiting for the typical long silence to seep through the phone.

"You're calling," she says. The sugar completely dissolved.

"Yeah. Hi. It's late. Sorry."

"He's not here."

That's another thing: My parents are divorced, but still live in the same house. Actually, separate wings of the same huge house. There's no acrimony. It's definitely love wedged between them despite all the physical space they don't share.

After Benjamin and Bryant died, somehow it was more harrowing to crawl into the same bed at night, together alone. The
agony of looking into each other's faces and seeing those similar features of the lost boys—chin, nose, the way the mouth
turned down in the deep of sleep—seeing all of that staring
back was simply too much for either of them to bear. That's
what my father told me when he called my dorm one early
morning. They filed for divorce three weeks after I left for university, six months after the funerals. But the idea of living in
separate homes seemed absurd—if only to them—so they
moved to a larger house and took opposing wings.

"Oh, he's already gone over to his side?"

"He's at the lodge," she says.

"Really? I didn't know he started that again." I hope I
sounded casual and not suspicious just then. But my father and
that lodge don't mix well. It's not like he's a stranger to the
drink; the rum shops in Trinidad carved out their influence early
in his life. The lodge—with all its secrecy and pomp—it was
different, and it pushed his drinking toward something more severe and sometimes scary.

"He goes on Thursdee now. A special committee."

"That's good. They miss him—I'm sure."

"You want me to leave word that you called?"

"Yes. Thank you."

"A'right then."

"Wait. Mum?"

"Yes . . . I'm still on the line."

"I wanted to let you know that . . . I don't think I can come up
this time. It's work. There's a big story—an important one—
that I'm working on for the issue. I know this is important too.
Ten years, I know, but I can't get the time off. I hope you understand."

"I understand that you're not a child. You make your own choices."

"I tried to get the time, but this story . . . it's a big one. They're counting on me."

"They're counting on you," she says, without tone, just my own words repeated.

"They are, Mum. It's a big story. Actually, that's why I'm calling Dad. I think he can help me with it."

"Do you want me to let your father know you're not coming?"

I know the question is really instruction. "No, I can tell him. I'll call back, if that's easier."

"Good enough. You take care, then."

"You too. Good night, Mum."

I slide the phone in my skirt pocket; the coins clink around it. I wiggle out of my coat, letting it fall wherever it does. It's cold out here. I can see the shadow of my breath pluming around my nose. I'm shivering and my shoulders are up to my ears again, but it feels like something. Not necessarily good, but something. I'm going to stay out for a while longer, exchanging knowing looks with the clock tower.

CHAPTER 6

They've posted another *Tell Me More* piece, about Grant and me, and this one doesn't rely on old photos from past stories from legit publications. With Grant, they used a studio pic from his new mid-season replacement show "that's spilling over with hot-bod dudes barely wearing shirts, flexin', sexin', and also fighting crime." (Barf.) The pseudo-candid photo, an expertly posed behind-the-scenes shot, probably came from one of his asshole costars. Or maybe the studio happily handed it over. Any light is considered shine by that lot. And for me, they have not one picture, but an entire click-through photo gallery of me stomping the night, cobblestone street in the Meatpacking District, throat laughing (with my mouth wide and head back) in a dim-ish bar, smiling like an idiot on the sidewalk, walking arm in arm with what looks like Tyson, and generally having a grand time in life *while my cracked-egg boyfriend cries alone in a half-full bathtub in a deserted mansion in Vermont.* Vermont? Jesus. How these people refer to themselves as journalists—and with a straight face—takes some serious balls.

My work phone won't stop, because Clark Bauer, the stalker "reporter" on the case, won't stop. Even with the ringer completely muted, I'm still harassed by the fucking flashing light. And here goes the phone again.

Shit. It's a 514 number. My parents never call me at work.

"Bathsheba?"

"Dad, is everything okay? Is Mum all right?"

"Yes. She gone out for a home visit with she church."

"In the morning?"

"You know I don't know."

"Right. But she's okay?"

"Bathsheba, I didn't call you to talk about your mother. She is how she is. She stays on her side and I keep to mine." The song of his Trini accent doesn't cover up the sharpness of his tone. "However, she did come to me the other day telling me that you say you have no plans on coming home this year. Now, you know I don't fault any person, especially a young person who's out there working, trying to claim their own, but they are your brothers. And December twenty-fourth will be ten years."

"Dad, I know—"

"I am still speaking."

"Yes, Daddy."

"I said it will be ten years. Are you trying to tell me that you can't look past yourself to see the significance of that?"

(I know better than to utter a word right now.)

"You are needed here," he says, his voice rising. "So you will be here. You can sort out your travel details and let us know when we can expect to see you. You have a good day."

And *click*. He's gone.

The tears aren't rushing; they're already here. When Trinity barges in, her face is flushed too.

"Oh my God. You saw it already," she says, sliding the door closed with a bang.

I can only squint.

"What the hell happened? I thought she was getting help, treatment," Trinity says. "Maybe she got tired of fighting. Got to the end of her rope and figured it was easier to let go." She puts her hand over her mouth, shaking her head. "So sad. She was stunning. And now she's just gone."

I lean into Trinity and try to talk, but no words come.

"The blogs are saying that she hanged herself. Ugh—so awful. I'm sorry. I know you know her. Knew her. You probably don't want to get into all the horrible details about Lana Scott and—I'm just really sorry, Best."

"I—I didn't . . . she was. I didn't know that—"

"Oh my God! I thought you heard. I'm sorry. I came in and you were cry—you looked upset. I thought you knew."

"I didn't know that she—I don't know what to . . . I'm sorry, Trinity, do you mind just giving me a minute?"

"Jesus. I'm sorry, but . . . um, Joan wants to see you. I told her assistant I would get you because I thought you'd be in here *upset* because of the Lana Scott news."

"See me? About what?"

"Oh, shit, this is the worst." Trinity runs her hands up over her face and through her hair. "She saw the gossip stories, about you secretly dating Grant King, and . . . she wants—they want you to do a first-person about dating a celebrity and all this other stuff rolled into it."

"What?"

"I know. Miyuki came up with it, I think. It's for the shame issue. I'm sorry, Best. It's totally shitty and I'm sorry."

"What the fuck? Who are these people?"

"I know. I know. But, she wants to see you. I have to tell her something. Do you need a moment?"

I don't even realize I'm standing until my heels are clacking against the tile. I'm running. I can hear my labored breath in my ears, my pulse thumping high in my throat. I don't know where I'm heading. I push through a band of blurred people gathered near the fashion closet. They're saying something to me. Yelling, squawking, cursing—I can't tell. The noise only turns my run into a desperate sprint as I break for the glass doors. I run into the deep elevator lobby, past where I should stop, and barrel right into the silver cage reserved for Millhause-Steig's golden few. I don't care. I need out of here, and if it means hijacking the special elevator, then that's what's happening.

As the sleek doors finish their slow close, I can't even muster a sigh of relief. All I have are stunted gasps, like hiccups but painful, and the tears are practically raining from my face. I'm a mess. Reduced to a dull stereotype: the sloppy, weepy girl running away from it all.

It takes four floors before I realize that there's a man in the elevator. He's been standing there since I poured myself in here. My breath gets loud, uneven. I'm reaching for a railing, a wall, anything. That's when he says it. "Take my hand." He says it and I'm instantly in a movie—a thriller or horror story—something with blood on the floor.

"Take my hand." Three words, said simply, with the ease of a man who knows his strength, a man who knows that there's safety within that one uncomplicated action.

"Take my hand." His eyes sparkle. Who in real life, besides babies and Aunt Lucille's cancerous cat Telly, has eyes that sparkle?

He inches his cupped palm toward me. Of course it looks soft and firm and capable. The one out-of-place thing about it—the small red line, a paper cut at the base of his index finger—is the only thing I can relate to. It's the one thing assuring me that this man, this whole moment is actual, no figment.

His face finally comes into focus. I've seen him many times before: talking quietly to editors and underlings in the hallways of the important floors, leaning in slightly, an attempt to cut his height down a level. In the main lobby, the lofty, lean figure breezing by the chattering cogs—one arm resting limber with the hand tucked casually into his pants pocket and the other swinging forward and back, back, back, as if waiting for a baton. He's all charm and grace and a thin layer of hubris or aplomb, or whatever it is that allows him to walk the long stretch of high-polished marble from the oversized revolving door along the enclosed breezeway and farther still, down to the executive elevator bay without so much as look down at his pristine shoes. I've seen him out front by the curb, sliding—never hurried, always collected, always cool—into a taxi. Once, maybe (but ask me tomorrow and I won't be so sure), I saw him in the cafeteria; the juice line, or maybe it was the sushi kiosk. It never matters when I think back to it. It doesn't matter now. What matters now is that he's real and he's trying to save me.

He's saying something. I can't hear. My brain is locking up. I strain, lean in, but nothing is getting through. It feels like I've pulled a muscle—everywhere. But honestly, no one has any sympathy for me right now. I should know better. This elevator is famous. I have no business on it. People have been crushed, their insides splayed out in color, because of something said, suggested, decided in this wintry, steel box. It's no place for the weak and considerate. But here I am, snotty, sweaty, and in pieces, following his advice—his command—and grabbing for his hand.

"In and out," he says.

Breathing. He's talking about breathing. I smile—or try to curl my lip—because I can hear again.

"Slowly. In and out," he says.

My eyes finally adjust to the room, to the moment, and I notice his mouth first. It's his turn to smile. His lips are full, plump, especially the bottom one. They're not thin, as one expects on a man his age. But then not much about him fits under that column. He's excellent; dapper and slim, not even a hint of paunch can be seen through his now-unbuttoned suit jacket. His hair is mostly gray, but thick and groomed. The lines—around his eyes, his mouth, above his brows—etched into his yacht-tanned face look right and intentional. He smiles again, wider now, and I trust him, instantly. The noise in my brain is quieting to stage whispers.

He's squeezing and stroking my hand with his thumb at once. I try to focus in on his paper cut.

"I'm here. I'm here with you," he says. He nods; small, even nods, as if confirming all of this with me. "This elevator isn't going anywhere. It's the ground floor. We're here. Just keep going, in and out, that's your job. When you catch your breath, get a rhythm, I'm going to open these doors and we're going to walk out of here like everything is okay, because it is." He pushes his suit jacket open further. I can make enough time-place connections to know that it's freezing outside and the man's just wearing a suit. There's a cuff link peeking out from the trim jacket. It looks like a face. A profile. It looks like one of my coins. I feel the flutter return to my temples, my chin is back on quivering. I'm trying to catch the rhythm he mentioned, but it's not working. My ears tingle and too quickly those pins and pricks spread to my jaw, my neck, my chest. Now black clouds are circling, getting bigger, crowding the light. My knees, they're wobbling. Did I accidently lock them? Shit. This is it. I'm going down, and all I can hope is that he's still holding my hand.

<hr />

"Hey, hey." He's got me propped up on him. His knees are bent and he's close to my face now. "You're good. You're doing fine. Back to breathing, okay? Watch me, watch my chest. It's rise and let go. Rise, let go."

The nods, they're helping.

I take a deep one and let it go. My breath is hot and tumbles out of my smeared, chapped lips. I do it again and another, slower still, in and out. I get more nods, a soft squeeze to my hand, and finally I'm standing on my own, I've caught a rhythm.

"You don't have a coat," he says as the elevator doors open.

"Right."

"Do you want to go back up to seventeen and grab it?"

"How did you know I'm on seventeen?"

"*James* magazine, I know," he says.

"Of course you know. You're Nik Steig."

"And you're Best Lightburn. I know that too."

"Yeah. I am. Making this whole elevator meltdown that much more fantastic. This is . . . mortifying."

"Come on. Leave that in there." He tilts his head toward the closing elevator door. "We're out here now."

Nik Steig does up his jacket buttons as we walk to the main entrance. He pulls out a scarf from a black hat, or some other magical place next to a rabbit, and ties it in that cool, European loop. "So, what now? Heading home?"

Say yes. "No."

He nods. "Do you want go somewhere else?"

Say no. "Yes."

"Well, since you're missing a coat, do you want me to get you a cab? Or my driver, he's circling, we can take you where you're going."

Decline. "Yes, thanks. Your driver."

"Good. But we'll need a bit more to go on than yes and no. Hank's going to need actual directions, I'm afraid."

"Actually, I just need to go home. Brooklyn."

"Let's go," he says without a pause, and gestures to the revolving doors. "Wait." He slips off his jacket and scarf. "I know you're Canadian and all, but I can't let you go out like that."

"How do you know . . . wait, I can't take your jacket."

"Sure you can." He opens it up for me. I should refuse again. I *should*. "Come on. Hank's probably crawling up to the curb now. Take it. It's nothing. I've got a meeting. I don't need it."

I turn, he helps the jacket over my shoulders and hands me his scarf.

This is not happening. This is not a soap opera. I must have fallen down the elevator shaft, because this is Nikolai Steig and this is not happening.

"Shall we?" he says and tilts his head toward the door. *Just go with him. Say yes.* "I'm sorry, Mr. Steig—"

"Nik."

"Nik. I'm sorry, but I just need a minute here alone to just pull my shit together. You have a meeting. You should go ahead. I'll get home all right." I raise my phone to his eye line like an idiot. As if the thin thing holds the salve for all that just went down.

"It's not a problem"—my cell phone's ringing cuts him off—"Listen. Take your call. I'll be in the car with Hank. No rush."

Before I can refuse again, he walks off, and I just watch him glide away. He knows I'm staring at him too.

I press *yes* on the phone, blindly. "Best here."

"Ms. Lightburn? It's Clark Bauer from *Tell Me More*. *Pleasedonthangup*. Please. I'm reaching out because . . . well, we want to run a proper profile on you. It's nothing bad. We're talking regular story about you, no rumors. It just that . . . well, I had a few questions for you . . . about your brothers."

CHAPTER 7

Brooklyn
Three Months Earlier.

He hands me the torn-out scrap of paper, damp and trembling, like his hands. On it, an uneven collection of wobbly letters colliding into each other—the directions to his uncle's home in northern Connecticut. I rest the paper on my lap; the crumply thing sticks to my bare leg. It's late August, near the end of a relentlessly hot, unkind summer, and we're sitting in his convertible with sun-warmed leather seats. There's a breeze, though, a slight one. It's odd that no one else is on the street yet. When it's hot like this for this long, people tend to make moves early in the morning, get to the subway before the oven of it all clicks over to broil. But there's none of it, as if the neighborhood decided to grant him some privacy to come unglued in peace.

Actually, if I were writing this as a feature story, that's the headline right there: *Grant Him Peace*. And for the subhead something like:

When a young actor living the dream life in New York City suddenly finds himself on the sharp edge of a nightmare, he

figures he has two choices: sink or swim. Grant King de-
cided to just drift away.

"This makes no sense," I say, looking down at the direc-
tions.
"I know. I just feel fucked up, like my brain's sweating."
"No, this, these directions. There's no house number. Par-
tridge Hollow, Finders Way. Is this irony?" My chuckle sounds
nervous, forced.
"Best, I'm a mess—I can't."
"I know. I don't want you to. But I just don't understand
these directions you wrote. I can't punch this into my phone,
even."
"Drive. I'll guide you."
Grant wants to believe this. He wants to believe a lot of
things right now, but none of them are true.
"It's okay. I'll figure it out. Don't worry about any of this."
I'm cringing at my own voice, all flossed like cotton candy.
How is this reassuring? The man is crumbling, caving in on
himself, and I tell him not to worry.
He looks horrible. Watching him, his mouth ajar, lips cracked,
and his face ashy, I want to offer something he could use: a
cold compress, a blanket, a kiss. If this were flipped, he'd
know exactly what to do for me, because Grant is the guy. He's
the guy. The guy who can fiddle around with that broken thing
and actually fix it. The guy who knows how to skip rocks, mix
a stiff drink, waltz, play the guitar, massage my scalp, and recite
"The Raven" in full with the perfect layer of gravitas. He's the
guy posted up in the dim corner at a party, simple, just sipping
a beer, while the room buckles and rolls toward him. And when
he dips out only twenty minutes after he arrived, everyone
misses him, instantly. He's the guy and he stays in character.
Now he's sitting next to me helpless, overcome and sweaty.
The magic spell started wearing off about a month before, in

the middle of summer. We had a fight. One that I wasn't even sure was real until he smashed his phone against the kitchen cabinet and stormed out. We had been talking, in bits and pieces over the course of a few days, about how a quirk becomes a habit and when either could be considered a flaw. Typical chatter for us (even sober). I said quirks were just smaller habits—the little, peculiar things we regularly do that make us adorable and interesting, like how Tyson refuses to drink anything cold that doesn't have lots of ice in it—cubed or crushed. Or the way Grant insists on wearing socks to bed, despite sleeping nude. Or how I check to see if a kitchen appliance—toasters and electric kettles, mainly—has been resting in water by swiping the plug prongs against the back of my hand before pushing it into the outlet. (Forever scared by that sloppy horror movie I saw when I was nine, where a mother standing in spilled milk touches the overflowing coffeepot and is electrocuted.) Each of these things is unique and tinged with a little weirdness, but nothing in them spells *flaw*. They're not defects in character like greed or jealousy, I told Grant.

"Or dishonesty," Grant said, and reached into his front pocket for his phone.

"Right. Or dishonesty. Um, aren't we talking here?" I said, exaggerating my wide-eye stare at the phone in his hand.

"Yeah, we are. I'm just check on something. Shawna, she's supposed to e-mail me sides for that movie I told you about. I actually have to send in a taped audition, which is always weird."

"But taking out your phone in the middle of a face-to-face is also weird, and rude. You've told me that—repeatedly."

He looked up from his phone, a smile hanging off the edge of his lip. "Best, come on. You know I'm listening, and you know I'm waiting for this e-mail. This audition, it's PT Anderson. It's important."

"So when I'm on deadline and doing my phone stuff, that's not important?"

He looked up again. The smile was still there, but fading. "We're not doing this. I'm not doing this. You're kidding, right?"

"I'm saying that you're setting these rules here and then breaking them. You were the guy, just last week, complaining about how we don't pay attention to the moments in our lives, how we're missing all the good stuff and basically walking around empty, just pretending we know how to respond to life. You then proceeded to mock me for having a Twitter account and caring about my following. That ringing any bells for you? Do you remember saying all that?"

"No, because I wasn't mocking you about Twitter followers. Who gives a shit about Twitter? I remember talking about how being an actor often makes you feel like a vacant shell, always standing outside of things, observing, recording, just filling up with notes on how people are *supposed* to feel, how we're supposed to behave and experience everything, so you can re-create that in a performance. And in the end, you're walking around with all of these other people's stories, their lives, their weird hang-ups and fears—you still feel empty. More than empty, you feel nothing. And the really fucked-up part is, you're stuck there, alone, with nothing."

"Grant, you didn't say any of that. You were scolding me— and our generation—for always being on some lit-up device. You were going in on us millennials for being vacant. I think you even used the word *cipher*. You were basically one line away from shouting, 'And get off my lawn!' It wasn't about loneliness at all. You were pissy because you felt like I wasn't listening to you talking about some actor thing."

"Some actor thing?"

"This is nuts. It's like you're presenting this revised version of history—how you wanted things to go or sound or be. I mean, it's a well-shaped story, but it's just not true. I would remember you saying that you feel lonely or empty sometimes, regardless if I were on my iPhone or not."

"This is some shit. Here you go, reducing me to some bullshit stereotype—again. And all because I'm out here on a grind, working to keep working. Like that's a crime? But maybe that's just some actor thing." By then, Grant's lips were stretched across his face as tightly as he gripped his phone.

"I don't know . . . you tell me. Maybe you should check your trusty black notebook and see." I said it, but wanted to hit *delete* the minute I did. His jaw was clenched as he backed away from me, tilting his head. "Grant, I'm sorry. That wasn't— look, I would remember if you said that. I would remember and I would be with you in that; talk it through. Just like we did at the hotel with the French fries and the bathrobes, when you told me about your mother, about missing her, wanting to go back to before—I would remember that. You know I would remember."

Misstep.

I saw his arm move; it was quick. Then the dense clash of his phone meeting the hardwood. And he was gone. For three days and two nights. When he came back, I said nothing about the fight or the phone, nor did he. We greeted each other sweetly, but something else was there in the interstices, something that Grant dragged in on the bottom of his shoes, nested in his clothes, resting on the very surface of his skin. It was dark and quiet and strong, and just curled up inside of him, stowed away with no clear plan to leave.

It was like that for the next few weeks: Grant sequestered in his bedroom with his black notebook and twenty pillows. He never bothered to get more than a thick futon mattress. He was only supposed to crash at my place for a few weeks while he waited for news about his HBO project getting green-lit. I blinked and he was full-on living with me. But just because he was in my bed didn't mean he needed to be *in my bed*. The second bedroom was free—in theory. Small and dim and always the wrong temperature, I'd often watch movies on my laptop in there, hugging a body pillow on the hardwood floor and wearing this ugly robe my parents gave me in high school, a bra (maybe), and my pilling yoga pants. It was supposed to be my office, then my meditation room, then my wardrobe extension/showroom, but primarily remained my dark hole until Grant tumbled into it and stayed.

When I left for work in the mornings during those weeks post-fight, his door would be closed. Same when I returned. After the first couple of times I stopped doing the sneaky ear-to-door listening thing. Maybe he was in there, maybe he was sleeping, maybe he was in there wishing he were sleeping. I figured he'd come out when he wants to, when he worked this dark, quiet thing out of his system. But one late night, when I got home from *Sex, Ovaries, and Office Politics* episode 12, I found the apartment in total darkness. Strange, because I always leave the lamp in the corner of the living room turned on, burning all day long—habit from my mother, who was always spooked about entering a pitch-black house. There was a slip of light leaking from under Grant's door, and a familiar bottle of water on the bar counter in the kitchen. There was a star-shaped sticky note on the bottle:

Best Lightburn's
HANDS OFF IF YOU'RE NOT BEST LIGHTBURN
THIS MEANS YOU, MURDEROUS BURGLAR

Whenever Grant was in town and made it home before I did, he would leave out a bottle of water for me. We had gone back in time somehow, and I was too thrown to submit to chuckling or feeling nostalgic about any of it. I just wanted to magically jump time again and cut to the scene where I'm recklessly drooling in my own bed. I grabbed the bottle of water and I tried to breeze past his room.

"Hey, you're home," he said through the cracked door. I pushed it open more. He looked just as his voice sounded, hushed and sweet. He was propped up on all of his pillows and had that goddamn black notebook cradled in his lap.

"Thanks for the water." I rattled it near my face.

He reached out his hand. It's this thing we started doing early on, giving each other five—up high, on the side, down low. Stupid, I know.

I slipped in. Gave him a soft, lopsided five. He gripped my hand, pulled me into him, into his bed, slowly. I went with it. He kissed me high on my cheekbone, right under my eye. It's his move. *These cheekbones, they're like ledges. I can't get enough.* Always appraising my bone structure, running his finger and, often, his lips along my collar, my cheek, jaw, hip bone, commenting on the angles.

"Sleep with me tonight?" The look that followed, all deep and doleful like a torch song pouring out of his eyes, only confirmed my plan to break up with him. Grant wasn't getting too close; he was already there—and it's not a safe place.

"Grant, I'm wiped. I've been staring at crappy copy all night about how dieting fucks up your boobs. My eyes are shot, plus I'm almost certain I'm wearing period panties for no legit reason. You don't want none of this, guy."

He nuzzled my ear, when he knows how much I hate that. I even hate the word.

"No, *sleep-sleep*," he whispered. "Nothing but sleep. Promise."

Again, I went along with it. Couldn't figure out how to turn away from the ache at the base of his request. Saying no, it didn't feel like an option.

"Okay . . . well, let me go get my jammy-jams on, wash this gross day off my face."

"You can wear this . . ." He reached for the blue T-shirt on the floor next to his stack of books, "and we can just turn off the lights."

"Um, so there's no sex, but I'm slipping into your cozy T-shirt? And, if history is any indication, you are likely nude under those covers—with socks."

"You know me well. Does it make me a dick to say that that's what I love about you most—that you really know me? That's major, because anyone who knows me would tell you that they don't really know me."

"Was that a riddle?"

"No, I change my answer. That—that right there, the jokes, the wry fly shit—that's what I love about you. Actually," he said, a drowsy, crooked grin creeping up the side of his face, "it's everything. I just love—"

"Grant, don't. I don't think we should—"

"Oh, but we should. We definitely should." He smiled again, but this time it was his smile—the earnest one that starts in his eyes. "It's just sleep, B."

The next night, he asked me again. Despite having common sense and better judgment and self-worth and all the things (according to every woman's magazine *ever*) that a girl should hone before stepping foot one into these kinds of relationships, I said yes—again. Lying in his bed again, awake again, staring up at the skylight again, tracing the cracks from the high window down to the top of the door, and trying to figure out how I might follow that same route. The moment I slid out from under his hot, heavy leg, some other part of him would wrap around me, pull me close. I was sleeping with an anaconda. And it had noting to do with his penis—which, of course, was also unleashed and twitching against my thigh. He smelled like beer and whiskey or maybe it was ethanol. Normally, this would be fantastic. I like kissing a man and tasting alcohol on his lips. But nothing about this was normal. Grant, this beautiful man with the famous jawline and "I got this" swagger, was becoming ordinary, a maudlin and needy cliché, desperate to have someone swoop in with answers and solve it all for him. And I—this woman with the cheekbones that he loves and the scent he loves and the list of detailed, sweet and wonderful things he notices and loves—was choosing to help him by leaving him. Later he won't see it as me quitting on him or rubbing salt in his eyes or kicking him as he's falling down. The truth is: He doesn't need me, with all my broken-doll parts. I was never going to be good for him, because I'm just not good. And later he'll know this. Later he'll see that leaving him was the most loving thing I could ever do for him.

We ended up having sex that second night, but it was a mess, and not in the usual sticky way that mixing parts can be sometimes. It was sloppy and sad and just a bad idea. He couldn't stay hard. He cursed himself, a murmur of hot words breathed into my neck. He pounded a fist in his pillow. He dug his nails into my hip. He cupped my face in his hands, connecting our heads. He stumbled over a scattering of muddled words. And finally, after all of it, he apologized, over and over, before sliding off of me to get dressed—shirt dragged over the head, legs pushed roughly into the pants—and walked out. The hollow *click* of the front door echoed in my chest. More than ridiculous, I felt relieved. Whatever ledge he was sliding toward, it didn't matter; I wasn't going to be there to watch.

I look down at the scrap of paper with its janky directions to the woods of Connecticut, and then over at Grant.

"Just get us the fuck out of Brooklyn, and I'll help you from there," he says.

"No need. I've figured it all out."

He's already curling into the seat, eyes closed, spirit fading. I adjust my rearview and glance down at the paper again. *Partridge Hollow. Finders Way.* I know exactly where I'm going. I toggle the mirror again, willing it to reshape the road ahead of me too.

CHAPTER 8

My introduction couldn't have been more awkward or awful. I called Grant's uncle from the road when we were forty-five minutes out. I had spoken to Uncle Richard exactly zero times before that. The wife, Rosalie, I knew about from the two or three mentions Grant made of her in passing—perfectly pleasant bits, but not enough to go on when meeting a guy's family for the first time.

I'd never even met Grant's big sister Gisele, and they were extra-close, especially since their mother died. Cerebral aneurysm. I used to think about the mother a lot, back when Grant and I first got together almost a year ago. From the stories he told, it was clear she—this quiet, white woman from the quiet, white Prairies—lived for him. Even his name—she chose it so carefully, created it to last: Grant King. She changed their surname after he—not Gisele—was born. Hecking wasn't doing anyone any favors, and with Grant's black father being a complete deadbeat—and then simply dead—she was happy to shed the terrible, clunky thing. Grant said his mother had long dreamed of being a sculptor, but never found the nerve to step toward it. She remained a grouchy chemical engineer who instead shaped her son's life until she lost hers.

But there I was, this basic stranger calling them with unsettling news about their fabulous, famous Grant.

Rosalie answered. Her voice was steady and calm, even after I told her what happened—as if I called to reminder her that her dentist appointment was on Tuesday. It was probably the British accent. Her only questions: Where exactly we were on the route and whether I needed directions. We were at a gas station in New Haven, and no, but thanks. I called Gisele next, while Grant was still inside buying more Diet Coke and licorice. Voice mail. Thank Jesus. I'm sure I sounded rambling and ridiculous.

When we arrive at Partridge Hollow, Grant's whole twitchy-sweating-weirdness is on level orange. He doesn't want to be here. He barely wants to be in his own skin. Rosalie—short and slight and nothing like I imagined—is charmingly sweet with Grant. She wraps her arms around him; her hugs long, but not lingering, and her offers of tea and blueberry scones and anything else we might need to be comfortable are warm and motherly, but not overdone. Richard is, as my mother might say, your *box standard* older, white gentleman. He's tall and also slim, better described as wiry, and he seems more interested in hearing about our drive up and the kind of mileage the car gave us than whatever is happening with his only nephew. *Mind if I have a look inside?* That's the only thing Richard has said to Grant in these first few hours since arriving. And he disappears right after. Richard is busy, clearly, and must go bury himself somewhere in the manor.

This place is massive; simply calling it a house is downright disrespectful. And no detail has been left unstudied. Everything in here is considered: from the drop-in, fireclay sinks and footed double-wide tub in the bright bathroom to the giant, yellow French range ($11,000—yes, I'm a stealth Google master) and the ladder in the kitchen. I said, there's a ladder in the kitchen, *on a track*. And the bedrooms—the handful that I've seen so far—are magnificent. When we step into the one Rosalie says is mine, I gasp. Like literally gasp. The ceiling's wood beams come to a perfect pitch like a tent. The bed, all white and wide and inviting, is covered in a beautiful quilt that I'd bet was handmade and passed down through someone's family tree. And the flourishes: rusted, old-fashioned lantern on the edge of a worn-down wood crate used as a night table; bench made from recycled railroad tie; junky-treasure Corona typewriter sitting on weathered cedar bookshelf. It's as if Aunt Rosalie created the room specifically for me, curated from all of my dreams. I want to fall into the bed this instant, and tell them all I'd prefer to be left alone and only woken when dinner is being served. Decadence suits me.

As soon as we come to the end of the tour, Grant heads back upstairs with Rosalie carrying his flat gym bag for him.

"You can stay down here and have some tea," Rosalie tells me, gesturing with her chin at the small, round, lacy-top table near the brick fireplace. There's a full tea service set out. "Or we can carry your things up as well, get a rest. There's always time for tea later."

During daylight hours Grant remains in his room in bed or he's gathered up, small and feeble, in one of the Adirondack chairs that Rosalie has lined up neatly on the west porch. At night, Grant roams around the compound with that notebook. I can hear him—the creaks and shuffles and deep sighs—from my room.

I knew the knock was coming that first night. I could have timed it. He stood leaning on the opened door long after I had said *come in*. He was smiling, sort of. I moved my reading short stack aside and pushed the layer of covers back, showed him there was room for him. He poured himself into the guest bed, his cold, tight arm rubbing against the top of my leg, and stared up at the ceiling. He was lying back in that way that I hate—like he's in a coffin. I offered a back rub. He nodded and rolled over. His body was icy and tense. I slid on top of him, straddled, wrapping my warm thighs around his lower back. He arched up to remove his T-shirt, unleashing this scent—his scent, a mix of soap, sea breeze, and fresh sheets—and he went back down into the pillow with a long sigh. He took more deep breaths and let them seep out slow—I felt each of them pressing lightly inside of me. Running my hands along his back, shoulders, neck, I wanted him. My breath got heavy and I felt my heartbeat quicken. All my bad ideas floated to the surface; my solid reasons for why there could never be an *us* started to fall away, replaced by this sure craving for him. Splintered and hurting, Grant was still pulling me in. I was leaning into it too, and about to go for it, slip off my tank top and everything else, when he said something.

"I'm sorry."

"Sorry?"

"Yeah. Sorry to drag you into all my bullshit."

"Grant, you're just going through it right now."

He let out another one of those deep sighs, and I slid right off of him. "Look, there's nothing to apologize for here. You're in a rough patch and need some time to figure it out. Just do that. Do what it takes to figure it out."

"You're good. Really good—to me, for me."

He squinted his eyes and I swear I saw a flicker of something, a glint of Grant the guy as his head tilted toward me. I let mine fall back, making it easier for him to get to my collarbone. But instead of burying his face in my body, he was sinking into the pillow, sobbing.

There are things that I know and there are things that I do not know. At the top of my list of things I don't know is this: What to do when a man starts crying. It's bizarre and terrible and I have no clue where to put my eyes, much more where to lay a comforting hand. What's the best move? Touch his head? Brush his wet cheek? His jerking shoulder? Like I said: things I do not know.

I haven't been around too many crying men—not men who mattered to me. Bryant was shy and quiet and often picked on—for general nerd reasons—but he wasn't one to cry about any of it. Benjamin never once shed a tear in my viewing. When he broke his femur in a bad hit during a football practice, he winced, he punched at the air, he cursed like a drunken pirate (or like the fourteen-year-old that he was), but he didn't cry. Something he learned from our father, I guess. With the shitty cards that my poor dad was dealt—squeezed into the sides of a derelict life in Trinidad, always without enough food, shoes, help, love, luck—if Bertram Lightburn chose to sob for hours each day, it would be completely understandable, maybe even expected. But once—and my memory sometimes clouds around the specifics on this, twenty years later—I woke up in the wee hours to the sound of what I processed in my kid's brain as a hurt cat mewling. It was coming from downstairs. Groggy, confused, I made my way through the darkness, following the hurt cat's call. There was light in the kitchen and the whimper was coming from there. Both things were strange, out of order, and it frightened me. I remember stepping toward the kitchen, right up to the edge of the archway, my body flat against the wall, as if I needed to sneak up on whatever was making that noise. Just as I was about to bend my head around the corner and capture the intruder, I heard it clearer: It was my father. I recognized his voice beneath the snivel and mumble. "*I'm sorry. Lawd Gawd have mercy. I promise to change. I promise.*" He was pleading, begging with all that he had. I ran back to my room, tucked my body into a tight ball, and buried myself under the blankets at the foot of the bed. The rest of it is blank. I don't remember how the next morning went, or the next week. Sometimes I do think I recall this one detail: my mother warning him about "next time" and his drinking, but I'm never sure that part is real.

I still make like a ball and hide under the covers when something freaks me out. And tonight, even with Grant sniffling in his sleep right next to me, that's exactly what I plan to do.

⸻

The simple silence of the Connecticut morning wakes me. Not a garbage truck, not a car alarm, not an elephant-footed upstairs neighbor, just a deep quiet. It kind of startles me; I pop up looking around the room, disoriented. Grant's gone. No surprise. I felt him get up in the night, but I pretended I was asleep. I pulled a Benjamin. That guy was always faking sleep. Like when I was fifteen and tried to sneak out of our house via Ben's bedroom window. He knew I was there. He had to; I used his back as a stepstool. He knew I was heading out to the see the ass clown (as he called him). And he knew I was going to steal our dad's car to do so. Benjamin's room was on the ground floor, sharing a wall with the garage. He heard everything: the reliable Honda in neutral rolling backward, and that clear crackling sound of the unpaved driveway under the wheels. He heard. He knew. But he still acted utterly shocked when I was busted by a couple of my dad's police buddies eight streets over. (Sneaking around in a crime reporter's un-mistakably pristine white car—the only black crime reporter, to be sure—is just never going to work out.) I was grounded for months and barred from going to driver's ed for longer—an entire year—because of that failed midnight escape. And despite the fact that Benjamin *knew* I knew that he was faking deep sleep, he never once copped to it. But then he was the one who taught me about mutually-assured destruction.

⸻

Rosalie set out a spread for breakfast with everything a person would want to see arranged on a bright white tablecloth when they wake up. And the Filipina chef, who keeps slipping in and out of an unseen door, would obviously prepare that one missing thing you desire, without a second word. Rosalie likes hosting. That was clear from the gate. The table is set for six. She pulls out a chair at the head of the table for me. Uncle Dick obviously ate already and retreated. His white, cloth napkin and newspaper sections are in a sloppy pile at the other end of the long table. My cursory scan for signs of Grant produce nothing. So I stay on alert.

"Good morning, Best. How did you sleep?" Rosalie is replenishing a basket of jumbo croissants. "I hope you were comfortable."

"Very much so. Thank you, Mrs. Copeland. You have a lovely, lovely home."

"Please—" she refolds an already crisp napkin. "Call me Rosalie, dear. Can I get you something warm, tea or coffee? I'm happy to make you a latte or hot chocolate."

The way she says *chocolate*, her little mouth forming a tiny O, and the accent cheerily clipping away the hard consonants. I'm tempted to say "pardon?" just to hear it again.

"Tea is great, Mrs. . . . Rosalie. But I can make it myself. You've been through enough—you've done enough, I mean."

She smiles, but it's pinched. "It's no trouble, dear." And she's off before I can finish nodding.

Quiet classical music serves as the steady background noise throughout the rooms. I keep looking over my shoulder for Grant to pop up, but only Rosalie returns, carrying a beautiful teapot.

"He's outside," she says, and sails that same stiff smile my way.

"I figured."

"I'll leave you to fix it—your tea."

This style of conversation, coded and awkward, continues a little while longer until finally Rosalie excuses herself, something about running into town for this thing or another. It doesn't matter. She wants out of this performance and I don't blame her. I'm going to grab a shower after breakfast, although the wide, footed tub is alluring. But soaking in one's dirt was never really appealing to me. I still don't get why it's the thing to do if you're a woman in *any* movie and need to think or calm down or cry. Showers are my jam. That's where I start my writing, although for the past six months, my mind has been drifting off on its own, traveling back in time to places I'd rather not go, so now I usually spend my shower time coming up with quips for Twitter. I have a public, you know: 209,000 followers and growing. But even that has been tainted. Now I think, *What if this is the last tweet anyone will ever read from me?* Do I really want it to be some shit about saggy breasts (tough break) or my real thoughts on blow jobs (kind of against them)? It's like when Lana Scott attempted suicide earlier this year. People were combing through her old tweets for months until her account was deactivated, hoping to be the one who spotted the first signs of a struggle or discovered the deeper meaning behind her words, especially her last ones:

Even after all this time/ The sun never says to the earth, "You owe me."

That half-poem stayed with me, stalked me, and—somehow—attached itself to these lingering thoughts about my brothers. I started to wonder: if they had a chance to leave their own epitaphs scrawled across the internet skies in that permanent ink, what would they have said? With Bryant, I know for certain it would be something brilliant and complex, speaking to the intricate cause and chaos behind all that this universe has shown us. And Benjamin: He would have kept it simple and cool, but funny, probably quoting some professional jock. *Straight cash, homie*, or something perfect like that. Instead, they were refused that chance and left this earth in vicious silence, terror steeped in their bellies.

The night Lana Scott's Twitter account went dark and then disappeared, my old and buried panic returned. I was alone at home, pretending to care about the piece I was working on ("How to Make Him Beg for More"), when I went to her page to read those fifteen words for the thousandth time. There was nothing there but an error page. I closed and reopened the app over and over before it settled in my brain that the words, this rough tether that I had been clutching, was gone. The rumor that she had attempted suicide earlier that day started to spread throughout Twitter in the seconds after I—and everyone else—realized that this vanishing wasn't about an online glitch. The tears rushed in so fast and hard my eyes stung, and before I could catch my hot breath, I was on the floor, curled into a trembling ball, praying to a god I despised to make it stop, and my brothers—their destroyed faces, their swollen bodies—were all I could see. I was still holding my phone, trying to think whom to call, but also how to do it, how to physically move my locked-up fingers to press the right buttons and beg for help. I had finally removed Dr. Monfries's contact info from my quick-dial emergency list two years ago; my parents' home phone was the only in-case-shit-happens number that remained, and I knew I couldn't call them, not like this.

I think I passed out or fell asleep right there on the cold hardwood. When I opened my eyes, it was dark in the room and the light was just building in the skyline outside. I was still balled up in the corner, still gripping my phone, now dead, but the vile visions were gone. I spent the rest of that early morning trying to pull my shit together in time for work. This meant hot, extended showers where I actively push my mind into a different space and tried to apply the idea of *a triumph of hope over experience* not to a second marriage, but to this second life I was given, this fresh and restored start. Nobody plans to backslide or wants a relapse when it comes to drinking or drugs. Same wishes apply to those of us who have come up against soul-shattering terror. The aggressive nightmares, the mental breaks, the bottomless sadness—I didn't want those, not again. So I let the hot water wash over me and then carefully patched up my force field—makeup, clothes, obscenely expensive shoes—and reentered the world with my forehead toward the sky, ignoring the storm roiling inside.

———◦•◦———

I'm barely dressed when Grant comes knocking.

"Come with me?" His eyes are wide, alert, close to sparkling.

"Grant, I'm not even all the way dressed."

"Well, get all the way dressed, and come with me."

I grab my shirt, slide it over me and go, without another pause or question. He's taking the stairs two at a time and I'm trotting behind him, like a nervous child.

"Going for a drive, Richard," he says, talking to the air. I hear some kind of acknowledgment, maybe coming from the grand living room, but the door closes behind us before I can be sure.

"I don't have my stuff, my wallet."

"It's okay." Grant reaches back, takes my hand. "Don't need it." He opens my door and kisses my shoulder as I get in the car.

We pull off and I notice, for the first time, the horizon behind the Copeland compound. It stops me, stops my busy thoughts, and makes me stare at it.

"It's beautiful, right?" he says. "Makes me wish I came up here more. Well, before. Anyway . . . I wish a lot of things."

We drive along the rolling hills with our top down, only the cool breeze mixing in with the quiet in the car. It's peaceful. He is too, not agitated and pained like yesterday.

"You know, there's a difference," he says, finally. "There's a line between feeling vulnerable and feeling afraid. I know that line. I have to, as an actor. But lately, it's gotten all fucked up, conflated, and I can't sort it out. Nothing's connecting." He shakes his head. "I think about this teacher at Circle in the

Square, she would always say that once you become aware of something it changes. Bullshit. I'm aware. I'm *aware* of this, but I'm still a mess. Nothing's changed."

"Grant, sometimes it has to look like a complete shit show before things come into a finer focus and you start making connections, start making sense of it. That acting teacher's kind of right. It's going to change. I don't want to sound like some AA-work-the-program wonk, but it's a process. You do have to work through it. Figure out what's making you feel so sad and what you can do to make it stop."

"But it's not about sad. I don't feel sad. I don't feel anything. I feel nothing, just . . . nothing. How am I supposed to figure out nothing? How do you make nothing stop? I've been putting all this energy into forcing myself to feel something, put meaning back into this empty, bottomless bullshit. The nothing is bigger than all of that. It's bigger than all of it. And I'm tired of trying to make a connection or make sense of it. It's like it's winning this thing, you know?" He rubs his scalp. "I mean, fuck. It won."

The hopelessness is choking the life out of him. I want to reach for him, but as I do, Benjamin's face jumps into my view—partially immersed in those dark, calm waters, frozen detritus bubbling up slowly around his eyes, by the bridge of his nose. I draw my hand back.

"Look," Grant says, pulling me back into the right-now. "I've got a lot of shit to work through. I don't know where to start, but, seriously, you don't need to stay for this."

I'm still rattled by the vision of Benjamin, but I don't want betray the earnest moment we're having. I want Grant to know that I'm listening, that I understand, because I am and I do. I rub his leg. He tenses up a little, but I stick with it.

"Rosalie and Richard, they really want to help too," I say. His leg muscles pulse.

"*Rosalie* wants to help me or adopt me or whatever the fuck, I don't know. But Richard, nah; he just wants me to get better and get gone. He doesn't need me hanging around, rubbing his dead sister's mistakes in his face. I don't blame him."

"I'm sure he doesn't want you gone, Grant. Maybe he's just weird about people in distress. Feels helpless, so he shuts down. My brother was like that."

"Your brother?"

"Oh, no, sorry, I meant my mother. But you know what I meant. We're talking about your Uncle Richard anyway, not my mother."

"Now who's being weird?"

"I'm just saying I get it. I can see how that happens. Nothing weird."

"But you said *brother*. You don't have a brother. That's weird."

"Slip of the tongue. Mother, brother, they sound alike. Cancel the page for Dr. Freud, okay? It doesn't matter."

"All right. Sorry. Look, everything's fucked-up enough already. Don't want us to be too."

"All right. It's fine." I move my hand from his leg and rest it on the end of the leather seat instead. Things were indeed fucked-up enough. "So, what are you going to do . . . about the *fucked-up enough already* stuff?"

"Well, today I'm going to the doctor, like a physician, then I'm off to some shrink Rosalie says is phenomenal. Maybe he does magic tricks or some shit. After that, I'll figure it out. But I'm going to stay here, at least for a little bit."

He turns into a miniature-golf place, complete with a grand, spinning windmill at the 18th hole near the gate.

He smiles at me; the first uncontaminated moment in days. "Are you sure you want to do this, Grant? I mean, I'm a master at mini-golf. A master."

"Somehow I knew you'd claim that shit." He turns off the car and his little smile vanishes. "One thing: I want you to take this back with you."

"What, the car?"

"Yeah. It only adds to the bullshit with Richard. When I bought it, he dropped some racist bullshit line about black men always being flashy and not frugal. But notice he can't take his eyes off it now." He shakes his head once more. "That guy stays being the crusty jerk."

"How are you going to get around? Them-there hills look hardcore."

"Rosalie has cars. It's fine. I'll be fine."

He put some weight behind this, like he's convinced that a few weeks away from the grind of his New York life, away from his shiny, showy car, and he'll be fine, mended. But I don't buy it.

Something real happened to Grant; something unhooked inside of him. People don't just bounce back from that after a few chats with a shrink, no matter how carefully the pieces of the cup are glued back together. It's all still there—the damage, the veins and fissures—they're still there. The best you can hope for is that later on, whenever *someday soon* comes, you can still hold water and it doesn't just leak out through the seams. Like with my mother after losing Benjamin and Bryant like that. It was too much, too fast—it was a rupture. Now she's just hollow and fragile, unable to bear even a feather's weight. My father's different. He's like one of those fat, bursting wallets held together by a sturdy rubber band. I don't know if that's better, but at least he can move through the days, carry on a conversation, look people in the eyes, and appreciate the sun on his balding head. His way, he's connected to the breathing world around him. Her way? She's dead to it all.

My mother has looked the same ever since the funerals: glossy eyes, stone-faced, everything flat, just checked out, never to return. When I was leaving for York University, she barely blinked when I said bye that afternoon. I hugged her—more like, she let me hug her stern body. My father, so sad to see me go, looked overcome. He didn't want to let our embrace end. He held on to me, wrapping me tight in his thin arms. Granted, it was only eight months after everything, and my parents were losing another child—this time temporarily and to another province, not some frozen abyss.

I had to pack up everything myself. Uncle Dobbs helped me with some of it, as much as his bony, bowlegged little body could. He hadn't gone back to Trinidad yet. Uncle Dobbs only left because he had doctors' appointments he could no longer put off. He would have stayed forever; it was his little brother, his only living sibling, who had to bury his two sons at once, and Dobbs couldn't stand seeing how he was suffering. What's more important than that? Cancer, it turned out. Uncle Dobbs's funeral was in Trinidad that November. Being the eldest, he was buried next to his parents (my grandparents) and his sisters Aunt Henrietta and baby Josephine—both gone decades ago—were next to him. That was the last trip my parents and I took together. It was the last thing we did as a family that didn't involve memorializing Benjamin and Bryant. It's entirely cruel that it was for yet another funeral that we huddled together. We sat in the same row on the plane, my father in the middle, and held hands going and coming back.

Over the last two years, I'd say my father has been trying to find ways to smooth out the cracks in his splintered soul. Mostly this involves being lubricated—Mount Gay rum, neat—but he's tried others things too, like returning to a longtime love, one that ranks higher than the drink: Food. Cooking. He's started taking classes at Académie Culinare. He even mailed me a couple of handwritten recipes ensured "to put some fat on my bones." I use one—the lamb *ragù* with pappardelle—as a bookmark. His penmanship is exquisite and I don't eat red meat anymore. That man could send me a thousand recipes featuring meat soaked in meat with a side of meat, and I would treasure each one.

I told Dr. Monfries about it, about my mother being this sad shell, in our last session before I left for university. We hadn't spoken about my mother in a little while—he preferred that we focused on my "own lens." His response was so basic and un-therapist-like, it felt as if I were listening to some cloying, internet-dubbed *life coach* on an echoey podcast. He said: "Sometimes you have to lose yourself to find yourself." I nodded, but had no clue what he was talking about. I couldn't wrap my head around it: Because I was leaving, I was given a chance to lose myself—on purpose—and I had no intention of finding this mess ever again.

CHAPTER 9

Day three: I need to leave this place. I've been wearing the same clothes in very limited states of mix-and-match for too long. There's only so much wash-and-drip-dry one pair of panties can stand. Going commando was never an option—not for Miriam Lightburn's child. Somehow, despite the years and miles between us, my mother's rules for life became the rules, for life. When Grant started spinning out, I only had time to toss some toiletries and my satin sleep cap (priorities) into a tote, plus I brought my work laptop, three back issues, and my thick, crumply honor-killing folder. I didn't plan on staying here long. A couple hours at most, just past dinner, that was my thought. It rolled into three days. Of course it's guilt. Last week I was rehearsing my breakup speech in the shower, so sure of myself, so sure of my plan to clap Grant from my hands like dirt.

There's some comfort, I guess, in seeing how well Rosalie cares for him. But it's also cartoonish: this petite, white woman arching up to touch his forehead, as if fever could explain it. And Grant, a muscled, golden-brown specimen, so wounded he allows her to do it, to dote on, pet, and coddle him. Strange and awkward as it is to see some of those moments play out between them, it also lets me know that I can let go. More important, that he can let go of me, stop reaching out, trying to pull me close, and just let me go. It's safer for him that way.

Cell reception is a joke in these parts, but I have to contact Trinity and it needs to be by phone, because Trinity is basically your grandmother packed into a twenty-four-year-old's body. She doesn't trust transmitting anything personal via e-mail or text. I want to let her know where I am and make sure there are no new fires. I'm still on edge about that edit situation last month: Rachel, the copy editor who actively hates me, went to the Yellow Doors citing *inaccuracies* in my alpha-wives story. Whatever. I don't even need to double-check my files to know that it's not true. I don't cut corners; I report shit out. Rachel's probably setting me up, but still, given The Mistake and all, the suits are tracking my moves.

When I step on the porch, I spot Grant sitting on a lonely bench under a massive tree deep in the backyard. I put my fingers to my mouth and send out a piercing whistle—I don't want to sneak up on him, even though there's no real *sneaking up* on someone who's chilling on incredible, private acreage like this. He turns around and waves me over. By the time I get to him, my temples are damp and I feel a little sweat gathering by the nape of my neck.

"Hey," he says, and makes room for me on the bench.

I turn my back to him and sit the opposite way. "Hey."

"Looking for me?" Grant rubs my shoulder with his.

"Not really. Just looking for a prime cell spot; need to call into the office. How was your night?"

He shakes his head. "No progress there."

"Yeah, I'm not sleeping so well, either."

"Did I wake you when I left? I should probably keep this batshit business contained in my own room."

"No, no. It's okay. Having you there, it's nice."

"It's nice? Don't do that, Best."

"What? It's nice having you in the bed."

"Come on. Stay level with me. Of all people, I need you to keep it straight."

Honesty is not a fixer. I know that as fact. Grant does too. If anything, honesty only ignites the bomb that razes everything to the ground. "All right, then: You need to get a handle on the drooling, sir."

He smiles and looks down at my cell; I'm rolling it in my palm. "You know you could use the house phone," he says.

"Yeah, I just don't want to disturb anyone. They've been so cool about me being here. I don't want to be *that* houseguest."

"No one's disturbed here—well, there's me, but then that's the other kind of disturbed. Making a call from the house phone won't change that."

"Come on—it's not—you're not . . ."

He looks at me for the first time since I sat down. "It's called dark humor. Has the New Yorker been completely squeezed out of you or what?"

"Well, we are in a town called Farmington. I'm already picking up a bit of a folksy drawl. Wait, isn't this a fly-over state?"

He laughs and looks at me again.

"Listen, Grant. I, uh—"

He nods. "You have to go."

"I have to go."

"Today?"

"Today." I swing my body around to his side of the bench and let our knees touch. "Walking down here to you, I was trying to come up with something to say, something not obvious and useless like, 'You'll be all right.' But that's all I keep coming up with. It's stupid. I don't know what to say to you."

"Why do you have to say anything?"

"Because it's good-bye. I'm leaving and people say things when they leave."

"But I don't want you to leave. So maybe if you don't say anything, my addled brain won't register it. You can trick me."

He smiles and slips his hand over my leg, cupping my knee. "Just trick me. Drive off with the top down without another word."

"Grant, I can't take your car. How am I—I can't take your car."

He moves his hand from my leg and raises it, palm out, in between our faces. "You'll be all right," he says. I give him a light high-five. Grant grabs my hand and brings it to his lips to kiss. "You'll be all right," he says.

I nod. "I'll be all right."

CHAPTER 10

New York City.
Day Before Thanksgiving.

Standing here at the massive window of this unending terrace, my eyes can't seem to focus on the beauty before me: Central Park, unobstructed, dim, empty, alluring. A view that only grew more charming when the sun showed up an hour ago, making even the dense skies of fall sliding into this early winter seem beautiful. But I don't really see it. Instead my mind's eye has taken over the optics, and it's playing a different scene for me: spring in Los Angeles. Beachwood Canyon, more precise. Grant flew me out to meet him there for the Golden Globes. We stayed at this incredible, fully restored 1920s Mediterranean villa perfectly perched above Beachwood Canyon. It was the home of a new Hollywood friend of his, Dylan or Declan, something that starts with D. He was in the music business, behind-the-scenes—a songwriter and producer, I think. There were lots of guitars and instruments all around, and an old-fashioned microphone in the corner of the cavernous living room. And candles. So many candles in varying states of being burned-out. Dylan/Declan was bouncing between Austin and London, Grant said, working with "some major artists"—though none that I cared to retain to memory. Grant and I had full run of that gorgeous house. The master bedroom was this magnificent corner of quiet and escape and the bathroom—the other place we spent all of our time—was vintage and without fault. We soaked in that tub each night, overlooking the canyon from the terrace window, until we were withered and thirsty.

Now the only thought circling my brain is how I betrayed all of that with one reckless night.

That's almost the cruelest part. Grant would love it up here, thirty-two floors above the real world. If he were standing here with me looking out through this wall of glass, Grant would be pointing out all that is hidden and waiting for us in the park, just past the Merchants' Gate. He'd make up a contest—bet me something silly, like loser has to belt out the entire first verse of Mellencamp's "Jack & Diane" in the middle of the subway car—to see who can name the most best Central Park movie movements. And as usual, Grant would win. He's always set to win.

Even if you asked me under the threat of violence, I still wouldn't have a complete answer for why I did it. I mean, I *wanted* to do it last night. Nik wasn't my boss' boss last night. He was just Nik last night, and he was what I needed last night. There was no slamming of bodies against walls or counters. No buttons popped, no panties torn. It was hands held and softly kissed everything. He gazed at me, cradled my face, smoothed my cheek with his thumb. He even did that thing where he gently led me to his bedroom by the hand. It must be whatever *lovemaking* is.

But it's not last night anymore. It's the early morning and I'm still at his penthouse, wearing his shirt on my back like a ridiculous rom-com trope, except I have crusted-over mascara on my face. I can barely look at myself in the window's reflection without shaking my head.

I want to call Kendra. Text her. Get her to tell me I'm right, that this ugly feeling is fleeting, that Grant and I didn't really break up, because we never had that talk to sketch out what we were to each other anyway, and who really knows what happens on those sets between takes with all of the hurry-up-and-wait and the back rubs. I want her to remind me that Grant and I came to live together by osmosis, and we have separate rooms and beds, and those last few weeks—that last month, really—there was nothing *together* about us, and when I drove away in his car there was an implied separation, a silent agreement to go to our separate corners, because that's what made sense.

Bullshit. I can hear Kendra saying it. *Bullshit, all of what you said is total bullshit.* You cheated on Grant the minute you stepped into the Emerald City, with its unreal private elevator that opens up directly in the Wizard's place, like it's the front door, and the extra bedroom masquerading as a shower, with all its fuss and fancy—this button for steam, that one for precision temperature setting, and the four others you have yet to figure out. You need to feel ugly, because this, what you did, it's ugly . . . she'd say.

Of course, my phone is still shut off and Kendra is still not talking to me, and Nik from last night is Nikolai motherfucking Steig—my boss' boss. There's nothing fleeting; I've messed up, big-time. But I'm still not turning on my phone. Not yet. I can't. Bauer's probably got twenty voice mails on there by now. I gave him the low-battery bullshit. He bought it, I think, and I bolted for Nik's idling car. I still can't figure out how this Bauer guy found me. I operate like a goddamn *Mission Impossible* agent when it comes to my cell phone. I know *everyone* who has the number. Unless Grant finally earned his iPhone back or got some internet privileges from softhearted Rosalie and read every ridiculous, humiliating word about him and his best bitch on *Tell Me More.* Maybe he emailed Bauer with *his side of the story* and tossed my number at him—the only reprisal card he had in his deck, but the most ruinous one. He must hate me. Even if Grant didn't believe all of it, didn't fully recognize his broken life on display like that, and didn't take me for a complete savage, he must still hate me.

I would. I do.

He may have handed over the number, but Grant doesn't know about Benjamin and Bryant or what happened. None of my friends know. Bauer must have an inside man in Montreal. But none of those high-functioning morons have any connections to me here; those old friends know nothing of my new life. Jesus. I hope Bauer didn't contact my folks. They barely answer phones there, especially not calls coming from random U.S. area codes. I wonder if Bauer found out about my dad, reached out to some old colleague still slogging through the crime beat at the *Gazette*. That makes no sense; too circuitous. Just to get bio on me? I want to believe that Robot and her able Asian sidekick are involved in siccing Bauer on me. I want to believe it, but I know better.

This would be the kind of thing that I would enlist Kendra and even Lindee on to help me crack the code. But those girls don't want to hear from me. Kendra might cut me some slack because of the Lana Scott stuff. Then again, her patience with me has gone anemic lately. And now, with me certainly flaking out on Thanksgiving dinner at the mom's house tomorrow, the Singh girls will be ready to cunt-punt me for real.

Trinity is the only one who knows that I'm not at the bottom of the Hudson. When I called her—from Nik's home line, no less—and asked her to messenger my stuff to my place in Brooklyn, she didn't even pause or pose anything besides, "Are you okay," which tells me that Bauer hasn't posted any new shit about me. I would've been able to tell if something was up from Trinity's voice, her elocution. She takes on this higher-pitched, fussy speak when she's uncomfortable or lying or anxious. It's what my mother's Jamaican church sister used to call *speaky-spokey*, but that was specific to Carib folk trying too hard to camouflage their native tongue with a forced American or British accent. For Trinity that meant slowed-down sentences swollen with ornamental vocabulary, a strained, grammatically overdone string of words pushed through her tight lips. I heard none of that on our call, brief as it was. But she must know Nik Steig's home address, his phone number too, and she didn't even clear her throat when I told her where to send my things.

Trinity will put it together at some point, if she hasn't already. Doesn't really matter anyway. Bauer, he's the one who's going to slice my neck to the bone. The sleeping-with-the-big-cheese part will be the least of my lost graces.

"Aren't you cold?" Nik wraps me up from behind, first with him and then a cashmere throw. "Morning."

"Morning. Sorry, did I wake you?"

"Standing there basically nude looking out the window? Yes, highly disruptive stuff, Best." He circles me, opens up the blanket and pulls me into another hug, burying his face into the top of my head. He likes kissing my hair. And each time I think, please don't let this devolve into the dreadful *your hair is so soft, like cotton* skit. Grant never went there. Then again, he dated a good many black women in his day—mostly models and actresses. He knows his way around satin pillowcases and our hair-washing mysteries.

"So, it's tomorrow. We didn't shrivel up and blow away."

"All right, all right. But you'll admit that it is time to face real life now. I'm about ninety-five percent sure the last twelve hours were part of one protracted, eerily vivid dream."

"Ninety-five percent, huh?" he says, grinning, and they appear. Not dimples—he's no child—more like long laugh lines sketched onto his face. I notice a flat mole on the jawline and another midway down his neck. He really is something to behold.

Nik squeezes my shoulders once more before peeling off of me and sliding over to the narrow sofa in his living room. "We can do real-world," he says and extends his lean body along the chair.

"The fact that you even said that without a pause tells me we definitely can't. Plus, you're Nik Steig."

"Yes, you have reminded me of this quite a bit."

"Look, last night was . . . it was good, fun; but what are we doing here? What am I doing here? I should just go."

"Why?"

"Why? Because you're—"

"Okay. Let's start a new thread," he says, and gestures for me to join him.

I follow his gentle chin motion, but sit at the end of the chair closer to his feet and wrap the throw cover tighter around me. He gives me a look that pulls me in, makes me focus on him, on his mouth. Before I realize it, I'm leaning on him, draped over his middle, and he's rubbing the nape of my neck.

"Why don't you stay?" he says.

"Stay here?"

"Yes. Stay the night, or the weekend or whatever feels good." Nik moves his fingers from neck to my shoulders.

"It's Thanksgiving Day tomorrow."

"True, and I do have a thing I'll need to go to tomorrow, but that's about it. You can come with me."

"To the thing tomorrow? Just like that? Wait, I thought you said you didn't have plans. What happened to 'I'm European. Thanksgiving is not a big holiday for us'? Now there's a thing? A thing that I should tag along on? I don't even have clothes here, and more than that—"

"Not an issue. We can get you some new clothes. I know a guy."

"You know a guy?"

"I do. Henry. He owns a label, he lives a few blocks over and he's an old friend. Not an issue."

"What is this, *Pretty Woman*?"

Nik laughs. "It's not *Pretty Woman* or *Cinderella* or whatever other damsel you may want to summon. That's not what's happening. I'm not trying to save you. I'm just enjoying you."

"And that includes dressing me up in your neighbor's clothes—"

"And shoes too."

I cut my eyes at him and choke back my laugh. "*And shoes*, so that I can be your escort to this thing."

"It's my foundation's thing, actually."

"Oh, Christ. Are you talking about the charity thing at the *soup kitchen*?"

He nods.

"Of course you're talking about the charity thing, because your family does it every year, because you're Nik Steig—and we're back to my main point: I need to go!"

In one smooth swoop he's up and walking to the kitchen. "So you'll go?"

"Not to the gala. Home. I need to just go home."

"Works. I can drop you at your place. Or you can take the subway, Annie Hall, and we can meet there."

"Nik. I don't think that's a good idea. No offense to the soup kitchen."

"None taken. Coffee?"

"Uh, no, thanks. I don't drink . . . Listen, my head's spinning. A shower. That's what needs to happen right now."

"Love it. Let's do it."

"Actually, I have to do this one by myself. I'm sweaty and pretty gnarly. All the parts and crevices are in need of freshening."

He raises one of his sparse eyebrows and steps out of the

kitchen toward me. "That sounds much better than coffee. I can give you a hand . . . or something. I've never been afraid of a little sweat, even in the crevices." Nik slinks over to me and runs his cold, damp fingers up my bare thigh. I have just enough time to grab the top of his shoulders as he's dropping to his knees before me.

"Not that. Not right now. I'm serious, I just need a hot shower—alone."

"Your choice," he says, and pulls himself back up with little effort. "I have a couple e-mails and a quick call. If you need anything, just holler."

It's my turn to nod. As I walk toward the bedroom, clutching the soft blanket around me, I want to tell him that what I need is not here in this millionaire's lair, it's not within reach. It's not even something I can give myself.

From the shower, still wet and wrapped in a white towel, I crawl into the middle of Nik's bed. It hugs me back and I stay there, facedown, near smothered in all his pillows. I like it here. I like how safe and tucked away it is here. I like that he likes me being here, that he looks at me as if I'm so original and different. I like that thing he does, how he connects with you in this way that commands your attention through everything: not breaking eye contact, speaking to you in these fluid, expressive sentences. You're instantly drawn in and compelled to stay put. I like how much he enjoys me, my body. I especially like that he likes going down on me, even when I'm unwashed and a little dirty. I like his knowing nods and his ease, the lack of fuss around whatever he does. I like that he's opaque and people fear him, this enigmatic stone of a man with a tepid disposition and ferocious authority. And I like that I've been let into the special back room of him, beyond the red ropes and given access to his secret other side that's warm and open and caring. I like that he knows a guy and always has an answer, never stumped. I like him—and that's the problem. If this had to be something, it needed to be an anomaly, a one-night mistake that I think back on years from now when I'm on the subway with a book that's not holding my attention, and I get flustered and turned on and warmed and perked up. It should be a story I weave into a larger novel, recast and reframed, faded so that any names, characters, places, and events are a clear product of my imagination: *Any resemblance to actual persons, living or dead, is purely coincidental.*

"You all right in here?" Nik says from the doorway.

I turn my head away from him, just enough to get the two words out of the side of my mouth. "Sort of."

He's sitting on the very edge of the bed; I feel the weight shift. "What's going on—you okay?"

"No, but that's not a new thing. I haven't been okay in years."

I hear Nik stretch over and feel his hand on my back. "What's going on? Do you want me to make you some tea, something to eat?"

I shake my head, but keep it turned from him. "Do you know what they call you?"

"Yes, I do."

"Does it bother you?"

"No."

"Because . . . you don't have time to study what people think about you, or something like that?"

"Something like that," he says.

"It would bother me."

"And where does that get you—being bothered by what other people think?"

I nestle my face into the pillows. "I see your point."

He rolls me over to my side with a gentle tug and takes a slow breath, as if shaping his thought before he offers it to me. "It's business. Life, work, the overlap, it's all business. And within those spheres, some people will line up well with you, your opinions, your ideas and convictions. Others will not. They will be against everything you do, everything you represent. They're roadblocks or maybe potholes. It comes with trying to get wherever you're going. Nothing you can do to change it—they're part of the terrain. Either stop and, as you say, study them, or continue driving forward."

It sounds like something my father would say, and instead of comforted, I feel gross all over again. I shove my face back into the pillows.

Nik laughs and pulls himself across to the middle of the bed. He's lying near enough that I feel the warmth of him, but without touching me. "I probably sound like a weary old professor," he says.

"You could say that." My words are half-muffled in the pillow and I can feel my ears heating up. I finally turn to look at him, and that's when I hear that little voice in the back of my brain, piping in for the first time since stepping off the elevator and into Nik's car: *Girl, what the hell are you doing here?* He must have seen the realization spread across my face, transmuting it instantly into a wash of dread and angst.

"What's really going on?" His face looks dim, almost stern. "On the elevator you were clearly in a state of . . . *something*. But you moved through that, it seemed, and by the time we got here last night, you were . . . better. Happy, maybe, and it was nice. Now this morning, you've changed again. You seem sad. Even your shoulders are slumped." Nik runs his hand high along my back. "It's as if you're carrying this heavy brick right here. You can almost see it resting there. Do you want to talk about it? That might help. They do call me the Wizard, right?" He moves his hand up to my neck and wraps his fingers loosely around it. For a split second I can actually see the *Law & Order: SVU* episode based on our true story playing out in my mind: the ingénue and the billionaire publisher-slash–charming serial killer. Who would play me, though? But he lets go of my neck and returns to rubbing my back.

"Right. Wizard. But then other people just call you Ol' Professor Pervy McPerv with the mixed signals and massages."

That does it; we both laugh. I slide my body back into his. He wraps an arm around me. "I'm just trying to find normal again."

"It's all around you, Best. Breathe it in."

"Just like that?"

He smiles. "Yes. Just like that."

When I wake up again in the middle of his huge crumpled bed the next day, Thanksgiving morning, Nik is already up. I can hear his whirling and whooshing coming from the kitchen. I wouldn't be surprised if he was in there cooking a full traditional turkey with fixin's or maybe, factoring in the German genes, it's one gigantic schnitzel with piles of bratwurst on a platter.

I stay lying on my back, taking low, slow breaths, afraid to open my eyes all the way. I don't want any of the details to escape. I need to keep things straight. At some point I guess I'm going to want to tell a person about what happened here. Maybe they'll be able to make better sense of it than I can. So I lie there, rooted, thinking about it: Dinner last night, Chilean sea bass made by his hand in that cold but lavish kitchen; and about the library, an entire wall stacked nearly to the ceiling with books, some new, but more of them dusty and smelling their age. Rare editions; old, unheard-of titles; authors both famous and unsung—all of it waiting in the quietest quiet I've ever experienced, filled with wide, beautiful, lived-in chairs, not one of them stiff or ignored. I actually spent a solid hour in there alone, flipping through some of my favorites. One of them,

To Kill a Mockingbird, even came to bed with us last night along with his newspaper. He asked me to read from it aloud. It was that scene where Atticus tells Scout the trick to getting along with folks is to climb into their skin and walk around in it, in their shoes, looking at the world from their view.

I paused there, after reading the famous line. He stroked my leg.

"Have you gone back to the elevator again?" he asked.

"No. I'm still here."

"What made you stop reading?"

"This is going to sound crazy weird—then again, crazy weird is our thing—but I was actually thinking about your skin. Like, how it feels to walk through this world as you."

He paused. "You want to be me?"

"Well, I mean how it feels to walk through a world that was practically created *for* you: male, rich"—I looked right in his eyes—"and white."

When he removed his reading glasses, he let out this long breath. I was sure he was going to use the next one to ask me to leave. But then that smile slid up one side of his face.

"Right. You're implying that I've been handed everything; that I haven't worked for any of this. Silver spoons and secret handshakes, is it?"

My back straightened and I felt my lips begin to purse. "Nik, I'm not implying anything, but . . . let's keep it real."

"Ah. So, you think my life is easy?"

"Maybe not easy, but *easier.*"

He nodded slowly and looked just past my shoulders. "That could be argued," he said, returning to me, a hint of a smile still hanging from the edge of his mouth.

"You know what? I don't know why I said any of that—God, such sexy, sexy pillow talk, right? Reporter me needs to see the line and shut shit down way before I cross it. It's . . . horrible."

"Nothing's horrible."

"Except it kind of is. I should go, Nik. This has all been unreal. Nice, but unreal, and it probably shouldn't have happened. I had no business getting in your car. Definitely had no business following you home, into your bed. It's just that everything has become . . . I should just go."

He eased the book from my lap, clasped my hands, and pulled me over to him, right under his chin. I wanted to smell his neck. Put my face deep into it and inhale him, but I knew that was creepy-chick 101. I stared at his Adam's apple instead and wrapped my arm around his steel middle.

"Do you really think nothing's horrible?"

A heavy pause lingered. He slid down toward me, his mouth pressed against my forehead, and kissed me there. "I do. Are you ready to go sleep?"

I really was; just tired of everything at once. "Yes," I said, looking up at him, "but I'm seriously leaving tomorrow, Nik. First thing. For real this time."

"There's no rush. The city is basically shut down. And I'm enjoying having you here. Stay as long as you need."

"We can't run this circle again," I said, and paused for what could have been seconds or stretched-out minutes. "You know I have to go."

The quiet fell over us like a thick cloud. We were spooned and fading. Nik finally broke the stillness and moved to turn off the light. It rustled me out of my zombie grog. (I still think it was my literal drool on his abs that woke him.)

"Don't. Lights out means it's over," I said through clenched teeth.

"This again?" he whispered.

"Yes. Turning out the lights means a new day's at the door, and the sun will come along and dry up all the magic dust that's sprinkled over everything."

"Magic dust. Are you dreaming right now?"

"Exactly."

"The sun will come up whether I turn off the light or not, Best."

"Then leave it alone."

He ran his hand along the side of my ribs, gliding over my breast, and it felt good. It was lulling me, soothing me. But then in one fast sweep, he pulled my body over his with the ease of a blanket. He kissed me again, this time just off the side of my lips, and moved his hand down my back, pressing all of me into him. And with some advanced yoga move, he flipped me over and like that, I was under him, under his plank. "Still thinking about the lights?" His voice was low and gravelly.

I nodded.

Nik slid down, his head just below my stomach. "Give me twenty minutes to fix that."

CHAPTER 11

This is some bullshit. I had just fallen asleep, finally, after slinking through my door from Nik's house. I actually tiptoed into my own apartment. Didn't even want to look at the cabbie long enough to tell him my address. Home, sleep, disappear—that's all I wanted. Now someone's buzzing my door. It's Thanksgiving. Thanksgiving morning, no less. What sane American rings a stranger's bell on the biggest holiday of the year? *If I had some hot piss right now . . .* It's something my mother used to say when we were younger and Jehovah's Witnesses came around. It was gross, yes, but also so damn funny, imagining my proper mother dashing a bedpan full of pee out the window like that.

It better not be Nik's driver Hank, or worse, Nik himself talking about going with him to that goddamn soup-kitchen thing. If he followed me home . . . Listen, that hot piss is sounding more like a pantry staple right about now.

I try to keep my eyes closed and barrel toward the door. If I don't let the light in, I'm still basically asleep.

"*Yessss.*" I'm practically swallowing the intercom. I want my voice to sound raw and abusive.

"Best? You okay up th—"

The voice, it's a man, but it's distorted. My hand is covering both the *talk* and *listen* buttons.

"Hello?" I start again.

"Best"—I hear the familiar chuckle—"it's Grant. Buzz me up, woman."

I'm awake now.

There are only a handful of seconds for me to settle on what to do next: take the fire escape to the roof or sink back into a half-squat fighting position with my fingers curled into claws.

More buzzing.

I could also do nothing. Don't press another button. Push all of this panic down to the bottom of my belly and let him walk away cursing and calling me crazy.

Buzz. BUZZZZ.

A quick glance in the mirror: My hair is in a matted high bun and still damp from that sexilicious shower with Nik. Jesus. I probably still smell like him and my nipples are sore and erect. I'm wearing my night retainer, an old shirt of Grant's, and my Bikram yoga shorts, and there are the beginnings of two diagonal sleep lines on my right check. Doesn't matter. One look at me—the redness still stretched along my collarbone and up the side of my neck, the nipples poking through—and Grant, he'll know. He knows my post-boots-knocked face, and he knows it well.

I hear Grant's voice through the closed-up windows and heavy brick of my building. It's faint, but I can tell that he's yelling, probably even cupping his hands at his mouth as he bellows up to my floor. "Yo, Best! Buzz me up."

As history tells, my building basically evacuates by crack-o'-dawn Wednesday for this holiday. But I can't speak for the neighboring brownstones.

I close my eyes and press *open*, holding the button for longer than necessary.

Grant reaches the top of my floor quickly and, like a wish come true, he's instantly standing here at my door, snatching my breath. And he looks good. I mean, really good. Healthy. Healed. Everything about Grant—his eyes, face, mouth—glows golden like he just stepped out from the sun. And like that, my steamy thoughts about Nik, that shower, that bed, are gone, eclipsed by this beautiful, radiating, warm star filling up my doorway.

"Hi," he says, as if it was that simple, and leans in to hug me. It's warm and tight. He smells like something delicious baked just for me. As his soft lips press against my cheek, I finally hear myself exhale.

"*Hiiiheeyy*. Hi."

He's grinning. "Hi."

"Uh. What—here to . . . come in?"

"If that's the final question, yes. I will." Grant unzips his gray hoodie. A plain black T-shirt, identical to the one I'm wearing, hugs his lean, taut torso. He slides by me. He knows what he's doing.

"You look great, Best."

"You're kind, but come on—I'm a full-time mess." He's still glowing, still grinning, still beautiful. "So, what happened? Wait, did you—does your family know you're—"

"Here? Yeah," he laughs, "they know. We're all here. My uncle's getting this award in the city, and of course Rosalie went along. I decided to hitch a ride. I have a lot of ground to cover with my agent." He steps over, reaches for my hand. "And with you."

"I—I kind of don't know what to say to you right now. Is this a fever dream?"

He squeezes my hand. It's comforting at first. I pull away as gently as I can and move toward the kitchen. This feels like a sick redux of a scene from Nik's kitchen earlier this morning. I pulled away then too, but that was about coy and sexy and wanting to be followed into the shower. This right here is plain old guilt and discomfort. "Do you want anything? I can make coffee. It'll be black, though. You know me and this fridge and the milks."

"No coffee," he says, tracing my path, easing over to me again.

"Okay, tea, OJ? What would you like?"

"I'd like to go for a run."

"You'd like to go for a run?"

"Yes," he says, laughing. "I'd like to go for a run."

"You run now?"

"Yeah, I run now. And I want you to go with me. So, come on, get dressed."

"I don't think that's—have you been reading . . . Grant, we should talk."

"B, no dis, but talking is not really your game right now. You're kinda bumbling."

He's smiling and happy and sweet, and clearly in the dark about everything.

"It's because I don't know where to start. And I don't want you to hate me."

"Hate you? That's not happening, one. And two, just go put on some workout clothes. We'll run it out. And if you still feel like *talking*," he makes dramatic air quotes, "then we can get into it then. Plan?"

"Grant—"

"Just go get dressed, Best. Please."

"What if people see you—see us?"

"Then they'll see us." Grant smiles once more and adds a nod at the end, in that Nik Steig way, and I want to vomit. But instead I do as Grant says and change into running clothes. It's the very least I can do for him.

———•◦•———

"Ready?" Grant says and leads me to the middle of the street. The air is crisp. I already regret some of my clothing choices. Didn't need the wind scratching at my ankles, mocking my capri tights/low-rise sock combo.

"We're running in the street?"

"Until we get to the intersection," he says. "The sidewalk's no good for your knees, your hips, lower back. You'll be fine. I got you."

The street is rather deserted. Not even a lonely fool walking their dog. It's sunny, but cold and quiet. There's a rusted-out car to our immediate left. The whole thing is giving me opening scene in a zombie dystopian YA novel. I'm half-expecting some dusty hero with a high-powered assault rifle to step out from behind the neighbor's rickety fence, demanding that we prove we're red-blooded breathers.

"Where we going?" I mimic Grant's stretches.

"Not far."

"I don't run, not even for the damn F train, Grant. I'm going to slow you down."

"You won't. You'll be fine. Trust me. Ready?"

We start off slow, but five brownstones down the road, he's speeding up. Grant's got a good, smooth pace. Looks like he's adopted an impressive running posture too. I'm putting in a solid effort to keep up with him as he glides toward Atlantic Avenue. I can't remember the last time I went running. Long distance was never my thing anyway. That was all Bryant. He was on the cross-country team from young. Benjamin was basketball, and I did track—sprint and relay. Bryant always played against type: cross-country running, Dungeons & Drag-

ons, and of course, astronomy. Jesus, Bryant and that tele-
scope. Anything that was happening in the night sky, Bryant
knew how to explain it. He planned on becoming an astro-
physicist. And he would have done it too. I used to blame
everything that happened, all of it, on Bryant's goddamn obsession with the stars, but the truth is, we went out there, resting on our young, foolish trust, oblivious to the raw truth that
bad things don't give a fuck about what you've planned for tomorrow, no matter how honorable.

Grant turns around, starts trotting backwards. "It's not as
cold, right, once you get going?"

The winks, the grins, the high energy—and on a cold morning. What brand of drug is this guy on?

"I'm not agreeing with any of this, you know that, right? I
don't happy-run through the cold city streets, Grant. *You* don't
happy-run, like ever."

He trots back to me. "People change, they improve."

"Are you life-coaching at me right now?"

"Best," he slows to a quick walk, "why are you acting so
grouchy?"

We stop running altogether. "Maybe it's because I'm grouchy.
You show up at my door randomly, drag me out into the cold
to go running. Who are you right now? What are we running
for?"

"Hey, listen, listen . . . I'm sorry." He rests a hand just off my
shoulder, at the top of my breast, like he's trying to calm my
heart. "I apologize, okay? You're right, I should have let you
know I was coming." His hand moves up under my chin. He
strokes my jaw briefly. I want to lean into the cup of his hand,
but it's gone before I can even second-guess it. "And the running—I just thought it'd be nice to get some air, see the place
in fresher light. The last time I was out here . . . that shit was
not fresh."

"No, Grant. You shouldn't be apologizing to me, about anything. I'm grumpy because I'm . . . because I fucked up. I've done a lot of crooked shit and it's starting to come up through my pores; all of the crooked, horrible shit; it's taking over."

For the first time since he showed up at my doorstep, Grant's grinning glow dims. I want to pull him aside, out of the middle of the street, and tell him everything. Tell him about the gossip stories and where I think the leak is (his agent), tell him about Bauer, about the accident and my brothers. I even want to tell him about Nik. But I don't have the words or the guts.

We see another running couple moving toward us, but they cut a sharp turn by the lights. Soon there are other people milling, two holding dog leashes and blue plastic bags, and another woman walking with a purpose along the opposite sidewalk. It's as if an alarm sounded, letting people know it was safe to come out all at the same time. Grant seems to notice the influx too, but remains at ease, relaxed in his runner's high. Maybe people do change, improve. The old Grant was always aware of outsider eyes on him. He knew when he needed to pull his ball cap down more, when to head to the back of the room behind the velvet ropes, when to smile, nod, and offer up the firm wave. *I see you seeing me, but respect my space.*

One of the things Grant said he liked most about Brooklyn was that people were so wrapped up in their own shit—writing the play, creating the app, delivering the sofa, pushing the stroller, getting to brunch—that celebrity, extra-large or medium-sized like his, didn't count for much. They like your work, maybe you'll get an "*ay-yo!*" from the rolled-down window of a barely slowed car, maybe you'll get a head nod or a pound, but really, you're just another anybody doing the brownstone walk-up like the rest of us. But really, who's he kidding? Grant King is six-foot-one, 180 pounds of lean, caramel-coated man. Even if you don't immediately peg him for some kind of cool-world hyphenate (actor/model/singer/jock star), you will—man or women—give him that double take. You can't fight it.

"Hey, come on, B. Let's not do all of that. You're not crooked or horrible or whatever."

He rests his hand on my hip and lightly squeezes. It feels good, but I don't want it to. I want to feel bad, shitty. I want him to stop being so kind and gentle with me, dig his fingers into me instead, pinch me, yell in my face, tell me that I am sickening and deserve nothing good. But he doesn't know any better. He looks at me, his eyes shining with hope and sweetness and full futures, and it's clear that he has no idea what he's really seeing. He doesn't recognize what's really standing before him: a basic savage dressed in human skin. It's like this comic-book series that Bryant used to collect about a young genome scientist named Dr. Scribner, who goes mad after an escaped lifer rapes and murders his wife and three daughters. He locks himself away in a secret cloning lab for decades where he makes these creatures, animals that walk and talk and present like natural human beings, but who are missing hearts and brains. Despite their convincing ability to appear sad, mad or happy, loving or concerned, they have no conscience or character. They have no intentions, only raw instincts. They act only when Dr. Scribner tells them to, following his instructions to the letter. He sends these pseudo-human goblins out into the unsuspecting, unprepared world to infiltrate and eventually take over. In the beginning his creations follow the rules and do helpful, upright things, but somewhere in the story they snap and return to their innate lawlessness. They're animals, Dr. Scribner says, and that's all they can ever be.

"Are you hating this?" Grant says, squeezing my hip bone again. "You're hating this. I can tell you're hating this. Let's just head back. I don't want to force running on you. It ain't for everybody."

"Is it helping you, with everything—the running?"

"Yeah, it is, actually. Right after you left, I started running every day. And I'm kind of deep into it now. Don't miss a run. I enjoy being out there alone thinking—or not. A lot of times I just run and take in the quiet of it, you know?" He shakes his head. "Listen to me. I sound like the typical New Jack, trying to force the feel-good thing down your throat. Sorry. Look, let's head back. It's cool. For real."

Grant takes my hand and guides me over to the dog-park entrance by the fig tree, the one we used to huddle under whenever we got caught in the hot summer rain. Now bare, scraggly, forgotten, it looks like it should be dug up and replaced. "Real talk: I'm low-key nervous here, and running felt like a solid stall tactic," Grant says.

"Nervous about what? Being spotted?"

"No. I don't care about that bullshit. I'm not the first person who flipped his wig a little. Not in this town. Please. Freak-outs are basically a rite of passage in this fucked-up city." He gives me a tight grin that seconds later slides off his face, and he's back to straight and solemn and perfectly vulnerable. "Listen, I want say this to you, so I'm going to say it all in one shot. I just need to you listen."

"I know what you're going to say—"

"No, Best. You don't. Just . . . *ssh*. Let me get it out, all right?"

"All right."

"Okay. So, I've been talking to my agent, a lot, and she's been patient and mad cool and really good with everything that happened. She thinks I'm ready to come back. My doctor does too. Ready to rejoin regularly scheduled programming, he likes to say. But he's corny like that. Anyway, the point is I'm moving to LA, try to tackle pilot season again. I already have three meetings, serious auditions, and—"

"Moving to—"

"No. You can't talk yet. I have to say it all." He takes a breath like he's starting from the top. "I'm moving to LA and I want you to come with me. Because I love you, I'm in love with you. But you knew that. You do, you know that. Even alone in my dark pit, I loved you. Being away from you and this, it just got clear: I need to do something about it. And it's this, it's me here nutting up and asking you into my life for real. I don't want to do this without you next to me, Best, in the center of this thing."

"I . . . Grant . . ."

"Zip it, woman . . . not your turn yet. Anyway, I already told my uncle and Rosalie. Gisele knows, of course. Everybody is down with this, Best. They're happy for me. I mean, crusty old Uncle Dick actually gave me the head-nod on this. And he wants you to come to dinner with us, tonight. I mean—yeah, I know, the Thanksgiving business is total bullshit, but this isn't that. It's a dinner to celebrate my uncle's award and also a little farewell: the loon bird is being set free."

"Grant—"

"Come on, man. Did I stutter? Simple instructions: Don't speak. Give a brother some space to roll out his shit."

"But Grant—"

"Richard and Rosalie have a reservation at Renard, which is pretty fucking fancy, right? And Gisele is flying in. She lands in about an hour. It's a legit family affair."

"Grant, stop—"

"A happy gathering for the Copeland-Hecking massive, for once. No drama. Finally. So"—he laughs, sounding relieved and nervous at once—"it makes sense. Feels right, and you need to come to dinner with us. Come to dinner and let's start this whole thing off right, with a thick-ass steak and some—"

"Gr—"

"Hell. I say we go baller with an endless bucket of bub. We

can fake the funk, tell the hostess we're rappers celebrating our *dawg* who got sprung from the clink early."

"Stop, Grant . . ."

"Uncle Dick might actually choke on an oyster with that one. And Rose—"

"Grant, Grant, Grant! Just stop! Stop, please. Just . . . stop. Look. I'm happy for you. I really am. I'm happy for you. I'm happy that you feel renewed and mended. I mean—look at you—you're glowing. And it's good. But I can't do this with you anymore. I can't be a part of all this fantastic that you are bursting with right now. I can't fuck that up for you. The thing is, I'm not good for you, Grant. I'm not good. I'm just not. I don't think I'm ever going to figure out how to be good at being a person. And you keep reaching for me, trying to pull me into you. That's the problem. *I* am the problem. You'll end up with my foot on your neck, unable to get your breath. You need to push me away with both hands, and let this end."

Grant's face looks like how I feel. Twisted, hurt, sickened, and sad.

The narrow park is filling up with more people walking their dogs. I see this black one with what looks like a curly perm. It's off its leash and running so fast and free. I don't know where its owner is and I can't take my eyes off of the furry thing, all loose and giddy. I watch this pup running and rolling for twenty seconds that felt like twenty months. I can't look up at Grant anymore, so I stay on the dog. "I'm sorry," I say to Grant's shoulder and take a step toward it, toward him. He moves back, as I knew he would, and cocks his head to the side. He's squinting now and his lips are tucked in tight.

I step to him. "I know how this is going to sound, but it's the truth: I never wanted to hurt you."

He nods and his face loosens.

"Grant, I'm really—"

He tilts his head back and slips his hoodie over his head, never breaking his stare. He's looking right in my eyes. I move in closer, reach my hand to touch his arm, his elbow, his sleeve—anything—but he spins on his heel before I make contact, and launches on a smooth jog straight down the center of the street.

I want to turn and walk away too, but can't, and instead watch Grant gliding until he's nothing but a long, lean blur.

CHAPTER 12

There's this squat, middle-aged security guard at my office building who seems to delight in my forgotten ID badge. It's his moment to be useful. He taps on his slim podium as I rifle through my loaded tote, and he says nothing. Just *tap-tap-tap* and that heavy breathing. I call him Puff Daddy or Puffy—a few times to his face too. He never hears me. He's not listening. He's not even looking at me. Not my face, anyway. Puffy is straight clocking my boobs. There's never been anything stealthy about his ogling either. I've caught him licking his lips, grunting and—occasionally, on late-evening shifts—playing with the convenient change in his horrible, ill-fitting, gray workpants. All of it is gross, but I could have French-kissed him just now when I showed up at the building on a locked-up, long holiday weekend and he would have let me in.

That he was there was no surprise. Eldon, my Trini homeboy in the mailroom, mentioned a while back that what's left of Puffy's family is in Mexico, so he usually volunteers to work all the prime holidays that everyone else on the security team wants off. He gets paid double-time while leaning up against the podium with his old-timey portable radio-TV hunk-o'-junk combo. Despite my matted hair, pilled coat, grimy Timbs, general homeless look, and layered stench (no shower since Nik's),

Puffy still unlocked the doors and let me in. Might be time to start calling him by his government name. But considering he's practically leering at my breasts right at this moment, we'll table the name-change thing.

So annoyed that Trinity never messengered my stuff over to my place. But riding up in the elevator—the one I'm *supposed* to be on—a nervous wave rushed over me, pushing that irritation aside. Brief never felt so long, and I cannot wait to get out of this box. The overhead lights feel dimmer, the miniature flat panel is frozen on a night image of the Empire State Building, and the almanac section to the top right of the screen is grayed out, the time stuck on 02:00. I'm trying to think of a song, a funny scene from that *Golden Girls* marathon last night, anything to cover over the wallpaper in my mind of Grant's sunken face before he ran off. And playing on loop underneath that is the flashback to three months ago: Grant is handing over his keys before curling up in the passenger seat to sleep like a scared child. His head is propped along the door and angled so that the reflection of his rumpled, blowing hoodie fills the entire side mirror. He's so sweaty. Even with the wind rushing in all around us, prancing along his expertly shaped and barbered head, he is just so sweaty. I can see that strip of wet, there above his perfect brow, glistening in the sun. Of all the strangeness that soaked through that cool August day, it's a frivolous strip of sweat that comes to me the quickest, and so clearly.

He must hate me. I wish he knew that it's better like this—he's better like this, without me muddying up his fresh pool. I've never been good and I'll never be good for anyone. Trying to reach out and hold on to me is the worst thing he could do. It's like Benjamin all over again. Grant doesn't deserve that.

I expected the elevator doors to open on a dark floor and prepared myself for the spookiness, but there were some lights on up front and farther down the halls. I open my mouth and almost say it, almost follow through on the scary movie trope: white girl calls out into the sinister darkness, "*Hello, is anyone there?*" and meets her gnarly end shortly after. I still toss an easy glance behind me every couple of steps as I walk toward my office. At least I'm not wearing ridiculous heels and a tennis skirt.

There's a strong, weird scent in my office, despite the frosted door being open. Both things are odd. It smells like old food that's been reheated in a microwave. It's distinct and disgusting. I set my bag on the desk and follow the odor; it feels like it's coming from somewhere down the hall near the mailroom where the lights are on. Still feeling brave or reckless, I head toward it. But as I get closer, my heart begins with its nervous twitch. As my mother would say, I'm walking with my two arms swinging, no weapon, no shield. I don't even have my phone with me. In fact, it's still off and shoved deep into the bottom of my bag. This moment needs to be added to my disturbingly long list of *what the hell was I thinking*—all items highlighting my lack of good sense.

I take a breath and hold it as I line my body flat against the wall by the mailroom entrance. I've seen this done on *Law & Order* a million times. Of course, they are actors trained to look like trained law-enforcement officials with loaded Glocks drawn and ready. I keep going with it anyway, whispering a rhythmic one-two-three before jumping into view of the hungry creeper . . .

"*Whatdoyouwant?*" (I'm actually brandishing my bony fists as I bellow.)

"Father Gawd!" Eldon yells and leaps back, dropping his plastic food bowl.

"Oh, Jesus. I'm so sorry, Eldon. I thought maybe—Look, I'm sorry. I didn't mean to scare you like that. I thought you were—"

"What, a robber? You thought I was stealing envelopes and packing tape?"

"I'm sorry. My mind is a wasteland of syndicated TV shows. It's ridiculous. Here, let me help you clean that up." I rush over and grab the paper-towel roll near him.

Eldon laughs; his mouth still has some chewed-up food stashed to the side. "Don't you dare. That food was well and old. Had no business reheating that. You did me a real favor and saved my belly some future disorder."

He takes the paper-towel sheet from me and stoops down to rake together the flood of rice and greenish peas and pieces of brown-drenched chicken from around his feet. He's shaking his head and chuckling. "Boy, you give my heart a real jump, gyal."

Maybe it's the steel-pan ping-pang melody of his Trinidadian accent or his lean, six-foot-five frame, muscles pressing through his smooth, bronzed skin. Whatever it is, Eldon's simply a treat, a walking feel-good story. He doesn't do the day-to-day mailroom runs anymore. Promoted. But sometimes he does my better sense a favor and pops up outside my office door carrying something heavy and important just for me. "Wait, what are you even doing here? It's Black Friday. Shouldn't you be watching football between food comas or something?"

"Yeah, I should. But I had t'ing I hadta do here for me bredren. He girl just had a next baby, so I tell him I go'n hook him up so he can miss a couple days next week, you know? Play daddy and take care of the new fam."

"That's really sweet, Eldon."

"Yeah, I try, y'know? Karma."

"Please. Karma doesn't want anything to do with me. Trust."

"How you mean?"

"It's a long story. Anyway, let me get out of your way."

"You could never be in my way, Madame Lightburn."

"That's kind, Eldon."

"Why you here, though? You not hitting the shops? My girl left since before dawn to line up in that cold."

"No, that's not my thing."

"No shopping? So w'as yuh t'ing, then? Wuk?"

"Right now, working is the best thing for me."

"Yeah, you ain't solo on dat, gyal. I catch boss lady in here earlier."

"Who, James Kessler was here?"

"Gurl, please. Not she. She ain't coming in here for a holiday; not for all the rum in Port-au-Spain. Nah, dred. I talkin' 'bout the next one, the black one, new boss lady."

"Wait, Joan?"

"Yeah, das who I mean. She did in here earlier and I spy she in yuh office." He steps in closer and lowers his voice. His essential oils—patchouli? kush?—take flight, floating right under my nose, replacing the stink of the sour food from the floor. "Yeah, man. In there peelin' through yuh papers, gyal. Flippin' through all dem on the desk and t'ing."

"In my office?"

Eldon raises his eyebrows twice, adding a slight nod to the maneuver.

"The fuck? What did she say to you?"

"She ain't see me. Man like me move in silence. Ninja styles, dred. Lis'en. I tellin' yuh this to say: watch yuh back, right? Is real crabs in this barrel he'e."

Eldon slides behind the main mail table, probably to demonstrate his ninja flow. Meanwhile, I do not know what to do next. Eldon basically just told me that there's a mini-IED under my feet; tread lightly.

"Yuh al'right, Lightburn?"

"Uh, yeah. I—I guess I'm trying to process what you just said."

"I *overstand*," Eldon says, kissing his teeth. "Yuh caant trust even yuh muhduh 'round this place, boy. But you, you go'n be al'right, Lightburn. And I not just sayin' dat because you's my people. I watch yuh, and just know that you ain't go'n let dem bad-minded people draw yuh down. You too ready, dred."

"Well, I don't know about all that, but thanks for letting me know, Eldon."

"Never a t'ing."

"Can I at least buy you another lunch?" I glance at the greasy film on the floor beside him.

"Nah, dred. My girl have nuff cook food back at the crib. This," he swims his hands around the wide stain, "this was just me being craven. Don't bother giving it another thought, Lightburn. And don't stop in here too long, man. You don't need to be breathin' in all this wretched stale air in here."

"I won't. I'll be in and out. I promise."

He winks, gives me a nod and starts walking toward the *Mailroom Employees Only* door with the key-code knob. The minute he clears the corner, I bolt back to my office. Something about the Robot rummaging through my files has me instantly nervous. The woman is all about subterfuge, yes, but old-school snooping doesn't seem like her style.

I turn my cell phone on, finally; this is an emergency. I'm pacing and can't think of whom to call first. Who would take my call, that is. My voice mailbox is full. Scrolling through the numbers, I can practically see the moment—to the date and time—when the Singh sisters collectively said, "Fuck her." It was Thanksgiving night, just after midnight. There's a long list of private-number calls:

Private number, Wednesday, 5:36 p.m.
Private number, Wednesday, 6:10 p.m.
Private number, Wednesday, 6:20 p.m.
Private number, Wednesday 6:32 p.m.
Private number, Thursday, 11:34 p.m.
Private number, Friday, 9:45 a.m.

It's Bauer. Has to be.

Tyson called somewhere in there. My guess: an "if you're feelin' it" casual invite to come over for his annual turkey soup and sweet-potato pie and *The Wiz* viewing party.

Nothing from Grant (as it should be).

And there were two calls from a 212 number within an hour of each other early this morning. Really early, like Nik Steig–early.

I'm taking the chance and hitting *call back*. I can hear myself panting through the phone as I wait, hoping that Nik will answer. *Please don't let this be a Bauer fake-out.*

"You're alive?"

"Nik?"

"Best?"

"Yeah, it's me."

Nik laughs. "I know it's you. Are you all right?"

"Yeah, I'm good. Fine. I missed you—missed your call. My phone. I just turned it on—the battery—and saw that I missed your call. So, I'm calling. You. Calling you back."

"Are you sure you're all right? You sound, I don't know, weird."

"Well, weird is our thing, right?"

"Right. But you're okay?"

"Yeah . . . I'm just sorting through stuff, trying to work it through."

The desperation in my voice is so thick I almost choke on it. But I'm long past humility and acting coy. I need his influence, his I-know-a-guy connector pull. I need his help to make this story really happen or all of this—all of this work and focus—will be for nothing. The choice isn't even a choice. I whisper one of my father's sayings: *Big mout' does get all de food*—the Trini equivalent to the squeaky wheels-oil idiom. I have to let the steam out of this boiling-over pot. I clear my throat. "Actually, I could maybe use your help on something."

"Sure. What do you need?"

"I'm working on this story, and it's kind of taking over my brain."

I can hear the *clink* of Nik pouring himself a glass of something—an adult, generous pour. "What's the story?"

"It's pretty grim. It's a crime story, but it's more about this girl—the survivor of the horrible story. This man named Bashir Imam drowned his four daughters in the backyard pool. His son—the eldest of five kids and the only boy—helped him do it."

"Sounds horrific. And this is for *James*?"

"Yeah. Yeah, it is. Of course, it is. A little different than the usual . . . but, yeah."

"A *little* different? This is a total departure. I'm surprised that Kessler is going in this direction."

"It's for the shame issue. And it's not about the actual crime or the father-son murderers thing. That's already been played out in the courts and the papers in Canada."

"So this is an international story?"

"I mean, Canada isn't exactly international . . ."

"Fine, but I'm still not seeing the connection to the *James* brand here."

"Again, it's not about the blood-and-gore stuff. That's not the focus. Okay, yes, Bashir was on trial for drugging the four daughters—the youngest was only seven. He crushed up meds in their rice pudding, then took them to the yard and drowned them one by one. The son helped with the pool part. I know. Completely hardcore horror movie, I agree. The media called it an honor killing; he's Muslim. Somehow the girls brought shame upon the family, so he killed them. The father denied all of it, naturally. Said the girls were messing around with drugs and mingling with a bad crowd or some other twisted-up fiction. But the thing is, one of the daughters—the eldest, Fatima— she survived. All the stories I've researched and collected never really got into how she survived. She was in a coma for a short while, but she survived."

"This story sounds familiar now that I think about it. Was this in Ottawa or something?"

"Yeah, kind of. That's where the trial was held. It was a couple years ago."

"So in addition to being brutal, it's also an old story. Where's Kessler's head on this? Is she even thinking about the advertising side?"

"It wasn't really her call."

"Whose call was it—Joan's?"

I know I'm on the borderline of taking too long to answer, so I push out a "yes." It sounds like a sneeze, blurted out, wild.

"Still doesn't sound right. But Joan does have a strong news background. Kessler trusts her, so there must be a thought-through plan here. In fact, if they are going for it, I might be able to help you."

"What do you mean? Do you know a guy?"

"Don't start. But, yes, actually I do. An old friend; Brian Thompson, he's the—"

"He's the big-ass cheese over at CBC. I know exactly who Brian Thompson is. He's a legend."

"That would be him. Let me give him a call. See what he can do to advance things for you. He's got wide reach. Good man."

"You'd do that?"

"Sure. It's clear you're invested in this story, and I can help, so let me."

"Nik, I don't know what to say. Thank you."

"My pleasure."

I hear his smile sliding up the sides of his mouth. He's going to say something dirty—I can smell it. The sticky words haven't yet left his lips, but I'm already embarrassed. It's when I spin around coy in my chair that I see her: Miyuki Butler filling my doorway. I almost choke, and jump out of my seat. "Uh,

I have to go. I'm at the office, actually, and I—yeah, sorry. I need to go. Let me call you later?"

"Oh. Uh, sure."

I hang up before Nik can say anything else.

"Jesus. What are you—how long have you been standing there?"

"Sorry," Miyuki says, her hands up at her face. "I just walked over here."

"You haven't been standing there this whole time?"

"No. I swear. I arrived here when you saw me," she says.

"You scared the shit out of . . . Put your hands down. This isn't a stickup." I'm too irritated and freaked to even bother masking my loathing. I say, semi-whispering, "Of course *you'd* think I'm some thief."

She hears me, and her face shifts from startled to clearly nettled.

"I didn't know you were in here until I saw your light, okay? So don't hate-speech me. I was coming over to say hello."

"I wasn't *hate-speeching* you. Anyway, it's Black Friday. Why is everyone here?"

"Who's everyone?"

"My guy from the mail—uh, the marketing department and now you."

"Oh, that is *everyone.*"

"Whatever, Miyuki. Why are you here?"

"I was in the 'hood and I came in to grab some work. Next week is going to be totally bananas. I wanted to get the jump on a couple of things. Why are *you* here?"

"Me? Same. I've got that story for you guys about . . . the shame-sex stuff, which is going really well and . . . yeah. So, that's me."

"Right." Miyuki looks suspicious. This is the first time I've ever seen her without her elaborate eye makeup, so maybe suspicious is her baseline. "How's that other story coming along?"

She slips into my office doorway, uninvited like some ballsy vampire, and leans against my open file cabinet.

"What other story?"

"Uh, *the other story* we talked about." Miyuki's voice is petulant and grating. I know she's fighting her tongue right now, and desperately wants to pop some smart shit like, "*Duh. Obvi. I mean, hello?*"

"I'm not doing that other story. What makes you think I'm doing that other story?"

"Because Joan told you to do it."

"Wait. What other story are you talking about?"

"The first-person? About you and Grant King, plus the Lana Scott angle. We e-mailed you about that new part of it." A low tide sweeps in and adjusts Miyuki's disposition. "Listen," she says, completely devoid of that fucking creaky-voice thing she does. "We were sad to learn the news about Lana. We know you were really upset. Heard about last week, your . . . departure. Sorry for your loss."

"Thanks, but I didn't lose anything. Lana and I, we weren't close."

"Oh. Okay. But still, that's a lot to deal with, on top of the Grant King stuff and all the gossip stuff. So, that's why we e-mailed you—about the extension."

"What extension, and who is *we*?"

"Joan and I, we—well, the e-mail came from me, but Joan and I had discussed it—that we would push your deadline on that story a bit. You didn't see the e-mail?"

"I haven't been checking that lately . . . which is exactly why I came in today, to catch up on e-mails from the last couple of days. Voice mails too; I left my iPhone charger here." (There needs to be a word for the relief that sets in when a perfectly shaped lie falls into your lap. It's akin to choosing the right colored wire to cut—*red! or blue!*—to diffuse the bomb, with two seconds to spare.)

Miyuki nods. "Makes sense."

"So, I should probably get back to that."

"Right. But one quick thing? A bit of advice, actually."

"Are you giving or asking?"

Miyuki slides the door closed, which baffles me, and I think she knows it. Mind games don't take breaks, not even on Black Friday. "Look, we're on the same team. And Joan is serious about making changes. She wants to do some cool things with the magazine. It's best to jump on board, not paddle against it, you know? She's different from Susie and James. She's in more of a hurry to get to the point. She's tell, she's not much for asking, and she's not waiting to see how you feel about things. It's about the work for her; that's what she looks for. That's what matters."

Typically, Miyuki's entire presence is annoying, but there's something in her face, something unvarnished and sincere that's edging up toward considerate. I take what she's saying for what it is and settle back into my irritation. "Okay. Good to know."

She gets up and opens the door. "So . . . about the piece, then?" She's returned to her usual comportment, which means the vocal-fry thing is back and glitter has magically appeared on her brow bone. I swear it wasn't there before. "Can you get the first draft in to me by, like, next Wednesday, by noon, latest? It's bordering on super-late and Joan has already noticed. I can't cover for you beyond this."

"You've been covering for me?"

"Yeah, totally. When you get to the e-mails, you'll see."

"I guess a thank-you is in order, then?"

She fans her hand in the air around her head. "No worries. We're all just washing backs here, right?"

"Sure."

"Great. Good talk." Miyuki pushes out her bottom lip.

"And I know it sucks; I'm totally ruining your holiday weekend with all of this work stuff. *Sahreeee.*"

"Not a problem. Thanksgiving's no big deal for me. I'm Canadian. We're not big on celebrating genocide and all."

"*Oh-kaay.* I'll just look for the draft first thing next week, then," she says. Before slipping out the door, she turns back and cocks her head to the side. "Cute scarf, by the way. Love brocade."

This bitch. *Love brocade.* The minute I start thinking maybe I need to relax my hardline stance on her, she shows me that it's not wise and not worth it. And here I was actively ignoring her whole animal-print-explosion situation.

I need to get out of here before she swoops back around to drop more bitch bombs at my door. This is probably her calling with one more dig, some more advice, maybe about the perfect Anthropologie candle she could loan me to deal with the odor problem in my office.

"Yes, Miyuki."

"Ms. Lightburn? It's Clark. Bauer. I'm a little surprised to catch you. I was just going to leave a message here. Your voicemail box is full on the other number. This one too, I think. Sorry about that."

"What do you want? Why are you stalking me?"

"Whoa. I'm not stalking you. I'm doin' my job. You know how that goes. Reporters never take holidays, right?" he chuckles. "I'm sure your dad always said that. Wait, is he still working for the *Montreal Gazette* or did officially retire? I think he might be still poking around on a few things, from what I gather."

"Listen, asshole. I'm not doing this. You're not doing this. It's not your job to flood my life with your nonstop messages. And hounding my folks? They're old and quiet and private. You have no right."

"Ms. Lightburn, hang on. Wait. I think you've got the wrong idea. And I'm sorry if I did anything to give you the wrong impression about me or what I'm doing here. This isn't an attack or staking or anything like that. *Tell Me More* is doing a nice holiday feature about one of *James* magazine's star staffers. I'm just reporting it out. That's all. Maybe I got a little ahead of myself. When I heard that your father was a big-time crime reporter . . . I kinda nerded out. That's it. Promise."

"You're not allowed to talk about them. I don't talk about my parents. I won't talk about my parents."

"What about your brothers—will you talk about them? I can barely find mention of them in any of the—"

"You know what? I don't have to put up with this bullshit. Don't call me again . . . or I'll be reporting *you*." I slam the phone down so hard the echo trickles out into the hall. I'm starting to sweat and the spoiled-food stench is making me feel light-headed.

I need to call home. See what my parents know, what they may have said. But I can't do it here. The muffled clumping sound of Miyuki's power boots stomping about is only adding to the nauseated thing taking over my body.

My cell phone's ringing now. Turning it on was a mistake.

But it's Nik. He's probably got information. Something from Brian Thompson. "Hi, can I call you back? I know, I know. Let me just get out of here. I'll call you right back. Promise."

CHAPTER 13

Pickuppickuppickup. Dammit—

"Hey. It's me. Yes, I know what time it is. I know it's Saturday. I know you're going to check this voice mail right away to see who the hell is calling you at this time in the morning on a Saturday. It's me and I sound crazy, I know. But I haven't slept. Like, at all. And I need to talk to someone. I need to talk to you. Shit. I'm talking too much on this. Listen, if this message cuts out, know that you need to call me back, *right.fucking. now. Please.* I've already left you, like, eighty emergency 911 calls. Actually, just call me back. Or I'll call you back in twenty Mississippis." I hit *disconnect* and start counting. As I get to twelve Mississippi, my cell phone vibrates.

"May, what in all the hells are you doing? I told you about people—"

"Playin' on your phone, I know. I know. But this . . . this is different and not a game and I can't believe what's happening."

"First, slow it all the way down, May. You are talking much too quickly for this man to follow. Now, before you open your hot little mouth to say the next spill of words, answer me one thing: Are you safe?"

"Tyson, I need to explain this."

"Now, May, all you need to do is answer my questions,

please. That's the only way this is gonna work. So, where are you? Are you safe?"

"Yes, I'm safe. Thank you. I'm at home."

"Good. Now, what—in fifteen words or less, May—what is going on?"

"Please, just trust me when I say that I can't say exactly . . . not yet. I'll explain everything, but I need you to do me a favor—a big one."

"No."

"No?"

"No."

"Tyson, you're about the only person I can call right now, and I need your help."

"Where are the Wonder Twins?"

"They're not really talking to me."

"Really? Because the rude one called me on Thanksgiving Day seething, asking where you are."

"Shit. What else did Lindee say?"

"May, I did not answer my phone. She left some fire message asking if you were with me and if you called me and something about her mama's house in Queens or some mess. Look, that shit got deleted, okay? That little girl didn't even say hello or 'happy turkey day' or nothing. Just launched into this long song for which I did not have time or tolerance. You know how I am about phone manners."

"Look, I'm sorry. She is pissed at me—they both are. She had no business throwing all that on your plate, interrupting *The Wiz*. I get it."

"*The Wiz?*"

"Yeah, every year, Thanksgiving, you and the boys watch *The Wiz*."

"That's Christmas Eve, May. We watch the games on Thanksgiving, like every other big-bellied American. *Girl . . .*"

"Sorry. I just—I got confused."

"This entire collection feels confused. Are you coming down off something?"

"Has anyone else called you? Any messages from a reporter—a guy named Bauer, Clark Bauer?"

"What is going on? A *reporter*? Are you in trouble with the law, May? Is this call being recorded or something?" He raises his voice, enunciating: "Because I, Tyson H. Turner, I do not know anything about what has transpired in the last seventy-two hours."

"Christ. This call is not being recorded. It's nothing like that."

"What is it like, then?"

"I don't know where to start."

"Start at the top. What's the big piece of chicken on the plate?"

"The big piece of chicken is I fucked up, royally."

"Wait. If this is about a certain King, this queen is staying out of it."

"King, queen. Right. You had that one in your pocket for a while, huh?"

"For a minute."

"It's not about Grant, not directly. He's in there too, but it's not the big piece of chicken. Wait, did you talk Grant recently?"

"May, I told you, don't pull me into that. You and him are *you and him*. It's not us. I said that from the start of—"

"I slept with my boss."

"The Robot?"

"No. Her boss, the big boss . . . *Oz!*"

"*Whuutt*? As in the Wizard? Oh, fix it, Jesus."

"Yes, okay? Yes. Yes, I fucked up. And, yes, I fucked the Wizard of Oz. Judge."

"No judgment here—you already know. But the way it sounds, the way *you* sound . . . May, what else is going on?

"There's a story coming out—or *might be* coming out—and it's a dirty bomb. I think. I don't know what he even really knows. It could all be some shenanigans, trying to get me in a corner to say things I don't want to say. I mean, ten years, denying it, lying about it . . . it becomes the truth, you know?"

"No, I don't know. I don't know what the hell you're talking about. Lying and denying and shenanigans. Do I need to come over there?"

"It's this reporter—Bauer. He wants to expose me or maybe use me to expose Grant. I don't know his game yet. I'm not seeing the whole board."

"Expose what?"

"You haven't read the *Tell Me More* stories about me and Grant?"

"*Tell Me What*—please. May, I do not drink that brand of tea. If it's not the *Times*, *Variety*, *Vogue* or my homeboy Frankie's blog, it doesn't rank in my media reads. I operate on facts only, not made-up bullshit."

"My relationship with Grant is smeared all over the inter-webs, for anyone to discuss. It's all coming from *Tell Me More*."

"So everybody knows about you and the King. And what of it? Like that makes a difference."

"It's not just about me and him. They exposed his recent . . . *problems*, and the break he was taking in Connecticut."

"What did I tell you about him before you two got braided up together?

"That he's solid."

"He *is* solid, May. That is a good man right there. Who gives a dry fuck about what anyone has to say about you and him or what he does for rejuvenation?"

"There's more, Tyson. I can't get into any of it right now. I'm juggling a lot of balls."

"Better than gargling them balls, honey." Tyson's old

smoker's cackle rumbles from his chest and cracks my stone-cold tone. I chuckle too. "Now, what's this favor?"

"I need you to come with me to the Singh sisters' holiday thing. It's next week."

"The *whut* next week? I will still have turkey leftovers rolling around my belly next week. What is the rush to get to jingle bells and ho-ho-ho?"

"You know they do the friends-and-relations gathering at their spot downtown. This year they bumped it up way early. They didn't get into the why of it, and honestly, I was just happy to still be on the e-vite list. I'm going to need you to work your magic too. I need to look glorious, like everything's curry."

"Ooh. You know I like when you talk your island talk, *mon*. Everyt'ing curry, mon."

"Not this again." I wait for Tyson's Ja-fake-can accent to peter out. "So, are you going to come with? I don't think I can pull it off solo. Not right now. I'm basically getting a shit pizza delivered to my lap every other day. I need support."

"Damn, a shit-pizza delivery service? That's vivid, boo."

"Well, aside from the fuck-uppery with Mr. King—*which you are not getting involved in*, I know—and then personally finding out where the sausage gets made at the Wizard's penthouse, I'm also about ninety percent sure that the Robot is spying on me. And she's using this other hater-bitch at the office for backup."

"Spying? You write sex stories, young girl. Unless you're actually having the sex at work in your office, then what in the Lord's good, green earth is there to spy—"

"Look, I know how it sounds. But trust me on this, please, Tyson. I feel like things are about to fold in on themselves at work, and I need to set myself up to come out on the other end of it unscathed. My head is all over the place. I don't have the armor to take on the twins when they're still breathing flames."

"All right, May. I'll come with you. Text me the particulars and I'll bring my secondary kit. I'll come by early, so we're not rushing as usual. But two things need to be in place for this to go right: A: I'll need a warm chicken patty *with* coco bread from Dutch Pot's bakery—your whole Carib flavor just now gave me a hankering, and B: There will be no discussion of Grant for the entire time I'm there working. And I'm so sincere about that last stipulation. Clear?"

"Clear. Thanks, Tyson. One question?"

"One."

"Will you help me fix things with Kendra and Lindee?"

"May, you are testing the limits of my talent and tolerance."

"Come on, please. I have to make it right with them. The fact that they invited me to their holiday *bashment* doesn't necessarily mean I've gotten the all-clear to land. It might only be the very tip of an olive branch from them. I've got to be smart about this or basically it's a wrap for me and the Singh sisters, and I need them."

"Just work on the warm Jamaican patty and coco bread, May. We'll tackle the other stuff, time permitting."

"Thanks. I'll let you get back to sleep."

"Oh, please. The bed is already made, hospital corners. I'm going to try to catch that early hot yoga class. That instructor is always what I need for the weekend, all hairy and hot, with them thick thighs. Mmm. What're you gonna do?"

"I really don't know."

"Okay. I'm talking smaller here: What are you going to do this morning, in the next hour?"

"Probably go up to the roof deck and brace myself."

"For what?"

"For the call home."

CHAPTER 14

When other subway riders leave the seat next to you empty on a wintery rush-hour morning, you know you look bad. Caught a glimpse of myself in a window reflection and *death warmed over* is being kind. Out of thin air, a wretched cold materialized and implanted itself in my lungs and bones and skin. I actually started feeling like something was brewing after I hung up from Tyson. It's almost as if I wished the thing into being. Not sleeping more than three hours just before dawn, and spending two days shut-in literally under the covers staring at a glowing laptop screen didn't help, either. I felt even worse than I looked. Everything hurt or trembled. I was sweating and chilled at the same time. When I got to my office chair, the whispers had joined up with the gasps and were building into blatant pity.

"Hey, girl-pie."

"It's not a good time, Maggie."

"For realz. No dis, but honey you look cray—"

"I think I know how I look, Maggie. Thanks."

"I said *no dis*."

"Right. You did say *no dis*. Is there something you needed?"

"Not really; I was rollin' through. Wanted to grab some time to chop it up with Joan, but Kristen's not at her desk—as usual.

That bish be tryin' it, right? Anyway, I heard you were back after your . . . thing last week. Thought I'd pop in and say wassup."

"My *thing* last week?"

"Yeah, I heard you had a moment. Like a *moment*. Full-on froke-out and collapsed in the elevator and everything."

"So that's the talk—I *froke out*?"

"You know it's impossible to keep shiznit on the DL 'round here. But something else will happen—it always does—and everybody will be sipping the tea on that. You'll be back on top."

"That's reassuring."

"You know what I mean, Best. My mother always says that the best revenge is looking great. And—normally—you look fucking fabulous. You're a total dime. And like they say, who cares what all the fives be sayin'. They're always going to be on your jock about something, right?"

"Totally." I cough, barely covering my mouth. Energy's fading fast. I don't listen to rap music, no reason I need to have it on full volume right here in my office. More rattling coughs blast through my dry mouth, over my cracked lips. And right on cue, Maggie hustles out of my mini–germ factory.

"Anywayszz, I'm out," she says, backing away. "Check you later, girl-pie."

"Sure. Do you mind closing that?"

"Totally," Maggie says, and slides my door closed with the sleeve of her sweater.

Bauer's calls started this morning. At least he gave me the weekend off. Nothing from Lindee or Kendra. Nik hasn't reached out since we spoke Friday. The phone was on and quiet for two whole days.

In a text, Tyson let it slip that Grant was in Toronto with his sister—a wedding or engagement party for his homeboy Luke. The minute Tyson hit *send*, I could practically hear him cursing at himself through the text-message screen. And my mind filled with visions of us, Grant and me, at this event having drinks and dancing and gorging on love and laughter and the good times under our feet. But despite the sharp images in my brain, I know that brand of happy is not owed to me, not with Grant. Not with anyone.

Speaking of drinks, I need to call my folks, for real this time. They didn't answer when I tried them Friday, same thing on Saturday. (Sunday was reserved for drinking really bad wine alone in Grant's dark room and passing out on his stack of pillows.) Each time I called, I got the answering machine, which was like hearing a Christmas carol in spring. I didn't want to leave a message. I doubt they even check the thing. So this call has to happen right now. If I show up at their door on Friday, arriving by car service, my father will not be pleased. It's more than the missed opportunity for him to make an airport run. My dad is the only person, besides cabdrivers, who actually likes picking people up from the airport. Whenever Uncle Dobbs would fly in late at night, I would always volunteer to go with my dad for that airport ride. Benjamin called me sucker to my face and Bryant usually got carsick. But I liked going with my dad. I remember how dark it would be outside and feeling special, seeing what the wee hours looked like. It was always cold too. My dad still had the front windows rolled all the way down. The wind, loud and mean, thumped at my ear, and the whole right side of my head. He said it was to keep us both awake. Obviously I figured out later—or maybe I knew it then too—that the brittle breeze to the face was an attempt for him to sober up. But I liked the cold air filling the car. We were being so different, wild rebels, that's what I told my child's mind. Kids can convince themselves of anything.

The other issue is, even before the accident, my parents never did well with surprises. They like to know who was coming and when, what was going to happen and how. The un-known is a factor they prefer not to entertain.

I've been chanting Tyson's curt advice on how to approach the angry Singh girls. He called me back after I drunk-dialed him late Sunday night. He didn't give me a hard time about it or anything, just said, "You talk to them by talking to them." That's it. That's all he said, and somehow it made sense, even for dealing with my folks. I sent an e-mail—with full sentences and sentiment—to both Kendra and Lindee early this morn-ing, apologizing for my rude flake-out and subsequent MIA assholery. They haven't responded yet. But that isn't going to deter me from the task at hand. Now is now and I'm going to talk to my parents by talking to them.

My father answers and it throws me off. I was prepared for the cold breeze that is speaking to my mother. He sounds pleasant enough, but weary; more so than usual.

"So, some good news: I'm coming there, coming home."

"As we expected," he says. It's clipped and stiff and clicks on my nervous ramble.

"No, I know. I mean, I know you told me to do that, to come home, but I was going to say that I'm coming home ear-lier than what we talked about." I take a breath and let my jumbled words dissipate. *Talk to them by talking to them.* "I'll be there later this week, Dad. My boss, he did me a huge favor and hooked me up with an interview, a crucial interview for this story I've been working on for a few months."

"I thought your boss was a lady."

"Yes. Yes, she is that. She's a lady. But it's another boss who helped me out. My boss's boss."

"I see. Your boss's boss is sending you here on assignment. That's interesting. This is a love life story?"

"No, no; oh, no. Nothing to do with love life. This story is . . . um . . . different from what I normally cover, but it's a good story and I think, if I report it out and line things up bird by bird, this could really change things for me here, change my career for the better."

"Hmm. Now I'm intrigued about this story. Sounds big."

"Right, yeah. We should talk about it, Dad. Just not right now. There's a meeting. I have a meeting soon, so I can't stay on here long. I wanted to share the good news with you and Mum. I'll call you later with my flight details and stuff."

"And your interview, it's downtown?"

"Actually, it's not in Montreal at all. It's in Ajax, so I'll fly into Montreal and then pick up a rental to drive to Toronto, for one night. Then I'll be back with you before I . . . uh, head back here, to New York."

"That's a lot of turnaround. You can't do the interview later, closer to when you'll be here anyway for your brothers' ceremony? Seems to make more sense that way."

"It does make sense that way, but I am on deadline with this story and I need to get in there before this woman changes her mind about the interview. You know how that goes. I really want to see this story through."

"I hear yuh on that. So, you book your flights already?"

"No, not yet. I still need to clear up one thing."

"What's the dates of the second trip out here, then?"

"Uh, I still—I'm wor—I—I don't know that for sure yet."

Silence. It's so full and awkward and laced with disappointment that I'm squirming in place. I wait for it, because it's coming. Not a bark or a bite, but a slow sprinkling of words that will certainly pierce my worn skin. I already feel like an imposter adult and my father is about to make sure we both see that I'm still a child, still operating at half-as-good, falling well below expectations.

"Bathsheba, I've already said my piece, and we're not going

to have this conversation again. You know your responsibility when it comes to this family. Exercise agency here, girl."

"Dad, I know that. I know about responsibility and this family. More than I can even stomach sometimes. I just"—the desk phone lights up with Lindee's number and a low, muffled trill follows—"that's my phone, Dad. I'm sorry. I need to take this call. It's work."

"That's fine. I said all I had to say on the matter."

"Right. So, I'll call later with my flight info."

"Good enough. I'll pass along your very best to your mother?"

"Yes, please do. Thanks, Dad."

I take a quick breath before picking up. "Best Lightburn." Shit. I should have just said *hello, Lindee*; she knows I have caller ID. I try to shake it off.

"Hey," she says, sounding like her regular self. It sends my shoulders back down.

"Hey, Lindee. Thanks for calling . . . I mean, to be honest with you, I'm a little surprised—I'm *glad*. I'm glad that you called, but just surprised. I only sent that e-mail a couple hours ago."

"Well, to be honest with *you*, e-mails are bullshit. You know how I am. I mean, if you have something to say, come at me straight, to my face. Call me, even."

"I know. I hear you. I guess I was nervous that you were going to shut it down, not give me a chance or hear me out."

"But we're not children, we're grown-ass. Or, what did you say your mom called it—like, the *one* time you actually talked about your family, you said something . . . what was it, hard-shelled?"

"Hard-back."

"Right. We're *hard-back* women here. We can handle a couple of hot words going back and forth for a minute. It's not

that serious. Deal with me straight. How am I going to shut
that down?"

"I know," I say, rolling my eyes. "I kind of panicked. Anyway, I'm glad you read it and called me."

"Kendra read it to me. She knows I think e-mails are—"

"Bullshit. Right. So, is Kendra there with you now?"

"No. She's busy, wrapped up in something with Flav. She's
going to reach out to you later to talk about things," she says.
It's strange and disheartening to hear Lindee offer up limp excuses like this for her sister, especially after all the talk she just
threw down about coming at her straight. Not her style and
therefore not at all believable.

"Look, again, I apologize for my dick move on Thanksgiving—and beyond, really. I've been operating on a wack chan-
nel for a bit."

"But it was my mother, though," she says. "It was disrespectful to her, and that's what set me off."

"I know. I totally hear you." We each let out long sighs. "So,
did New Mark work out? Gold stars for him?"

"Please. New Mark took home the most-liked award after
talking to our mother for forty minutes about Indian spices.
And that's just for starters. Oh, he got gold stars and a few
other things." She chuckles. It sounds dirty and I love it. It's
only been a week since we fell out but this minute, this moment, I miss her. I miss Kendra. I miss us being us and not giving a single damn about anyone else. But there's still something
there underneath it all—something that's not lying flat between us—and it's making my stomach knot up. I want to blurt
it all out, the truth, vomit up my story, but instead a belch spills
out: Grant.

"Grant showed up at my door Thanksgiving morning with a
whole move-to-LA-for-pilot-season scheme. The kicker being:
'And I want you to come with me, live life with me.'"

"Is that how he dropped it? Just tag along, be my plus-one in life?" I can practically see her sneer through the phone.

"Not like that, but kind of like that. He said he doesn't want to do life without me, that he wants me standing with him through all of it."

"So, he's on some new meds, then," she says, almost through a yawn.

"Lindee, it wasn't like that. I know you're not the biggest fan of the guy, but he was serious. He wants me to come with him. *Wanted* me to come with him."

"But you don't really know if he's all right. Like, he could lose it again, but this time you're out in Los Angeles all alone trying to convince him not to jump into the empty pool out back."

"That's not fair. First of all, he didn't snap like *that*, and second, he's better now. He seems better, looks better."

Talking to Lindee, choosing my words about Grant so carefully, I sound like I'm trying to convince myself that he's fine and ready to head to Storybookland. I get why his agent Shawna wants him back up and running. As agents go, it's all business with her. She's never once pretended to be friends with Grant. But his doctor, I don't know. I'd like to see *his* prescription pad. *Psychotropics for everyone!* We had a doctor like that. He was assigned to my dad. Always trying to suggest this drug and the third. I mean, Klonopin? Ativan? Abilify? Christ, the man was devastated, shattered, yes, but he wasn't seeing faces in his shoes. The antipsychotic stuff was way beyond the line. And Bertram Lightburn put the kibosh on that bullshit once he could see the road that quack was trying to lead him down. He just stopped all therapy and never went back. And my mother turned to the church from day one; you can guess how much good that did her.

Lindee is clearly irritated talking about Grant, so we move

on to Nik. I confess my workplace sin. Lindee starts to cackle when I get to the *Pretty Woman* thing. I know she's laughing at me, but I'm so relieved to be back in her circle—desperate, really—that I'll let her take her punches and I'll just try not to flinch.

"Wait, was it *Sex and the City* where Samantha slept with that old guy? Not the rich weasel one. This one was like super-white and saggy and wilted and gross. Was it like that with him? *Ugh.* I can't even imagine." She snickers. "Or did he try to kick it old, old, old school and make like he's Thomas Jefferson and you're his sweet Sally?"

That's enough. I need to break her concentrated and unfamiliar efforts to slut-shame me. Returning to the subject of New Mark does the trick. She is fully gushing about him—yet another out-of-character move for Lindee. But the heat is off of me, so I'll gladly keep asking about Mark, letting the saccharine flow, adding a few enthusiastic verbal nods and encouragement in opportune spaces.

"Well, damn. I guess I should look forward to meeting this fresh prince of"—there's a shadow outside my door—"actually, someone's here at my office. Sorry. I have to go."

I've never thought, "Oh, good, it's Miyuki" until this very moment. She's wearing her over-the-knee, black leather boots, a deliberately tattered army jacket and thick, dark-rimmed glasses. I've seen this look from her before; I call it *hipster stripper who codes.* She's got her hand clutching her over-accessorized chest and her mouth is ajar, gasping.

"Oh, my *gawwd.* I heard you weren't doing too well. Are you going to be okay?"

"Yeah, I just picked up a bug or something over the weekend."

"Like I told those girls, you didn't look so great when I caught you in here on the holiday. I could tell you were getting sick—I could smell it on you. I mean, like, the air in here just smelled like sickness."

"You told which girls?"

"Just, like, my team."

"Your *team*?"

"Yeah, you know, Maggie, Isabelle, Trinity—the girls. Anyway, so this is kind of awkward, and looking at you now, maybe I'm getting my answer. I mean, it's totally rude and out of line, and I don't even know if it's, like, illegal to ask this, but it kind of changes the story that you're working on. Maybe you can just confirm or deny or . . . add a comment—"

"I'm sorry, as you can see, I'm not really one-hundred percent right now. In fact, I should probably head home. Also, I really don't know what you're talking about."

"Oh, my bad. I'm talking about the story. The new *Tell Me More* story that just posted about you and"—Miyuki looks behind her, then lowers her voice to a creaky whisper—"your secret."

My stomach rolls and my chest seizes up. I hear a popping in my ears and then my voice: "Oh, fuck!"

"So, is it true?" Miyuki looks horrified. Her hand flies to cover her gaping mouth.

I leap from my seat. I don't know what to do. It's threat level *go ape shit* and I can't breathe.

Miyuki rushes over to me, forcing me back in my desk chair. "Best, calm down. You have to calm down. I'm sorry. I shouldn't have brought this up." She's yelping: "*Somebody? Anybody? Can I get a hand here?*" Trinity appears in between blinks. She adopts Miyuki's panicked expression and joins in wrestling me into the chair.

"In your condition, Best, you have to calm down," Miyuki says. "This can't be good for the baby."

Trinity's eyes bug. And I finally tune into Miyuki's frantic pleas.

"Wait, what? Whose baby?" I say, breathless.

"Yours," Miyuki says. "Isn't that what this is? You're pregnant. Aren't you pregnant?" She's still gripping my arm; utter shock building between us.

"Jesus Christ! Is that the *Tell Me More* story? Is that what you're talking about? They're saying that I'm pregnant?"

"Yeah. Yeah, that's the rumor . . . from sources close to you. They're saying that you are pregnant."

"Wha—with whose baby? Grant's?"

Miyuki releases me from her bear hold and steps back. She's looking to Trinity for backup, or confirmation, for a reaction; but instead she's leaned against my desk, stunned and mute. "That's the thing. They kind of hint that it's maybe not his, and that's why you guys broke up?"

"Holy shit. Is that true, T? Is that the story out there?" I'm practically growling.

Trinity nods, but keeps her eyes on my shoes.

It starts in the back throat, works its way through the coats of phlegm and soars out of my mouth, this laugh, so hard and so huge that I startle myself. "I'm out of here."

"Wait," Miyuki says, stopping me with her hand on my shoulder, "so it's *not* true."

"I'm out; sick day," I tell them both. "I'll keep you posted on how things go with *this cold*."

Redness is crowding Miyuki's face, completely overshadowing her already bright pink blush. She looks like she wants to sink into the earth. I cut my eyes at her as I grab my things and glide through the door. Even though I can barely breathe without my chest tightening up, I still need to rub this in, make her feel like an utter, out-of-line fool. As I breeze by, something in me wants to reach out and grab on to her, steady myself on her bony shoulder, anything to stop the spinning, but I know I can't do that. Not with her. Instead, I wrap Nik's brocade scarf tighter around my neck and keep moving through the door, trying to act as though all is right within my crumbling world.

CHAPTER 15

"You know I didn't invite you over to rummage through my fridge, right?"

"What I know is that you did *not* just say *rummage*, May. Because, Miss Ma'am, this fridge never, ever has a thing in it, but today specifically? Listen, sis. I could stretch out all of my six-foot-three-ness in there on my fainting couch *while* playing dominoes and be chilling, literally." Tyson closes the fridge door, leaning his shoulder on it. "You don't even have a single, struggling, sweaty bottle of vodka in the freeze box like these regular day bitches out here. Now that is some sad shenanigans."

"Don't do me like that, Ty. I've been at home sick, remember?"

"You lucky I come prepared for all things. Look in my wine bag, boo." He grabs two tumblers from the cabinet. "At least your glassware game is tight."

Of course Tyson's wine bag is fine leather and label. Inside there are two bottles. None of them are wine. "Hold on, you walk with your own minibar?"

"Sweet May, your fridge always looks like heartbreak and country music. I know my audience. Now bring them bottles over so we can clink and drink."

"The worst. You're the worst husband yet."

"Jesus knows my heart."

"Seriously, thanks for going with me tonight. The Singh sisters and I . . . it's still a little bumpy."

"Behind that disappearing act you pulled for turkey day? Girl, please, that was basically four years ago. They need to move along." Tyson slides open several drawers near the sink until he finds the coasters. He motions with the open vodka bottle to follow him into my living room. The light—even the manufactured kind—is better in there.

"Well, wait. In their defense, it was a bit more than the no-show thing. They said I was selfish, self-interested, and maybe I was."

"Do you have anything on or are we working fresh here?"

"Fresh. I washed my face just before you got here. No moisturizer, nothing. Clean canvas." I take the seat Tyson set up for me by the window. He's meticulous about his art and I know the rules. "I should have told them what was really going on with Nik and the blowout with Grant. I was being stupid, not selfish."

"You know you're my boobee, my top May. Your skin is that creamy peanut butter, these cheekbones be calling out to me in my sleep, and the wig is always laid, right down to the slick baby hairs, plus you crack my shit up—like, for real, have me rolling—but them twins ain't lying: You are all about yourself."

"What? You think I'm selfish? I'm not selfish."

"Oh, because you say it's not true, then it's not true? Hmm. My mistake." He folds his lips and arches his brow as he works on filling in mine.

"No, really, Ty, what makes you think I'm selfish?"

Tyson splashes more ginger beer into his glass. "Listen, you asked me to accompany you to this li'l holiday function." He walks his fingers along his brush belt and reaches for the one with the longest handle. "I'm making sure all the glam is in proper position before we get there. I'm going to beat your face, sign off on what you pull from your closet, brush a little bronze over my own flawless before killing these tasty Mules and heading out to nibble on some obese shrimp—with my pinkie sticking high to the sky. That's it, May. Nothing in that blueprint says anything about being Dr. Phil."

"Wow. You don't mince a word; pull not one punch."

"What did you expect me to say? I deal in real words, May. That's me. But if you want to keep it gully, I can do that too. The only reason you called on me as your plus-one is because A: You did Grant dirty and you can't call on him to be your sweet and silky arm candy tonight. He's back in New York, by the way, shooting an indie, but you ain't heard it from me, and B: you damn sure can't roll up in the spot holding Thurston Howell the third's hand. The baby-bump watchers are real *outchea*. And that scandal would be straight lava, honey. Can you imagine that scoop: *Preggo Best Lightburn spotted canoodling with the publishing Wizard Nik Steig.*" He starts singing into his blush brush: *"Ooooh, Love child, never meant to be. Love child, scorned by society."*

"Hilarious. Just fall-over hilarious, Tyson. Do you feel good about yourself now?"

"Oh, May, always. The fact is: You just don't want to walk into the room this evening alone and have to face up to them power twins with the truth dragging on your heel like some goddamn toilet paper, okay? That's what's really hood."

"Jesus, Tyson, you know I don't speak Queensbridge."

"Translation: You're selfish."

"I'm selfish because—what, I'm embarrassed about the Nik mess?"

"No, you're selfish because you're still pushing this conversation to be about how you're not selfish. Now close your lids and your sweet little mouth. Need quiet to work this gel liner like a bad bitch."

"But I need—"

"You need to sit your little behind quiet, let me work my magic."

I do as told. Last thing I need is a full Tyson read. When he arches away from hovering over my forehead, I start again. "Can I say my piece now, sir?"

He takes a step back, reaching for his glass without a blink. "Speak on it, sis."

"The Grant stuff, agreed, it was jacked up; it is jacked up. I need to get right with Grant. I know that. And I will. I owe him explanations and clarity and all of it. I know I do. Kendra and Lindee too. I need to level with those girls. Not at this dinner with Flav and New Mark and everyone there, but before this year is out I'll do the right thing. And you"—Tyson raises his brow again, dips his nose further into his drink—"I'm not using you. Not tonight. Maybe a little before, but can you blame me? Look at what you can do to a face. Sickening. *Beat to the gods,* as the kids say." His pursed lip relaxes, spreads into a smile. "But tonight, I just want you with me—part shield, part wubby blanket—to protect me a little, you know? It's been hella rough these last few. I still have to get my head around this Nik stuff. I do like him, in this dumb, rebellious this-is-the-way-to-ruination. And if I'm honest, I like the power part. He was able to hook me into an interview that I doubt I would have been able to get on my own. All on some *I know a guy* deal. He can probably help me move this story up the chain, in a real way, and I like that he can do that, that he wants to do that; he wants to help me. But that's the thing: It sounds gross, like some borderline sugar-daddy thing."

"Oh, *borderline?*"

"Hey . . ."

"Real words, May."

"He wants me to come by before I fly out. To thank him, I

guess. And I sort of feel like I should go there to say thank-you in person."

"With your vagina?"

"Ugh. It's gross again."

"Is it good, at least?"

"Actually . . . yeah, it is. It's really good, and then that shower. I probably shouldn't even be talking about this with you, because . . . well, Grant."

"See? Selfish," Tyson says, and rattles his glass.

"Funny. You're killing it tonight. Really, the whole set is murderous." Tyson pops his fake collar. "But seriously, I'm not selfish. I'm not. It's not being selfish. It's self-preservation."

"What does that even mean, May? And don't think you can run circles around me, girl child. I'm magna cum laude, Princeton. Facts."

"You know exactly what I mean, Tyson. You've got your own stories as proof. Your parents, that mother, the rejection, the reckless shots are your heart, at your core. That's real shit. Destructive, hard-knock, real shit. But you're standing. You're not cowering on a ledge somewhere timing when to jump. You did that through self-preservation."

"You don't need to tell me twice. But I already know I'm selfish. You need to see that you are too. Own it, May. It's not always a bad thing. It's not this evil way to be; like kicking puppies and hoarding cake. That's not what this is; it's not about being wrong and horrible, cooked all the way through."

"I am, though. I am wrong and horrible, all the way through."

Tyson tosses his head back and drains his drink, letting the few shrunken ice cubes roll around his mouth like mints. His eyes linger on me, on my entire face. His silence is forceful and deliberate—or it's not. Maybe it means nothing more than a man gnashing on ice, but it's making me uncomfortable. Finally he cocks his head to the right, crunching up the last slithers of ice, and speaks.

"Best, you keep us all at arm's length. For years, at a distance. That's how you move through this world. We don't know you any other way. But I see shit, I know shit, and I've been living in this city longer than I haven't. You're not evil or horrible or wrong. I put my good name on that."

My eyes start their flicker dance, a ridiculous strobe moving around the room. I feel the quiver in my chin first. It spreads too quickly to my bottom lip.

"Do not upset the first-class sunset I just painted on that lid, May. You will not like the words that will exit my mouth if you fuck that up, boo-boo."

We both fold over into cackles. Tyson can be sweet. I know this. He doesn't hug it out, though. Doesn't like people brushing up on him. I know this as well. He tops off my drink before pouring a straight shot of vodka in his own glass.

"Let me give you some lash and lip and get you in that closet to set this shit off."

"Thanks, Tyson"—I break form and clasp his wrist—"thank you."

He doesn't tense up or even pause, but briefly meets my eyes and smiles.

———※◇※———

The minute Lindee catches us from across the room, as we come through the door, my nerves kick in. She heads over our way. I grip Tyson's leather arm tighter.

"Easy, May. I got you," Tyson says, patting my cold hand. "In a minute you'll be luxuriating on one of those plush benches. You can serve haute realness from the seated position."

"It's not the boots; my feet are fine. It's Lindee. She smiled at me just now; a big, toothy *Hee Haw* grin. She doesn't throw those things around like candy. Something's up. Fuck—is this an intervention?"

Tyson slows his stride. He gently takes my hand from the crook of his elbow and holds it, turning to look right at me. "Honey, you okay? You've been all in your feelings the whole day. Is this going to be a situation or are you just having a moment?"

The sneer and edge from his voice are gone. He's warmth right now—his hands, his face, his whole mien; it's warmth. I don't know what to say because I don't know what to say. Maybe this is a situation. All the panic, the fainting, the lapses in good judgment, in good choices, they were all moments charging up to this one unavoidable, uncontrollable, ugly situation.

Tyson rubs my hand. He's waiting for words. I don't have them. But I do notice his coat now, and I can't believe I didn't see any of this earlier. It's buttery smooth, deep black, thick but thin. He said it was vintage. It looks like Benjamin's.

"May, for real, you all right? We can always fake and flake this shit. My homeboy Bobbito lives like three blocks from here, and there is always something crunk and fabulous happening for the kids at that loft."

"No, I'm good, Ty. Just had . . . a moment. And we can't leave now; they saw us. I'm trying to move back over to their good books, not the other way."

"I heard that. Purgatory ain't no kind of fun."

"Purgatory?" I say with a squawk. "Wait, how do you know about purgatory?" I shake my head. "Don't think you know fact one about Tyson Turner, people. Do not bet on it, because you will lose."

"Truth. Try your very best and you will indeed still lose, whippersnappers. Done at the door. Word and good night, okay?" Tyson daintily pulls some pretend blinds down over his faux window and laughs. *Dramatics are requisite*: another part of Tyson Turner's code. "Now let's get them *shramps*, please. They be callin' me, sis. Reposition your swag and let's roll."

I take Tyson's arm again and we walk over to Kendra, Lindee, and crew. Lindee pops up, waving me over to her end of the table. A collection of stumpy candles are gathered low on the table beneath her, illuminating the pretty ropes of gold necklaces draped along her chest. It makes everything about her shimmer. She looks beautiful, but strange. She's still grinning as Tyson and I glide over to the empty bench seats next to her. Lindee's eyes seem brighter, her hair shines—she's happy. When she hugs me, it's tight and dense, and the sugary perfume from her hair shimmies up my nose and nests somewhere high in my sinuses. I pull away a little. I need to get another look at this one's face. Maybe they finally fooled me. But she speaks with that twisted mouth and confirms that it's really Lindee.

"Where's Statutory Steig?" Lindee says softly, but directly in my ear. "Was excited to see the old perv maneuver the narrow aisles here with his walker."

I lean away from her and let my eyes speak for me.

"Come on, Best. You're not the only fact finder in the game. I've watched *CSI*."

Tyson pokes his face in the slim space between us. "Hi, Miss Lindee Singh. Figure I need to show my manners first, 'cause you working that caste system hard."

"Hello, Sir Turner, I was getting around to you." They do their thing: air-kisses, curse words, then compliments. "Fly hat. A Homburg, right? The feather, though; that is fire," Lindee says to Tyson, barely touching its brim.

"You know how I do." Tyson gives her a short hat-tip. "And don't think I didn't notice the boot, Miss Singh. Just vicious."

"So, are you the stand-in for old man Nik Steig?"

When I told her the Nik stuff, I assumed it was under our usual strictest-confidence rule. Clearly I can't assume anything anymore. And I'm a bit stunned that she actually said Nik's name all loud and in public like that.

"Never that, darling," Tyson shoots back. "I'm always the selection, never the substitute. Don't get it jumbled. Speaking of selections, are you going to introduce us to your new amuse-bouche over there." Tyson uses the slightest purse of his lip to gesture at Lindee's now-boyfriend, the lived-everywhere director New Mark.

The ball of stress clogging my throat dislodges and starts to dissolve. I can always count on Tyson to throw sugar into Lindee's hot snark soup, making it less bitter.

"Mark, this is Sir Tyson Turner. He's the most legit makeup artist in the game today. If you've seen a killed brow arch at the movies, then you've seen his work. And this is our sister from another mister, the fabulous Best Lightburn, but you already know all about her and her work." Lindee comes in close to Tyson and me, but yells anyway, "Mark follows you on Twitter, Best. Clicks on all your flirty sex-story links and everything"— she reaches back to Mark, seated, and rubs his shoulder—"so really I should be thanking you."

Ew.

"She's already started messin' about with the highballs," Mark says, rising. "Dark 'n' Stormys, can't trust 'em." He's quite tall, like Grant—well over six-foot. That's where any sameness ends. Mark is long, but lanky, and is a few shades darker too. He reminds me of my Sri Lankan neighbor when I first moved here, Nishad. They have very similar hair—deep black, rumpled, flooded by waves and curls. New Mark is wearing thick-rimmed, Ray-Ban Wayfarers, but it's hard to tell if it's because he's an authentic nerdboy or doing faux artist (*fartist,* as Grant calls them). He steps from behind the wide table, closer to Tyson and me: "Mark De Silva." His voice booms over the music, and he greets Tyson with a firm hand-shake and moves quickly and somewhat apprehensively into the bro-hug. I get a two-cheeked kiss and shoulder-pulse combo. "Jokes aside, I do really enjoy your work, Best. Even before I found out you two were mates. It's brill; you keep it fun. I like that."

The accent—it's exactly how I imagined Nishad would sound, if I had ever found the stones to talk to him. I would usually wait, watching through my cloudy peephole, for Nishad to clear the stairs before I even unlocked the first of the eighty bolts on my door. I don't know what my problem was. Just fear. Fear that the other giant shoe would finally drop, torpedo-style from the skies, and flatten me for good.

"Um, are you exchanging vows down there?" Kendra yells from the other end of the table. She walks over to us, slow, almost slithering. "Hi, honey. You look gorgeous," she says to me in one breath, and moves to kiss Tyson. "Your handiwork, I already know," Kendra tells him. "But this girl is a diamond. Your work is easy."

"Sweet of you, Kendra," I say, unsure if I should take the compliment or prepare for a sucker punch to the neck. "Are we that late?"

"Why, 'cause we're drunk already?" Kendra laughs. "You already know that the Singh girls are cheap dates. Cheap, slutty dates. Right, Flav?"

Tyson and I swap looks and clench our teeth at the mere mention of Flavio. The man is many things: talented, handsome, freakishly fit and rippled, and a bubbling pot of hot, dirty sex boiling over. He's also the chief corruptor of Kendra. Nearly every bad idea (cocaine weekend in Vegas) and messed-up call that she's made (threesome with his photo assistant Emma) has Flavio Di Luca's grand and loopy signature all over it.

"Hey, Flav," Tyson and I sing in limp unison. He nods and jabs a peace sign in the air in our general direction.

"He's so hot and bothered right now," Kendra says, draping herself over my shoulder. Her mouth is pressed up on my ear, and it's moist and warm and gross. "I promised to give him a mini–hand job under the table if he quits speaking Italian with those randoms at the next table. I just might do it too. He's been good these last weeks."

I give Tyson our sign, which is really just the universal distress signal—it's all about slight, but deliberate eye movements.

"We want whatever the hell you're having, Miss Kendra Singh," Tyson says, peeling her off of me in his smooth, artful way. "Glass us up, honey."

"That waiter will be back around again, any minute. He likes our table." Kendra pulls my hand. "Come sit with us. Tyson, you can hold down this end and talk pretty faces and camera angles with New Mark."

With a sweep of her arm, she's made Flav and the two others next him—that assistant Emma and Kendra's work wife Melinda—slide down the bench to make room for me. I try to stop it, tell them it's fine, I'll sit wherever, but Flav does his grand gesturing thing with his arms and chest and chin and before I can close my mouth, I'm ensconced. Flav's veiny arm drapes around me as he continues yapping with Emma, and Kendra is inching her face up to mine, grinning like a fool, her eyes glassy.

"So, Montreal, huh?" she says.

"Yeah, Montreal. I leave in a few days."

"Your parents must be, like, shitting themselves with excitement. When's the last time you went home?"

"Not that long ago. They're fine. No one's shitting."

"You know what I mean. It's hard to get you to go anywhere." Kendra's smile droops. She looks like she's thinking it through, focusing on selecting the next group of words carefully. I'll give her more time with that.

"You got plans?" I say it so quickly it sounds like a belch.

"This year my mother kinda shook up the snow globe with something different. They're going to India for a month. Her oldest niece is both graduating from med school and getting married. So it's a big-deal trip. She leaves in a few days too. She told us about it at Thanksgiving, but was quietly planning it for months. Guess anybody can be slick. Right?"

The weighty pause has crept back in. She's looking at me. Her smile's completely gone and she's irritated. She has a tell: biting the corner of her lip. "It's like you and your boss, right? Who knew the Wizard was down for on-the-sly booty? We can all be sneaky bastards."

"Can you lower your voice? Why would you—and Lindee— want to bring that up here, now, with everyone around?"

"Oh, because a reporter might be lurking behind us or squatting under the table so he can report on all your little se-crets?"

"Why are you doing this? I apologized. I sent you an e-mail and tried to reach out to set things straight between us."

"I know. I got your e-mail and Lindee told me about the call, about Montreal and the interview and Grant's offer and the Richard Gere thing with your boss—"

"So why are you still punishing me?"

"Punishing you?"

"Yeah, punishing. It feels like you're trying to be mean and punishing me for something I've already apologized for and keep apologizing for. Just get it all out now."

Kendra shakes her head. "It's our holiday party, Best. Now's not good."

"How is this a holiday party with all this bullshit between us? It's mad tense right now. You're being out-of-line rude. Let's get it all out in the open and squash it."

Kendra rolls her eyes. "Have a drink, Best."

"That's not going change this, Kendra. All of this, the looks down the table to your sister, the stiff convo—what, are we going to chat about snow accumulation next?"

"What do you expect?"

"I expect that, as my friend, we can talk about this and move through it."

"The time to talk is later. It's not now. I'm having a good time. All I'm looking to move through right now is another glass of that Shiraz." She tilts her head past me. "Flavio, *amore mio*, is there another pour left in that bottle?"

"No, it's *finito*. Empty. *Permesso*, I go to the bar immediately for more of this for you and the table, *cara mia*. I'll return quickly, okay?" Flav leans over me, like a pile of coats, to kiss Kendra before jabbing my forehead with his pelvis as he wedges his way out of the tight table. I've never been clear on whether Flav like-likes me and does things like that to keep it confusing or if it's all steeped in unfettered disdain.

Kendra's grin has returned as she sways to the Usher retro set blaring above our heads. I catch a glimpse of her sister. She's doing something similar, shimming in her seat. The Singh girls are happy, possibly in love and content, at the same time, for the first time. Watching them, blissed out and free, I feel the sharp pinch. It hits my face first then picks up force rolling down my chest. I've fucked it up with them and I don't know how I'm going cut through this rigid space between us.

"Kendra, I'm sorry."

Her eyes are still closed, her empty glass moves with her, the last two sips of deep burgundy wine bump around its bowl.

I touch the back of her arm, easy, lean into her, and start again, louder. "Kendra, I'm sorry."

She brings her groove to a crude stop and opens her eyes, looking right at me. Her face is straight. There's no joy there anymore. It's something else, something blue and heavy—regret, maybe? Pity? Either way, it's a cold stare and it's intended for me. My mother had a name for this kind of thing: dead lion. She was looking at me like a dead lion. And what do you say to a dead lion?

"I know you are. I know you're sorry. You're sorry that things are weird now, but that's about you, again, as usual. It's about you. See? This is what I mean. I told you this wasn't time. I'm having fun, finally. It's our holiday jam, our time to get together, be merry and bright, and once more here you are forcing the stars to shine on you."

"That's not true, or fair."

"Look, my sister and I have been your friend, all the way. We've let you in, happily. You, you've kept the doors closed, blinds pulled, making us push our way in, and we're done. Who wants to keep doing that? Connection, bonding, friends, it's not meant to be this way: pushing, difficult, agitated. This doesn't feel good. We all have things we'd rather not share or rather not remember, but when you're in something with someone, they're in it with you. They want to be there, in the mush of it with you. It's not meant to feel like work. This—" she moves her empty glass back and forth between us—"this is work, and I don't want to do it anymore."

Flav returns with his bad timing. He has two opened wine bottles in hand and two long-necked beers tucked into the pit of his cardigan's droopy pockets. "The beer is for my friend there"—he points his elbow to his Italian neighbor—"his football team is shit. He needs to drown them in this." He hands a bottle of wine to Kendra.

"You mean drown his sorrows, Flav," she says, chuckling.

"No, this team is so shit. Fuck the sorrows. Drown the men." He winks at us both.

Kendra starts her pour.

"Need some air," I say. "Did you want to step out for a smoke?"

"No, I'm good. I don't do that anymore. Cold turkey."

I sling my coat over me. "That's great, Kendra. That's really, really great. I'm happy for you. And your lungs." When I grab my purse, the heavy end of the buckle hits Emma in the back.

She's too engrossed in the wine and merry and bright to even notice. I say *sorry* anyway. "I'm just going to step out for a sec, then."

"All right. We'll be here," Kendra says. Her smile is back, but it's pinned with that same blue heaviness as before. She's quick to move off of me; starts in on something animated and light with Flav.

The cold air feels good on my face—even when it starts stinging, it's still refreshing. There's a buzz on my hip. I answer without checking, "Tyson, let me take a breather, pl—"

"Best? It's Trinity. Sorry to bother you so late."

"Is everything okay?"

"I don't know, but they're calling a big meeting tomorrow morning."

"Who, Joan?"

"Joan and James and Isabelle and . . . Miyuki too."

"But I called in sick—officially. And remember I told you I leave for Montreal on Friday? It's for the interview, but I put it down as vacation. I'm seeing my folks."

"I know. I told Joan that you were out sick and that you had vacation days on the schedule, and they said to call you in anyway. They're having it first thing Friday, because I mentioned that your flight was in the evening. Sorry, I panicked a bit. It's Joan, she was all over me, over my desk, gawking at my screen. And everyone looks pretty fucking serious about every fucking thing. So, I don't know. Plus, they told me to block time in the conference room downstairs for this. Said it's an all-hands. Seems major. That's why I'm calling now. I had to wait for people to clear out of here."

"It's not in JK's office?"

"No, it's on twelve. I think someone from legal might sit in on it. I'm sorry, Best. I don't know anything else. I even asked JK if she needed me in it. She said no, and not another word after that. I have no clue what this is about. Do you?"

"Maybe. I think. I don't know. Thanks for the heads up, Titi."

"Okay. No problem. See you tomorrow," she says.

"Right."

My fingers were already trembling from the cold, but my brain was spinning, churning out its own heat. This is about the Robot's snooping around my desk. I know it. Actually, I don't know shit. Maybe Nik fucked me, and this time there were no belly kisses and glorious showers afterward.

I watch this young couple trying to hail a cab from the center of the street. They're giddy and groping and probably drunk. He's wrapping her up, as best he can, in his coat as he wears it and they dance, rolling, edging back from the safety of the sidewalk until she stumbles off of it completely and drops into the slushy street. She's shrieking and horrified; humiliated, I'm sure. And her man, after a strange and long pause, slides down to join her in the melting snow.

I'm still gripping my phone. I start typing as fast as my frozen fingers allow and hit *send* just as quickly, before I can change my mind—about any of it.

I'm sorry. We'll talk when I'm back.

CHAPTER 16

Going straight to Nik's place feels lame, but also kind of last-resort. My nose, my fingers, my face, everything's still cold, but the shivering is less about the chill outside and more to do with this crazy fire-drill meeting going down tomorrow. My e-mail to Trinity was brief and precise. Storm coming; switched to earlier flight, can't make meeting.

That's the thing about telling stories for a living: You get really good at shaping the narrative, crafting things to be exactly as you want them to read.

Once I hit *send*, my phone went to *off* mode. I hope my brain can follow suit.

Nik is wearing his specs on the edge of his nose and a heather-gray knit work shirt with stone-colored chinos. He's got his thumb slipped in the middle of a slim hardcover while balancing the rest of the book in his palm. He looks old. He *is* old. But then the sly curl of his lip happens and none of that matters.

"So, what exactly would Richard Gere say right now?"

"I earned that one."

"You did, actually." He nods a few times in his easy way and steps aside, gesturing to the now-open path from the elevator into his home.

"I can't stay long; the car's waiting. Just stopping by—"

"Before your flight. Yep. I got that part on the phone.

"Sorry, I'm nervous."

"About the interview?"

"No, it's that, plus other stuff. Going home, being in Montreal, it can be . . . complicated."

"Right. So you're going to see your family, that's why the earlier flight?"

"Yeah, something like that."

"Something *like* that?"

"I need to visit with them, properly, and I didn't want to swoop in, go do the interview, and then moonwalk out of there without taking the time I need to with my parents. So I bumped up the flight a couple of days."

"Makes sense. Family time is important."

A creepy quiet settles in between us. I don't know if he can sense that I'm lying or maybe it's talking about the importance of family that has stirred up the weirdness, highlighting the sheer impracticality of him and me. There is no meeting my family on the horizon for us, and we both know it. I reach for my coins in my coat pocket, and he shifts the book between his hands.

"Well, I wanted to stop by to say thanks, again. I know it's crazy-early and I could have said it on the phone this morning, but I kind of feel like I never got the chance to tell you personally how much I appreciate all you've done for me these last couple of weeks, Nik. You really bet on me here, with this story, this interview, and I want to let you know it means a lot. Thank you."

He steps closer. "Hey. Listen. I'm not betting on you. This isn't a bet." He moves in even more and wraps his fingers low and loose around my neck and jaw. "You've got a solid story on your hands, Best, and you're a talented writer. You're going to kill it."

"Well, maybe not *kill it*, since this is about an honor killing."
Nik smiles, raises his chin and tucks my head under it.
"What do we do about you?" He's holding me tight into his
chest; the book pressed in the thick of my arm.

I close my eyes and let the embrace just happen without
judgment. This might be good-bye for good for us, and I want
it to at least be sweet.

⤐•⬅

The plane is half-full. I was able to jump ahead several rows
and spread out. I hate being at the back of the plane. I don't
fuck around with wing seats. If anything were to happen, being
in the front, closest to the piloting crew, seems like the safer bet.

There's a plump mother and her all-pink-everything daughter behind me. The girl looks like she might be two or three or
five. Who the hell knows with these tiny humans? My only
hope is that she's got an Elmo app on her mama's iPad or an
American Girl doll in her pink backpack or whatever is needed
to keep that young brain away from boredom. I need some
sleep. Across the aisle there's a guy my age gabbing on one
phone through headphones while fingering another. He's so
wrapped up in himself, his thumbs gliding across his glassy
screen, that he's oblivious to the fact that he's in the way. His
brown cool-kid, leather messenger bag, along with his dangling foot, juts out into the aisle. His boots are deep brown,
rugged, leather high-cuts with bright blue laces. They look
nice. So does he. He's not giving off total hipster asshole vibes
either, but people still have to skirt around him, step over his
shit as they move to the back of the tube, to the death trap. It's
a little early-morning fun watching this, a brief case study,
guessing who will quietly grumble about the imposition and
who will nut-up, as Grant says, and say something to Two-
Phones. A huffy "excuse me" from one of these people leaning
on the better side of valor would certainly do the trick, but so

far they all seem content with undercover eye rolls and gritting their teeth. Plus, he's black, so they're probably all scared as hell.

The flight attendant finally strides by—his straight-edged crisp blue shirt tucked into the trim waist of his navy, undeniable slacks—and says something. Two-Phones repositions himself and all his crap, smooth and easy, without inserting as much as a groan into his phone convo. Of course, he shoots a look my way: brow cocked, eyes sloped, and half a smirk. It's a mildly put-upon, insider-y look, like I already know where he's coming from: busy and bustled and important and willfully aloof. Also, these white people, *amirite?* I should turn away from him, show him my sharp shoulder. *Sorry. No audience given, Two-Phones.* But instead I smile and shrug. It's easier.

He powers down all his shit without being told—shocker— and it looks like he's going to lean over, try to holler. Yes, it's happening; he just licked his lips. Here it comes.

"Seriously," he says, smirking a beat too soon, "it's always the male stewardess trying to flex that power, right?"

"Think they're all called *flight attendants.*" I give him my most authentic smile. It has served as an anti-irony shield in the past.

His smirk stays put as he gives me the once-over. I must have passed the sniff test because he's edging closer into the aisle toward me. "You're right. I'll take that hit. *Flight attendant* it is. So, are you going or coming?"

"Are you asking me if I'm from Montreal?"

He chuckles and looks down at his boot. "Yeah, that's what I'm asking."

"Yes."

"Yes?"

"Yes, I'm from Montreal. You?"

"Transplant-ish. As they would say in your hometown, *à temps partiel.*"

"Actually, no one would say that."

"I thought Canadian girls were all sweethearts."

"What made you think that?" I smile again. This one's definitely forced. He knows it. Listen, it's barely 8:15 and I should be rightfully stretched out, my feet pointing toward his face. He need not be surprised by anything attitudinal that floats his way. Plus, *I thought all Canadian girls were sweethearts?* Do better, Two-Phones.

The airline-safety speech audiovisual kicks on. The volume level is downright disrespectful. I actually catch myself tossing a look over at Two-Phones.

Shit. Now we've imprinted.

The flight is only an hour and some change. If he thinks it's appropriate to chat me up through this whole thing . . . Lord, reveal yourself to me now.

"Hey, I'm Miles."

As he twists out of his wires and seat belt to extend a proper hand to me, I decide right then to accept everything—the gesture, his curiosity, his interest and longing—even his e-mail address or cell number when that's offered. And it will be offered. I know Miles, his type, his game, his speed. I know plenty of Mileses, with the dark, skinny jeans rolled up at the bottom and iconic fitted T-shirts, and hipster-hop hats and hoodies. Actually the last Miles I met like this was a young brother with long, thick dreadlocks that he wore tied and tucked atop his head in a beautiful, fat bun. He was a skateboarding, code-switching type, studying to be a doctor at McGill. We met at a block party-slash-beer crawl in the Village. He was on a week's leave from med school and thought "visiting the Big Apple" was a sure way to give his brain a break. We gelled on the McGill-Montreal thing right away and five beer-stops in, we were holding hands and making a plan to get ice cream later that night. Because the best thing to put in your belly on top of all that beer is some thick and cold dairy, naturally. At no point did I mention that I actually hate ice cream, nor did he disclose the fact that he's a high-functioning alcoholic. As in: crack open a beer . . . in the shower . . . at 9:00 . . . in the morning. (Yes, I crashed at his hotel. It was close, and I wanted to see what all that hair looked like draped over me. In the end, nothing beyond a brief, but decent, old-school Frenching session and some light under-the-shirt groping went down. He wanted to watch porn together and have more ice cream, but I felt I had already compromised myself enough with the earlier cookie-dough foolishness. Topping that off with hotel-room porn felt like a bridge too far.)

"I'm Best." I take his hand and count it down. Three, two—

"Best? The best what? What makes you the best?" He's letting the hand lock linger and trying his best to charm his way into my bra or at least some over-the-shirt petting in the gross airplane bathroom. You can tell that someone told him more than once that he had gorgeous eyes. They're very dark and sharp and shining, and he's got the volume turned up on them as he looks at me now.

"Guess we'll have to figure that out at some point." I take my hand back and leave Two-Phones there on a slow simmer.

"Do you want me to slide over, sit with me, so we don't have to keep yelling over the engines?" Miles says.

He looks so pleased with himself, excited by the possibilities here. He doesn't know that none of this counts. It's not real.

"No, thanks. I'm going to try to catch some winks, you know?"

"Yeah, of course. Totally." The shine from his face dims slightly.

I throw him a bone. "Did you check a bag?"

"No. Why? Did you?" he says, perked up like Pavlov's dog.

"No. Is someone meeting you?"

"No, no one likes to come to the airport," he says.

(Obviously he's never met my father.)

"Let's share a cab," I tell him, with no inflection. No need. His goofball grin is already stretched clear across his face. I want to tell him to calm down; I haven't yet decided how far I'll let him go. We may get to the cab and it's a ticklish hand-shake, an e-mail exchange, and *c'est tout.*

"Sure. Sounds good," he says. "Okay, I'll let you get back to . . . being the best."

Groan, guy. You just took two steps toward Handshake City.

I put my head down on my balled-up coat. The minute my eyes close I see my dad's face. He's shaking his head and looks sad—more than usual, that is. I know he's not going to be pleased that I grabbed the earlier flight without telling him, thereby robbing him of his precious airport jaunt. But I had to do this. I'll deal with his irritation as it comes.

Walking to the taxi line in silence was kind of cute. I felt Miles glancing my way every few steps, then acting like he was looking just past me, over my shoulder or down at his flyboy, leather carry-on. It was midway charming.

Miles and I proceeded to jump into arguably the rankest cab on the road—just musty. And the stench was warmed-over, be-cause the driver somehow felt it necessary to crank up the heat.

"Thought the point of the cab-share thing was to talk, not stare out the windows like strangers." He's wagging his leg slowly. Nerves, maybe, or it could be a tech-junkie side effect from not once checking his phones since the start of the flight almost two hours ago. He didn't even do the auto-reach when the wheels touched down at Trudeau. Neither did I. But, I have reasons.

I turn to him. "So talk."

"I wonder," Miles whispers, "would ol' dude notice if we crack these windows? It's fucking deadly in here."

"I've been thinking about it, but he looks like the Creole cuss-out type."

Not only did our Haitian cabbie elect to drive the smelliest car in all the land, but he also refused to so much as spit a word of English. Miles tried some Franglais foolishness at first, but our cabbie Frantz was prepared to stay stuck on *jerk*. I had to dust off my second-language skills and lay it down nice *pour mon ami puant*.

"Did you give him my address first?" Miles asks.

"I *only* gave him your address."

He's struggling to play it cool. That grin is taking over, though.

"How long have you lived there?" I ask. "That's a nice spot."

"Yeah, I love it. Close to everything. Top of the mountain. I only moved in this past summer. I was in Outremont before, when I first got here."

"Do you have roommates?"

"Not anymore." The grin is back. "Do you?"

"No. I don't live here."

"I think I figured out what you're the best at . . . being cryptic. Every answer is like halfway shaded. Like peeling away a mystery."

"No mystery. Just ask better questions."

Miles's knee picks up its wagging pace and he's chuckling. "Okay. I got you. Better questions. I can do that." He stops moving, drops his smile, and angles his body toward me. "What's your real name?"

"Best. Short for Bathsheba."

"Come on. That was a real question. A good one."

"And that was a real answer. My real name is Bathsheba, but people call me Best. Seriously."

"All right, *Best*. Where do you live?"

"In New York, Brooklyn."

"Then who lives here?"

"My parents."

"You coming home early for the holidays."

"It's more of a work trip. Tacking on a visit to it."

"How long will you be here, visiting your family?"

"A few days."

"Would you want to see me again—dinner or something?"

"Maybe."

"Wait—do over. Better question: Will you have dinner with me . . . tomorrow?"

"Still maybe. Family obligations."

"Yo. This heat is ridiculous. And the smell—it's worse than camel breath."

Miles is tearing off layers. He's down to a rolled-up, crinkled everywhere white V-neck tee when I notice them: horizontal lines, grooves running the length of his otherwise smooth, brown arm. Scars, some short and others—the ones along his tensed bicep—are longer, deeper, fresher, and slightly raised with added texture. He's a cutter.

All the flirty games end here; it's not fair to him. He's got his own troubles, clearly. Deep ones.

Now I need to figure out a quiet way to tell the driver that there's been a change. There will be a second stop after the mountain after all.

CHAPTER 17

It's the red door that fools you. It leads you to believe that you're entering friendly territory. Once you step through it, cross over the welcome mat, you'll know that you've punctured the reality of things at this home. It's decidedly charmless and unwelcoming. Even the doorbell is a ruse. The melody it chimes is the first and last upbeat thing you'll hear at my parents' home. The house itself is large but doesn't quite commit to being garish. There are a few tasteful touches: the marbled foyer, the piano in the main living room, the sunroom addition where the books live, the old woodstove in the perfect corner of the kitchen, even the reimagined fourth garage in which my father stores all of his filing cabinets looks thought-through and appropriate. But there's sadness here too, so real and familiar I can hear it trudging through every room of the house.

I'm busy thinking about Miles and his self-harm situation and I don't have time to rehearse what to say to my parents, like I typically do. But I'm not too worried. These folks aren't the type to deviate from the script. My dad will be a mix of surprised and low-key disappointed that I'm on their doorstep, early and delivered by taxi, while my mother will be my mother: a chilled hello and a hesitant, stiff one-armed hug before telling me in which room to set my bags.

Not gonna lie. Seeing a slight dash of surprise in Mum's raised forehead when she opens the door will be an interesting twist to our usual performance. The woman's default look is that she couldn't give the thinnest slice of a shit about you and whatever it is you have the effrontery to step to her with. She's always had that "don't try me" face, but there used to be warmth there behind her crinkly eyes. Over the last ten years, the whole thing has crystallized, forming this rigid screen, a steely layer, beneath it only more hardness.

But twist on the twist: She barely blinked when she opened the door to me. And after the first hello in the doorway, not another word was exchanged until we were well into the kitchen. As I walked behind her down the wide, bright hallway, I scanned the walls and tried to angle my eyes into the nooks of certain rooms to see what looked different. The last time I was home at this house was two years ago. I was able to skip out on the memorial last year because the gods showed me grace and kindness and placed pneumonia in my lungs. I was actually thankful for the legit excuse to miss out on the Montreal mourning because I'm awful that way, but when things moved from fever, chills, and bone-rattling cough to diarrhea, delirium, and blood-tinged mucous realness? I was chanting the Act of Contrition and praying the rosary like I was in a goddamn nunnery. Tyson, the only one still in the city for the holidays, would stop by every evening with Gatorade and flat ginger ale and to sing his grandmother's greatest gospel hymns over me. Of course I didn't tell my parents how bad off I was. All they knew and all that mattered was that I wasn't coming home to honor my brothers.

I noticed some new framed art on the wall in the living room, and the piano is gone. All of our school photos had long been boxed away. The only picture that remains, looming large by the winding staircase, is the one of the whole family, extended—aunts, uncles, and all brands of cousin—at the Grantley Adams airport in Barbados, when we arrived for our grand and rare vacation. I learned not to linger on those smiling faces in the photograph. It sets me back.

Watching my mother's body move slowly toward the belly of the house, I see that she's slimmer—scrawny even—and I think about how much more of her there was back when I was a kid. There was real comfort for me, nestled in her literal form. Walking behind her in the mall, or to our car in the parking lot, or up the church aisle to our usual pew, her wide sturdiness made me feel strong and safe, like nothing bad could get past her and brush up on me and drag me toward awful.

We all felt some version of that. Benjamin had this habit of stroking her arm, up near where it met her shoulder. I jammed my hand up her sleeve a few times to see what all the fuss was about. It made sense; her arm was soft, smooth, and thick and warm like the most perfectly perfect blanket. Bryant got in on the action too, though he latched onto her unwarm, unsmooth, uninviting elbow. Such an odd egg, that guy. Our father teased both his sons about all of it, of course. Li'l leeches, he'd call them. Didn't bother them. I should say, it didn't bother them until real-live girls became a viable option for them—for Benjamin, really. He started kicking it to girls early, like nine or ten. Bryant took the tortoise route. He'd rather look up at the stars than clock girls. He only got his first run-to-the-bedroom-close-the-door phone call from a girl a few days after his fourteenth birthday. Michelle. I can never remember her last name. Two things come to mind when I think about her: First, that she was really cute—Bryant showed me her picture in their yearbook. And second, how horribly upset she was at the funeral. Michelle sat with her parents several pews back, but I could hear her crying, this hollow weeping. She cried through the whole thing. I kept glancing back, checking on her, making sure she was still standing. That wailing was tough to hear, but it also served as a distraction, and I have to say, I was kind of grateful for it.

"You want something to eat?" My mother pulls out a chair for me, sets a place mat on the table. "I not too long made some plantain. I could fry up an egg to go 'long with it, and there's bread from Vincey's bake shop in the tin."

"Oh, don't worry yourself, Mum. I'm fine. I had some tea and stuff earlier."

She sits in the seat she had pulled out for me. "Your father said you were coming later in the week."

"I know. I got an earlier flight last minute. It was easier. You know, the storm." She's trying. Why shouldn't I? "But I apologize for not calling, letting you know that I was coming early. This morning was a rush, and then the roaming charges . . . anyway, sorry."

"That's all right."

"I'm also sorry about before, when we talked, and I said I wasn't coming. It was work and I couldn't get around it, but—"

"You're here now."

"Right, I'm here now. I still have to work, though. An interview in Toronto; Ajax, actually. A day trip, maybe overnight. It's just an interview. Otherwise, I'm here . . . for you guys, and stuff."

"Your father will be happy."

"Right." I take a few steps farther in, peek through the bay window out to the yard. "Where is he, anyway?"

"He gone to the market."

"Ooh. That's good. What's on the menu?"

"I couldn't tell you. It'll be tasty, though."

My mother returned the place mat to the short stack under the fruit bowl in the center of the table and promptly got up. Her sudden moves jolted me out of my blurred ideas of actually having a real and sustained conversation with her.

"Should I get my bags and . . . ?" I say, pointing with my thumb through the archway behind me.

"I have to iron some sheets," my mother says. She's standing close to me, true arm's length.

"I can help with that, if you want."

She frowns and I turn toward that archway. I know what's coming, what she'll say next, and I wait for it.

"That'd be nice," she says.

(As this early-morning trip has already shown, I don't know anything.)

My mouth is open a little and I stutter out a delayed response. "Oh, okay. I can do that. I can help. Lead the way."

I hear him padding around the room, the change in his pockets clinking together, but I keep my eyes closed anyway. As he gets closer to the bed, I smell the alcohol. It drags me out of make-believe and I turn to greet him.

"Hey, Dad." I pull myself up and out from the thick covers. My voice is sufficiently groggy, and I'm sure I look confused. It's dark out; the blinds are half-open and the lights are dimmed. My purse is open and jumbled, scrunched up by the pillow next to me.

"Didn't mean to wake you." He doubles back to the small table near the door. "I was gonna leave this for you." It's a tray with food.

"Oh, you didn't have to—I'm sorry I missed dinner. You weren't back from . . . the market. I came in here to chill for a bit and wait until you got back . . . anyway, I'm sorry I slept through it."

He's smiling, but clearly concentrating on balance, both his and that of the wide tray. As he draws closer, I see my favorites: Trini chow mein, *pow*, and Chinese cakes. There's even a short glass with pale orange fizziness. "Is that my fave—pineapple soda? Dad, this is great. You really didn't have to do all of this, bring all of this food to me on a tray."

"Nonsense. You're here now." He rests the tray down next to me on the bed and sits on the wood chair at the foot. "You took the early flight this morning?"

"Yeah, it was easier. You know, that storm and everything. I'm sorry I didn't call. I know you like the airport run."

He nods his head slowly, gentle like Nik would. "Glad you reach here safe." More nodding. "You go 'head and eat while the food is hot. You know my feelings about them microwaves."

I lean into the plate of golden noodles and inhale its tangy heat. The third bite is even more delicious than the first. His smile is wider now and seems to delight in each forkful I savor. I take a deep sip of the sweet soda, letting it tickle the inside of my nose as it likes to do. After that, I'm full, but it has nothing to do with the food. I slide the tray off my lap. I don't realize the words are tumbling out of my mouth until they are. My eyebrows hoist my forehead to the ceiling and I trying to swallow the lump expanding in the back of my throat. This is a mistake; I know that much—but I also know that I can't stop it from happening.

"You've always taught me to speak up, don't shrink in a corner—for anyone."

"That's right. That's what I always tell you children. You're nobody's sheep."

"Right. Not sheep." I swallow hard; the sound is loud in my ears. "I'm not a sheep. I can't do this anymore, Dad. Can't just follow along."

His eyes narrow and his chest rises to take a breath and maybe speak, but I keep going, keep talking, putting my focus back on the tray. "Can't keep reliving what happened that night, Daddy. It's not about not honoring them. A day doesn't pass—not in these ten long years—that I don't think about them." I finally glance over at him. "And I don't want to upset you or Mum more than you already are, more than you always are, but I can't let this continue to define me, define my life here. It can't be the only thing that brings me back home to you. I . . . I want to have Christmas back."

The look that takes over his face makes me want to suck all those words back in, gobble them up and stuff chow mein in my mouth down behind them. He's not ready to hear any of this. His lip quivers, but he's trying to fight it.

And now I feel empty, despicable.

"I'm sorry, Daddy. I'm still tired from the flight and stressed over work stuff and I don't know what I'm saying. I'm sorry."

"I know," he says, finally. "I know."

"I'm out of place. I'm sorry. I have no business saying any of th—"

"No. No, it's your business, Best. It's fair and it's your business to say it. Truth tell it, those first three or four years, man, I didn't want to do it either. But the pictures on the wall, all the memories, I can't do nothing else but let them in and remember. It's my business to remember. I make it my business to honor them boys." He leans back on the side of the bureau; his gaze resting on my plate of food. "When they birthdays come 'round and I pull out them birth certificates from the files, study each crack in the little black-ink footprints, draw over that messy scratch of my signature with my fingers . . . it's real cruel, and I feel that at the base of my heart, at the seed of it. It's like a torture. I don't like doing it, but I do it. I honor them because I loved—" He brings his hand, balled up in a tight fist, to his mouth, and I wonder if he's going to be sick.

I don't reach out. That's not what we do here. But I want to. I want to squeeze his hand, hug him, pat his back, pour him another drink—anything that would pick his shoulders back up.

"Dad . . . They're always going be in our lives, in our minds, circling around us. They won't disappear. They can't. We wouldn't let them disappear." Tears blur my vision. "They're not in the ground, under those stones. They're here, with us. Always."

My father's sad, heavy gaze falls away from me and then to the floor between us. After a long pause, he shakes his head once and says it: "They're not here."

Before I can draw my next jagged breath, he's standing straight and moving over to me on the bed. I brace for something: a tight squeeze, his total collapse, a wash of tears. I try to be ready. But he only leans into the side of the bed and gently pushes the tray toward my crossed legs. He shakes his head again. "They're gone."

I can see him straining to steady the low bounce in his chin, and it breaks me. He's moving to the door with quick, even steps.

"Dad"—my voice is cracked and gravelly—"I'm sorry."

"Nonsense," he says, barely looking back at me. "God need be sorry. Not you."

CHAPTER 18

Is there anything gloomier than a cracked snow globe? (Spoiler: The answer is always *no*.) My dad has one sitting atop some crinkled papers on his dusty desk. And I say *dusty* because there isn't yet a word created to aptly describe the thick, fuzzy grayness that coats every surface of this man's narrow lair. The clunky computer beneath the shaky desk, the stained keyboard draped over old international newspapers, the jumbo fax machine (yes) teetering on the tower of Yellow Pages, even the old-school brown extension cord stretching across the room: all of it chalky and gross.

I could say that this isn't like him, that things have fallen away over the years given everything that happened. But that would be a shameless lie. My father bought into the archetype of reporter-as-natural-mess a long time ago. The way he sees it, who has time to neaten this and organize that when you're too busy being dogged and relentless while driving the truth home?

I want to check the train schedules, but can't bring myself to reach for my phone. The truth is, I just don't want to deal with the toxic crap waiting for me on it. Between Bauer's voice mails and Trinity's the-sky-is-falling squawks, I'm fairly certain the hard, shiny plastic thing will self-destruct by week's end. I already turned it on quickly last night to retrieve Fatima's cousin's phone number and house address, and the notifications on that fucker nearly sent me into a seizure: e-mails, tweets, texts, Facebook; just endless. And Jesus, the number of voice mails was truly staggering. Turning that phone on again is a fool's errand.

What a steaming mess, and I've stepped all the way in it. But my focus needs to be like a laser right now. This interview, this story, it's all that matters. I'll just do it classic-style and make a landline call to Via Rail from my mother's side of the house.

I dip into my dad's office anyway. Maybe his grandfather clock of a computer could dial-up the internet or his favorite ancient AOL or something so I can see what's happening in the news up here. But visions of some random wire catching and the whole dingy deal going up in smoke has me shook. I don't want to make any swift moves in this Luddite cave.

The newspapers on my dad's desk catch my attention. Two are French-language papers and one is in Arabic, maybe Farsi? Strange, but also not strange. This is my dad, after all. There's a bulky folder in the pile of papers. It's labeled in his crappy, wobbly handwriting. I can't make it out. I try to push things around without leaving tracks. Something I credit my mother for teaching me. Back in the day, we all referred to my mother as the detective. The credo around our house was simple: Don't bother, Mum already knows.

Using an unsharpened pencil—there are, like, eight of them gathered in a grubby mug—I'm able to drag the folder out more, even lift the flap a little. The paper to the very top looks like a faded form, maybe something medical, definitely official. There's a seal and possibly a stamped signature to the bottom.

"You in here noseyin'?" my dad says.

I'm sure I look startled. There were no tip-offs this time: no change in his pocket, no reek of booze drifting into the room just ahead of him. I can feel my eyebrows shoved up to my hairline.

"Oh, no, Dad. I'm just sitting, waiting." I tap the pencil like it's a drumstick on the arm of the mug and slip it back into place without once shifting my glance from him.

"You got a fax coming through?"

I glance at the jalopy. "What, from 1995? No."

"People still send faxes, you know?"

"No, they really don't, Dad."

"You don't know," he says and swats his hand at me. His mood seems stable, bordering on fine. "When you leaving for Toronto?"

"Probably in a couple of hours. I have to make some calls, reach out, check in on things with my interview."

"So why you so nervous then?"

"I'm not."

He steps in, but stays close to the door. "Denial. Now I know for certain that you're really nervous."

"I'm not denying anything, Dad. I'm not nervous; I'm just . . . preoccupied. There are a lot of moving parts."

"Do you want to run through your questions?"

"You followed the case?"

"Here and there. Don't have the stomach for that kind of thing these days."

"Yeah, it's pretty gruesome. But this interview is less about all the horror-show stuff, more about her, the survivor." My dad looks instantly uncomfortable, like red ants are scratching at him from the inside. "I don't really have a list or anything. Just some notes, you know? I'm going to do what you've always taught me, and let the story tell. The most important question I have is: And then what happened?"

"Good. That's how it's done," he says, and moves into the room, walking over to his black cabinets. It gives me a chance to slide the fat, mystery folder back under the newspapers.

He's backing me still, with one hand resting on the corner of his filing cabinet, the other shoved deep into his pants pocket.

His head is down and his bony shoulders are pulled up to his ears. He looks so small, fragile. The Trini Lightburns are a spindly crew, and my father's always been slim, but here he looks flimsy—almost transparent—standing in the sunlight and dust, like a fading outline. He has something to say. From his stiff stance, I can tell he's not sure where to start.

"So, I'm going to . . . head over to Mum's side, get something to eat or whatever. You okay? You need anything?" I'm already standing. He doesn't know where to start and I have this distinct feeling that I don't want him to start. It can wait.

"Bathsehba, before you head over. There's something." He's still gripping the cabinet. "We've never asked you, but I want to, I need to ask. It's ten years and I need to ask." He's turned around now, switching hands so that he's still holding onto something sturdy. My father's eyes, bloodshot forever, it seemed, are brimmed with tears and the tip of his pointy nose is red. His jaw is clenched and that vein down the middle of his forehead is bulged. There are blotches along one side of his neck— I've seen them before, in the mirror, back in those early days when I could barely look at myself without a fury rising to the surface. "I need you to tell me what happened that night," he says. "I need to know how this happened. I want to hear your voice say how you're here now. Please. I need to hear it all."

My mouth is open. The tears rush in and I feel myself starting to buckle back into the wobbly chair. I let the tears fall, but stay standing. I'm shaking my head, willing the words to come. "I—I'm sorry. I can't do this right now, Dad. The interview and the train schedule . . . I can't do this right now. I'm sorry." He's calling for me, his voice cracked and strained, but I'm not listening. My bag was already packed and in the hallway. The back of the red door is in my sights. I'm out.

It's not until I've rounded the corner and heading downhill that I feel the raw chill against my face. Even with the sun in the center of the sky, it's miserable outside. I don't bother buttoning my coat and my hat barely hangs off the back of my damp head. If I don't see a taxi, I'll just keep walking until I hit the Metro. With my luck, the closest station is not for another nine blocks.

The cold air stings everything—exposed or covered—and my coat flaps in the cutting wind, but my fingers are too frozen to do anything about it. My tears have hardened on my cheeks or maybe reversed their tracks back into my eyeballs. Either way I can see clearer: buildings, signs, people; they are no longer blurred clumps. Now it's a fancy SoHo-style gourmet market, a bookstore, a boutique, a high-end yoga shop, a shoe store, all of them bustling. There are dazzling Christmas lights strung beautifully, connecting rows of twin pine trees, and people look delighted despite the snow and frost.

The salesgirl at the yoga store looks at me with her face slightly twisted when I ask to borrow the phone at the checkout counter. I start to tell her some concoction about a dead battery, but it's clear she could not care less and hands me a black cordless.

"It's local, right?" she says, her face still bent out of shape.

"Yeah, very. You can dial for me, if you want."

"Uh, no. I have customers. If you could just stand over here, to the side of the cash wrap . . ." She shags a limp hand in the general direction and turns her attention to the *next guest in line*. At least her expression has warmed up for them.

"Hey, it's Best. Lightburn."

"Hey, wassup? This is weird. Did you just get my voice mail?" Miles says. He sounds surprised and hopeful and beaming all mixed together and it's spilling through the phone. "I left another one for you, like, an hour ago . . . anyway, so did you want to just make it official and hop on lunch? The brunch window is kind of closing out. Wait, are you at Yoga Sense?"

"Yeah, I'm just using their phone. Long story. I'm actually out already. On Greene Avenue. I thought I'd just try you from the road." The sales chick with the morphing face is shooting daggers at my left temple. "My phone died," I say loudly and boomerang cut-eye right back at her. "I haven't checked voice mail—"

"Oh. So you didn't get my voice mail from last night either?"

"Miles."

"Ask better questions, right?"

I can hear his goofy chuckle bubbling up. "No, just answer mine: Do you have time to meet me?"

"Yes. Most def. Where on Greene Avenue?"

"Maybe the bookstore. Or I could meet you . . . there?"

"At my place?"

"If you want."

"Yeah. That'd be cool. Do that. Need the address?"

"No. I have a good memory."

"Of course. You're Best."

━━━━◆◆━━━━

Miles does this dramatic, sweeping door-opening thing that's common among little kids playing house. He looks like he's running late for a men's fashion-mag shoot—the lounging issue. It's all sleek everything: a gray-black, thin cashmere-y sweater and slim black sweatpants stuffed sloppy-style into these black leather, extra-high-cut sneakers with gold eyelets and gum soles. No earbuds or cords or devices are dangling anywhere. Maybe it's the rad pad spread out just past his shoulder or the considerate dim lighting in the foyer, but Miles just turned completely cute and charming. I want to fall into his cozy sweater and never leave.

"*Aunt-tray-voo*," he says. His French accent is adorably abysmal. "It's cold as balls out there." He opens his arms, waiting for me to step into them. And I do. It's easier.

"Do you want some coffee, tea, to warm up?" he says, resting his chin in the top of my head. I'm wearing a hat—well, partially—so I allow it. All of Miles's moves feel likes he's been watching a lot of teen dramas on television and taking notes. I'm halfway waiting for this one next: He'll clutch my face in his palms and swear to me, in a weighty whisper, that he'll *never let anything or anyone hurt me ever again. I promise.* And then turn into a werewolf or some other supernatural.

"Thanks. Tea would be nice."

"I can do a latte too, or macchiato with caramel or espresso, hot cocoa. It's the machine. It does everything."

"Tea's fine."

"Right," he says, smiling. I'm sure he was told at some point postpuberty that his smile is winning and wonderful. If we're being honest, it's none of those things, but the consistent effort he puts into it is definitely special. "Tea it is. Milk, honey, sugar?"

"Straight, no chaser. Thanks."

He laughs. "Make yourself comfortable. The remotes for everything are there on the bench. I'll be right back with your tea, in a shot glass."

There's that fly leather bag, sitting plump and ready by the coatrack. His slim, silver laptop rests on the sloping side of the bag's bulge. "Where you heading out?" I say, throwing my voice toward the kitchen. "Feels like I caught you heading out."

"I can never hear anything back here. Gimme a sec."

I've seen enough. I'm going in. "Hey, listen." I'm trying to adopt that TV heartthrob whisper he used on me earlier. Miles's head is buried in a wide cabinet by his shimmering stove. "You know, I'm good. I don't really need tea. I've already warmed up, pretty much."

"No, no. I have it. Just gotta find the pods," he says. "They're in here. I swear."

"It's okay. Really." I ease up behind him. And, sidebar: That cabinet is fucking ridiculous. Every box lined up, stacked and exact. Labels face out and possibly alphabetized. "Forget the tea." I touch the small of his back. "I want to try something."

"Oh, word? What's that?" He turns around, grinning like a goof.

"I want to ask you something."

"Wait: Do you want try something or ask something?"

"Both."

"Okay. Let's do both, then."

I see the giddy in his eyes. He thinks we're going there, thinks we're going to connect or at least rub up on each other. But that's not in the cards. I don't feel it. I don't feel that thing, the undeniable pull that makes you want to completely ingest the person, gobble them up or wrap yourself around them as tight as ever possible and press their entire being into yours. I like Miles; there's an openness, a willing that feels good to be around, but the mere idea of actually kissing him isn't sitting well with me right now. It's actually kind of making me uncomfortable.

I try to look past his thirst and stay on my course. "Do you have family?"

"Hol'up"—his face stiffens—"is this more verbal tricks?"

"No, no tricks."

"So what are you trying, then?"

"Telling the truth."

"All right. I'm down with that. My family. They're mostly in Atlanta. I'm not real close to them. Kind of what brought me out this way. Just a lot of fucked-up old history that nobody's willing to let go. I don't even go home for Christmas anymore. I usually meet with some old friends, other holiday orphans, and we snowboard for a week. I'm going up to Mont-Tremblant tonight to check out this chalet with my boy Justin." He cocks his head. "My turn."

"Your turn?"

"My turn to get some truth from you. Why are you here—as

in, here at my place? After the cold-ass one-eighty in the cab . . . and then I called you a few times and nothing. I kind of figured it was a wrap; I wouldn't see you again. But here you are, at my crib with a bag and red eyes and even more mystery. So, what's up?"

"I'm a journalist, a reporter, and I have this interview in Ajax, so that's why the bag. As for the one-eighty in the cab, I just got the sense that you were dealing with some stuff on your own and you didn't need more complications. And, if you're looking for truth, you've got to know that I'm one big walking complication. Not an exaggeration. And about going home for the holidays . . . we haven't had a regular Christmas in ten years."

"Fucked-up family too?"

"Yeah. What's left of it." As I turn my head, I spot the pesky box of pods. It's mint tea; my favorite. I slide it out of forma- tion and hand it to Miles.

He pops one into the machine and the dull, whirling sound begins. "What do you mean, what's left of it?" he asks, frowning.

"We're still doing the truth-telling thing?"

"Hell, yeah, we're still doing it," he says, and the crooked smile creeps in.

Like a jerk, the fancy brewing machine falls quiet. It's just my voice circling now as my stomach folds in on itself. I can't even take a breath or blink or turn back on this. The words feel like fire behind my lips. I actually want to say it, what hap- pened, so I do. "On Christmas Eve, ten years ago, there was an accident. My brothers . . . they both died. Now it's just me, my folks and their constant heartache. That's why I don't like com- ing home and why I don't talk about my family." My entire chest settles back into place and I feel—literally, physically— lighter for this one perfect and brief moment. And then I see my father's red, sad eyes, his trembling self, trying to coax a tincture of truth from me for once, for good. I couldn't find an opening for him, but here I am, letting it stream out of me with a stranger that I met on a plane. That's the dividing line: Miles is a stranger. He only knows the parts of the truth that I tell him. My father, he can't know even the thinnest parts of the truth. He couldn't bear it. I can't, most days.

"That's fucking fucked-up, for real. Shit." He stirs through the steam billowing above the large white mug and hands it to me. "I'm sorry, man. I'm sorry about your brothers."

There's no pity painted on his face and it's refreshing. In fact, he looks distressed, almost angry. The heat of the mug feels good against my palms. "That's maybe the best description I've heard in a while: *fucking fucked-up*. It's definitely that." Miles is still frowning and shaking his head as he slides the misaligned box back into place. "My turn," I say, blowing on the scalding tea. His face softens. "When we were in the cab, I saw your arm, the scars. I've seen that before; my college roommate. That's why I changed my mind in the taxi and why I didn't come up here with you, why I didn't plan on calling you back. I stuffed your card in my coat pocket and let the whole idea of you go. I thought you were dealing with some raw stuff and didn't think some one-night-stand bullshit would help." His eyebrow shoots up. "Come on, Miles. I don't live here. It was only ever going to be a one-time, hookup thing."

"Oh, so you were doing me a favor by ignoring my calls? That's pretty fucking presumptuous. Is that what you're doing now, laying things out for me, helping me sort through my problems? Is this the interview?"

Of course I have to follow him out of the kitchen, but I hang back, keep a smart distance and my eye on the closest exit. "Calm down, Miles. I'm not trying to upset you. I just want to be straight with you. Remember, trying the truth?"

"Yeah. Got it." He walks over to his glass-top table in the corner of the living room near the window and leans over another slim, silver laptop. "All right. You want to go for truth?

Let's keep it real, then," he says, without looking up from the screen. "Yeah, some of those marks are exactly what you thought. High school shit. But the other scars, and the ones that cut across my ribs and the big-ass one that runs down the part of my leg that's still real flesh—those are from this." Justin spins the laptop around with one rough push. I have to step in closer to see the photo, and when I do, when I see it, I feel sick and sorry and foolish.

"I was in an accident too. Ran over an IED in Afghanistan. I didn't lose my life; I lost my leg and probably a lot of my good parts; my mind, for sure. But I got it all back, mostly." He juts out his foot. "Shit, this new leg is probably better than the old one. Bionics. Ain't never been a day that I was lying around here feeling sorry for me. We all get raw deals, man. It's the fucking human condition, as my CO liked to say. That's one thing the army taught me: Don't take none of this shit personal. You can't play the game right if you out there takin' shit personal. Otherwise every day will be a fight to tap out, just put a gun in your mouth and tap out for real. Misery and fucked-up situations, that shit's go'n come regardless of who you are. But it's how you deal that makes the difference. Adjust, accept, shake hands with yourself on it, and keep it moving. That's the truth I know."

"That's really . . . real. And I'm sorry. I don't know why I had to push and poke and assume that I know anything about anything. I'm sorry."

Miles closes the laptop with a soft swat. He seems less agitated and I'm actually wishing for the return of his goofball grin.

Nothing. Only a short exhale leaves his lips. He's still leaning on the table, not looking at me. Trying the truth was a bad idea.

"That tea's probably chilled now," Miles says.

"It's fine."

"Do you want me to make you something else?"

I shake my head and rest the cup down on the edge of the frosted table. "But I could go for one of those hot chocolates doused with bourbon. They make 'em at Old Dublin, if I recall."

The creases in Miles's face loosen and that wonky grin takes its sweet time spreading across his mouth like the thickest molasses. "Next time, say that first. I'll get our coats."

⟫•⟪

Using Miles's cell was a no-brainer. Plus, the "my phone is dead" thing was still working in my favor. My mother doesn't answer calls from numbers she doesn't recognize. She's always been slightly funky about the telephone, and the introduction of caller ID really let that beast free.

I left a hasty message telling them first that I was okay—as if that was a concern for my parents—and that I was taking a night train to Toronto, back late tomorrow night. I knew Miles was giving me sideways looks for the duration of the minute-long mumble message; I could practically hear the questions rumbling in his chest. The second round of special cocoas took care of that, though. He got lost on some looping tangent about the trouble with TV cop dramas and procedurals. We were about to leave the chocolate sweetness behind, move into the well with our drinks, when good sense showed up and cut us off. Miles had a long drive ahead to meet up with his boy Justin, and he offered to drop me off at Via Rail for a 5 p.m., nearly sold-out train that I absolutely could not miss.

We made it and the good-bye wasn't strained or strange. Getting Miles slightly lubricated made him that much more enchanting and sweet. I tucked his business card deeper into my pocket as he drove off from the station. He's definitely going to be added to the contacts . . . that is, whenever I finally decide to turn my phone back on.

The train was full. I had to grab the first available seat: back of the second car, no one next to me. Not bad.

Sleep was not an option. I didn't want to be jerked awake by some random rattling twenty minutes later with a headache and dry mouth. Tried to chill instead. But that wasn't happening. Did the crossword and sudoku in the *Destinations* magazine—Ryan Gosling's on the cover. That's a BFD for a flimsy, on-board, freebie train mag. But the Gosling piece was all cotton candy. Probably a phoner or worse, a bullshit write-around. (I still jammed that glossy thing in my bag. I mean, it's Ryan Gosling. In a tight shirt.)

I've already pulled out my notes about twenty times and flipped through the grubby copy of my father's "How to Interview Workshop" handout. What's one more time?

Macro Strategy: Work the Answer
Blend—Make them Active; Establish Common Ground
Extend—Pick a Blend Point; Follow Your Blocking
Control

I highlight the questions from his top ten that I'll likely use most:

10. **What's an example?**
8. **What were the options?**
6. **In what way?**
5. **Why is that?**
2. **What do you mean?**
1. **What happened?**

And I've also stared at these pictures just as much. Fatima was the prettiest sister. A hard thing to discern given how beautiful everyone in the Imam family was—even Bashir, with his thick, arched brows, bronzed skin and deep-set, twilight-

moon eyes. I can never look at his face for too long; the darkness of it, the torment steeped in his face starts to feel too alive
and sinister. I know it sounds crazy, but there's something real
and wicked bubbling behind the flat photo of this man, and it
creeps me out every time.

I've turned into my mother and instead of triple-checking
the door locks and stove knobs, it's my printouts that I keep
looking over: the car-rental info, hotel reservation, directions
to get to Fatima's place (even though I'll have GPS.) I've also
visited the dining car four times and ate nothing, dipped in and
out of the quiet car for no good reason, switched from the window to aisle seat a few times back-to-back—like a complete
weirdo—and there are still two hours of tracks to cover before
we pull into Union Station tonight. Clearly, true boredom has
set in. Maybe a quick call to Miles would help. He keeps circling my brain. I'm hearing him say *It's the human condition*,
with each glance at these Fatima photos. He's worked it all out.
Figured out where to put things, useless things like shame, re-
sentment, pity, guilt. They're not weighing on Miles in the
slightest. I could have sat with him at that bar for hours more.
And him being easy on the mind—and eyes, with his bionic
leg—that doesn't hurt.

Looking around the train, every other seat has that distinct
blue glow hovering above, tickling the ceiling—I've counted.

Fuck it. I root around my coat pocket for Miles's card and
actually mumble the words "just do it" to my cold phone. I
press the raised, rigid button on the side of my phone and rest
it on the seat next to me. Not going to bother with the deep
breaths and pep-talk bullshit. I don't want to sound rehearsed
with him. I like this truth-thing that we're doing. (However, I
will take one quick exhale for centering purposes.)

My phone rings and it's loud. The clang of it gets me a mean-
mug from the older couple seated nearby. I'm startled too. I literally just powered up the thing and already it's ringing? I

don't even have time to check the ID. "Hello?" I whisper and arch my body away from my annoyed neighbors.

"Best! Best?" Trinity sounds breathless, panicky.

"Hey. Yeah, it's me."

"Oh my God. Best. You're alive. Are you okay? Where are you, in Montreal?"

"Yes, alive; yes, I'm okay. Yes to all. Actually, I'm probably in Ontario now, though. Train ride is ongoing."

"Ontario? Train ride? Wait, I thought you were flying home."

"I did. I'm heading to an interview, for that honor-killing thing I told you about a little bit ago."

"Jesus. That thing."

"Yeah, it's gruesome, but that's not what my story—"

"No, I know about the survivor angle. Everyone knows about the survivor angle. I can't go three minutes without hearing about the goddamn story around here."

"What do you mean?"

"You haven't heard my voice mails? I've left like eleven thousand. I've been trying to reach you for-fucking-ever. I even sent a couple texts. *Texts.* Me, sending texts. And you know where I stand on that shit."

"My phone is . . . I've haven't checked really anything yet. What's going on? Who's talking about my story—in what way?"

"Everyone, and not in a good way. Why didn't you just come to that all-hands meeting, Best? Honestly, you could have sorted all of this out. Now it's a shit storm. You should have just come to that meeting."

"But you know that I was traveling. My flight got changed. I told everyone. I sent the e-mail to all concerned parties."

"Hang on. Let me just change locations. Ears are everywhere now," Trinity whispers, "especially around my desk, since I was the last person to speak to you—which I had to lie about, by the way, so remember to say that we didn't actually talk. Say I left you a voice mail about the meeting. Remember to say that when you're questioned. It's important."

"Slow down, Trinity. Questioned? Who's questioning me—Joan? Is this a Joan-led witch hunt?"

"Okay, I'm in the breast-pump room." She's still hushed. "No, it's everyone: Joan, Miyuki, Isabelle, Maggie, James. Like, James is super-pissed and you know she doesn't do pissed well. Countdown is on 'til she's asking me for her pills."

"What's the problem? I cleared my vacay with these people."

"It's not the time off. You know that. It started with that sex story you turned in for the shame issue. There were questions from fact-check, some red flags in it. Next thing I hear, people are saying you've been working on that honor-kill survivor story for some other magazine, but using our name and resources, and now there's all this talk about fraud and—"

"Fraud?"

"Yeah. Best, it . . . it doesn't look good for you here. I think there was a meeting on twenty-eight with the lawyers today."

"Twenty-eight; that's Nik Steig's floor."

"Yeah. He's been in James's office too. It's just not looking good for you."

"What do you mean by that?"

"Best, I think they're going to fire you."

"Jesus. Is that coming from twenty-eight, from Nik Steig?

"I don't know. I don't think so. He has been kind of quiet about all of it. But when is Nik Steig *not* quiet about anything, right?"

I'm running through our last moments again, trying to slow it all down, look for signs. Nothing. Nik was as warm and sweet as he's always been. But you don't get to be the Wizard of Oz without a stony underbelly, without showing that the cutthroat begins with you. "Look, thanks for the warning shot, Trinity. I'm sorry I dragged you anywhere close to the middle of this."

"It's cool. I just wish there was something else I could do. Actually, I just wish you came to that meeting."

"Me too."

"When are you back?"

"That answer's shifting."

"I should go. This door should never be locked. Lawsuit waiting to happen."

"Yeah, those lactating mamas do not play."

Trinity attempts a laugh, but the poor thing limps through the phone, sounding more like a whimper or held-in sneeze. "I don't know how you're doing it. With all the stuff going on here and then all the *Tell Me More* stuff—I'd be hunched under a desk somewhere, just catatonic."

"What *Tell Me More* stuff? Was there another story?"

"Not yet. This reporter called me and I think Kristen too, maybe. He was basically ringing around the low end of the masthead looking for you. Guess he knows editorial assistants are the only dummies who still actually answer desk phones and—"

"He was looking for me or asking about me?"

"Looking for you. Said you were helping him with a story, which was—to be totally honest—kind of surprising after they posted all that shit about you and Grant King and this sup-posed baby bump. Thought you would have told them to go straight to hell."

"Yeah, I think that guy's already there, making these inces-sant calls."

Trinity chuckles. "Wait, what?"

"Nothing. I'm not helping with anything. If he calls you again, tell him . . . actually, don't tell him anything. You're not obligated to talk to him, like, at all. It's totally within your rights to hang up on him. Tell Kristen too; you don't have to tolerate that guy."

"Whoa. Is everything okay?"

"Not yet. It will be. Let me get through this interview and it will all be okay."

"I'm sorry this is happening, Best. I don't know what else to say."

"I guess, See you when I see you?"

"Okay, then . . . What you said."

I stay there, clutching the phone, watching its brightness fade and letting the pathetic symbolism of it settle in.

At this point, there is no point, so scrolling through the phone makes sense. It's clear that Bauer's going for a record this week. There are eleven (so far) missives from him, a healthy mix of voice mails, texts, and e-mails. In the three most recent notes, there is no message, but instead a handful of ALL CAPS phrases in the subject line.

YOU NEED TO CALL ME BACK!!
YOU'RE AVOIDING ME, THIS IS IMPORTANT
MAKE IT EASY ANSWER MY CALLS!!!

The texts are basically carbon copies of all his bellowing e-mails. As each new one pops up in the line, I trash it. Delete on repeat. It's so mechanical now.

And then I see it, lying there quiet and special, sandwiched between Bauer's heavy directives: an e-mail from Nik. My thumb hovers over the trash icon as a mini-panic sets in. What if Nik pulled the plug on this Fatima meet? Maybe he's calling to personally let me know how big I fucked things up and to throw down that hacky bad-movie line, assuring me that *you'll never work in this town again.* He could still be in the dark—intentionally. Like every other penis-free woman in this penis-focused industry, JK and the Robot want to appear ever-confident; decision-makers with grit and resolve who don't need to a man to step in and carry shit when things get unwieldy.

Or maybe he just wants to make sure I'm all right, talk through our weird parting and flesh it all out, like adults do. I'm really hoping it's the latter.

It's this last embarrassing wish that pushes me to listen to the message.

"Best, it's me." I can almost hear his quick nods through the phone. "Listen, when you get this, call me. Okay?" Nik's voice is smooth, pleasant. I think. Smooth and pleasant could also be detached and disappointed. I play the message again and three more times after that. I can't be sure until I'm sure.

CHAPTER 19

Ajax, Ontario

Nerves take over the instant I pull into the driveway. I don't remember anything about this morning, not my shower or the tea and toast or the drive over here from the hotel. Automated everything. It's the best I can do to avoid thinking about that call from Trinity. Jesus Christ. *Fraud*? And Nik's voice mail; I came up with about forty-seven different ways to read his tone. Actually, that's all I could think about last night. That is, until I decided to investigate the minibar. Dinner was so-called healthy $16 popcorn surrounded by mountains of plush pillows on the quicksand-like bed. I don't know when sleep came to me—it just did—and it was deep and heavy, like the kind that rinses the brain clean, fooling you into believing that you earned a fresh start the next day.

It feels like it's been an hour that I've been staring out at this tiny playground in the center of this large crescent. It's covered in snow, but I can make out the slide and poking out next to it, I see some painted-green steel. Monkey bars. Or is that not PC now—monkey bars? *Jungle gym* can't be much better. I'm stalling and it's too cold for this shit.

Before I ring the doorbell, I feel I should say a prayer or a
wish, a chant, something to will this to go the right way. But
whenever I've looked to a higher power for help in the past it
was useless. I can either continue staring at this frosted-over
play yard thinking about the many ways faith failed me or I can
ring this goddamn doorbell. My toes are frozen despite my
doubled-up wool-sock action. (I don't mess around. Fashion
never trumps function when windchill is involved.)

The door chimes out some muffled sonata. It kind of brushes
back my prickly edges a little. Tempted to ring it again.

A woman answers. She's pretty, but looks stern. There are
no smiles. Her long black hair is swept across her left shoulder
and she's wearing a plain, spotless green apron over a long
black skirt and gray turtleneck.

"Hi. I'm Best Lightburn. The reporter." I hand her my card.
Of course it's pink and ridiculous. It's *James* magazine. At least
the font is legit. Power and elegance. No curves or flower
bursts.

She takes the card and purses her lips as she reads it like it's
a search warrant.

"I know you've traveled a distance to come here," she says.
Her voice is even and low and there's a slight British lilt to her
words. "My husband has only good things to say about Will,
and he in turn said nice things about your friend in New York
City. But Fatima has been through utter torment. I don't think
this—"

"I'm sorry. I don't mean to interrupt, ma'am, and I apologize for disturbing you this morning on a weekend and all, but
I'm not from the papers or TV or anything. I'm a writer for
James magazine"—I glance at my card in her hand—"a
women's magazine in New York, and I think it's important,
crucial, for the millions of young women who read the magazine to hear from Fatima, to hear about her strength. Really,
I'm not here to gawk or prey on her. I know she's been through

the unthinkable. I don't want to add to that in any way. With all due respect, I just want to talk to her, hear from her. So, may I see her?"

The woman softens her gaze ever slightly, while keeping her eyes locked in on mine. I smile, also slightly, and hold my calm stance. In my head, there's shouting, throwing up invocations to God, Yahweh, Buddha, and whoever else might be watching this standoff.

"All right," she says after a few beats and offers me her right hand. "I'm Parveen Asad, Fatima's cousin. Please, come in."

She steps aside and gestures for me to enter. The gust of overhead heat in the foyer is strong, but feels good. Before she can close the door behind me, I'm taking off my boots. I haven't lost all of my Canadian habits, thankfully.

"This way, please," she says. Her steps are light, heedful. I follow her, trying to keep my movements slight as well.

Despite the large bay windows toward the front—and on such a bright, white morning—the house is dark. The hardwood floors, the area rugs, the half-drawn drapes, the paint, even the framed art sparsely hanging from the tall walls—it's all dusky. And the heat is on high throughout. It's hot and dark, like some well-appointed cave.

There are a lot of photos, professional ones, of what seems like family crowding the walls of one room. A large piano is in there too. I only glimpse a few of the photos as we glide by. Looks like sunnier times. I see smiles stretched across brown faces set against blurry watercolor backdrops. It's very Sears photo studio and it's familiar. We did the plastic photo session every year too, for Christmas.

As we get deeper into the house, I can hear talking, but it sounds like it's coming from a TV or radio: quick and animated in that *this is not real life* tone. Parveen takes a sharp turn and stops abruptly.

"Please, you'll wait here?"

I nod like a witless puppy, even take a few steps back from her.

Parveen cracks the door and slips through the slim space. She's not whispering, but talking in this low hum. The background burlesque is gone, turned off or muted, and a silence sets in. I feel scared and strange and near tears, choked up by the eerie quiet.

The door *click*s open. Parveen's head floats out. "Please," she says, and opens the door wide. The silence dissolves and a heavy thumping noise replaces it, getting louder by the second. It's my heart throbbing behind my eyes, in my throat and ears. This is the moment I've built, created out of scraps and thirst. There's definitely no going back now; that was clear months ago. This is my moment and I can't let it melt away. So why can't I move?

Parveen steps out to meet me. "Is everything all right, Miss Lightburn?"

My mouth is dry, so I just nod.

"Would you care for some tea?"

Nod.

"I'll make some for all of us. Please," she says again, gesturing to the open door, "allow me to introduce you to Fatima."

Parveen's voice is stronger now. It's practically pulling me toward the room.

"Of course," I say too loudly. Can't worry about modulation right now. I'm just surprised that a word found its way out. "Thank you, Pa—Mrs. Asad. That'd be great."

Eyes up. Connect. Common Ground. Control.

Fatima sits stuffed into the corner of a large wraparound couch. She is frail. Her face is long and faded, the color of unbaked bread. Everything about her—from the shrunken baseball cap barely covering her crude-cropped hair to the dirty pink slippers peeking out from under a patchy, stained blanket—it's all gnarled and dingy, like some long-forgotten sock discovered years later behind the dryer, rolled up in clumps of dust.

She smiles anyway. Her teeth are gray.

"Fatima, this is that magazine writer we discussed, Miss Best Lightburn," Parveen says. Her voice sounds more pleasant, kinder than just moments ago. I want to turn to Parveen, see if she's smiling too, but I can't take my eyes off of Fatima. I can't read her yet. Is she drug-loopy or lucid? The two news stories I've read about her recovery only talked about how fast and astounding it was—*miraculous* was the word they used. They also liked to say that she's a walking example of courage, most notably with her gut-wrenching testimony at her father's trial. The details, what she remembered, were heinous. It shattered even the slimmest chance of a not-guilty verdict. For the father, anyway. The brother worked out some deal early on that got him some bullshit lesser sentence. I never did wrap my head around him: a brother helping to end his own sisters' lives. He didn't even claim insanity. He just did it, he said, because his father told him to. A wave of virtue crashed into his zombie brain at the last minute, thank God, and he called 911 when he realized that Fatima was still alive. But he was the big brother. Instead of watching out for them, he did this. What brand of abomination is that?

"And, Miss Lightburn, this is my dear cousin Fatima Imam."

"Hi, Fatima." I move slowly to her, as if anything sudden will send her scurrying deeper into the couch cushions. "It's a pleasure to meet you. And thank you for agreeing to speak with me."

When I make it to the couch, I extend my hand, but she does nothing, not a flinch, not a blink. Before I can realize it, Parveen is standing next to me.

"My darling Fatima, I am about to make some tea for all of

us," Parveen says, and gently covers my hand with hers. She doesn't break eye contact with her cousin as she lowers my hand back down to my side again. "I'll bring a few kinds, so you can choose, all right?"

"You know my choice," Fatima says, slow and low.

Parveen taps my wrist and somehow I respond; I step back from the couch with her. "I will be in the other room, just beside this wall," Parveen says. She's looking at Fatima but there was no *darling* attached, so I know the message—a gentle warning—is meant for me.

There's a solo chair directly across from Fatima. It looks odd, borrowed from another room, possibly from another time, and it is backing the door. Figure it's mine.

Fatima's clocking me, each move my hands make as I unpack my things: notebook, pen, digi-recorder. It's not a curious thing. It's more suspicious.

"This is just a tiny recorder I like to use." I hold it up and offer it across the table. She's not disarmed. She doesn't budge, just more staring. "Anyway, it's easy. I touch this button on the side and it's on. I still take notes. It's a weird habit, more a distrust of technology, really. I get that from my father."

Fuck.

Fatima takes a deep breath. I can see the top of her tiny body rise.

Christ on high.

"It's okay," she says, her head down.

"Um, it's okay to start?"

"It's okay to say *father*."

"I'm sorry. Sometimes, when I'm nervous, I don't think it through and I say things, all the wrong things—I'm sorry."

"No apology. It's just a word."

"Right. Still, sorry."

Fatima raises her head to look at me. She's smiling, I think, but it's so vague and ailing I'm not sure. "Do you want to talk about him, your father?"

"What do you want me to say about him?"

"You don't have to talk about the trial or anything. That's in the papers, in the past. Maybe you could talk about what it was like living with him, before what happened. I mean, what was he like? Was he loving, gruff, funny?"

"He was just my father. And now he's not even that," Fatima says, leaning back on the chair's thick pillow. She's warmed up, eased up a little. Even the agitation in her eyes is clearing. I need to follow her lead.

"From what I understand, he was strict. Part religious dedication, part Middle Eastern ideology and socialization. But was all of that pressed into the walls at home or were there sweeter, more generous moments, pockets of warmth and graciousness from your father?"

Fatima's face is blank. No signs of a struggle to reach for memories from the very back of her mind and hold them up for me.

"Was yours?"

"My father?"

"Yes," Fatima says. "Was he warm, shy, generous?" She's not angry. Her voice is committed and she's not looking anywhere else but right at me.

"Uh, yeah, my father is those things: warm, always, and shy; used to be. He's a reporter, retired now. And he's a loving, nice man. He likes to cook and read about the news of the world and—I'm sorry, Fatima, this is not how it usually works, these interviews; I'm not supposed to be answering questions about my life. I'm not important to the story. This is about you, your life, your experience. I don't count. I shouldn't be anywhere in the story."

"Just curious."

"I know. It's okay. I'm curious too. Listen, do you want to just skip this part about your father for now, come back to it later?"

"No. I can say it now. I won't talk about him later."

"Well, let's go back a bit. What was it like for you growing up with a very religious father, with all the rules about what clothes you wear and the friends you can talk to and where you could go?"

Her eyes dart around the room before settling on the top edge of my notebook. "Can I change my answer?" she says.

"Sure, but you haven't really answered anything yet."

"Talk about him later"—quick whisper—"Cousin here."

Parveen backs into the room carrying a large tray. "The tea's here," she says. In each interaction with this woman, she grows more pleasant. However, Fatima's face hasn't really changed much at all since the first stale smile. Of course, Parveen notices her grim look the minute she spins around. I click my pen closed, slide it in the center of my notebook and close that too. It's only a matter of minutes before Parveen shows me the door, back to the cold driveway with a scowl and flinty *please*. It won't help, but I do it anyway; I hold my breath and wait for Parveen's reaction to unfold in full.

"Is everything all right in here?" Parveen says calmly and sets the tray down on the narrow coffee table. There are two cups, not three, and she's almost done filling the first one. I keep holding my breath, watching to see if she moves the teapot over to the second cup.

She does fill it, without a pause.

I watch the steam rise and let my breath go with it. "Oh, yes, ma'am. Everything is fine. We just started."

"Very well." Parveen looks to her cousin for confirmation,

maybe a nod, wink or some other secret signal that I'm telling the truth. "Do you need anything else, darling cousin? More covers?"

Fatima shakes her head. It's slow and uneven, and she's gazing at some fascinating spot on the wall behind me. I can't tell if this drunk-toddler thing is a side effect from her injuries or something that had been there long before her father and brother tried to kill her.

"Thanks again." I smile at Parveen. "This is great." *Now . . . please,* I want to say, with one of her servile hand gestures. I won't get anything good from Fatima this way. I won't get her to let down her quirky fences if this cousin stays perched at my shoulder.

"All right, I'll leave you to it," Parveen says after a weird, long lull, and shuffles backward to the door. "I'll just be in the kitchen, next to this wall."

The click of my pen is loud, almost like a snap of my finger, and Fatima's attention is back with me. "How about we start with you instead, your recovery. How are you feeling?"

"Different. Strange, most days, and tired."

"Why strange?"

"My sisters are dead and that's strange. It's strange and different that they are no longer here with us, with me."

"I'm sorry, Fatima. It's unimaginable, that level of sadness and loss."

"Aliyah would be nine right now. Her birthday, it was last month."

"Tell me more about her, Aliyah, and about your other sisters." I grimace a bit here, thinking about the big no-no I just committed. My father would have kissed his teeth hearing me go with *Tell me about.* "*Tell me about* is not a question," he always says. "It's a statement. It's limp and not specific. And the answers you hear back will be limp and not specific too." To my slight surprise, Fatima takes a breath to answer anyway. Rules will have to be set aside for this one—that's clear.

"My sisters, I miss them, each one and all of them together. I miss them."

"Are you physically in pain still?"

"I go to doctors. They check different things. But I don't really feel anything."

"Do you mean you feel numb?"

"Maybe. It's more a way for me to avoid getting overwhelmed."

"Overwhelmed by . . . guilt? About being the one who survived?"

Fatima sits up, arching closer to me. It doesn't feel angry, but who knows? She might be getting ready to throw that scalding tea in my face. She says nothing for a long, uncomfortable stretch. I start to reach for my recorder. A pause might be good here.

"The guilty ones have been given their sentences to serve."

"You mean your father, your brother?"

She nods.

"So what overwhelms you, then? What makes the numbness come?"

"The questions," she says, in her flat way. "There are a lot of questions coming from different directions. I don't really have any new answers. I've stopped looking for new answers. I wonder when everyone else will stop asking the same questions."

"Does it bother you that I'm asking you questions right now?"

"No. You're not really asking me anything," she says. Fatima sits back into the couch. "Your story, it's supposed to be about me as a survivor, my strength and courage or will to live or something, right?"

"Yes, exactly that. Being as young as you are, having to shoulder that kind of nightmare . . . I want to know about that experience. I want the readers to see into that, see your heart and what the burden of survival means."

Fatima slides the creased baseball hat off and rubs the top of her head. "That's what I'm saying." Her voice is loud now and as choppy as her jet-black hair. "Parts of my body are demolished: eardrum, bones, muscles, nerves. I've had tubes shoved everywhere. Dull pain, searing pain, it's all there still, two years later. It hurts and it's hard to do small, simple things most days. I'm surviving *that*. I'm living with it. But I'm not a survivor. My sisters died. I didn't. I'm not a survivor, I'm just lucky."

"Do you really believe that? You honestly think it's about *luck*?"

I can't even veil the outrage. This girl made it through poisoning and drowning alongside her three sisters and she's boiling it down to luck? Luck is for suckers. Fools who think that things remain floating in the air until some arbitrary combination of ingredients settles to the bottom of the jar and you wind up on this right side of chance. Fuck that. It's ludicrous and simply untrue.

Fatima is looking at me, probably because my face is screwed and streaked with irritation. Hers remains composed and cold. I'm trying to pull out the journalist, the third-person and scrape together some kind of integrity.

I'm failing.

"I'm sorry, Fatima, I find it shocking that you don't see yourself as a survivor. You don't see your strength driving through all of this. I mean, you were the last one drugged. Maybe that's where luck played its one small part, but everything else? That's all you. You were able to hold your breath long enough and, in the midst of that horror, have the genius idea to play dead. That is incredible and extraordinary and the definition of survival mode. You did that. You did. That's not luck. That's you."

"And my sisters, they welcomed death? They didn't fight it enough?"

"No. That's not what I meant. This isn't a judgment about your sisters. I'm saying that your story is inspiring and astounding, and it has nothing to do with being lucky."

Fatima reaches for her teacup. She moves slowly, deliberately, and her hands are trembling a little, rattling the cup against the saucer. I grab mine too, as if I'm thirsty at the exact same time she is, and try to blend in some clanking sounds of my own.

She sips and sips again. Her eyes go to the tray. Maybe she's thinking about what to say to me next. Maybe she's thinking about how to get the cup back on the saucer more steadily this time.

"There's a book I was reading before . . . It's called *Civilization and Its Discontents*. It's Freud, his theory that humans will fight for life, even involuntarily sometimes. Our bodies will just take over and fight the death, no matter what."

"That's heavy reading for a high-schooler."

She shrugs.

"But, Freud, didn't he also have a theory about a death drive too?" I say. "A death wish?"

"Yes, he goes into that in *Beyond the Pleasure Principle*," she says. "I read that too. The theory is that the goal in life is death. All self-destructive behavior we humans display is really our unconscious desire to die coming to the surface. The behavior is an expression of the death drive. Violence and aggression are really the death drive, or more the energy behind it, turned outward."

"So, if both of these theories are true, we're—what—fighting to die while fighting to live? How does that even make sense?"

"Jekyll and Hyde, I guess," Fatima says. She rubs the top of her head once more, but this time there's irritation there, impatience, and I don't know how much longer she'll entertain me.

"You seem tired. Do you want to take a break?"

I sound like Dr. Monfries, and Fatima is playing the role of Me like a true understudy. This whole scene—quoting scholarly books, the removed comportment, stray smirks—it could have been ripped straight from any session I had with him in those first years. Only instead of sitting in a dim den, we would be at Dr. Monfries's office in the mental health institute. On warmer days we left his office in the pavilion and walked the grounds, down by the sculpture garden. I liked when we did that, but I would never dare tell him so.

She's looking off to the side. I push for more. "Maybe we can bundle up and go over to that snowy playground out front. What do you think about that?"

"I haven't been outside in weeks," she says.

"And it's like shrivel-your-balls cold out there, so why venture—I get it."

Fatima chuckles. I'm talking a half a snort, thin smile, and actual noises rising up from her throat. I send a smile back, and for the first time since getting off that train I don't feel like this is a losing game. I've cracked through some kind of shell with her, and I'm going back in.

"I have an idea," I say and close my notebook with added drama. "Let's just talk. The recording is on, so let's just talk, about everything or nothing really or whatever you want to talk about."

Jesus. All we need now is a shabby tweed sports coat, pleated chinos, and a pair of thin, gold frames, and my transformation into Dr. Monfries will be complete.

"I don't really know what I want to talk about," she says. All grins are gone, the meager gains lost.

"Really? Just nothing—we sit here and wait for the walls to whisper?"

Fatima squints and cocks her head. "Waiting for walls to whisper. That's a weird thing to say."

"But so was bringing up shriveled balls, right?"

Her tamed grin returns. "True," she says.

"The balls thing is all me. I don't have balls, obviously, so it's funny to me when I use them as a point of reference. The wall-whisper bit, that's something my mother used to say whenever we complained about being bored. 'Well, go sit on the bed and wait for the walls to whisper to you.' And we actually did it those first few times. Waiting there on the edge of our beds with our ears pointed like hounds. Can't blame her fully, though. We could be kind of annoying when we were ready."

"We?"

"Yeah, me and my brothers," I say, caught-up and breathless.

"Do they still live at home, your brothers, with your parents?"

"No."

In the stillness I hear myself, everything I just said, echoing. I shake my head.

"We're not supposed to talk about you," Fatima says.

"No. We're not." I grab my notebook from the table between us, but with her eyes set on me so heavy, I feel like I've stiffed her on a promise and close the notebook again, tossing it to the floor on top of my slouching bag. "Not for this story. Maybe if we went out for a drink sometime. I could get into all my stories, exchange views on the fucking human condition." I smile, but she flinches. "Oh, pardon my language. It's just something this guy—a friend—says, and it stuck with me."

She pauses, wrinkling her brow as if truly considering my loose, undercooked offer for a drink "sometime." We both reach for our cooled tea.

"Do you drink alcohol, Fatima?" I say between gulps. "Is that something that got you in trouble at home?"

"I tried some—twice, in the summer. I didn't like it. Made me sweaty and dizzy."

"Did your father find out?"

She nods and looks down into her teacup.

"Were you punished, when he found out?"

"He tricked my sister," she says, speaking directly into the cup. "He told her no one would meet trouble. He said he needed to make sure I wasn't going to get a disease in my stomach. She was frightened of him, always. She didn't see it was a trap."

"What do you mean by *trap*?"

"He beat us both with her jump rope and tied us up—rough box string on her and an extension cord for me. We stayed like that past dinner through to the night. My sister, she was so scared—she vomited on herself, but he still kept us there by the furnace, chained up like beasts."

"Where were the others, your brother and sisters, when this was going on?"

"Upstairs with him, praying."

"Praying?"

"Praying for our forgiveness. We betrayed the creed, he said. We betrayed Islam. Betrayed our family, bringing shame on all of us."

"Jeez. Did that kind of thing happen a lot?"

"Yes—the punishment and the praying. He believed that we were doomed, us children. The more time we spent with non-Muslims only sealed our fates."

"So why not homeschool you all? Why bother introducing you to this country, its culture? I read that the move to Toronto was your mother's idea in the first place. Why stay after . . . well, after she passed?"

"My mother, bless her rest, was the one person who could speak to him plainly. Never with disrespect, but in this way that he'd listen. She wanted her children—especially her daughters—she wanted us to have education and opportunity. The things she wished for herself and, with his careful permission, was planning on getting."

"How was she planning on getting these things?"

"She took a drawing class. My mother was very talented like that—born with it. She longed to do more things, but the cancer came and took her first. He stayed, I think, because he didn't want to leave the memories of her here to get cold. And he also believed there was still work for him to do here."

"Like what? Run the town off its sure path to hell?"

"Not the town. His children."

"Did your father tell you that? That you were doomed, going straight to hell?"

"Nothing was more important to him than honor and family. He believed that here, we were turning out backs on both."

"What did you believe?"

Fatima keeps her eyes on mine, but says nothing for a long while, maybe sixty seconds of complete quiet. I notice a twitch, left side, just above her top lip and rippling up to the bottom of her nostril. The movements are tiny, but near constant. The silence allows me to zero in on the spasm.

"I believe that my father was a very scared man," she says. There are tears gathering at the base of her eyes, but we're in it and I can't break now.

"Scared of what?"

"Of everything. Of being here lonely, without his wife, trying to move along in a world too fast and foreign. He was scared of losing control of the life that he understood. Losing his children. Life here was like a bright light beaming on us, drawing us away from him daily. He didn't know how to fight against that light. He didn't know where to even stand in that light. Instead, he retreated into himself, afraid and unraveled and leaning on these wild, unbalanced ideas about what he needed to do in order to survive it."

"It almost sounds like you feel sorry for him. You're a thoughtful person—I mean, that's clear—but do you? Feel sorry for him?"

She pauses.

"Do you forgive him?"

Fatima pauses again, but this one isn't as heavy or long, and the twitch has all but disappeared. "I forgive the man who was my father," she says.

"What about the man who tried to kill you—do you feel sorry for him?"

"I don't know him," she says. "I don't feel anything for that man."

Now I'm the quiet one; not sure what to say next. I can't string anything together to articulate what's bubbling up in my gut: anger, confusion, sadness, pity. It's all there, when it shouldn't be. I want to grab Fatima by her bony shoulders and shake her, remind her of Aliyah, Hafeeza, Mariyah—Christ— even that corrupted brother Majid. How can she forgive all of that, forgive all of those lives snatched from being, so cruel and cold?

"I know what people think about Islam, about Muslim families like mine," Fatima says. She's sitting taller as she speaks, and the frowsy covers are off, piled up at her feet. "I know how the world sees us, but it's not like that, you know. There's honor in us, and goodness and decency. The truth is, a Muslim's faith rests in things like mercy, peace, and forgiveness. I chose to forgive so that I can be free of fear and suffering. I didn't want to be afraid like him. I didn't want to carry it around, shackled to my leg, like him. There's no guilt or terror or shame growing inside. I'm free."

I didn't feel them coming. They were just there, tears, sliding into the corners of my mouth. She's crying too, but her tears seem happy and light, and she looks relieved. We catch ourselves at about the same time and do that girl-giggle while patting the water away from our eyes with fingertips and backs of hands.

Fatima smiles at me. "Are you okay?"

I nod and smile back.

"Do you want to take a break?" she says, and drops her crushed hat back on top of her head. "I have an idea"—she grins—"we can go outside, to the playground. Who cares about the cold; we don't have balls, right?"

CHAPTER 20

I've written fast before, to meet a deadline, to spit out all the details on paper and clear my head of whatever this expert said or that study showed, so I can move on to something else, something more important and preferably not involving a vagina. I've stayed up stupid late to write before too, finish the term paper or type my way through a hangover. But I've never written like this. Furious, barely blinking, pausing only to briefly smooth away a relentless, thin streak of sweat from the nape of my neck. The sweat wasn't because of any heat, not the external kind. The hotel room was near freezing and I was wearing a bra and the complimentary, chintzy white-cotton bathrobe wrapped at my waist. This heat was coming from inside. It sounds like a cliché, I know, but it's the truth. I was burning up, a fire inside of me pushing its way out, blistering my fingertips, singeing everything in its path. This Fatima story was raging through me. I had to get it out, start to finish, and it had to happen immediately.

It started the minute I left Parveen's home. I was writing it in my head driving back to the hotel. It got so wild and crazed in there, it all jumbled together and basic skills like concentrating on the road and figuring which gear to shift into were pushed to the darkest back corners, beginning to leak through my ears. I had to pull over at the closest Tim Hortons and pour whatever I could into my notebook. I know how I looked to anyone walking by my car, crying and scribbling, shaking my head and nodding, but I didn't give a shit. *Go eat your dough-nut, lady, and leave me be.*

The way I asked the front-desk girl to check me back in, tossing my credit card at her like some spoiled mall rat. Just rude. She cursed at me under her breath, in French too. I heard it, but I didn't care about that either.

And let's not get into the other poor front-desk dude, who I berated into bringing the printed pages up to my room from the business center at two in the morning. You can't even call it a bark that I unleashed on him for—what I perceived as—having molasses in his ass. Yes, I actually said: *Is there molasses in your ass, guy?* I know. But I needed those pages like it was life or death, because it was, and it is. My job at *James,* my overall magazine career is hanging in the balance. I'm *thisclose* to re-deeming myself with Nik, JK, the Singh sisters, Robot, Susie, just everyone with this one story. Surely, had I a spare minute to explain myself to Mr. Slowy McSlowerson, he would under-stand what all the rudeness and bluster was about. (I did apol-ogize to the guy for the molasses thing, though, and for snatching the stapled stack from his pale hands too. When he returned with the second-edit printout, I gave him forty dol-lars, plus let him take a generous gander at my boobs each time, since I never bothered to pull the robe up. That peep show alone is *atonement* by definition. It's fine. He'll be fine.)

Reading my story over and over, the tears come each time, at the same line. I can hear Fatima's voice, explaining plainly how and why she's forgiven the man who once was her father. I see her, with her fucked-up hairdo and concaved upper body melding with that droopy couch. She's somehow pushed her hand through my gut, squeezing my insides and twisting in a way that will leave marks. I can't shake her, and really, I don't want to.

I know Nik will love this story. I do, I know it. But he thinks I've gone rogue, a crook committing one of the top three crimes against journalistic integrity. There's plagiarism and fabrication, and then there's me, rounding things out with mis-representation—which I still think is wildly inaccurate.

He will love this story and he will champion it, get it into the best open space for it to shine. Definitely not in *James*. They're too fool for school. No, it's got to be a more legit pub, one that is all about the big, ambitious deep-dive.

I attach the polished document to the e-mail and start typing, quickly pounding on the keys before I have a chance to talk myself away from the narrow side of this burning bridge.

To: Nik Steig
From: Best Lightburn me@bestlightburn.com
Subject: BL_Filing: "Forgiving Dr. Jekyll, Forgetting Mr. Hyde"

_____

Dear Nik,
I know I have much to explain. And I will.

You believed in me before. Please grant me an extension on that and read the attached Fatima Imam story. This was all possible because of you, because of your kindness and trust. I haven't wasted any of it. I can't thank you enough for all of your generosity. Know that I will make it make sense, if you let me.
Always,
B.

I'm open. The thin film that's been resting on top of everything is gone. I need to keep this going. Another e-mail.

I include my mother in the salutation, even though I know she won't ever see it. I was supposed to be back at their house already, and running out—literally—the way I did wasn't a good look. They're both worried. I can feel it. At this time in the morning, my dad is already up reading his international papers and newswires. I keep it brief, skipping limp apologies, sticking to facts instead:

> There was a delay with the assignment. All clear now. I'm at a small hotel near Mississauga. Home on the early AM train tomorrow. Grabbing cab. Please don't worry about it. Don't worry about me either.
>
> Good news: A) Story filed, B) Bringing guava jelly from Nick's Bakery with me.
>
> Always,
> B.

The minute I hit *send*, her name rings in my head like a bell. If anyone would offer a sympathetic ear right now, it would be her. My office mom—former, anyway. And if things crash and burn with Millhause-Steig, she'll probably have a couple leads for me too.

I start tapping away at yet another e-mail.

> Susie!
> Yes, it's me Best, coming at you from my personal e-mail account (so you know something's kinda up, right?). I've been meaning to get back to you, but it's been . . . uh, the same at the mag, which you know means it's border-

line batshit over there. Plus, there's the added "I think I'm already fired" bit topping the deep-dish crap pie like the worst whipped cream ever made. I'll have to fill you in on the details on *all of that* in person at a bar. I'm actually in Toronto right now . . . in a faux boutique hotel . . . wearing half a flimsy bathrobe . . . while writing the story of my career. So there's that.

Anyway, let's catch up soonest. I'm sure you're out doing something fabulous in a city with big lights adding more bright stories to your already brilliant life. Happy, Merry, Joy!

B.

Before I could blink away more sleep, I hear the soft chime. The flickering in my heart stops when I see the reply is from Susie. I feel silly that I actually thought for a half-second that it was Nik writing me back, telling me he still believes in me and that my story ironed out all the knots between us and that it was okay to come home again. I know. It's like: *Get some sleep, Lightburn; your dreams are seeping out.*

To: me@bestlightburn.com
From: Susie
Subject: WHAAATTTT???!!!!

*WHAT IN THE HOT HELL IS GOING ON?? Forget the bar,
I'm calling you now. Up with the dogs. Answer your
phone!*
SDW

I turn on my cell and put it back on the desk faceup. I'm ready to talk to Susie. The rest of the world can keep waiting.

CHAPTER 21

Montreal

My mother doesn't like driving. She's been riding shotgun in every car for the last seventeen years. She doesn't like waiting. Be on time or be left behind, that's one of her top three rules of life. From all that I've gathered, my mother barely likes me. Her ovaries force her to tolerate me. So walking out of the train station and seeing her sitting there in the driver's seat of my dad's car waiting, I'm immediately worried.

"Mum? Are you all right? Where's Dad?"

She waits for me to close the car door before she loosens her grip on the steering wheel and looks over at me.

"I'm glad you reach home safe," she says. Her voice, like her face, is bare. I wait a beat for her to say something more.

Nothing.

I quickly scan her torso, buttoned up tight in her oversized wool coat, searching for a hint, for any clue about the strangeness of her being here with me alone. But even her body language is mute.

"Is everything okay?" I nod, trying to coax her into doing the same.

"I don't want you to panic," she says. "I have a lot of information to say at once, but if you panic, you won't hear anything."

"Mum, please, just tell me. You're driving and you're here to get me. Panic is already with us. Just say it. Where's Dad?"

"In the hospital. Montreal General."

"What? Oh my God! What happened—is he—"

"Please don't start panicking."

I'm already crying. It's too late. She knows that. "Just say it, Mum." My breathing is choppy. "Is he gone?"

My mother rushes to touch my arm. Her hand is gloved in black leather and the sleeve of my coat is thick, but I feel it: warmth.

"Oh, no, no. He's not. Thanks be to Jesus. He's not," she says, gently patting my arm. "He's stable, but the situation is grave. It's his liver. All the drink . . . it caught up. There was bleeding in the esophagus. He passed out yesterday evening and got rushed in by ambulance."

"Jesus Christ"—she stops patting me—"I'm sorry; I'm upset, Mum. I'm sorry."

"It's taken me a good while to get here this morning," she says. "Would you be all right to drive instead?"

"Yeah, yeah, I can drive. I can do it." My nose is running and I'm sniffling and gasping like a sick baby as I move to open the door. I feel my mother's grasp again.

"Here." She hands me a handkerchief. It's white and starch-pressed into a perfect square. I recognize it, the baby-blue swirls of the calligraphy monogram running off toward the bottom right corner. It was Bryant's. We all had our own handkerchiefs in our own assigned "signature" color. Benjamin's is forest green, and mine, red.

I take it from her, but can't make myself rub snot in it, and instead use my sleeve when I walk around the back of the car to the driver's side. She went around the front and we meet back inside in our swapped seats.

"Here," I say, and push the folded white napkin into her yawning coat pocket. "Thanks, but I didn't need it." My breathing starts to steady itself and I adjust the mirrors, strap in, and turn the heat down a little. "I'm not all the way clear on how to get there from here. Can you navigate me, if I start struggling?"

"Of course I will," she says.

I watch her for a handful of seconds—her head is already swiveling, checking my blind spots, clutching her seat belt—and I wish she would reach for my arm again and hold me like that for the rest of the drive.

———— ◦ ————

There's a very distinct, disturbing smell that typically wafts through the air of North American hospitals. It crawls into your nostrils, digs into your sinuses, and settles in the minute your foot exits the elevator. Taking the stairs is no way to escape it, either. The stench is stuck to the brick and plaster walls, soaked into the resin flooring. Honestly, if you can get out of life without once ever having to inhale the funky cocktail of sick, sadness, and disinfectant, then you've won.

Aside from the extra-short, older black nurse who greeted my mother by first name and told her she's saying a prayer for us all, we get to my father's room quickly and with no interaction or detours. He's awake, reclined to less than 45 degrees, and looking over at the neighboring empty bed. Except for his swollen belly protruding through the sheets, he's so very thin. He looks exposed and frail, like a bug caught without its hard shell. I don't want to cry, but have nothing else to offer.

"Go on in. He's up," my mother says—another soft touch, this time to the top of my back. "He knows I went for you. He's there waitin'."

I rush in to him, throw my arm wildly around his neck and shoulder and squeeze. It's not until I feel his weak tapping that I realize this hearty hug is not only unusual for us, but also possibly too much for him right now. I peel myself off and make sure to look him in his eyes, bleary as they are, because I want to see him and I want him to see me. With my hand still resting somewhere near his heart, I smile down at him. He attempts one too, but his lips are dry and cracked, especially the bottom one, and it comes across like a grimace.

"Daddy, are you . . . okay?"

He blinks but takes a long while before opening his eyes again, and gives me a light nod. "It's my liver," he says. It sounds like he's gargling small stones.

"Yes, Mum told me," I say, cutting him off so he doesn't have to drag more words through the sandpaper in his throat. "She told me about the bleeding and the ambulance. I'm sorry, Dad. I wish I was here when it happened." My tears are back once again. I let them race down my face, free at last. Miles flashes into my mind. What would he say about this, this brand of the human condition? It's not fair. My father is a good man. He doesn't deserve this; he's already suffered enough for twelve men. I shove my hand into my pocket for my coins and my heart is no longer beating out of my chest.

My father inches his hand toward me and drums two fingers—the most agile ones—on the side of the bed. My mother steps out of the corner where she sat too quietly, as if called by way of the Morse code of my father's finger patter. He turns his head slowly to look at her and she nods. I don't understand what's happening despite my front-row seat to this weird show.

My mother hustles over to the door and closes it. And she's back by his side in a blink, raising his bed slightly, while I stand here confused. She's moving so quickly.

"Your father wanted to talk to you," she says. He taps the

bed with his full hand and winces. "And me too. Me and your father, we both want to talk to you about the plan for tomorrow."

"Wait, tomorrow?"

"Yes, the memorial for your brothers."

She says this as if she's reminding me of something simple and everyday, like I forgot that the recycling goes out tomorrow.

"Wait, I don't understand."

"Your father and I were talking, before he took sick, and he said instead of having you go to come back in a few weeks, we would just do the ceremony tomorrow. That's what we were planning."

"How are you planning anything when he's in the hospital? You're in the hospital, Dad. You're in the hospital barely able to talk, with a bleeding liver."

"My liver ain't bleeding," he croaks.

"Whatever . . . just look at you. This is serious. You're barely listed as stable. I know it's ten years, and that is . . . well, it's ten years, but you're really sick. Mum, you're a nurse. Back me up. You know what this means. His liver is basically a lump of coal. He'll be lucky if he gets out of here by New Year's. You know this."

"Bathsheba, let your mother finish, please," he says.

"No, I'm not being rude, Dad, I'm being realistic. We can do everything at the cemetery as usual, later, after you get out of here and have some strength back. That's all I'm saying. Maybe it's just us this time, private, we can tell the others that you're recovering from this and it'll only be us. And if you're still not better when the time comes, we have our ceremony here in the room. Or we can ask about wheeling you into the chapel."

"Bathsheba," my mother says, and nothing else. She lets her eyes rest on me. It's kind, her gaze, and there's more softness and affection living inside her saying my name right now than in all of the compact exchanges we've had over the last nine months.

I'm trembling and lean on the bed to stop the shiver in my knees. My mother is fixed on me. I don't know where else to look but back at her.

"Mum, you know it. You see it"—I shake my head, whimpering—"You see it. He's really sick. He can't—"

"He's all right," she says. "It's nothing fatal, but it is nothing light, either. He knew it was bad before the bleeding ever started. The doctor says it might be cirrhosis, but they want to rule out cancer." She takes a few slow, measured steps away from my father's side, moving around the bed toward me. "But we wanted to talk to you about tomorrow, even before this happened to your father, before you left for your work trip." More steps. "We want to go back there this time. For the ceremony, we want to go back to the water, to the ice."

"No. No! I can't do that. You can't ask me to do that. I can't go back there, Mum. Dad. I can't. I'm not doing that."

My father's gray face droops even further. He's sweaty and slimy and looks like he's about to pass out any second now. "You need to," he says from the pit of his stomach. "We all do, or we gonna be stuck like this forever."

"We got to go back there," my mother says, as she continues slinking her way to me, determined. "It's ten years we've been carrying them. It's time to let them go, let those brave, sweet boys rest in the Lord's peace." She takes her final few steps and is standing next to me, close enough that I hear her heavy breath. "Your behavior is not your character. You can let go too."

The second her arm settles around my shoulder it sends a jolt everywhere and I shrug her off.

"You don't get it. You don't know what it's like. I can't go back there." I'm shouting and sobbing and can't do a damn thing about it. "I can't do this . . . I need some air."

My mother steps in my path, like she used to when I was younger and about to do something stupid. "This is not nature, a parent living beyond their child," she says. "But what you're doing isn't right either."

I push past her, just as I used to back then too, and head for the door.

"Don't run," I hear him say, but I'm already gone.

Like your average coward, I kept running. I got my bag from the car and left the car key at the front lobby with a blond woman at the circle desk. I added a note for my mother and took a cab back to the house. I was about to grab the rest of my things and bounce, when a drop of good sense—as Mum likes to say—landed on me. Decided to stay here, at least through tomorrow. It's time I face them, get clean with them before I leave for real, and for good. I can't keep coming back here. Not like this. And my poor parents, with their cracked-open hearts, they've suffered enough for nine lifetimes. They don't need me ringing these horrible bells in their ears.

They want to know what happened that night. Jesus, they already know. They have to know. My father is a crime reporter, a really good one. They probably just want to hear me say it. And I should, I should say it, even though I've never told anyone. Dr. Monfries brought me to the edge of it once, but that was back when I was conflicted about leaving Montreal for university. I thought that coming clean with Dr. Monfries might somehow help me close the door on all of it, leave it in my dust. But there's no shirking that kind of thing. It follows you everywhere. It lives with you, in your dreams, in your quiet corners. It's part of you. Then you look up one day and it's swallowed you up, it becomes all of you.

I've known for a while that I'm an animal; a scared, feral animal. And everything that's happening to me, I deserve it. I really do. Chickens coming home, karma playing the bitch, whatever you want to call it, it's justified. I think I'm ready for it.

Fatima's been on my mind, obviously, but I've also been thinking a lot about Lana today, on the train ride here. Wondering about her state of mind at the end, when she made the decision to leave. Was she relieved? Did she think that all the ugly and horrible would finally be gone? She'd be free, like Fatima is now.

I used to think about checking out like Lana did. But those thoughts only popped up in the very beginning. I couldn't bring that kind of pain to my parents. Soon I was okay with waking up the next day and the next one after that. The pills went back to their respective bottles and uses. Dr. Monfries called it progress. I called it acceptance: This was who I was, who I am. And I do things like step on my sinking brother's back and neck, claw into his bloated arm, into the side of his face, kick in his jaw and head so that I can drag my own body out of the raw ice to save myself. I can look into his eyes, filling with blood and fear, and not instantly reach for him, grab him, pull him up, get him out too. Instead, I roll to my broken side and watch his stiffening trunk—his soaked, slack leather arm first, his lopsided shoulders next, and his neck, face, top of his head—dip under and be gone.

I saw it and did nothing. When they came in their thick, dark parkas with neon stripes and badges and white faces and they saw what was left—me sprawled out, half-naked and in shock—I told them nothing. *I don't know how. I can't remember. I don't know.* They stopped asking and just called me lucky. Lucky to be the last one in. Lucky to be a girl. Lucky to weigh under 45 kilograms. Lucky to be wearing thin, light clothing. And my parents, they were lucky to not lose all three. They had a survivor, a lucky, brave survivor, and for that they should be grateful.

It was all luck. It saved me from drowning in that frozen pit. But now, it's run out. All of that glowing, special golden luck— it's gone. I need to face the unpleasant payback that's been accruing over the years. And this is it. Right now. It's Nik and the Fatima story, the Robot, JK, Kendra, and Lindee hating me, the magazine, the fraud, the grasping, the selfish everything. This is what I'm owed. It's time I stand still, no running, and accept it.

CHAPTER 22

Mum slept at the hospital. I knew this only because when I arrived, she was still slouched on the cheap leather chair-bed in my father's room, wearing yesterday's crinkled clothes, asleep. He was resting too. His eyes were closed, head tilted back and mouth ajar. His machines were awake, though, chirping and clicking along while the scent of sickness filled every corner of the room.

It's creepy, watching them like this from the edge of the door, but if anyone in this family deserves some sleep, it's these two. I knew it wasn't going to happen for me, so last night I just stayed up watching old episodes of ER—of all things. They had been airing a straight run of the entire series, from pilot to finale, 331 episodes, which started last month. I tuned in at the top of season 6, but shut it all down after watching one of the most haunting episodes: a yet-to-be-diagnosed schizo-phrenic patient, in the midst of a psychotic break, stabs two hospital workers. Two young, beloved physicians, on Valen-tine's Day, no less. The last scene is a disturbing overhead shot of med student Lucy Knight and Dr. John Carter lying in deep red pools of their own blood on the floor of an exam room, looking at each from under a hospital bed, unable to move, un-able to call for help because the rest of the ER staff is having a

Valentine's Day party with music, goodness, and laughter. Even watching with a throw covering my head and barely able to see the TV screen properly, it was still too much for me. I retreated to my dad's office—with the blanket still draped over me—looking for a visual palate cleanser. He always has interesting books and old international newspapers, and is incapable of tossing anything away. I didn't want to disturb his stuff too much, because he'll know. Yes, it looks like a file cabinet exploded in here, but the man will know if that specific piece of paper dangling from the windowsill actually belongs on the floor next to the shelf. There's a definite system to his mess madness.

The cracked snow globe was still sitting slanted on his desk. I picked it up, nice and easy, trying hard not to shake its remaining white flecks around. That's when it clicked. I remembered where he got the thing. It was a souvenir from a work trip he took to Niagara Falls. It was for Bryant. Benjamin and I got other things; fleeting, flimsy things that slipped from our attention as easily as they've slipped my memory now. The snow globe was actually a thin veil of an apology for what happened with Mother and Bryant while he was gone. My parents ran that house on a straight line. Pity the fool who decided to come in with some sideways bullshit. They never beat us, but the threat was real, like a third rail. My father had this broad white-and-brown belt—I'm sure it still lives in a box somewhere. The thing was wide and breathing hot disco-ugly. It stayed in the back of their bedroom closet on a failed belt-hanger contraption. My father never pulled it out or used it, but we all knew that he was fully capable of doing both. Ben showed me the belt when I was six, like it was a ghost story. All quiet and tiptoeing and spooky whispers.

I don't think my father ever mentioned the belt, but it became the star of most of my mother's threats during this stretch when Dad was pulled deep into this spate of gruesome home invasions in Westmount. He would stay out late, working. It's what sent him off to Niagara Falls, if I remember it right. I was eight or freshly nine. Ben was eleven and Bryant was ten. We were mini-terrorists, constantly pushing Mum's buttons, testing the clear boundaries. Mum took the belt out every other week, waving it around while growling warnings at us. Once she rushed at me with it. I said some smart shit about not being allowed to go to a sleepover or some other simple preteen right revoked. My mother did not tolerate *lip from children*. Being mouthy and staring up in her face when she was setting us straight about bad behavior, that was the height of disrespect in her book.

I think I said it was unfair or that she had us locked up in the house like animals or something equally dramatic, and that's when she came at me with the belt. She would have gotten me good too, but Ben being Ben, he threw his body over mine. It shocked her, put a stutter in her step, and when she drew her arm back to reverse the sure cruelty coming toward me, the belt slipped from her hand. The heavy metal buckle landed to the top of Bryant's head, cutting it wide open. He had been coming up behind her, about to lunge for her arm. That's what he told Ben and me after he got back from the hospital. We were both rather impressed with his action-hero plan—such a departure for that peaceful kid. Seven stiches and a ludicrous cover story about falling out a tree: those were Bryant's takeaways from the bloody ordeal. But Ben and I knew he was proud of the whole thing, in his quiet way. My mother never so much as raised her voice at any of us after that. Cool and deadly. That became her way and it was truly effective.

As I slid the globe back into its teetering spot, I saw that folder again, but this time it was open and the papers are fully exposed. Death certificates—Benjamin and Bryant's—and beneath them, a short stack of photocopies: the coroner's reports, their files from our old pediatrician, studies from medical journals on hypothermia, a piece from the *International Journal of Aquatic Research and Education* called "Drowning Survival in Icy Water," magazine stories and newspaper clippings on how people have survived a fall through the ice, plus pages and pages of his scrappy, handwritten notes torn from a yellow legal pad. I couldn't read anything clearly, but I did recognize my name as well as my brothers' names and the name of the horrible lake. There were also loads of numbers, data: times, temperatures, and weight stats.

And another click, this one more like a punch to the gut: It's me. My father was investigating me, trying to crack the case of the girl who watched her brothers die.

I fell back against the chair, knocking the snow globe from its perch. I heard the heavy *thud* against the matted carpet along with the swish of papers drifting to the floor behind it. I sat there in his chair, sickened and still, replaying that scene from *ER* over in my mind: Lucy and Carter splayed on the cold tile, locked in on each other's petrified eyes. No one reaches out. No one screams. They can only let what's happening, happen. I finally got up from the squeaky swivel chair and spread the throw on the carpet by its wheels and waited there for someone to come find me.

CHAPTER 23

My mother started to stir first. She slept through two different nurses sidling up to my father's side to check this pouch and that pump keeping him metabolized and functioning. When the third one came, she sat up straight in the chair as if startled out of a bad dream. If only it were that simple.

The nurse—she said to call her Ellie—apologized to my mother for waking her. That's when Mum noticed me sitting in the corner skimming one of her daily meditation books. It wasn't for show; I was legit looking through it.

"Oh, how long have you been there?" Mum said in a whisper.

"Not too long. I didn't want to wake you."

"Yes, I didn't realize I was so tired. I didn't mean to stay here last night."

"You were wiped out, Mrs. Lightburn," Ellie said. "The ward nurse told everyone to leave you be. I just wish there was a better place for you to sleep than in those awful chairs."

Ellie was quite plump and waddled around the room. With each step there was a symphony of sounds coming from different parts of her: a squish from her white shoes; a light wheezing from her nose and heavy breath; a hissing *shoosh* from her stockings and pants rubbing together. She was pleasant and so gentle with my father, like when she caressed the side of his face and shoulder to wake him up for a vitals check. And every time she caught my eye, she'd wink at me.

"I'm gonna be out of your hair in just a minute, Mr. Lightburn. Then I'll let you get back to your lovely family here."

My father nodded and tried to orient himself in this new reality.

"Helen, the overnight nurse, she mentioned your two sons. Are they coming by later?" Ellie said, her voice high-pitched and sweet.

We all stayed quiet, not even blinking, as if someone told us to make like statues. Ellie sensed that she had plucked at something raw and sore. It was obvious by the shift in the room. Ellie folded up her smile, tucking it under her chin in an instant. "Let me get out of your hair, sir," she said through clenched teeth and quickened her steps. Her face was flushed and the *whoosh*ing sounds from her pantyhose picked up the tempo. I felt bad for Ellie. When she finds out from the other veteran nurses—the ones who knew the Lightburns before and now, after—how inelegant the simple question was, she's going to feel horrible. I even predict tears from Ellie because of it. She's still the sweetest.

I decide to jump right into the rigid silence, not let it settle in.

"Are you feeling a little better today, Dad?"

He nods and props his lips up into a drowsy grin.

"And you, Mum, did the rest help?"

"Yeah, you could say so."

They're both looking at me with strange, incredulous expressions on their faces, bordering on scared.

"I was thinking, maybe we should do a little ceremony here, just the three of us. If your doctors say it's okay."

Mum stands up ramrod-straight. She's awake, her eyes bulging and watery. She's flustered in a way I've never witnessed.

"I—I—I don't have my prayer book nor nothin' so," she sputters, waving her hands around.

"It's okay. I brought it for you, Mum. It's in my bag, along with some other things for us, from home." I look over at my dad, nodding. "This is going to help us, just like you said."

When I hand my mother her worn book, she doesn't look up at me, but I see her chin trembling, her lips pulled tight. It's all on the surface, but she doesn't want to let it out. Not yet.

I move over to my father and place the folder with all of the notes and evidence at the foot of his bed. His face crumbles. A scratchy seal-like bark falls out of his mouth as he sobs quietly in his stiff bed. I touch his foot and then his knee and last his shoulder. I'm looking at him through our tears, keeping my face as pleasant and open as possible. "It's okay, Dad. It's okay. I'm ready."

My mother always starts these ceremonies with a long prayer. She's been able to make it through it without breaking down these last three or four years.

"Mum, are you ready to begin?" She looks at the room door that was quietly closed without her noticing. "It's okay. I spoke to the ward nurse, Phyllis, already. She knows to leave us alone for a short while. It's just us. It's okay, Mum."

Her prayer is short this time. She's overcome and can't finish. Saying their names is a struggle and she keeps pausing to wipe away the wetness from the pages in her thick book. She fills these spaces with a *Jesus, Jesus, Father God, Praise Him* singsong refrain. I feel my stomach lurch watching her; it physically hurts. So protective of her little birds. My mother was the only one allowed to speak a single sour word about any of her kids. All of our teachers and coaches and friends' parents knew not to mess around with the Lightburn children. Each one of us born "by the grace of God," she said, fighting our way through fibroids, preeclampsia and prolapsed umbilical cords, nothing was going to happen to us once we took that first breath. Not an arrow or sling, no harm, no scorn would ever come, she liked to say. Not while she was taking in the same air. But that's what broke her. She wasn't able to keep her birds afloat that night, and it broke her.

Toward the end of her prayer, she reaches out to me by the bed and clasps my hand. No gloves. No stiffness or apprehension. I'm so distracted by this that I miss the part where I'm supposed to say *Amen*. She continues to hold on to me, standing close enough that a few of her stray tears land on my sleeve.

My father goes next, as always. He reads a poem by heart from Derek Walcott. It's his favorite poet from a long-ago lost life, before children, before deadlines, before mortgages, when he still cradled this dream of being a writer of plays and prose and believed it could one day be real. The poem is called "Love After Love," and when he read it to us that first time four years ago, I thought maybe he misunderstood it, read it through a cloudy lens. It's about a breakup, I told him in an e-mail the following summer (I couldn't bear tell him to his face after he shared it at the memorial).

"Dad, I think it's more about learning to love yourself again after the love of another goes away."

"Yes, that could be true. But how is that any different than what's happened here?" he replied in an e-mail several weeks later.

I had no answer for him.

The poem became one of my favorites too. And though I've written it across my own heart, hearing my father recite it every year since makes me feel like it's brand new each time.

My father's voice is low and pained, but he gets through the whole thing, stopping when needed.

For my turn, I pull out my special gold coins and lay them out at the foot of the bed on top of the folder. I don't want to let go of my mother's hand, but I need to—I need my fists clenched and arms folded against my chest to do this.

"Dad, I know you have questions about what happened, how it happened. But this story starts before all of that. These coins, it's the best place to begin. We each had pockets full of them, all three of us, just cheap tokens that we used to play games at the ice fair. We spent nearly all of them trying to win crappy stuffed snowmen and reindeer and junky plastic toys that we knew we had no uses for." My father chuckled at that, and asked to hold one of the coins in his hand. But Mum just stared through me with fierce sorrow in her eyes. "There were rides. Benjamin and I went on a couple, but Bryant just wanted to go. There was a constellation, a star that he said he couldn't miss. He went on about it, bugging us to leave. We surrendered, finally, and left. One of them gave me their leftover coins as we started out of the gate." My father's bent and spindly fingers wrap around the coin he's holding and places it up by his chest. He's moving his dry lips; it's slight and quick as if reciting an incantation, a plaintive chant to face what he knows is coming next.

I've paused here, trying to reclaim my resolve. But watching him cling to the coin sets an ache in my bones. My mother's face is plastered with torment. I don't know if I can look over at her any longer. The snot and salt from my tears appear without notice and slide into my mouth—the taste of it is so heavy, so nauseating, I want to stop talking, stop breathing and moving, stop all of this for all of us. I've changed my mind. Nothing will be mended from this.

"Please," my father says, and I know that he's begging me to continue, not stop. He wants to hear it and maybe my mother does too. Everything in my body is screaming for me to run, run fast and far from this, and spare these good people. Leave them with the coins and whatever's left of their shredded souls.

But he says it once more: "Please."

Digging my fingers deep into the palm of my tight fists, I stay where I'm standing and force the next piece out. "Bryant told us about the shortcut. We didn't know it was ice. We didn't know."

I see Bryant in a flash—his backpack first, then his coat, and finally the back of his head. It's dark all around us except for some faint brightness shining down from above: stars joined up to create a nightlight for us. Bryant, he's so sure, confident as he leads his siblings home—I could tell from his stride. He's practically marching out on that cold, slick earth, not once looking back at Benjamin or me. I need to push this vision from my mind in order to keep talking. But shaking my head isn't working. The scene continues to play in my brain, only sharper than any time before, even clearer than in real life. I can see the very stitching in Bryant's bag now, the curl pattern of his precision-cut hair peeking out from the bottom of the dark gray toque on his head, the grooves of his thick soles on his boots as he takes each step. I just can't see his face. I never saw his face.

The lurch in my stomach is violent now. I squeeze my fists even more until the pinch of it starts to sting. I'm sure there's blood. The neckline of my sweater is wet. I have long stopped wiping away the sludge of tears and mucous gathering there. And all I can hear is my mother's breathing. It's dense and uneven and growing louder.

With my eyes squeezed shut, I start again. My voice is raised—I need to be louder than that breathing. I can't listen to her breathing. "Bryant was out ahead of us, looking up to the black skies. He didn't hear it, the thunder beneath our feet. He didn't hear it." I focus on the other gold coins, the leftovers resting on the bed, and try to make it replace the vision playing out in my head. "He was gone before I could blink."

Mum leans forward on the bed as if the strings that were holding her up had been cut. They're not ready for this. Looking at them, their crumpled faces, I want to end the torture, spare them the wet gore of it and just tell them a plainer truth instead: The daughter they knew, the one that they still hold space for in their dilapidated hearts, does not exist. She died along with their other children that sad night, and in her place a brute was born. That's the thing that stands before them now.

Both of my parents look destroyed, but my father's soggy eyes continue to plead with me to keep going, keep dragging them through the shards of this dreadful story. I promised myself that no matter what I wouldn't run, that I would stand and receive everything that comes from this. So I take another breath—it's shaky and pinched—but it helps me get to the next part.

"Benjamin, he was weighed down by something. His jacket, I think. He was trying to escape it. He flailed and grabbed at the broken pieces of ice around him, but that only crushed them even more. His teeth were chattering; mine too—it was so cold. It felt like angry, frozen fangs digging into our thickest parts." I'm still fixated on the gold coins. It's the only way I can pull the words from my grinding teeth. "Somehow he thrashed enough to get close to me . . . reach for me. But it was too much weight. He was too heavy and his reaching turned into pulling, dragging. He was dragging me under with him. I couldn't breathe or think or see and something in me took over. I started clawing at whatever was solid, whatever my hands could find. And then I felt something clawing at me. It was him—my neck and my head, he was just pulling and grabbing. He was dragging me under. I had to. I had to get out." I hear my voice loud in my ears. But it's muffled, as if I'm under water—again. My father has dragged himself up from the bed. My eyes are blurred-out, but I can still see him: he's practically crawling toward me at the end of the bed. I step back and hold my palm up between us. He needs to let me finish this. "I had to, Dad. I had to get out. And before I could even realize it, I was stomping on him, climbing and kicking and scrambling to break free. And then he was gone. He was too heavy. He was dragging me in. He was too strong and I watched him drop beneath the frozen boundaries, no floundering or fighting, just gone."

My father, through tears, tries to reach for my open hand. He's mumbling soft words about forgiveness. "You didn't know," he says. "You couldn't know." All the warmth and soothe have evaporated and a thick smog of sorrow drifts up around us. He stretches out his feeble arm and connects with me, pulling me closer to him by my wrist. I give in and let myself lean into his wobbly embrace. "You didn't know," he whispers into my forehead.

What I know is, I don't want to hear that. Just like I don't want to hear that I'm lucky to be alive. I don't feel lucky or spared, only ruthless. I try to tell them this, but Dad interrupts again, assuring me that Benjamin knew that I never meant him harm, that I was delirious and doing what anyone would do: clutch at life as it was being violently dragged away.

I nod and let him carry that line for as long as he can, as long as his quivering voice will allow. Mum is sobbing now, hunched over; her fingers are pressed deep into the blanket on the bed. Part of me feels like this was a mistake, upsetting this sick man and his shattered wife. It was enough for them to just honor their two sons, ten years gone. This pushed them too far.

But then a different thought springs forth, a forceful one that makes me immediately see the finer point in all of this: I did it. I told the truth and nothing swallowed me whole. I showed them who I am, what I am, and somehow they still want to love me. And for the first time in years, I feel good, shameless, and free.

CHAPTER 24

It took a lot for me to get on a plane and fly back to New York while my father is still in the hospital. But I told him about the Fatima story and the boiled crap soup that was waiting for me at Millhause-Steig. He practically demanded that I head home on the next flight out, face my accusers with my head high. I promised him I would and that I'd also be back to wheel him out of that smelly hospital when he got the all-clear. Never one to shy away from a friendly wager, he took my bet (fish cakes fried up by my hand) that he would be out of there and home in a matter of days.

I came directly from the airport here, to the secret second lobby of Millhause-Steig on the twenty-seventh floor, where I'm waiting for a pair of leggings on top of clacking heels to come collect me and show me to my fate.

There's a ghost town-y feel to everything up here. The receptionist barely looked up at me when I gave her my name. And the same four people who have walked by repeatedly as I sit here act as though making any eye contact with me means catching the uncorked virus I represent.

I don't need to bet on this; I know it's bad. The anvil will be dropping on my head any minute now. They should have just sent me straight to HR and be done with it. Why make me come in, so that they can perp-walk me right back out? The snarky insider blog *MagDrag.com* already called it: *James' Best Lightburn (ALLEGEDLY) Out*. They quoted only nameless sources, of course, and made sure to SHOUTY-CAPS every mention of the word *allegedly*. That blog is consistently the worst. Always doing the most with the least. One "source" in the post claimed that I had fled to the UK and was hiding out at a former boyfriend's house—sorry, a *former flame's flat* (like they just discovered alliteration). And hiding out? I was in Canada for five days, mainly driving between my parents' house and the hospital . . . with a couple visits to Miles's place when I couldn't sleep. We mainly watched 90s TV shows together and talked—and also made out. A lot, actually. It felt good to hang out with someone who didn't want anything, didn't have questions with no real answers, happy to see what I show him, happy to just share the space with me and rub my feet sometimes. Miles is exactly who I need him to be. But no "source" could possibly know about any of that.

Twitter's on it too. Folks are all in my mentions making guesses at why I'm getting the boot, which magazine I'll head to next, and who the mystery British ex-loverman could be. People are actually naming names and linking out to photos of random English men. Jesus be a fence.

Tell Me More has been surprisingly quiet. I scanned through the site on the plane. They were trying out a new, *revolutionary* (their word) in-flight iPad loaner program in business class. The flight attendant slipped one my way. Coach-class pity, I guess. I was able to check a few local gossip sites from 30,000 feet in the air, and still felt like I had crawled through mud after reading most of it. These people, they're out to gut all the fish, in big ponds and small. All sarcasm and spite, these sites seem to delight at the destruction of some young journo's reputation and dreams. And for what—a snarky headline and a viral post? It can't be worth it.

"Hey."

"Trinity? Hey. What are you doing up here?" I pop up and my coat and bag roll from my lap, landing on the floor with an echoed *splat*. Trinity bends down, helps me scoop things up.

"Well, I got promoted," she says, beaming, and hands me my scarf and gloves. "I'm the assistant editor, special projects for *Hudson*, so I'm up here now."

"Word?"

"Yeah, word."

"Holy shit. That's great, girl. When did this happen?"

"I know, it's kind of crazy. I applied on the low, like, back in September and they told me I got it around Thanksgiving. But I told you about this already; I left you a voice mail a while ago."

"Yeah, I haven't really been checking that thing. Actually, I haven't checked it at all in over a week. E-mail, same. I only got the urgent message about this meeting at the crack of dawn from Ashley. Or Tiffany. Amber?"

"Summer."

"That was next. Summer."

"Summer Harris. She's nice. She's like me, when I was working for JK, but she's that for this whole floor."

"So basically, she knows where the bodies are buried."

Trinity barely smiles and starts her nervous tic—brushing away bangs that are nowhere near her eyes or forehead. I call it her phantom sweep. She nervously looks over her shoulder and I notice she's chopped off all of her hair.

"Your hair—whoa. The new cut is banging, T. You look great."

"Yeah? Thanks. I went super-short and fringe, plus darker with the color, you know, trying to do the total fresh-start thing. Still getting used to it this short, but I like it. It's easy. Oh, and you look great as well."

"Don't bother. I just flew back early this morning and had to rush over here for this meeting. Trust me, I know how I look right now. *Hot-ass mess* would be a very apt description."

Trinity looks flustered; she's blushing. "You always look great, Best."

"You're kind. Anyway, I should get back to waiting for Amber—"

"Summer. Yeah, she's not coming. It's me," Trinity says. "I'm in this meeting and they know I know you, so I said I'd come out and grab you."

"What . . . wait, who else is in this meeting?"

"Best, I just started . . . I don't want to—"

"Don't want to what—treat me like a human being? Finish a conversation?"

Trinity steps into me and lowers her voice further. "It's like hawk-central up here," she whispers. "Everyone watches everything."

"What does that have to do with what I'm asking?" I say, trying to keep my voice low and controlled too.

"Whoever you think is in the meeting, is in the meeting."

"Nik Steig?"

She shakes her head. "He's not back in the office yet. Traveling." Trinity glances past me and waves at someone, adding the widest, toothiest, open-mouth grin of her life; I could count her fillings. I glance back. The horse-laugh is for the receptionist, the same one who acted like I was an annoying but harmless ghost. "Let's just head in," Trinity says to me, loud enough this time for all the listening walls to hear. "They're waiting."

I stare at her for a breath, trying to glean anything I can from her typical nervous tics and tells. Nothing. She's keeping all her cards close to her chest. I still can't believe that my part-time protégé has grown up, got herself a smooth pixie cut and a schmancy new post in the upper room, and just like that, she's bettered me.

Trinity gives me the no-touch-hand-by-my-back move that diplomats, official gentlemen, and condescending businessmen like to do when trying to usher you—the dawdling woman— along. I'm so stunned I barely hear the snort-chuckle that falls out my own mouth.

"Are you okay?" she says through her teeth. She is, after all, still cheesing hard as we move down the empty hall. "Do you need a minute or something?"

"Do I? Are you telling me I should take a minute to call legal counsel or something? Just scratch your chin if yes."

"I meant, did you want the restroom. You're sweating a bit, but it's fine; let's just go in, get it over with." Her grin is wiped clean away and she's back to her stomp-the-ants mustang walk.

"Yeah, let's do that, get it over with."

Trinity leads me into the bright conference room and says, "Found her," without so much as a smirk thrown back at me. Really, Trinity? First the sweaty remark and now this? Forget the loyalty, where's the love? Trinity takes her seat next to Agnes Wolf Freedman, the features director at *Hudson*. She's been at the company going into dog years now, starting out as someone's secretary. Every few years she's offered a specially-created VP, EVP or some other kahuna post at Millhause, but famously declines, preferring to stay put at the flagship *Hudson*, "just working the words," as she liked to say back when she still gave interviews. Agnes is extraordinary. Exceedingly smart and talented, and she still looks unthinkably fabulous. She's a classic: style and substance commingled, walking around like her days could never be numbered.

Of course Agnes is at the head of the boat-shaped, glass table. Trinity looks comfortable there to her right, like an able XO of this ship. On the other side of Agnes, an empty chair, but not give-her-space empty: it seems reserved. Next to the chair is the Robot and beside her, two others—one a young man—who I don't recognize from anywhere. They all look up at me as I walk toward a chair. Hell, yes, I took the other head seat at the table. I'm going to act this thing out to the very end.

"Thanks for coming in," Agnes says, smiling. "Glad you could make it. I know everyone's attention is turning toward the holidays."

"Oh, no problem. I was due back today anyway."

Trinity clears her throat loudly. Yet more shade from her! (What's up with this chick?) And now I have to clarify my opening statement.

"I mean, my flight was today, so I'm back . . . from Montreal . . . where my parents live." Jesus. I'm stuttering like an idiot. This is not how I wanted things to start. But I'm stunned. I can't believe Trinity is pulling passive-aggressive throat-clearing. I invented passive-aggressive throat-clearing. The understudy is coming for me and she's taking "break a leg" rather seriously.

"Good. So glad we didn't make you cut your holidays short," Agnes says, still smiling. She seems perfectly pleasant, but I'm pulling the mask over my grill anyway.

"Not a problem at all, Ms.—"

"Goodness, call me Agnes, please."

"Oh, of course. Right." *Smile served back at you.* It's clear that locking in on Agnes is best, because I'm pretty sure Trinity is busy packing her musket with more gunpowder. I'll clock her in the peripheral; make her think I'm not paying attention.

"So, I'm definitely excited to hear what you want to talk to me about," I say, cheerful.

"It's about this story, on the young woman who survived that harrowing ordeal at her father's hands. Just horrific. She's quite remarkable. Fatima, was it?"

"Yes, Fatima Imam. And yes, she is remarkable. Fascinating, inspiring, but so humble and so solid, especially given everything she's had to endure."

Agnes nods as I speak. And she does that thing where she makes you feel as though you're the only one in the room with anything important to say. Nik does something similar, although he takes it up a notch, leaving you giddy and giggling inside because he chose you to show his magic trick up close. Part of me is waiting for him to swoop in, take that empty seat next to Agnes and start singing a psalm about my story, about me, and we all chuckle about the minor missteps I took to land this thing.

"Speaking of *solid*, I found your writing throughout the entire piece to be just that: solid." It's the Robot chiming in, and I think I just passed out. "You did a really great job on this, Best. Great command of your voice. You really knew what you wanted to say, and the organization and flow of the piece was really strong."

Holy. Shit.

The Robot looks legitimately pleased with me, and even sat up in her chair excitedly midway through saying all that. She's defanged and brushed back—even her outfit is softer (muted colored cashmere separates replace dark wool suiting). It's less Robot and all human Joan right now. It's all so unbelievable. I should really pinch myself. Maybe I've already had the heart attack and am now witnessing this whole thing from the afterlife. I'm a hologram.

"Agreed, Joan," Agnes says. "Really fine job all the way around. Actually, that's why Trinity and I are here. We want to work together—*Hudson* and *James*—on this story, and I think there's a smart way to hold hands on this as a special project. We can go multipurpose, multi-platform without being redundant." She gestures to Trinity: "This one is falling over with great ideas on how we can do it."

Trinity gives me that horse-grin. The growing nut sack on this girl, she's got to be bowlegged by now.

"That sounds great, Agnes. Thank you. Thanks, Joan," I say.

"And Trinity has worked *for* me before. We can definitely come up with something sharp and fresh."

"Actually, a quick step backwards to dot all of our I's and cross our T's," Robot says. "Let's make sure we have all your research notes first, Best. Would you be able to file those today?"

"Yeah, of course. No problem, Joan. I would need to head back home. Everything's on my laptop."

"Excellent. So we'll wait for source copy from you, then, before we take next steps," Agnes says, and goes around the room waiting for a nod and visual confirmation from each of us. "We have a plan. Fantastic." She gathers her short stack of papers and her signature blinged-out lanyard with her fourteen keys, and turns to Trinity. "Did you want to walk with me back to my office to finish talking about that shoot?" Trinity quickly nods and collects her things from the table too: a green Sharpie and a notebook, which is orange and neat and glossy and basically a total replica of the one I always carry. What part of the game is that? My eyes want to jump out of their sockets and roll over next to her rip-off notebook so she sees (clearly) that I see (literally) that she's biting my style, and that I do not approve.

Damn it. She just caught me looking at the notebook. And now she's roughly scooping the thing up to her chest.

"Thanks for coming in," Trinity says. "I know you were probably—"

"Nonsense," I say, again cheerfully. "It was a total pleasure. I've always been such fan of *Hudson* and, of course, a fan of you, Agnes. I'm honored and excited to finally have an opportunity to work with you and learn from the best. So, again, thank you." I give them each that New Age, bullshit, hand-to-heart, modesty head-bow (even the two silent partners get one, despite sitting there on mute like they're conducting an audit). On Trinity's bow I add a side squint. *I'm the battle-tested champion of these war games, young'un. Stand down.*

Walking back to the spooky lobby, I want to pass by the receptionist's desk on my way out and drop a snark bomb, just for shiggles. Maybe a drive-by cut-eye will suffice. But, really, who cares about that lame receptionist? I'm going to have a story in *Hudson* while she's still going to be sitting there answering the phones. My dream is finally coming true. I'm moving on up to all those bigger-better things that were waiting for me to claim. At least I had the decency to hold off until the elevator door closed before busting out my boogie-breakdown move. (It involves a slim portion of Janet Jackson's "Rhythm Nation" choreography, and should really be contained behind closed doors anyway.) When the elevator opens again on the main floor, I'm basically jittering in place. I want to tell the first person I see to hold fast to their dreams or keep reaching for the stars or the world is their oyster if they float on cloud nine next to the silver lining or whatever. I'm feeling corny and happy and excited, a combination that I haven't experienced in a really long time. It's good.

Everything feels brighter, better. I barely notice the black snow on the curb below me. All I can see when I look down is my foot tapping out some jittery, joyful beat. These people jostling me and calling me a dumb tourist? Ignored. I only see the gloriousness that is the Rockefeller Center Christmas tree shimmering in the crisp, clear sky.

I'm taking a cab home. I don't want to fuck up my mood with any subway struggles. One hit of warmed-over urine under the subway stairs can puncture even the sturdiest glee bubble.

My cabbie is so breezy and kind, he actually just got out to open the door for me. In the brick of winter. On Fifth Avenue. I'm tempted to ask if he's new to this cab-life thing, but a hearty "thank you" seems to work better. We reach Brooklyn without any objections from him or any traffic, not even when we hit Flatbush Avenue. It's all going my way. Finally. And it's not just the *Hudson* story or talking through all that stuff about the accident with my parents. It's more. It's palpable, and it's more. Something has switched over to the other side, opened up for me, and I feel saved. I feel good. I feel like I want to share all of this with someone.

And like an obvious brick, it hits me: I want to share it with him. I want to be in it with him, rolling around in the grass of it like blissed-out fools with our shoes kicked off.

I need to tell him. I need to tell him now.

As I hit the top of my stoop, he's taking over my mind, playing large in every corner. I can picture his face, hear his voice, his laugh. I want to talk to him. More than anything, I want to see him. It's urgent and desperate and I can't think about anything else but him. It's settling in, this truth, so quickly and sure that I'm taking the steps two at a time. I need to be near him, with him for any of this goodness and happy to feel real. The fact that he probably doesn't want to have anything to do with me feels like a minor setback.

I reach the roof, breathless, and push the heavy exit door open with everything inside of me. The freezing air, the snow-covered concrete, none of it matters, and I rifle through my dumb, jumbled bag for my phone, deadweight I've been carrying around for too long. I turn it on. The bars drag to a climb. This search for a signal feels like an eternity.

Seeing his name in my contacts, I'm frightened and thrilled and about to burst or scream or all of it. I'm committed to hitting this *call* button. I have to talk to him.

But the goddamn thing vibrates, bouncing almost clean out of my hand.

"Mum, is everything okay? What's wrong?"

"It's your father, he's gone to ICU. This time they say it's likely cancer in the liver. I think you should come back, if you can."

"Of course. But, is he—"

"No, no. He's alert. No pain at present," she says, the cool undertone completely missing from her voice. She sounds dazed, flattened. "It's not late stages nor nothing, but he did ask after you a few times already."

"I have to do a couple things around here first, then I'll look into another flight out. I probably won't get there before tomorrow or tomorrow night."

"That's okay. I'll tell him we spoke. Your father gon' be pleased to know you're coming back. He has . . ." There's a long pause. I know the call didn't drop. I can hear the busy atmosphere buzzing behind her loud breathing. I press the phone closer to my ear as if that changes anything. "He still has the coins," she says.

Now I go silent.

"Are you there? Hello?"

"Yeah, I'm here, Mum. I'll call when I know my flight info."

"All right, then. Good enough."

"Okay. Bye."

I definitely can't call him now.

I glance down at my phone. The notifications are out of hand, everything is lit up and red. It's clear that Bauer's back on stalker duty, but his messages have become curt and impatient. It's giving me a bad feeling. I scroll through my favorite numbers again and dial. I need to bolster the bridges before they're completely burned to the ground. It can't be left up to Bauer. The apology, the explanation, the details; it all needs to come from me. This is going to be rough, that's a given. Might as well start from underneath the heaviest, most unmovable rock and push my way up from there.

———✦———

I couldn't read anything in Lindee's voice on the phone, and there was nothing specific behind it when it came through the downstairs intercom, either. But then everyone sounds like they're broadcasting through a static storm when they use that thing.

"Hey," I say and step aside so she can come in. I've left enough room between us, in case this goes way wrong and there's a bottle of hot cat piss hidden in her super-deep coat pockets.

"Hey," Lindee says. She walks in, easy, relaxed, as if the last month never happened. "So, this whole cryptic text-message bit, is that going to be your thing?" Lindee slips her coat off and drapes it next to her on my couch. "What was it again? *'I'm sorry, we'll catch up when I get back.'* Then *poof*, you disappear, never to be heard from again, like the Ghost of Christmas Yet to Come. And now you're back, but the mystery . . . that seems to live on."

"Lindee, look, you and Kendra have every right to feel like that."

"Oh, Kendra is particularly pissy about all of it. You already know I'm made up of scraps of bone and skin; I don't feel much. But my sister's totally different. She's all about caring and shit."

"Is she coming later?"

"No. She and Flav are in LA for a wedding. This photographer friend of his is getting married to a model on a beach in Malibu, of all places. Dress code said all white and barefoot. It's like, can you buy a bottle of originality somewhere? Just a sixteen-ouncer."

"I'm guessing you didn't want to go? I mean, barefoot on a beach isn't completely horrendous."

"Please, you don't know that crew. The whole thing is just a hair above reprehensible," Lindee says. "Plus, I have plans with New Mark. He's taking me to a party in Chappaqua with his family—well, his mother, stepdad, brothers and their wives, and his great-aunt or great-cousin or something."

"So basically his entire family."

"Basically."

"Holy—Lindee?" I plop down next to her. "That's fantastic. So you and Mark are doing this thing for real. That's . . . I'm really happy for you."

She lets a grin break through her stone-locked jaw, nodding. "Yeah. I think we are. I know, it's corny as all what-the-fuck. I'm like a giddy idiot from Planet Girl."

"You're hardly giddy and never an idiot. You're just happy."

Lindee looks around the living room and spots my open laptop on the flat side of my suitcase and my coat bunched up beside it. "So, guess you *literally* just got back."

"I did. But I'm gone again in a minute. That's why I asked you to come over, to try to explain a little. There's a lot going on. I thought I figured out where to start this, but now that you're here, I'm kind of losing my nerve."

"Nerve? You don't need nerve. Just say what's going on."

"What's going on right-right now is my dad. He's not well. It's his liver. My mother called just before I called you. It might be cancer. I'm looking for a flight back up there."

"Shit. Is it late-stage?"

"No, I don't think so. But he's been drinking for more than half his life and that liver is basically saying, 'Peace out, bitch.'"

"Cancer is the fucking worst. I'm sorry, Best." She rests her hand on mine briefly and shifts positions on the couch so we're closer, but not touching. "That's just so fucked up. Is your mother freaking out?"

"Not really. She's not the outwardly freaking-out type."

"When our stepdad went through some shit with his heart, my mother tried to do the steady-rock thing for a minute, but then she started to crumble and that was rough on everyone. Plus, it's just you, so she's going to want to lean hard on you. Get ready."

"Actually, it's been rough for a while for her, both of them. They've leaned hard on each other and I haven't really been there for that, for them. They have no more room to lean on anything. They're practically lying flat."

"What do you mean? Is this a return of the big, bad cancer thing?"

"No. This is reason I called you and Kendra over. There's a story—maybe a story. There's this reporter from *Tell Me More*—"

"Still them? Jesus."

"Yeah, this reporter Bauer, he's been kind of hounding me about a story that's going to post—or might post—about me soon."

"With Grant again? People still care about this shit? He's back in New York; I read that. But so are George Clooney, that disgraced mayor, and that cute kid from the werewolf show. I'm sure there's more juice that they can pump from their celeb stories than stale Grant and his ex-girlfriend troubles. "

"It's not Grant. It's me and my family. I don't even know what he's going to write, how much he's going to say, but he's been asking questions about my life in Montreal, before I moved here."

"What, do you have a record or something?"

"No." I want to take a beat here, a breath, but I also know that I can't stall this further. Not anymore. "There's something I've never told you or Kendra or anyone. And now I think Bauer knows and he's going to expose this private thing that—"

"You're killing me here. What are you saying? Did you murder somebody? Oh, Jesus Christ. You're on the run!"

I shake my head before burying it in my lap. I need to keep talking through detached breath and the tears and snot slinking down my face. "It wasn't always just me. I had two brothers, older, Benjamin and Bryant. There were three of us." I keep my head cupped in my hands. My ears are on fire and I can't look up to even glimpse Lindee. She's moved back and away from me—I felt the shift in weight on the couch. "We were in an ice accident on Christmas Eve ten years ago. We were taking a shortcut home, across a lake. The ice, it was too thin. We all fell through. They didn't make it out. I did. So now it's just me."

Lindee shoots up from her seat. "Are you fucking kidding me?" she barks. I raise my head. Her mouth is staring open and her eyes are as wide as plates; she seems to be holding her breath. I want to say more, but I don't know if she'll even hear me.

"Jesus fucking Christ!" Lindee's moon eyes are tearing up and her brows are twitching. I can see the broken words gathering up in her throat. "You're serious. You are fucking serious right now?"

I can only nod.

"That's really horrible. Shocking and horrible, what happened to your brothers. Really, it is. Your poor parents . . . But, honestly? I can't even begin to process how you could go along all this time and never once say any of this. You've been lying to us *for years*. And now because there's some gossip blog that might out your whole fraud life, you're *now* saying something. Who does that?"

"Lindee, it's not that simple."

"No, it is that simple. You have another fucking life with real people that you've never once thought to mention. How sick is that?"

"Please, just—"

"Just what, Best? Just act like this is normal? You know, I've been representing you, defending you against my sister these last weeks. Kendra has this ability to see good where good is. But she also uses that to sniff out when something isn't right, like with an apple days before it turns into ruined fruit. I couldn't figure out why she wouldn't let up on you, let you off the hook. I told her to give you a chance on all this shit that happened. And she just couldn't. She knew. She knew you were ruined fruit."

Before I can get another word out, Lindee snatches up her coat and heads toward the door.

"Lindee, I'm trying to do right here, tell the truth."

She throws her arms into her coat and whips around to me in one smooth motion. Her mouth is twisted, more than usual, and her scowl is the most prominent thing about her. "That's the thing: You're not you. You're a whole other person, with another life. Do you even know what the right thing is?" Lindee shakes her head. "Good luck with all that," she spits, and flies through the door.

CHAPTER 25

This time the receptionist looks me straight in the face and holds her gaze throughout our interaction. It's still quiet and creepy up here, but I'm not nervous this time. Not about this meeting. I'm definitely curious about why they've called me back for another meeting, but not nervous. My anxiousness centers around the fact that I still need to book a flight to Montreal. Yesterday was all about wrapping things up with this Fatima story for *Hudson*—and recovering from the Lindee blizzard. I don't know if there's a way back with her. I was half-expecting her to be usual Lindee, in a constant state of just DGAF. But she showed me. That was *definitely* Give A Fuck mode. Somehow I thought she'd appreciate the straight-talk and want to hear me out, give me a chance to do better by her.

Wrong. I was so, so wrong on that one.

And with Kendra—this is the longest we have ever gone without speaking or texting or anything. I started writing her a letter last night when I couldn't sleep. It took me hours, the attention placed on getting the right wording; plus, it's handwritten. I left a small mountain of ripped-up stationery by my bedside. I still need to finish hers today—a couple more lines and it'll be ready. The one to Tyson wasn't as grueling, and I know he'll definitely read it and get back to me. He's good that way. Our thing is different. He has plenty of his own secrets and shaded-out bits of life tucked under his fly fedoras. I doubt he'll judge and jury me. As soon as I get out of this meeting, I'm not going home. Straight to Starbucks with these letters and off they will go. I even have special Love stamps held over from the summer. (Kendra always made fun of me for that, still buying stamps. Maybe the stamp will be the sliver of heart and levity that I need to break through to her.)

If only this meeting would start already. I should probably use this time to figure out how to tell Agnes and Robot that I'll be taking more days off to go home because my dad's sick. I have a feeling they'll understand. I *did* just drop a stellar story in their laps, for chrissakes. Actually, maybe that's what this is. Maybe they called me back in to tell me that they're making Fatima the cover. I'll probably bust out in laugh-cry when they tell me. Or maybe I'll just hold firm and keep it moving, start talking about the details of the cover shoot, like how they should handle her hair makeover. Nothing drastic; keep it understated, modest. Either way, I'm dressed for war, right down to my back-zip, high heel, suede Gucci boots. Trinity will never catch me sleeping again. I've even got a few stinging quips with her name on them just frosting up my back pocket, should the need arise.

Here it comes, the clicking heels. I'm basically forcing myself to not look over my shoulder right now as she approaches. I'm going act like I'm so deep in my super- important thoughts that she'll have to say my name twice before I acknowledge her. Like I said, I invented this shit.

"Best?"

It's not Trinity, but some knockoff standing there with a weak smile and UGG boots. Her hair is long—like T's was before she went *Devil Wears Prada*—and she has a tattoo snaking up her arm: a flock of flying swallows.

"Hi, I'm Summer," she says, jutting out her hand right between my boobs. Her voice is raspy like a hungover sorority pledge and her handshake feels similar to squeezing a package of frozen peas. "Finally, right? I feel like me and your voice mail should go out for drinks." Now, her laugh—how shall I put this? It's near identical to the sound of a cat choking on wet tissue. I want to reach over and cover her mouth with my bare hand, anything to end the grisly sound.

"Or maybe a smoothie," I say. "My voice mail's been sober for two years." Christ, what I'm doing? The yucky cackle is out again, louder this time. And she's bucking her head too—nodding, I guess. And I did mention that she's wearing UGGs, right? I'm being punk'd.

"I shouldn't be laughing," she says. (No, you definitely should not.) "It's been a weird week already." Summer gathers herself by physically pulling the smile down from her face. I've never seen anything like this from anyone other than a children's party clown on television. "Sorry about that. Goofy lately. Are you ready to head in?"

"Yeah, let's go."

"Actually, we're heading up to thirty," she says, and starts toward the elevators.

"Oh, really? Is legal joining the meeting?"

"No." The goofy TV clown is gone and Summer's face is dour.

"So, why are we meeting on thirty?"

She presses the *up* button several times, pauses, and goes back to the useless move. "You're meeting with James Kessler first."

"First?"

"Yes."

The elevator arrives and Summer rushes in. I don't. I'm not going anywhere until I get a sense about what's waiting for me on thirty. Summer is clearly agitated by my resistance. She opens her mouth to speak, it seems, but only a loud cluck of her tongue comes out.

"What's going on with this meeting? Is this about my Fatima story? Just tell me."

She looks like the unlucky hostage tasked with being the gunman's messenger, the point of his weapon sharply jabbing at her back. Summer's hand flies to the inside panel (the *door open* button, I imagine) while waving the other arm in the open doors' space.

"What is this meeting about? I'm not moving until you answer."

Her eyes widen. More tongue clucks. "Okay, yes, it's about your story. Now could you get on, please? The alarm's gonna go off any second."

"Who's up there?"

"Best, you need to get on here. Unless you plan to take the stairs."

"Just tell me, who all is up there?"

"James Kessler. That's who's up there, waiting. So please, could you just—"

"All right. Whatever. I'm on. Calm down."

Summer presses the button hard. We ride the three floors in silence. Getting my bitch face on straight is proving challenging with her ridiculous boots staring up at me. I pull something out anyway and keep my eyes away from the giant mirror to my right.

We approach a wide-open office door. The room is long and deep and with the manufactured brightness of a television soundstage. I spot JK first. She's angled away from the door, sitting on the edge of a high-back leather chair. Her hair is up and from what I can see she's dressed in total stark black.

My heart drops to my stomach.

James Kessler is all about softness and cloudless glow. It's whites, pastels, gauzy delicates. That includes her shoulder-length white blond hair, which is usually down, framing her milky face. She only does the cold, all-black clothes, high-bun combo if she's bringing bad news. When she told the staff about the company-wide layoffs: hair up, all black. Announcing the cancer death of Kelly Woodrow, veteran photog and the mag's first-ever art director: hair up, all black. Even when Hollywood's so-called hottest couple confirmed their breakup earlier this year: bun, black. (The better blond half of that power duo was on our cover that month, and advertising and PR were basically rolling around on the floor tearing off their clothes in a tantrum like toddlers in the toy aisle.)

JK is nodding while a woman I don't recognize speaks to her. I can't hear a word, not even a lisp. The woman is leaned back at her desk. She's wearing a navy suit jacket with something silky and draped underneath. I catch a glimpse of some sparkly, long necklace drooped down the front of the jacket— the whole outfit is exactly something the Robot would covet, which tells me two things: she's got to be from HR or legal, and this is the end for me. I don't bother looking to Summer for any confirmations, I can feel it. The only question now is *why*, but maybe that doesn't even matter. So I step deeper into the Coliseum and ready myself for whichever beast they send for me first.

Summer knocks on the door behind me.

"Ah, Best," JK says, startled. "Please, come in. Shut the door and have a seat."

There are two chairs near JK. I take the one right next to her. I want to see her raw blue eyes when she shanks me.

I read somewhere that one should enter into any potential rejection scenario with the biggest smile and shine you can muster (all right, fine—it was a piece in *James* mag about getting dumped by your man . . . and I wrote it). Acting like it's your very best day might lead the person turning you down to rethink their decision. It's very last-ditch, but there were actual studies and experts backing this shit up, so, worth a try. I think I'm about to get pushed out the side of a plane without a working parachute, so last-ditch is my speed right now.

Stepping right up to Power Suit's desk, I smile and extend a firm hand. "Hello, Best Lightburn. Thanks for having me in."

She seems a little stunned. (The desired effect.) She stands and shakes my hand. "Yes, hello. I'm Kathleen Martin. Of course you know James."

"Hi," I say to JK warmly and gently touch her forearm. "You look great."

JK is also baffled and tries to smile her way through it.

Before I can cross my legs all the way, Kathleen starts up. "Best, I work with both human resources and Millhause-Steig's legal departments as a consultant. I feel we should let you know straightaway why you're here."

"Yes, please do, Kathleen. I'm all ears." I'm trying to keep this relaxed brow and smile-from-the-eyes thing going, but I might crack at any minute.

"James, would you like to jump in here?"

I turn my hanging-by-threads sunny disposition toward JK; bat my lashes too. She actually looks sad—sadder than the day Susie left.

"Sure," JK says. "I'm really sorry, but we're ending our contract with you, Best. Effective immediately."

"Wait . . . what do you—I'm sorry, but ending my contract? I had a meeting with . . . They're running my big feature story in *Hudson* and our magazine, together. Both magazines. I just filed all my source info yester—huh. Right. *I filed all my background info yesterday.*" It's the sound of a thousand mousetraps snapping at once. "I was still on contract yesterday. So you own the story now. It's all yours. Of course."

JK's eyes shoot over to Kathleen, but I stay on her. I don't care. JK's been in the game a long time. She can handle my red glare.

"Ms. Lightburn, as you know, this was not a personal nor easy decision for anyone here at Mill—"

"Are you serious, right now? This is what you're doing to me?"

JK finally looks my way. "Best, this is not an attack. You know there have been issues and this was a difficult decision, for everyone."

"Issues? I just brought in a huge story for you. A winner. What issue do you have with that? You don't want to win awards—real ones that have nothing to do with red lipstick and workouts to help you drop five jean sizes in a week?"

"That's not fair, Best," JK says.

"Fair? Do you really want to talk about fair?"

"Excuse me, Ms. Lightburn," Kathleen says, "but this is not the kind of discussion we planned to have. The decision has already been made and it took a great deal of consideration on all parts. However, I should remind you that we have a full file with documentation about everything."

"Everything. Everything like what?"

"Dating back two years ago, your deposition is still in here. More recently, we had an incident with serious inaccuracies in a story you wrote"—she looks down at a notebook—"for the shame issue for *James* magazine. There were a number of attempts made from various and numerous coworkers at the magazine to contact you to discuss these inaccuracies. All efforts were unsuccessful. There are records of phone calls, voice mails, copies of e-mails sent to you that went unanswered. There was even a meeting called with the research department, your editors, and manager that you chose not to attend. It's also noted that you were contacted about the meeting by James

Kessler's then assistant—directly by phone—yet you still refused to attend."

"I was away in Canada, visiting my parents. I remember
speaking to Trinity, or *James's then assistant*, in person earlier
that week, reminding her of my time off—which was approved."

"There are also some serious issues with this last story you
filed. You falsely stated to a Mr.—"

"I'm sorry, but I did what I had to do to get the story. I got
it. It's good and two magazines here are publishing it. Everything in that story is true and the backup—which you now
have, by way of three-card monte—shows that. There's nothing false about any of it."

"Best, you falsely used the magazine and the company's
name and reputation to move through this story that was never
assigned or approved," JK says. "Trinity has proof of all of this.
No one's just making it up." JK is talking to me like a teenager
busted for cheating on the final or stealing Dad's car or whatever restless, uninspired children do.

"Trinity has plenty of proof about plenty of things, it
seems," I say, shaking my head.

"Best, that's not fair," JK says again, her face washed in disappointment.

"James, it's fine," Kathleen jumps in, holding her hand up.
"Ms. Lightburn, the purpose of this meeting is not for you to
argue your case or accuse coworkers of deception. It's been decided. We're letting you go."

"But keeping my story."

"Actually, it's Millhause-Steig's story, Ms. Lightburn, and
again, we're not here to argue through this. The section on
ownership rights and representation is clearly outlined in your
original and updated signed contracts. The purpose of this
meeting is not to rehash any of that."

"So what is the *purpose of this meeting*, then? To throw acid in my face, rub salt in?" I turn to JK. "Because that's what you're doing here."

"We called you in so that we may be clear about what's happening: Your contract has been terminated and we need your signed acknowledgement showing your acceptance of that fact. If you have any questions regarding severance or 401(k) contributions, there's information that might answer those concerns in this packet." Kathleen slides the thin envelope to the end of the desk toward me. "There's also contact information for Wendy Myers, who handles exiting employees, with a focus on editorial contracts." She looks at me and through me, as if pity would be too much for her to spare.

"And, Best, I just want to say that I'm sorry," JK says. "This is not how anyone hoped things would go. But you'll be fine. I know that much."

Kathleen keeps her frozen stare on me.

JK's neurons must be melting throughout her brain and she's likely grinding her molars to dust at Kathleen's brusque approach. JK hates the lack of grace more than anything, more than gum-chewing, more than stay-at-home mothers—and those two sit pretty high on her loathing list as it is. But she also can't stomach disloyalty.

"Are you prepared to sign?" Kathleen says, almost yawning.

There's something my father would often say to us when we were trying to argue a point with him about why we didn't want to do the homework or the chore or the whatever. We—usually Benjamin or me—would try to hold our ground in our arrogance, just wrong and strong, battling against Dad's clear experience and common sense. And he'd say: There's nothing more pitiful than a confident fool.

I feel JK's sad eyes on me, and I nod. "Yeah. I'll sign."

Chapter 26

MagDrag.com is doing me dirty. It's been three-and-a-half weeks since I got axed and there's been a crappy post about me every other day. Move the fuck on. If I ever meet "a source close to Lightburn"—clearly a good, caring friend who knows me so very well—I'm going to spit clean in their eye. All the bullshit this "source" person has been spewing about me, about my past stories, about my rumored relationships. The only reason I even read these dumb posts and the comments sections on these dumb posts is because I'm terrified someone will rip the covers off of everything between Nik and me. But nothing. Not even a whiff of something funky. Instead they linked me to Eldon, from the mailroom. How would that even help me, having a secret relationship with the head of the mailroom? First, that Eldon is sex on a stick. If you ever had the good fortune of bumping into him in the Millhause skylight gym—sweat nasty, rocking those basketball shorts, that tight tank—you will consider yourself blessed. Getting to roll around with that dude on the regular—please, I would not be keeping that shit secret. Poor Eldon, dragged through the social-media mud for no good goddamn reason. At least his picture popped up in a thumbnail a few times, looking princely and sweet with those chalk-white teeth. That should net him a few cell numbers and business cards from *hot-body gyals in a de* dancehall.

At first I could've sworn the source was Trinity, still digging her dagger in my back. Then there was the Miyuki Butler factor, but she had no clue how much I despised her, unless Trinity decided to enlighten her on my regular clowning fest. It still didn't fit. Miyuki Butler is not the "revenge is a dish best served" type. Plus, there's nothing in it for her. She has the job she always wanted and I'm gone. She's pretty set.

Some of the information in the latest *MagDrag* posts sounded straight made-up, and that smog blog has never been about integrity. The fact that they're trying to call mine into question is laughable . . . although I've found it hard to skin my teeth about any of this stuff.

Oh, but I did catch a reprieve earlier this week when the story broke about the Robot's marriage flameout. Bauer actually broke the story on *Tell Me More*; *MagDrag* picked it up, as did "Page Six," the real New York gossip god. The Robot's husband, Gordon Gregory, filed for divorce after finding out that she's been having an affair with a former Major League pitcher from the Mets. That she of buttoned-up navy suits and broaches was even sneaking around is mind-blowing enough, but add in the other bits—Affair going on for three years! Ballplayer's a longtime, good friend of Gordon's! Possible sex tape!—and we're talking paradigm shift. It turns out Bauer was trying to get ahold of me near the end there to dig up more dirt on the Robot. He figured, who better to know what's going on with the Robot than the *only other black journalist* at the magazine.

The explosion with the Robot may be the perfect distraction tactic for me to disappear for real. I killed my Twitter account and Facebook fan pages just before coming back here to Montreal. I've gone back to reading the newspaper—albeit the

Montreal Gazette—and rereading classics and favorites in my parents' library. Like right now I'm reading Chinua Achebe's *Things Fall Apart*, because . . . well, yeah. Next up is *Lord of the Flies*. You see the theme.

My father's liver is an asshole. The man's been in and out of the hospital since Boxing Day and they still can't tell him with any real certainty what's wrong. He's managing the pain, he claims, with the drugs that they dole out to him in buckets, but I think he's sneaking sips of his own liquid therapy when my mother's out at church. She still lives on her side, but spends a lot of time on his playing cards and dominoes with him. He's weak most days and prefers to sit in his tiny office "organizing affairs," he said. I found a low rum bottle in the bottom drawer of a filing cabinet in there. There was also a small stash of blue movies (as he would call them). I pretended I didn't see either thing. He's been really kind to me about this Millhause-Steig stuff and the Fatima story. "Don't bother yuh head with all that *commesse*," he said, when I gave him the full scoop on the swindle and drama. "Them people real *sometimeish*—and wicked on top of that too, *ent*? You shoulda tell them to kiss yuh ass." We laughed for a good twenty minutes after he said that. My father is not one for slack talk, but on those rare times he does drop the good-Trini-Catholic-boy veil, it is fucking fantastic.

Didn't bother telling Mum about the whole double-cross, not in any detail. Things have definitely defrosted with her lately, but it's not all sugar cakes and sunshine. Not even close. There's still a gulf there, with only a flimsy straw bridge across, and neither one of us trusts the thing enough to lay a foot on it. And lately her focus is on running circles with these doctors and church, in that order. Bothering with me and my simple drama, there's no space for it.

"You know your mother is happy to have you here," my father says. She had just left us alone in his office after delivering his special lunch before heading out to some church thing, again.

"I don't know about all that, Dad. It's good that I'm here with you, keep you company. That helps her."

"See, that's part of your problem. You play yourself small. You matter to her and to me too, of course, but you've always been her heart. You should know that, you know. You're her heart."

"Wait, are you seeing the white light, boss? Why are you talking to me like this?"

"It's my fault too. I shoulda been talking to you like this a long time ago. I shoulda been talking to you like this from the start. All of you deserve to hear me talk like this from the start."

His droopy tone wipes away my smile. "Dad, don't upset yourself. It's okay."

"No. It's not. I send you out into the world like this. Them people at that magazine, let them stay there. They *teef* yuh stories, but them can't steal yuh core, the meat of who you are, Bathsheba. They can't take that, unless you allow them to."

Of all the parables and life lesson-y things that he's laid out for me over these last couple weeks, hearing my own dad tell me I play myself small felt like a driving punch to the gut.

He's been feeling better, but not bounced back, so I'm heading to New York today. I have to sort through the rubble of things I left behind, figure out if I can still afford that apartment without Millhause money. Tyson said I can stay with him if things go salty with the rental company that took over the building after Mr. Bernhardt passed away last month. I've been going Luddite, steering clear of e-mails and smartphones and all things of blinking, buzzing brightness. Tyson actually calls the house, asks my mother for me and everything. It's strange, but I like it. Makes me feel like I'm fourteen all over again.

Tyson didn't react how I thought he would to my truth-telling letter. He was even better. "May, this is not living," he said before I could finish my "hey." It was one of the last calls I took before boarding my flight to Montreal and turning the phone off for good. I wasn't sure what he was talking about at first; I couldn't imagine that my letter had reached him that fast. But it had and Tyson was ready for me, ready to set me straight.

"This thing you've been doing, carrying all that heavy and all that sad and guilt and shame, that's not living. That's not living life. That's just surviving it. You need to let all that go. Forgive yourself. Get free, because you're here, May, and you are needed." It broke me down and everything inside that had been propping me up for the past several months just collapsed on itself. I cried on that flight like a lost child. The older woman sitting near me leaned over and slipped a thin pack of tissues into the bend in my arm. I nodded in thanks, because that's all I had. By the time that we landed, my face was a red, streaked, puffy dumpling. The cabdriver barely wanted to look my way to ask where we were heading.

I gave the driver Miles's address. It just spilled out of my mouth that way. Plus, there's no one else here for me, no other old school friend to pop in on. Not anymore. I threw salt over all of that, everyone from high school, long ago. It was too hard; too much pity and pretense. When we pulled up to Miles's place, it took me a solid two minutes to get out of the car. The poor cabdriver didn't know what to say to move me along and stayed frozen in his seat. After I finally got it together and got out of the car, the driver skated off like he was being chased.

Miles was home, but not for long. He was leaving for NoCal again in an hour. His internet company is in the process of going public. Something I should know more about since he mentioned the big news during one of our *Fresh Prince of Bel-Air* mini-marathon and make-outs. I wasn't really listening or watching (it was an episode with new Aunt Viv, and I'm partial to the original). I should have paid attention to a lot of things that night, because I could've remembered that we were actually on the outs *before* taking the damn cab to his house.

We fell out over foolishness; some spilled milk that spread across the kitchen table and soon covered every other nearby surface. I was leaving for New York like I am now, but it was pre-implosion and I was so focused on my own shit with the honor-killing story. Miles said something about hanging out with me in New York since he'd be there around the same time I was, and told me not to worry because even though he'd be around my 'hood, he wouldn't assume that he could stay with me, and that there's no pressure and that he just wants to meet my people, and how cool it would be to hang. Of course, I briskly changed the subject with little elegance or tact, and off he went down You're Ashamed of Me Boulevard. There was no stopping him, either. It started with some nonsense about class and Caribbean blacks snubbing African-Americans. And ended when he brought up his leg. His motherfucking missing leg. That's when I gave him the high hat. I'm a lot of things, but I'm not that: so hopeless and vain that the man's missing limb would render him a shameful hide-away.

The whole awful thing came crashing into my brain the minute he answered the door. He looked surprised and confused, but not angry. Then he noticed my soggy face and his awkward stiff-arm vanished.

"Hey. You all right?"

I nodded.

"You sure? You look . . ."

"I know. I was upset about—"

"Is it your dad?" He reached for my arm.

"No. Well, yes, he's back in the hospital. That's why I'm here. I mean, that's not why I'm *here-here* at your place. It's just—I, uh. It's—"

"Hey, hey. It's okay. Come in." Miles took my bag and ushered me inside. It was dark and a little chilled. "I'm—man, shit. This is crap timing, but I'm getting ready to bounce. I thought you were my boy Justin. He's taking me to the airport. I . . . I don't know what to do for you right now. I can't miss this flight. Meetings on the other side, you know? I can't even switch it to a later flight."

"I know. I don't want you to. I should get going too. The hospital." I backed up into the door and stumbled over his suitcase.

"Best, slow down. What's up? I mean, you came here—"

"I—I . . . I'm sorry. I wasn't thinking straight. I was upset on the plane and . . . I guess I wanted to apologize to you, get right with you."

He melted a little and let the goofy grin loose. "Done. Now, how can I help you get right with yourself? Do you want a ride to the hospital? Justin's mad cool; it'll be no bigs for him to swing by there before the airport."

"No. Thanks, I'm okay. I should go. My mother's probably watching the door for me right now."

He rubbed my shoulder and back. "Okay. Why don't you hit me later tonight. Let me know what's what with your dad and stuff. Let me know you're all right too."

"I will."

"You sure I can't do anything?"

Take me with you. I was tempted to say it, even as a halfway joke. Instead I told him I was all good. We hugged good-bye, but it was different, tempered with something; distrust, maybe. I let it go. There was no more room in my brain to hold onto anything else.

———◦◦———

I didn't call Miles later on that night. We haven't once spoken since then. I've thought about him, though, like right now as I'm sliding into this cab, again, to go to the airport, again. This cabbie, a middle-aged Jamaican man, is friendly and happy to see me. He calls me *dawta* when I get in and told me there's something very *upful* about me. His name is Robert Campbell. He told me to call him by his nickname, Skinny (short for Skinny Man, on account of his being the precise opposite of slim), but I prefer going the respectful route and stick with Mr. Campbell. He talks his face off for the whole ride and it's fine. Hearing all his chat 'bout the *bodderation* at work, especially the *facety ooman* in dispatch who has him ready to flex off on his own, *jus' now*—it's like hearing an oldie-but-goodie on the radio.

I left Mr. Campbell's pristine, white Ford Crown Victoria smiling, warmed from the inside, until I sat down here in the business lounge and spotted some guy reading *Hudson* magazine. There was Fatima on the cover looking groomed, glowing, and thoughtful in black and white, posed next to the large words:

THE SIN ISSUE
How One Woman Cheated Death
and Forgave the Man Who Tried to Kill Her

Christ. I'm staring at this thing appalled, like it just leaped across the row of seats and smacked me in the face. It hurts. It physically hurts. I only stopped cursing in my sleep about that colossal bullshit a few nights ago, and now here it is back to haunt my daydreams. It's not fair and it'll never be all right. Part of me—fine—*every* part of me, down to the bottom of my boots, wants to walk over there and ask that man for a quick look at his magazine. What if they took my byline off? Worse, what if they reduced me to some *additional reporting by* tiny-font fuckery?

Kiss my ass. They can kiss my ass. Let them stay there. No

time for their wicked, nothing lives. I refuse to play myself small. My moment is on its way.

I'm pulling out all my new mantras courtesy of Bertram Lightburn and trying to act like they are making an ounce of difference. I need a drink. Wait—a complimentary one. Honestly, if there's a better reason to have an airport lounge pass, I haven't heard it.

Even sipping on this stingy gin and tonic (it's basically crushed slush), I'm still staring over there at the man reading *Hudson*. I need another one of these drinks and a phone call home. Hearing my dad's voice might help me breathe through this.

Who am I kidding? All the pep talks in the world won't shake this. I don't need anyone else trying to pick me up off the floor. I don't even need this drink or the Fatima story or absolution from the Singhs. What I need, what's going to really save me is simple: It's him. I need him. I need him with me if I want to play this game the right way and live this life. And I need to tell him.

We've got a half hour before they begin boarding. Even if I have to start it now and finish the rest when we land in New York, I have to call him right now and tell him that he's it. He's the answer. He's what matters.

Voice mail. Of course.

No patience for his message, I press the star key and just leap . . .

"Hey. It's me. Don't delete me. Please. Just, please, listen. I know it's all fucked-up between us right now. I know my part in it is huge. I was reckless, stupid, and, yes, out-of-this-world selfish. All of the above, I cop to it. But the thing is, there's more here, with us. There's more to us then a bunch of bad choices and being afraid. I know we can be better. So much better than we were. A million times better. And we can be better together. But I know what you're thinking and it's true.

I've said it so much, it's like this wobbly piece of wood that I've built my entire adult life on: I don't need you to save me. I don't want you to save me. You know what? It's not even about being saved. I don't need you to save me. I just need you. I need you, because . . . I love you. I know it's fast and sudden, but if you're still listening—Jesus, are you? This message is a total screed and I'm sorry—but there's so much more, so much I should be saying, but not like this. Look, I'll be at my place in New York for a few days then back home to Montreal. But if you can, if you want to, come meet me and we can talk it out. Just come meet me tomorrow night. I'll text you where—safe turf, promise. . . . Bye."

My heart's beating a little faster now. But it's that exhilarated quicken that brings with it adrenaline and mettle and the sturdy belief that you can do anything; it's all possible because you're ready, willing to reach to the outstretched hand and grab it and never let go, no matter what tugs at you. I'm ready for this. I'm ready for him to love me and take care of me and never let me go.

Hudson-reader guy is gone, but he left the magazine behind on the seat. I'm going to take that as a sign to do the same damn thing.

CHAPTER 27

The words tumble out the minute we sit down. "Susie, can I tell you the truth?"

"Always."

"I almost cancelled on you. I picked up the phone twice and dialed all but one digit, both times."

"Well, I'm glad you went through with it. I wanted to see your face for this," she says, and refills her goblet with sparkling water.

"That's what I mean. I didn't think I could really face you. Jesus, I still don't think I can. If these tables weren't so tight, I'd probably bolt before the entrees get here."

I miss hearing Susie laugh like that. It truly is contagious, all loud and throaty. She looks great, ever calm and pleasant. Her hair is longer, curlier, wilder, and she looks rested and happy. Maybe after a few more months away from Millhause-Steig I'll be gorgeous and chill too.

"Why are you dreading face time with me so much?" Susie is picking through her salad for every last piece of crisp bacon. She frowns when it's clear there's nothing but greens left.

"Because it means facing up to all of it. Looking everything in the eye—it's not fun. I'm embarrassed. I feel like I disappointed you, betrayed all the confidence and good intentions you held for me. And it makes me sad and I don't want to cry in front of you . . . or into this bisque."

"Honey, I'm not any of those things. I don't think any of that shit about you. So you made some choices. That's what we do. We make choices. Everything comes down to that. How many of these people sitting in here right now haven't made a choice between doing the ambitious, slightly dangerous thing and sitting on the couch watching someone else do it instead? You went for a story—a good fuckin' story—because you believed in it. You took action and actions have reactions. So we deal with those too, as they come."

"But getting axed like that . . . You didn't see the way JK looked at me. The waters are so muddy now. And you vouched me."

"Oh, please. Kessler will get over it. Many have done much worse and they're still in her good books. Etched in there, actually. Trust me, you have nothing to feel bad about. You need to get over it. You took one or two missteps, Best. Minor ones. But now you know better. Now you're moving forward and you know better."

She's so certain I want to believe her. I want to believe it's that easy and that *truly* falling from grace in this town is nearly impossible. I want to imagine looking back on this whole thing as a speck, the slimmest slice of what mattered. But that's not where my brain is, and I don't know when I'll get there. Even when I unplug the speakers in my head blaring all the vile things I have to say about myself, and it's supposed to be quiet, I can hear the echoes, the whispering telling me—assuring me—that I will not bounce back. This moment will count. It matters. People will remember.

Looking at her across from me, painted several coats thick in her brightest expectations, I don't know how to just dismiss her and all her wishful thinking.

The waiter arrives with our steaming dishes and warns me,

with bulging eyes and panicky drama, that my plate is extremely hot and I Must. Not. Touch. It. Susie and I trade eye rolls as he leaves, but I hope he comes back a few times. I'm not clear where this convo is going, and who doesn't appreciate a little wacky-waiter skit to help keep things light?

"Did you read it? I mean, did you read what I sent?"

"Oh, I read it. I read it when you sent it to me right then. Woke up in the middle of the night to read it again. I also read the mag versions. *Hudson*, of course did the better turn, but Kessler and her people did a good job too. Some of the pictures were . . . well, you know what speaks to the *James* gal."

"I feel like an asshole even asking this, but is my byline—"

"Very much intact. Agnes did a fine edit job. You should be pleased all around. Two covers. Not shabby at all, dove."

"Wait, it's on the cover of *James* too?"

"You haven't seen them?"

"No, I've been kind of hiding from it. I don't even go online anymore. I read hardcover books and watch TV shows from the nineties. I'm a downright mess, Susie."

"You should stop that—the hiding from it part. I certainly approve of nineties TV and good old literature, but you should also pick up a few copies of the magazines. Keep them in your smile file and be proud. There's a lot there to be proud of. A lot." She slows the cutting of her steak. "Actually, that's part of the reason I wanted to meet."

"To tell me to start a smile file?"

"You and that cheek," she says, narrowing her eyes at me. "Love that your sense of snark is still floating on the surface."

"Sorry about that. I'm trying to curb the dickery these days."

"Curb nothing. It's what makes and keeps you interesting. I'm serious."

"Thanks for saying that, but I'm still pushing sincerity to the front burner and letting all the snide shit cool off in the back. Anyway . . . why did you want to meet?"

Susie puts her fork down mid-bite and pushes the plate to the side. SDW loves her some grass-fed red meat, so this has to be important. She actually looks a little sheepish, and glances beside her before leaning in a little to the center of the table.

"I told you I read your story and that it woke me out of my sleep, but I was waiting to see if my gut was right before telling you what I did next. But it's my gut and I can build houses on my gut."

"Okay, so you're the one who sent the piece to Agnes, not Nik?"

"No. Nik sent it to Agnes, from what I heard. I sent it to my two editor friends—book editors." Her grin stretches. "And they both got back to me in under an hour, because they loved your story, loved you, and they want you. You have two of the Big Five battling for you!"

"Big . . . Fi . . ." My mouth is still full of half-chewed tomato and I haven't swallowed since Susie started talking all hushed and wily.

"They want you. They want to offer you a book deal—a major one." Susie nods and takes a sluggish sip from her sweating water glass. "I'd say a bidding war's about to begin for your book, my dear."

"Wha—are you—they want me to write—is this for real? Are you for real?"

"I am. It is. It's all very real. And to add a little button to that grand news . . . you're also looking at your new literary agent. If you'll have me."

"Susie . . . you can't play around here. Are you being serious?"

"Deadly."

"Oh, good Christ! This is . . ." I cover my face with the cloth napkin from my lap. "Dammit, Susie. I told you I didn't want to cry in front of you, and here I am about to toss this napkin over my head and cow-bawl like it's an Italian funeral."

I hear Susie's giggle, then sniffles. She reaches up and lowers the napkin to look at me and lightly squeezes my hand. We're both wet, snotty messes, grinning like fools. She squeezes my hand again.

"It's real and you deserve it," she says. "So no more talk about disappointments and hiding away."

"But . . . I mean, what book? If anything, Fatima should be writing a book."

She breaks her hold to dab away some of her tears, leaving a complete Rorschach test on her white napkin. "Actually, it's an extension of Fatima's story . . . but from you. Shame, guilt, and absolution."

"What do you mean, *from me*? Am I ghostwriting this thing?"

Susie's face slides from elated to edgy, uneasy. I've seen the look before, but never on her. She doesn't wear it well and I'm waiting for the ugly-ass left shoe to drop right on my head.

"What is it? Just say it. My back is broad these days." I toss my napkin on the side of the table, right in my plate of mushy risotto. Whatever tears and smears I have will remain, and the waiter, the couple sitting beside us, and everyone in this low-light, cramped dinner box will just deal.

"I want you to know that I will always have your best interests at the top of my list, even if you decide to find another agent. You're not a writer or a client—you're a friend."

"Just tell me, Susie. Really."

"There was something there in what you wrote, behind the words, settled into the white spaces, which was so gut-deep that I could almost reach in and touch it. It was something wounded and sorrowful and it had nothing to do with Fatima's tragic ordeal. Not directly. This thing, it was coming from you and it was asking to be heard. Begging to be heard, finally, and I was wide open to it. I was ready to grab anything I could to help lift this wretched heap from your back. It was from you, not her. And then you told me about your brothers, the accident. All the dots came together and I saw the shape of it. My God. You're not even thirty, carrying that and for ten years. I could not begin to imagine . . . until I read your Fatima story."

"That's what this book is, digging up my dead brothers?"

"No. No, that's not—Best, this book is about you. I told the one editor a little about you, and surviving the ice accident—"

"That's not your story to tell. I told you that—the little piece of it—in confidence, when I was freaking and basically flattened out in that crazy hotel room. Why would you tell some random editor any of that?"

"First, she's not random. She's a friend, like you, and I've known her for close to twenty years. We grew up together in this industry. I trust her. You can trust her too. And you can trust me. I want you to get it off your chest, Best. You need to, honey. This book is how you can do it. It's creating life out of death."

My pause is so long, just me looking down into my lap. I know Susie's hanging on the ends of my loud, heavy breath. When I do look up, she's practically tilted, sloped toward my side of the table. "So, how would it go—just me exposed?"

"It's a memoir in essays. It goes how you want it go or it doesn't go at all."

Susie's expression shifts again; no longer are her eyes asking for pardon. The lull is back, filling in every inch of her face. I do trust her, but I'm still trembling in my seat. The rush of all of it . . . I can't think straight. Everything's coming at me lopsided. Although I've wanted this from almost the first day, I can't say I thought it would ever come true.

"Susie, before anything can happen, before even thinking about the words *next steps*, I need to talk to my dad. My parents—I can't peel things open on them. That's reckless."

"Of course. Of course, you talk to them." She sits back in

her chair at last. "You take a couple of days with this and get back to me. Just know that I'm on your side, no matter what, Best. I'm always going to be on your side." Susie drains the bottle of sparking water into her glass and pounds the thing.

I barely get around the corner when it all goes to pieces. My head is throbbing or maybe that's my heart lodged behind my eyes. I'm sobbing and my breath is choppy and I can feel the puke crawling up the back of my throat. I crumble where I stand, leaned up against the bus shelter, my bag a tiny mound at my feet. My iPhone is out and in my hand and before I realize it, I'm tapping out letters.

Meet me tonight. Please. Shit is falling apart. My place.

It's sent and my phone is dialing home without a break. I need to get my father's two cents on this.

"Mum, hi. Is Dad awake? . . . What—*when*? Okay, okay. I'm coming." I jump into a sprint, the phone pressed to my ear. "I'm coming. Just wait for me. Tell him to wait. Please. Just tell him, I'm on my way!"

CHAPTER 28

Packing up my dad's office, his room, his side of the house is hard. I don't know where to start and my mother is no help. I can't expect her to be. There is no try-to-be-strong setting on her. Not this time. She was a wreck on the phone, a wreck when I finally got to the hospital, a wreck when they asked to move his body out of the room—he had been in there, a white sheet up to his chin, for more hours than what's normally allowed. She told them they needed to wait until I got there. I missed his last breath, but I still must be allowed to see him and say good-bye. That's what she told them and what she told me more than twice. It was awful seeing her like that, unglued and heartbroken. She prayed and cried and prayed and cried. It was endless and unbearable and sad.

They showed me to a dim room just outside of the morgue. I kissed both his cheeks and just above his cold brow too. I leaned into his stillness, drowning out all the noises around us—the low whirl from the vents, the hiss from the overhead lights, my mother's gurgles and moans—and I told him plainly what he already knew, that I love him. I left it at that. I was saying good-bye to his body, not his being. There were no tears from me this time. The nurses said I was in shock. But I know what that is: I've felt shock before and this wasn't that.

⯈•◀

I have been taking longer and longer breaks while trying to go through the things here in his office. Sometimes I'll feel my nose running and taste the salt on my lips. That's when I take a break, walk outside, sit on the front steps. Tyson thinks it's too soon to be doing this, but what else am I supposed to do? The funeral was prearranged years ago. After my brothers died, my parents put their own *home-going* plans in writing and paid for all of it in full. Their plots are reserved, right next to Benjamin and Bryant.

His service is later this afternoon. I've been showered and dressed since five o'clock this morning, but still haven't figured out what I'm going to say. My father did the eulogy for his sons. I don't know how, but he did. I half-expect to find a folder in here with his own eulogy already written out, by him. The *Gazette* will run something—that's them, though, their take on his life as a tireless crime reporter. Mine has to be different. It has to come from my foggy brain and cracked heart.

I think it's time for another break.

She's probably resting again. The pills definitely help. I move quietly anyway. As I reach the door, there's a knock—a soft one. Another flower delivery, I'm sure. The flowers and plants and food baskets being sent here, it's endless. I brush back the wetness and stray curls pressed against my cheek and ease the red door open. I cringe as it squeaks.

And there he is, filling in my doorway.

"Hey," Grant says.

"Hey . . ."

We stare at each for what feels like a week before I pop the bubble. "What are you . . . how did—"

"Tyson told me." He smiles. "I got your messages. I was coming to you. But when I got there you were gone."

"I'm sorry."

"No. Don't. It's okay. I'm sorry about your dad."

I put my index finger to my mouth—as if my mother can hear anything beyond her own anguish—and motion to the front steps. Grant follows, but doesn't sit down. He's waiting for me. He stretches out his open palm. I do my part and give him a soft five. He pulls me close and I fall into him, burying my face into his chest, digging my fingers into the back of his black suit jacket. I inhale him, his familiar fragrance, and listen as his heart pounds against my temple.

"Can't believe you came." I speak directly to his shirt pocket because there's no way I'm looking up at him, at his face, into his eyes.

"Why wouldn't I? A million times better, right?" Grant nestles me deeper into his open jacket and wraps his arms tight around my whole body. He kisses the very top of my head. "Anyway, someone's got to help you off that wobbly piece of wood. Think I got that job on lock."

I laugh, but it comes out like an uneven exhale. He kisses my head again, squeezes me.

"When my mother died and everybody tried to talk to me, tell me things, none of it made sense. None of it mattered. The grief, it was constant, bottomless. She was gone. That's all I knew. And I missed her. People kept telling me and G that it was instant, that she felt nothing. But that didn't change anything. She was still gone and we were supposed to keep going forward without her? That sounded as crazy as telling me that the earth was actually flat after all." Grant pulled me in tighter under his chin. "I still can't believe that she's gone. I think about her every day. Literally, every day, at least once. But it's mostly the golden parts, you know? Like how her face looked when she was concentrating on a sculpture. Focused and beautiful. Or how she would put ketchup on everything—a couple times we busted her taking nibbles of it straight raw from a spoon. I think about that and she's with me again, in all the ways she'd want to be—all good things. I know that this, everything I'm saying right now, doesn't even sound like any language you understand, but it will. It will. And one day it stops being so incredibly sad. You wake up and the world looks like it did before, the color comes back to things."

I sink into him and breathe him in once more. "Thank you . . . for flying here, for being here and holding me up." The bones in my back come together in time and I can finally look Grant in the eye. "I couldn't do this without you."

"C'mon. You've *been* doing it, for years, Best. I just wanna be with you while you do, hold your hand from here on."

And like that, it came, my whole bitter grief, cracking through me like rolling thunder, burning a stinging path up my chest, my throat, my mouth, until I could do nothing but let it come, and then let it go.

———❖———

Looking out at the smallish crowd in this oversized church, I recognize some faces: my mother's chapel sisters, my father's old newspaper comrades, a few neighbors from the old house. The others are starting to blur together, though, like one broad brushstroke of black and gray. I turn my focus to the right. The faces sharpen again; clarity. I spot Aunt Lucille, my mother's sister-in-law from Ottawa. She's sitting in the exact same seat, the same pew as ten years ago, only this time she's with just one of her grown sons, Kenrick, who looks older now, haggard and balding. Kenrick meets my eyes and sends a deep nod—the kind that speaks whole sentences. I return one, trying to fill it with a similar sentiment. In front of Kenrick and his weeping mother is my weeping mother, sitting next to Grant. His arm is stretched along the top of the pew and my mother is resting back on it, resting back on him. He's saying something to her, quiet near her ear, and it looks like it's helping to steady the jerking in her shoulders.

Next to Grant is Tyson, followed by Lindee and New Mark, Kendra and Flavio, and right behind them, a mass of curly, auburn hair. Susie. She's here. They're all really here with me, for me.

I clear my throat and it echoes through the microphone. "Eulogies are supposed to be . . . I don't really know. This is the first one I've had to do. I don't know what they're supposed to be. But I think I'm already failing at it. More like flailing and trying not to curse or something rude like that." Muffled chuckles rise in a low wave. I think the pastor just laughed too. "I figured writing it down would help, but every time I started something, I was crossing it out before I could finish the sentence. Writers get used to staring at a blank page for a good chunk of the day, a good chunk of their careers, but this time I don't think there are any words to fill the space that my father has left. So I think it's better if I use some words that have already been perfectly strung together by someone else. There's a poem I'd like to share. It's by Derek Walcott, one of my father's permanent favorites."

I look at my mother. Her head is bobbing, but she stops long enough to smile right at me. "Dad knew this poem by heart and could recite it with such feeling and knowing, you'd think he cowrote the thing. The first time he read it aloud was at a small memorial for my brothers, Benjamin and Bryant, a few years ago. A little while after—okay, it was more like months later—I told my father that the poem was beautiful, but that the emotion behind it was about something else, it was about someone else, someone trying to mend a broken heart, trying to recover from the loss of a love. Dad didn't wait long before saying, 'That's exactly me. I'm exactly that someone else.' Of course, I left it alone. It's *his* favorite poem. Why try to force my analysis on him? But early this morning while trying to comb through some of my father's things in his dusty office, wrestling with those awful filing cabinets, that's when it clicked. And I get it now. Because now I'm exactly that someone else too."

I don't have what it takes to scan the room and connect with any of the faces watching me. I can only glance to my right at Grant. He's holding my mother close. Her body is folding from the middle, and her head leans all the way over, resting on the stable wall of him. I push back from leaning on the lectern and take a step to the side of it. I need to feel solid beneath my own feet. When I close my eyes, I see my father sitting in front of the TV, right up against it. He's fiddling with it, as he liked to do. But it's how he's sitting—kneeled, his scraggily legs tucked under him, resting his weight on his heels. It's how he used to sit when we were all younger, when were all untroubled and free. The picture of him warms me, and without taking another breath, I begin:

"The poem by Derek Walcott, it's called 'Love After Love,' and I want to dedicate it to one of my greatest loves, my mum.

>*The time will come*
>*when, with elation*
>*you will greet yourself arriving*
>*at your own door, in your own mirror*
>*and each will smile at the other's welcome,*
>
>*and say, sit here. Eat.*
>*You will love again the stranger who was your self.*
>*Give wine. Give bread. Give back your heart*
>*to itself, to the stranger who has loved you*
>
>*all your life, whom you ignored*
>*for another, who knows you by heart.*
>*Take down the love letters from the bookshelf,*

the photographs, the desperate notes,
peel your own image from the mirror.
Sit. Feast on your life."

When I open my eyes again, I see my mother looking up at me. She's holding one of the coins. It's shiny against the black lace of her gloves. The other coin is in the casket, tucked into the breast pocket of my father's oversized suit. I hold my mother's gaze for a moment longer. There's a splinter of light or life or maybe reminiscing in her face. And she turns, moving slow and slight, saying something to Grant. He slopes toward her and says something back, but he's fixed on me, staring at me, somehow still glowing. He gives me that grand, breath-grabbing grin. And I realize, with a swift certainty, that happiness isn't so far away anymore.

THE THUNDER BENEATH US

Nicole Blades

ABOUT THIS GUIDE

The suggested questions are included to
enhance your group's reading of
Nicole Blades's *The Thunder Beneath Us*.

Discussion Questions

1. What's underneath Best's pattern of pulling men into her only to push them away when they get too close?

2. Why is Best so insistent on pursuing the honor-killing story?

3. Best discovers evidence in her father's office that leads her to believe he's been investigating what happened on "that horrible night." Did he already know the truth before Best spilled the full story?

4. Why does Best feel she had no choice but to break up with Grant, despite his "mental health break"?

5. How is Miles able to push Best toward finally telling everyone the truth?

6. During the interview with Fatima, Best gets really annoyed at the mention of "luck." Why does the concept of luck rattle Best so much?

7. Who did you think Best called, professing her love? Did you know it was Grant or did you think it was perhaps Miles or even Nik?

8. Trinity appears to throw Best under the bus toward the end of the book. Do you think she was ever a true friend or was she plotting all along?

9. At the end of the novel, when Best was deep in grief at her father's funeral, what made her realize that happiness was "not so far away," and that it was also hers for the taking?

10. How does her father's death help to close the chasm between Best and her mother?

Acknowledgments

I've long been the weirdo who reads the acknowledgments of a book first. Of course, nine times out of ten, I have no idea who the list of people are, but I still like seeing how they've collectively rooted for the writer, and now it's time for them to be publicly thanked.

With that in mind, I want to shout my gratitude to the skies to the following people—and the many more whom, because of space and time, I didn't list on these pages. Please know that I wouldn't be here writing this without you.

I am forever grateful to my loving parents, Maureen and Tony Blades, for always supporting each dream, wish, endeavor, and story of mine. You have set the brightest path for me to follow. I love you.

Thank you to my siblings: Yvette, who would go hoarse cheering for me, and Sean, whose support of my work over the years is so appreciated. And Nailah, my wise little sister, I cannot thank you enough for being first reader and trusted ear on all of my stories and wild ideas. I am ridiculously lucky to have you as a friend and sister.

To the Burton family, thank you for your unwavering love and support over this last decade. (Also, Janet and John, nice job raising that son of yours into such a remarkable man, father and human being.)

Many thanks to my agent Sharon Pelletier and the legendary Jane Dystel for not only betting on this story, but also on me. I struck gold landing on Team DGLM. I also must send a special thank-you to Rachel Stout for walking me through this book deal with constant calm and kindness.

To Selena James, the editor who just "gets" me: Working with you has been like *buttuh*. Even though Best Lightburn doesn't believe in luck, I certainly do, and count myself so fortunate to have you in my corner. Thank you to the Kensington crew, especially my publicist Lulu Martinez for all of the hard work, attention, and dedication.

Colleen Oakley, I don't know how I can ever truly show my deep gratitude to you for digging into this revise with me. I am officially indebted to you, friend. Let's have Idris take us *both* out to dinner next week, yes?

To Kate Reed Petty, thank you for being one of the earliest readers of this book, back when there was still so much work to do. I will always treasure you and your time.

More immense thanks to my dear friends and band of ardent supporters: Saada Branker, Robert Edison Sandiford, Lloyd Boston, Ravi Howard, Sharon Pendana, Charles Bennett, Craig Carter, Phillip Moithuk Shung, Nicole Beland, Cheryl Della Pietra, Larry Smith, Kristin Wald, A'driane Nieves, my Sacred Heart crew, my countless cheerleaders on Facebook, Twitter and Instagram, my old-school print magazine friends and comrades, my design wizard Todd Wilson, and so many more.

To my little sweet potato, QB: You are truly the most delightful little boy on this spinning globe. I love you with every chamber of my heart (plus infinity with a googol added on to that!).

And finally, my Scott: I love you, for everything that you are and everything that you bring forth in me. You are exceptional.

In this thrilling debut novel from Carrie H. Johnson, one woman with a dangerous job and a volatile past is feeling the heat from all sides . . .

HOT FLASH

Available wherever books are sold.

CHAPTER 1

Our bodies arched, both of us reaching for that place of ultimate release we knew was coming. Yes! We screamed at the same time . . . except I kept screaming long after his moment had passed.

You've got to be kidding me, a cramp in my groin? The second time in the three times we had made love. Achieving pretzel positions these days came at a price, but man, how sweet the reward.

"What's the matter, baby? You cramping again?" he asked, looking down at me with genuine concern.

I was pissed, embarrassed, and in pain all at the same time. "Yeah," I answered meekly, grimacing.

"It's okay. It's okay, sugar," he said, sliding off me. He reached out and pulled me into the curvature of his body, leaving the wet spot to its own demise. I settled in. Gently, he massaged my thigh. His hands soothed me. Little by little, the cramp went away. Just as I dozed off, my cell phone rang.

"*Mph, mph, mph,*" I muttered. "Never a moment's peace."

Calvin stirred. "Huh?"

"Nothin', baby, shhhh," I whispered, easing from his grasp

326 / CARRIE H. JOHNSON

and reaching for the phone from the bedside table. As quietly as I could, I answered the phone the same way I always did.

"Muriel Mabley."

"Did I get you at a bad time, partner?" Laughton chuckled. He used the same line whenever he called. He never thought twice about waking me, no matter the hour. I worked to live and lived to work—at least that's been my story for twenty years, the last seventeen as a firearms forensics expert for the Philadelphia Police Department. I had the dubious distinction of being the first woman in the unit and one of two minorities. The other was my partner, Laughton McNair.

At forty-nine, I was beginning to think I was blocking the blessing God intended for me. I felt like I had blown past any hope of a true love in pursuit of a damn suspect.

"You there?" Laughton said, laughing louder.

"Hee hee, hell. I finally find someone and you runnin' my ass ragged, like you don't *even* want it to last. What now?" I said.

"Speak up. I can hardly hear you."

"I said . . ."

"I heard you." More chuckles from Laughton. "You might want to rethink a relationship. Word is we've got another dead wife and again the husband swears he didn't do it. Says she offed herself. That makes three dead wives in three weeks. Hell, must be the season or something in the water."

Not wanting to move much or turn the light on, I let my fingers search blindly through my bag on the nightstand until they landed on paper and a pen. Pulling my hand out of my bag with paper and pen was another story. I knocked over the half-filled champagne glass also on the nightstand. "Damn it!" I was like a freaking circus act, trying to save the paper, keep the bubbly from getting on the bed, stop the glass from breaking, and keep from dropping the phone.

"Sounds like you're fighting a war over there," Laughton said.

"Just give me the address."

"If you can't get away . . ."

"Laughton, just . . ."

"You don't have to yell."

He let a moment of silence pass before he said, "Thirteen ninety-one Berkhoff. I'll meet you there."

"I'm coming," I said and clicked off.

"You okay?" Calvin reached out to recapture me. I let him and fell back into the warmth of his embrace. Then I caught myself, sat up, and clicked the light on—but not without a sigh of protest.

Calvin rose. He rested his head in his palm and flashed that gorgeous smile at me. "Can't blame a guy for trying," he said.

"It's a pity I can't do you any more lovin' right now. I can't sugarcoat it. This is my life," I complained on my way to the bathroom.

"So you keep telling me."

I felt uptight about leaving Calvin in the house alone. My son, Travis, would be home from college in the morning, his first spring break from Lincoln University. He and Calvin had not met. In all the years before this night, I had not brought a man home, except Laughton, and at least a decade had passed since I'd had any form of a romantic relationship. The memory chip filled with that information had almost disintegrated. Then along came Calvin.

When I came out, Calvin was up and dressed. He was five foot ten, two hundred pounds of muscle, the kind of muscle that flexed at his slightest move. Pure lovely. He pulled me close and pressed his wet lips to mine. His breath, mixed with a hint of citrus from his cologne, made every nerve in my body pulsate.

"Next time we'll do my place. You can sing to me while I

make you dinner," he whispered. "Soft, slow melodies." He crooned, "You Must Be a Special Lady," as he rocked me back and forth, slow and steady. His gooey caramel voice touched my every nerve ending, head to toe. Calvin is a singer and owns a nightclub, which is how we met. I was at his club with friends and Calvin and I—or rather, Calvin and my alter ego, spurred on by my friends, of course—entertained the crowd with duets all night.

He held me snugly against his chest and buried his face in the hollow of my neck while brushing his fingertips down the length of my body.

"Mmm . . . sounds luscious," was all I could muster.

———◆◆◆———

The interstate was deserted, unusual no matter what time, day or night.

In the darkness, I could easily picture Calvin's face, bright with a satisfied smile. I could still feel his hot breath on my neck, the soft strumming of his fingers on my back. I had it bad. Butterflies reached down to my navel and made me shiver. I felt like I was nineteen again, first love or some such foolishness.

Flashing lights from an oncoming police car brought my thoughts around to what was ahead, a possible suicide. How anyone could think life was so bad that they would kill themselves never settled with me. Life's stuff enters pit territory sometimes, but then tomorrow comes and anything is possible again. Of course, the idea that the husband could be the killer could take one even deeper into pit territory. The man you once loved, who made you scream during lovemaking, now not only wants you gone, moved out, but dead.

When I rounded the corner to Berkhoff Street, the scene was chaotic, like the trappings of a major crime. I pulled curbside and rolled to a stop behind a news truck. After I turned off Bertha, my 2000 Saab gray convertible, she rattled in protest for a few moments before going quiet. As I got out, local news anchor Sheridan Meriwether hustled from the front of the news truck and shoved a microphone in my face before I could shut the car door.

"Back off, Sheridan. You'll know when we know," I told her.

"True, it's a suicide?" Sheridan persisted.

"If you know that, then why the attack? You know we don't give out information in suicides."

"Confirmation. Especially since two other wives have been killed in the past few weeks."

"Won't be for a while. Not tonight anyway."

"Thanks, Muriel." She nodded toward Bertha. "Time you gave the old gray lady a permanent rest, don't you think?"

"Hey, she's dependable."

She chuckled her way back to the front of the news truck. Sheridan was the only newsperson I would give the time of day. We went back two decades, to rookie days when my mom and dad were killed in a car crash. Sheridan and several other newspeople had accompanied the police to inform me. She returned the next day, too, after the buzz had faded. A drunk driver sped through a red light and rammed my parents' car head-on. That was the story the police told the papers. The driver of the other car cooked to a crisp when his car exploded after hitting my parents' car, then a brick wall. My parents were on their way home from an Earth, Wind & Fire concert at the Tower Theater.

Sheridan produced a series on drunk drivers in Philadelphia, how their indiscretions affected families and children on both sides of the equation, which led to a national broadcast. Philadelphia police cracked down on drunk drivers and legislation passed with compulsory loss of licenses. Several other cities and states followed suit.

I showed my badge to the young cop guarding the front door and entered the small foyer. In front of me was a white-carpeted staircase. To the left was the living room. Laughton, his expression stonier than I expected, stood next to the detective questioning who I supposed was the husband. He sat on the couch, leaned forward with his elbows resting on his thighs, his head hanging down. Two girls clad in *Frozen* pajamas huddled next to him on the couch, one on either side.

The detective glanced at me, then back at the man. "Where were you?"

"I just got here, man," the man said. "Went upstairs and found her on the floor."

"And the kids?"

"My daughter spent the night with me. She had a sleepover at my house. This is Jeanne, lives a few blocks over. She got homesick and wouldn't stop crying, so I was bringing them back here. Marcy and I separated, but we're trying to work things out." He choked up, unable to speak any more.

"At three a.m."

"I told you, the child was having a fit. Wanted her mother."

A tank of a woman charged through the front door, "Oh my God. Baby, are you all right?" She pushed past the police officer there and clomped across the room, sending those close to look for cover. The red-striped flannel robe she wore and pink furry slippers, size thirteen at least, made her look like a giant candy cane with feet.

"Wade, what the hell is happenin' here?" She moved in and lifted the girl from the sofa by her arm. Without giving him a chance to answer, she continued, "C'mon, baby. You're coming with me."

An officer stepped sideways and blocked the way. "Ma'am, you can't take her—"

The woman's head snapped around like the devil possessed her, ready to spit out nasty words followed by green fluids. She never stopped stepping.

I expect she would have trampled the officer, but Laughton interceded. "It's all right, Jackson. Let her go," he said.

Jackson sidestepped out of the woman's way before Laughton's words settled.

Laughton nodded his head in my direction. "Body's upstairs."

The house was spotless. White was *the* color: white furniture, white walls, white drapes, white wall-to-wall carpet, white picture frames. The only real color came in the mass of throw pillows that adorned the couch and a wash of plants positioned around the room.

I went upstairs and headed to the right of the landing, into a bedroom where an officer I knew, Mark Hutchinson, was photographing the scene. Body funk permeated the air. I wrinkled my nose.

"Hey, M&M," Hutchinson said.

"That's Muriel to you." I hated when my colleagues took the liberty to call me that. Sometimes I wanted to nail Laughton with a front kick to the groin for starting the nickname.

He shook his head. "Ain't me or the victim. She smells like a violet." He tilted his head back, sniffed, and smiled.

Hutchinson waved his hand in another direction. "I'm about done here."

I stopped at the threshold of the bathroom and perused the scene. Marcy Taylor lay on the bathroom floor. A small hole in her temple still oozed blood. Her right arm was extended over her head, and she had a .22 pistol in that hand. Her fingernails and toenails looked freshly painted. When I bent over her body, the sulfur-like smell of hair relaxer backed me up a bit. Her hair was bone-straight. The white silk gown she wore flowed around her body as though staged. Her cocoa brown complexion looked ashen with a pasty, white film.

"Shame," Laughton said to my back. "She was a beautiful woman." I jerked around to see him standing in the doorway.

"Check this out," I said, pointing to the lay of the nightgown over the floor.

"I already did the scene. We'll talk later," he said.

"Damn it, Laughton. Come here and check this out." But when I turned my head, he was gone.

I finished checking out the scene and went outside for some fresh air. Laughton was on the front lawn talking to an officer. He beelined for his car when he saw me.

"What the hell is wrong with you?" I muttered, jogging to catch up with him. Louder. "Laughton, what the hell—"

He dropped anchor. Caught off guard, I plowed into him. He waited until I peeled myself off him and regained my footing, then said, "Nothing. Wade says they separated a few months ago and were trying to get it together, so he came over for some making up. He used his key to enter and found her dead on the bathroom floor."

"No, he said he was bringing the little girl home because she was homesick."

"Yeah, well, then you heard it all."

He about-faced.

I grabbed his arm and attempted to spin him around. "You act like you know this one or something," I practically screeched at him.

"I do."

I cringed and softened my tone five octaves at least when I managed to speak again. "How?"

"I was married to her . . . a long time ago."

He might as well have backhanded me upside the head. "You never—"

"I have an errand to run. I'll see you back at the lab."

I stared after him long after he got in his car and sped off.

The sun was rising by the time the scene was secured: body

and evidence bagged, husband and daughter gone back home. It spewed warm tropical hues over the city. By the time I reached the station, the hues had turned cold metallic gray. I pulled into a parking spot and answered the persistent ring of my cell phone. It was Nareece.

"Hey, sis. My babies got you up this early?" I said, feigning a light mood. My babies were Nareece's eight-year-old twin daughters.

Nareece groaned. "No. Everyone's still sleeping."

"You should be, too."

"Couldn't sleep."

"Oh, so you figured you'd wake me up at this ungodly hour in the morning. Sure, why not? We're talkin' sisterly love here, right?" I said. We chuckled. "I've been up since three anyway, working a case." I waited for her to say something, but she stayed silent. "Reece?" More silence. "C'mon, Reecey, we've been through this so many times. Please don't tell me you're trippin' again."

"A bell goes off in my head every time this date rolls around. I believe I'll die with it going off," Nareece confessed.

"Therapy isn't helping?"

"You mean the shrink? She ain't worth the paper she prints her bills on. I get more from talking to you every day. It's all you, Muriel. What would I do without you?"

"I'd say we've helped each other through, Reecey."

Silence filled the space again. Meanwhile, Laughton pulled his Audi Quattro in next to my Bertha and got out. I knocked on the window to get his attention. He glanced in my direction and moved on with his gangster swagger as though he didn't see me.

"I have to go to work, Reece. I just pulled into the parking lot after being at a scene."

"Okay."

"Reece, you've got a great husband, two beautiful daughters, and a gorgeous home, baby. Concentrate on all that and quit lookin' behind you."

Nareece and John had ten years of marriage. John is Vietnamese. The twins were striking, inheritors of almond-shaped eyes, "good" curly black hair, and amber skin. Rose and Helen, named after our mother and grandmother. John balked at their names because they did not reflect his heritage. But he was mush where Nareece was concerned.

"You're right. I'm good except for two days out of the year, today and on Travis's birthday. And you're probably tired of hearing me."

"I'll listen as long as you need me to. It's you and me, Reecey. Always has been, always will be. I'll call you back later today. I promise."

I clicked off and stayed put for a few minutes, bogged down by the realization of Reece's growing obsession with my son, way more than in past years, which conjured up ugly scenes for me. I prayed for a quick passing, though a hint of guilt pierced my gut. Did I pray for her sake, my sake, or Travis's? What scared me anyway?

Stunning, suspenseful, and unforgettably evocative,
this debut novel glitters with the vibrant dreams and
dangerous promise of the 1920s Harlem Renaissance, as
one man crosses the perilous lines between the law,
loyalty, and deadly lies . . .

THE STRIVERS' ROW SPY

Available wherever books are sold.

CHAPTER 1

Middlebury College, Vermont
Spring, 1919

It was graduation day, and the strange man standing at the top of the cobblestone stairwell gave me an uneasy feeling. It was like he was waiting on me. With each step I climbed, the feeling turned into a gnawing in my stomach, gripped me a bit more, pulling at my good mood.

I glanced at my watch, then down at my shiny, black patent leather shoes. First time I'd worn them. Hadn't ever felt anything so snug on my feet, so light. Momma had saved up for Lord knows how long and had given them to me as a graduation gift.

Again I looked up at him. He was a tall, thin man, dressed in the finest black suit I'd ever laid eyes on; too young, it appeared to me, to have such silver hair, an inch of which was left uncovered by his charcoal fedora. Even from a distance he looked like a heavy smoker, with skin the texture and color of tough, sun-baked leather. I had never seen any man exhibit such confidence—one who stood like he was in charge of the world.

I finally reached the top step and realized just how imposing he was, standing about six-five, a good three inches taller than I. His pensive eyes locked in on me and he extended a hand.

"Sidney Temple?" he asked, with a whispery-dry voice.

"Yes."

"James Gladforth of the Bureau of Investigation."

We shook hands as I tried to digest what I'd just heard. What kind of trouble was I in? Was there anything I might have done in the past to warrant my being investigated? I thought of Jimmy King, Vida Cole, Junior Smith—all childhood friends who, God knows, had broken their share of laws. But I had never been involved in any of it. The resolute certainty of my clean ways gave me calm as I adjusted my tassel and responded.

"Good to meet you, sir."

"Congratulations on your big day," he said.

"Thank you."

"You all are fortunate the ceremony is this morning. Looks to be gettin' hotter by the minute." He looked up, squinting and surveying the clear sky.

I just stood there nodding my head in agreement.

He took off his hat, pulled a handkerchief from his jacket pocket, and wiped the sweat from his forehead. "You can relax," he said, "you're not in any trouble." He put the hand-kerchief back in his pocket and replaced his hat. He stared at me, studying my face, perhaps trying to decide if my appearance matched that of the person he'd imagined.

He took out a tin from his jacket, opened it, and removed a cigarette. Patting his suit, searching for something, he finally removed a box of matches from his left pants pocket. He struck one of the sticks, lit the cigarette, and smoked quietly for a few seconds.

Proud parents and possibly siblings walked past en route to the ceremony. One young man, dressed in his pristine Army uniform, sat in a wheelchair pushed by a woman in a navy blue dress. He had very pale skin, red hair, and was missing his right leg. Mr. Gladforth looked directly at them as they approached.

"Ma'am," he said, tipping his hat, "will you allow me a moment?"

"Certainly," she said, coming to a stop. She had her grayish-blond hair in a bun, and her eyes were some of the saddest I'd ever seen.

"Where did you fight, young man?" asked Gladforth.

"Saw my last action in Champagne, France, sir. Part of the Fifteenth Field Artillery Regiment. Been back stateside for about two months, sir."

"Your country will forever be indebted to you, son. That was a hell of a war effort by you men. On behalf of the United States government and President Wilson, I want to thank you for your service."

"Thank you, sir."

"Ma'am," said Gladforth, tipping his hat again as the woman gave him a slight smile.

She resumed pushing the young man along, and Gladforth began smoking again—refocusing his attention on me.

"I don't want to take away too much of your time, Sidney," he went on, turning and exhaling the smoke away from us. "I just wanted to introduce myself and tell you personally that the Bureau has been going over the college records of soon-to-be graduates throughout the country.

"You should be pleased to know that you're one of a handful of men that our new head of the General Intelligence Division, J. Edgar Hoover, would like to interview for a possible entry-level position. Your portfolio is outstanding."

"Thank you," I said, somewhat taken aback.

"I know it's quite a bit to try to decide on at the moment, but this is a unique opportunity to say the least."

"Indeed it is, sir."

He handed me a card. "Listen, here's my information. We'd

like to set up an interview with you as soon as possible, hopefully within the month."

He began smoking again as I read the card.

"Think about the interview, and when you make your mind up, telephone the number there. We'll have a train ticket to Washington available for you within hours of your decision. Based on the sensitivity of the assignment you may potentially be asked to fulfill, you can tell no one about this interview.

"And, if you were to be hired, your status in any capacity would have to remain confidential. That includes your wife, family, and any friends or acquaintances. If you are uncomfortable with this request, please decline the interview because the conditions are nonnegotiable. Are you clear about what I'm telling you?"

"Yes, I think so."

"It's imperative that you understand these terms," he stressed, throwing what was left of his cigarette on the ground and stepping on it, the sole of his dress shoe gritting against the concrete.

"I understand."

"Then I look forward to your decision."

"I'll be in touch very soon, Mr. Gladforth. And thank you again, sir."

We shook hands and he walked away. Wondering what I'd just agreed to, I headed on to the graduation ceremony.

I picked up my pace along the cobblestone walkway, thinking about all the literature and history I'd pored over for the past six years, seldom reading any of it without wishing I were there in some place long ago, doing something important and history-shaping. I may have been an engineer by training, but at heart, at very private heart, I was a political man.

I wondered, specifically, what the BOI wanted with a colored agent all of a sudden. I was certainly aware that during its short life, it had never hired one. Could I possibly be the first? I thought it intriguing but far-fetched.

"Don't be late, Sidney," said Mrs. Carlton, one of my mathematics professors, interrupting my reverie as she walked by. "You've been waiting a long time for this."

"Yes, ma'am." I smiled at her and began to walk a bit faster. I reminded myself that Gladforth hadn't actually mentioned my becoming an agent. He'd only spoken of an interview and a possible low-level position.

"It's just you and me, Sidney," said Clifford Mayfield, running up and putting his hand on my shoulder, his grin bigger than ever.

"Yep," I said, "just you and me," referring to the fact that Clifford and I would be the only coloreds graduating that day.

"The way I see it," he said, "this is just the beginning. Tomorrow I'm off to Boston for an interview with Thurman Insurance."

Clifford continued talking about his plans for the future as we walked, but my mind was still on the Bureau. Working as an engineer was my goal, but maybe it could wait. Perhaps this Bureau position was a calling. Maybe if I could land a good government job and rise up through the ranks, I could bring about the social change I'd always dreamed of. I needed a few days to think it through.

Moments later I was sitting among my fellow classmates, each lost in his own thoughts inspired by President Tannenbaum. He stood at the podium in his fancy blue and gold academic gown, the hot sun beaming down on his white rim of hair and bald, sunburned top of his head.

"You are all now equipped to take full advantage of the many opportunities the world has to offer," he asserted. "You have chosen to push beyond the four-year diploma and will soon be able to boast of possessing the coveted master's degree. . . ."

Momma had told me from the time I was five, "You're going to college someday, Sugar." But throughout my early teens I'd noticed that no one around me was doing so. Still, I studied hard and got a scholarship to Middlebury College. My high school English teacher, Mrs. Bright, had gone to school here.

"It seems," Tannenbaum continued, "like only yesterday that I was sitting there where all of you sit today, and I can tell you from my own experiences in the greater world that a Middlebury education is second to none. . . ."

I'd left Milwaukee, the Bronzeville section, in the fall of 1913 and headed here to Vermont. I had taken a major in mechanical engineering with the goal of obtaining a bachelor's and then a master's degree in civil engineering. I would be qualified both to assemble engines and construct buildings. Reading physics became all consuming, and I'd spent most of my time in the library, often slipping in some pleasure reading. Having access to a plethora of rich literature was new to me.

"I want you to hear me loud and clear," President Tannenbaum went on. "This is your time to shine."

As I looked across the crowd of graduate students and up into the stands, I saw Momma in her purple dress, brimming with joy. She was so proud, and rightfully so, having raised me all on her own. For eighteen years it had been just the two of us, Momma having happily spent those years scrubbing other families' homes, cooking for and raising their children. But now that I had turned twenty-five, I would see to it that she wouldn't have to do that anymore.

It was time for my row to stand. As we progressed slowly toward the stage, I became more and more painfully aware of my wife's absence. I'd first laid eyes on Loretta in the library four years earlier when she'd arrived at Middlebury, making her the third female colored student here.

I'd approached her while she was studying, introducing myself and awkwardly asking her if she'd like to study together sometime. She'd just given me an odd look before I'd quickly changed my question, asking instead if she'd like to have an ice cream with me sometime in the cafeteria. She said yes and it was easy between us from that day on.

"Sidney Temple!" called out President Tannenbaum, the audience politely clapping for me as they had for the others. I walked onto the stage, took my diploma from his hand, and paused briefly for the customary photograph. I looked at Momma as she wiped the tears from her eyes.

I longed for Loretta to be sitting there too, witnessing my little moment in the spotlight. Before coming to Middlebury she'd spent one year at the Pennsylvania Academy of the Fine Arts and another at Oberlin College. But she'd finally found her collegiate home here and earned a degree in art history.

Her graduation, which had come three weeks prior to mine, had been a magical affair. Unfortunately, that celebratory atmosphere had come to an abrupt halt. Today she was grieving the loss of her father and was back home in Philadelphia arranging for his funeral. His illness had progressed during the last year, and he'd rarely been conscious the last time we'd visited him together. I'd figured that would be the last time I'd see him and had said my good-byes back then. Still, it was comforting to know that Loretta had insisted I stay here and allow Momma to see me graduate.

With the ceremony over and degree in hand, I headed to the reception the engineering department was having for a few of us. My mind raced to come up with a good reason for visiting Washington, D.C.—one that I could legitimately tell Momma about. As I arrived at the auditorium, she was waiting outside. We embraced.

"I'm so proud of you, Sugar."

"I couldn't have done it without you. I love you, Momma."

The pending trip to Washington crept into my mind even during that long motherly hug.

———◆◆◆———

A week later I was standing in the train station lobby in downtown Chicago on my way to the nation's capital. I'd said my good-byes to Momma back in Milwaukee earlier that morning. My "good reason"? I'd told her I'd been asked to interview for a position on the Public Buildings Commission, a government committee established in 1916 to make suggestions regarding future development of federal agencies and offices. It was the first time I'd lied to her, and the guilt was heavy on me.

The Bureau had sent an automobile to pick me up at Momma's place in Milwaukee and drive me to Chicago. It was a wondrous black vehicle—a 1919 Ford Model T.

When my train was announced, I headed to the car where all the colored passengers were sitting. Unlike the South, here in Chicago there were no Jim Crow cars I was required to sit in, but I guess most of us just felt comfortable sitting apart from the whites, and vice versa. Was the way things were in public. But it was a feeling I never wanted my future children to have.

All the folks on the train were immaculately dressed, and I felt comfortable in my cream-colored three-piece suit and brown newsboy cap. We gazed at one another with curiosity, they probably wondering, as I was, what special event was affording us the opportunity to travel such a distance in style. The car was paneled in walnut and furnished with large, upholstered chairs. It was the height of luxury.

I began studying the brand-new Broadway Limited railroad map I'd purchased. Ever since my first year of college, I'd been collecting every map I could get my hands on. It had become a hobby of sorts, running my finger along the various lines that connected one town to another, always discovering a new place various rails had begun servicing.

The train passed by West Virginian fields of pink rhododendron, then chugged through the state of Virginia as I reflected on its history and absorbed the landscape with virgin eyes. This was the land of Washington and Jefferson I was entering.